A NOVEL BY
William Price Fox

ORLO*ff* PRESS

Athens, Georgia

Copyright 1971, 1997 by William Price Fox.
First published by J. B. Lippincott and Company.

This edition published in the United States by Orloff Press.

Orloff Press
P.O. Box 80774
Athens, GA 30608

Orloff Press and colophon are registered trademarks

Printed on acid-free, recycled paper
Manufactured in the United States of America

Library of Congress Catalog Number: 97-67939

5 4 3 2 1

For Sarah

Ruby Red

1

It was nine-thirty and Virgil Haynes and Agnes McCoy were parked on top of Needle Hill watching the Piedmont and Delta flights coming in from Atlanta. A full moon had risen and was shuttling between the low clouds blown up from the river. It would rain before morning. The radio was on 1010, the Charlotte Gospel Hour, and Agnes was crouched in close. "Listen here, Virgil. This next line."

The Renfro family, a husband, wife, three-daughter, and one-son group, were finishing up their ninth hymn of the evening. "Right here."

The mother throbbed. . . .

> "I am thy rock, thy way, thy light.
> Come take my hand, I'll be thy sight."

Agnes McCoy worked the first shift on the Customer Relations desk at Southern Bell Telephone Company and sang country and western and gospel on weekends with Ruby Jean Jamison. They called themselves "The Rose of Sharon Girls."

She slid back into the corner and tucked her dress down tight. "That's an original piece. I think Mrs. Renfro wrote it."

The spring-steel sound of an electric dobro shimmered in while Mother Renfro caught her breath for the finish. . . .

"I'll be thy sight, thy eyes, thy ears.
I'll be thy comfort through the years."

Agnes rested her cheek on the window slot. She could smell the river breeze as she watched the clouds picking up the loan office neon from Sumpter Street. "Virgil, I swear, there's just nothing like good gospel. Nothing."

Virgil drew on his cigarette and watched the ash flare in the rearview mirror. "Yeah, I like that one. It makes you stop and think."

"Don't it though."

Virgil, who did bulldozing for the Suttee Lumber Mill and drove whiskey for Spider Hornsby, was sucking on Sen Sen chips and thinking about Charlotte Gospel, but it wasn't about songs or salvation. He knew that at ten o'clock the show ended and he had an hour before the Augusta Golden Hour of Hymns began. He had memorized the radio schedule and knew he had a full hour of talk shows, rock music, and cotton and hog reports before the 50,000 clear-channel watts from Augusta would come on and stay on until midnight.

Agnes let him hold her hand during the next number, "I Walk With Jesus." When it ended she squeezed it. "Oh, Virgil, I really wish you'd think about coming back to the Washed in the Blood."

He moved closer. "I've been thinking about it. I really have."

"It's only once a week. And Lord, you get so much out of it."

"I know."

It was seven minutes before ten, one more long song and a commercial. He eased his hand behind her shoulders and crossed his left leg over his right to tighten his position. She made no move to pull away. The last hymn, "Where Would I Be Without My Jesus?" began. The Renfros' son was only fourteen and sounded unsure of the words. His voice dropped. Agnes turned the volume up.

(2)

"Careful, Ag. Watch that switch." A hot wire hung down where Virgil had had to chisel the switch out after he'd been drunk one night and snapped the key off.

The long song ended and Foster Renfro, the father of the group, moved in and in a sermonlike voice began talking about his used-car lot. "I want all you good folks out there in radio land to know we've got us a policy down at Renfro Motors that no other car lot in the country can stand up to. We don't have any bathing girls sashaying around or brass bands or plastic doolollies spinning in the breeze. We don't feature none of that nonsense. All we have is a simple, cold-biscuit down-to-earth policy of Truth. That's it folks, capital T.R.U.T.H. So when you come out to Renfro Motors, it's on the Interstate right at the Gastonia turnoff, you're going to see that we don't soap in one price and then hit you with another one back in the contract room. . . . No, sir, the price you're seeing is the price you're paying." A guitar and a dobro mixed two long chords. "Remember, folks, at Renfro Motors we Guarantee Satisfaction and we Guarantee—The Truth."

Virgil mashed his cigarette out in the ash tray and swallowed his Sen Sen. "I'm afraid that's it."

"Let's hear the closing prayer."

The prayer came to a chorded Amen closing, and the Renfro family went humming off into a station identification break and a Seven-Up commercial. Agnes tried the dial, searching for another gospel group.

Virgil reached over. "Here, let me try. This thing's sorta tricky." He paused at each station across the band. "That's it, honey. 'Fraid we're out of luck."

Agnes snugged her knees up. "You're getting so you kinda like it, don't you?"

"Guess I do. Guess they sorta grow on you."

He crossed his leg tighter, drawing himself closer. He sat still, trying to feel if he could go farther, and dried his right hand on the seat cover behind her head and his left on his pants leg. He wouldn't ask her how things were at Southern Bell or what was new at church. Only short questions with short answers.

"Where you and Ruby playing next?"

(3)

"Stark Street Baptist. You coming out?"

Shifting slightly, he pulled her in close. "I'll be in that first row."

She came easily, feeling relaxed and smooth, and he kept her head moving until her chin rested on his neck. "They're having a cake and pie auction after the show. I don't know what the money's going for."

He tucked her chin under his ear. "Fine, I don't want to miss that." He cleared his throat. "I've been missing you, Agnes. You know that thing?"

His ear tickled and buzzed when she spoke, sending hot and cold fast-moving icicles around his neck and down his spine. "I missed you too, Virgil."

Tipping her chin back and not letting himself pause, he slid his mouth to her neck and then to her ear. Then smoothly across her face to her lips. He brushed them lightly, feeling thin and feathery as if every move was light and right and perfect. He dried his hands again. And then, firming his hand behind her head, squeezed her mouth to his. Her hands gripped his shoulders as if to push away; instead they pulled him close. He felt his teeth on hers and her mouth opening wide, her hands clutching, scratching, pulling. He wasn't ready but adjusted quickly and worked his left knee in between hers. They opened slightly and he pushed up to spread them. They tightened but she wasn't resisting, she was squeezing. He kissed her deeper, longer, harder, rolling his lips and tongue over her eyes, her ears, back to the corners of her mouth and deep into it. One hand touched her breast; the other flattened on the wet spot of her back and pulled her closer. Slowly her knees opened and her dress slipped up. He could see her long white legs in the moonlight and hear his heart pounding. Her hands were in his hair and on his neck as he feverishly worked in under her blouse and to the two-hook brassiere. One released, the other jammed. He squeezed his hands under and scooped them up and around her breasts. Her wet hair was in his face. Her mouth was open; her eyes were closed. "Virgil. Virgil. Oh, Virgil." He kissed one breast, then the other. Then in between. She panted, gasped, screamed silently, and moaned. "Oh, Lord, Lord, I can't. I can't."

(4)

Her pants were wet when he touched them, and he slid them to one side. She was twisting, arching, on fire and out of control. He eased up and paced himself. He didn't want to get too excited. Nothing could go wrong. Nothing. His head was clear. He could see the stars and the moon over the radio tower. There were no cars in sight. She was ready; he was ready. It was ten-twenty. Even the Augusta Golden Hour of Hymns was forty minutes away. To stop and roll a rubber on now would break the spell. He would stop half way through. Maybe three-fourths. Maybe nine-tenths. He unzipped and unsnapped his pants and shorts and kicked them down until they hobbled his feet. He couldn't get them over his shoes. It didn't matter; all he had to do was slide her to the middle of the seat. She came easily, her body horseshoeing up and throbbing as she gasped for air and his lips and reached up, clutching for him. He reared up over her; she was his. Shifting his feet away from the brake pedal, he jammed the hot wire to the steel dashboard with his naked hip. CRACK! A blinding two-foot blue-white flash exploded and danced across the dash like a fluorescent snake. Agnes shrieked. "LORD!"

The car lit up like it was on fire. Virgil jumped. "SON OF A BITCH!!!" The hot wire had singed the hair, blistering his leg, and was leaping up, down and around the steering post, crackling and popping like Chinese firecrackers. He snatched it loose, tied it off on its insulation, and crouched back in to calm her. "Easy, Ag, easy."

She was shrieking, shouting, screaming, ice cold and rigid.

"It was the hand of God! I saw it! I saw it!"

"Honey! It was the damn ignition! It does that all the time! Look! Look, I'll show you!" He brushed the lead again and a three-inch spark jumped off. "That's all it is. It ain't even grounded. Now just don't you worry. Virgil's taking care of everything." He moved in to press her down and spread her legs. "It's going to be all right. All right."

She twisted hard, ramming her hip in his groin and scooting back into her corner. "Keep away from me! Keep away!"

He fought down the hot pain. "Honey, honey. It was only a little spark."

(5)

"No, it wasn't! I saw him! His face! He was turned sideways! He was angry! I swear before God! Virgil, I saw him!"

She scrambled with her bra and blouse and pulled down her skirt.

"Thank God he showed himself. Oh, Virgil, we almost did it. We almost did it."

Virgil, still trembling, lit a cigarette and running his fingers through his hair looked down at his pale legs. He pulled his socks up and then his pants. "Yeah, Agnes, almost."

"I've got to see Roebuck and tell him. Oh, Virgil, it was a miracle."

"Oh, for Christ's sake. Grow up; that was a damn short, that's all. Leave that moron out of our business."

"You listen to me, Virgil Hooper Haynes. Preacher Roebuck Alexander is not any moron. He's a saint and he's been put here on this earth to help poor sinners like me and you. You realize what would have happened if that light hadn't struck?"

Virgil buckled his belt, twisted the wires together, and kicked the starter. He slammed the car into reverse.

She raised her voice. "Tell me, Virgil Haynes. You know what would have happened?"

He idled the engine and slumped forward on the wheel. "I'd probably be in a pretty good piece of ass."

Agnes McCoy didn't say a word all the way across town.

As Virgil cut the corner in front of the Piggly-Wiggly he turned the radio on and jacked up the volume. The hundred-man Augusta Baptist Choir blasted into the car, making the dashboard hum and the ash tray rattle. It could be heard a mile away.

Agnes said nothing when he stopped the car in front of her house. She sat stiffly, waiting for him to open the door. He lit another cigarette and after taking three fast draws flipped down the glove compartment and pulled out a fresh fifth of Spider Hornsby's whiskey. He took a long drink and then a short one. He offered the bottle to her. She sat stiff and rigid, looking straight down the dark street. Someone up the block shouted, "Hey! You crazy son of a bitch! Cut that thing off!"

Virgil didn't turn the radio down or kill the engine or open the

(6)

door. He was fed up and furious and the taste of Sen Sen made him spit. He took another drink and then another. It made him even madder.

Agnes snapped the radio off and opened the door. "Good night, Mr. Virgil Haynes, and—"

He didn't let her finish. "Be sure and tell that shithead your pants were wet when the Lord got there."

She slammed the door. "—and good riddance!"

"Go to hell!"

Virgil, with his left hand gripping the rain drain on the roof, dipped under the Southern tracks at Lower Marion. Quick thunder bounced out of the cement underpass as he straddled the yellow line on the Bluff Road and flattened the Chevrolet out at ninety. The needle froze as if painted there, and he held it past the cotton mill. At the Fairgrounds cutoff he jockeyed down to fifty for the hairpin turn around the Texaco station and then, slamming the foot feed to the floor, headed for the green and red neon of Big Cora's.

Agnes McCoy stayed home only long enough to change her underwear and call Preacher Roebuck Alexander. She hurried down the two blocks to his house. At the door she brushed the flying ants away from her face. "I know it's late, Preacher, but I just had to."

Roebuck was tall and had to duck under the six-foot two-inch doorjambs in the living room. He poured two glasses of iced tea and sat her on the wicker couch facing the Late Show. He cut the sound off. "I've never seen you so upset, Sister Agnes. You look like you seen a ghost."

She told him the whole story. Roebuck rose. "Sister Agnes, you've been delivered back to us by the blessed hand of Jesus!" She closed her eyes.

He folded his hands between his knees and rocked back and forth. "This is glorious. Glorious! Sister Agnes, you have been through the fiery furnace. Been through it!" He turned the picture off and took her hands in his. "And lamb, you ain't even singed." In the half dark he scanned her as if he were looking for

(7)

fleas. "Not a mark, not a scratch. Oh, Sister Agnes, I'm glad. I'm so glad!" His arm was around her shoulder; his hand was holding hers. "Now you just sit back and rest your head on me. Oh, this is a joyous night. Joyous. . . . I think we ought to just sit here and thank and praise God."

He began humming and then singing "Love Lifted Me." Together they sang four choruses. The song ended and Roebuck raised his eyes to the dark ceiling. "I thank thee, Lord. I thank thee for protecting and delivering this precious lamb, this precious child, out of the hands of the devil and into your loving grace. I thank thee, Lord, for guiding her through the Valley of the Shadow of Evil. Oh, Lord, I truly thank thee."

Agnes prayed softly. "I thank thee too, Lord, for sending us Preacher Alexander as a rock on which we poor sinners can lean on and draw our strength from."

Roebuck patted her arm and held her other hand. "Sister Agnes, you're no sinner. Why, you're pure enough and fine enough and sweet enough to . . . Why, I can see you—" He swallowed hard and ran out of nerve.

"Where, Preacher?"

He had difficulty getting it out. "I mean, in a couple of years, with a little help and encouragement—why, I can see you with your own congregation."

"You mean that?"

He patted her closer, rubbing her upper arm and squeezing her hand. "I mean it. Why, in a few years I can see us standing in front of a great multitude. Yes, standing there and preaching, shouting and singing, and I can see that great multitude down on their knees, their faces streaming with tears of joy and God's own salvation."

"Yessir."

"Please don't say yessir. I feel like I'm seventeen when I'm with you. And I want you to be calling me Roebuck."

"I'd be glad to."

"And there's something else."

"Yessir. I mean, yes."

(8)

"I think it would be a step in the direction of salvation if you'd get shed of Ruby Jean."

Agnes paused. "Preacher, there's not a lick of harm in Ruby. I declare there isn't."

His right hand held her shoulder, his left patted her hand. "I'd consider it a personal favor, Sister Agnes."

"But we've been together since junior high school. I just don't know about that."

"Well, you turn it over in your mind. We'll talk about it some more. And now I want you to go home and spread that pretty black hair out on a nice white pillow slip and get you some sleep. I've got to work on my sermon."

2

Almost everyone on the six- and seven-hundred block of Cherry heard the singing and came out on their porches to watch the Washed in the Blood of the Lamb Baptist Church end their Wednesday-night prayer meeting with a march on Spider Hornsby's. Preacher Roebuck Alexander, squeezing his Montgomery Ward accordion, and Quendolyn Hightower on guitar led the thirty-six-member congregation marching two by two into the final chorus of "Onward, Christian Soldiers." Behind them down the red clay street of the Bottom one kid was pushing a Greyhound bus inner tube, two were tacking back and forth on bicycles, and Eugene Motes's twin liver-spotted hounds were loping in and out of the ranks and yapping down the drain ditch.

At Spider's yellow clapboard the insect-repellent 200-watt porch light went off; then all the lights. The jukebox stayed on. "Onward, Christian Soldiers" ended and the two columns lined up in the yard facing the geranium beds planted in whitewashed truck tires and the two-swing, no-chair porch.

Preacher Roebuck Alexander inhaled his twelve-chord in a long G flat. "All right, let's give them the 'Spelling Song.'"
Quendolyn's shrill voice took off like steel on stone:

"Some folks jump up and down all night
And D. . .A. . .N. . .C. . .E. . ."

The others followed:

"And then they got the nerve to say
They're S. . .A. . .V. . .E. . .D."

In the dark kitchen, with her red hair snapping in a tight pony tail, Ruby Jean Jamison hitched and jerked to the strong Ray Charles beat from the hundred-selector Seeburg. Her eyes were closed, her shoes were off. She danced close to the big blue and yellow juke, popping her hands on the back beat and picking up speed for the finish. Spider reached down and pulled the plug. The bubbling lights slowed down and died. The music stopped. Ruby whirled. "Hey! Oh, come on, Spider. The hell with them."

Spider sat back in his padded-armrest rocking chair and propped his feet up on the trash burner. His thumbs were hooked under his fifty-four-inch underbelted stomach. "Let's hear what that fool's got to say."

Virgil, sitting on the floor with his back against the wall, said, "Crap, let's hear the music."

As the congregation began humming "Rock of Ages," Preacher Roebuck put a foot on the bottom step and a hand on the rail. "Spider! I say, Spider Hornsby! If you're within reach of my voice you're close enough. All you got to do is reach out. Reach out, Spider, and you can touch that blessed hand of Jesus."

Ruby tucked her candy-striped blouse in her shorts. "Go on, hon. Reach out. Tell him you want to be saved."

Virgil was drinking Spider's moonshine out of a Dixie cup and sucking on a half lemon. "Better listen to her, good buddy. Could be your last chance."

Spider scratched his right heel with his left big toe. He wore no shoes, only short red socks.

Virgil kept his Chevy and International Harvester bulldozer

keys on a rabbit's-foot key chain. He slid over and trailed the hairy foot down Ruby's leg. She jumped. "Goddammit, Virgil! You stop that!"

Spider pointed at where he thought Virgil sat. "Damn your ass! Leave her alone or I'm kicking you out."

"O.K., no more. You got my word." He dipped the dipper in the five-gallon steel bucket on the table and poured a long one. "Must be getting near pay day. Old Roebuck's got a pretty good crowd out there tonight."

Ruby held her hair up and fanned her neck with the TV *Guide*. "Listen at that Quendolyn. I'd give me anything in this world if I could chord a tune like that. I mean it."

Spider rubbed her leg and squeezed her knee. "You keep practicing, sugar plum. You're going to get there. . . ."

Cupping his hand under her knee he sipped his corn and Seven-Up and listened to the singing. For fifteen years Spider had been going to the Washed in the Blood of the Lamb on Sundays and Wednesdays, and for fifteen years he had been the only one in the Bottom to put ten dollars in the collection plate every week. He had paid for the new piano, bought nine new pews for the Amen Row, and three months before, when Preacher Ben Breckenridge had spasmed, stroked, and died while water-skiing up on Lake Murray, he had bought one hundred dollars' worth of fresh flowers and a two-hundred-dollar Winnsboro blue granite headstone. Everything had been fine until Roebuck Alexander had gotten the call from Gates Street Holiness to come to Washed in the Blood. And then it had all happened at once. . . . It was during the second sermon that Roebuck had made his move. He was pounding on the Bible opened at Revelations and preaching about dancing, drinking, and fornicating in the backs of Fords and Chevrolets when suddenly he stopped and pointed at Spider, sitting in the first row. He began screaming like a turkey that the whole problem in the Bottom could be laid at the feet of Spider Harold Hornsby.

Spider had stood up and raised his hand. "Preacher, seems to me like you're getting mighty close to home." He had been calm and had kept his voice low and steady. "If the crowd don't buy it from me, they'll just cross the tracks and get it there." He smiled. "And everyone knows my stuff's ten times better."

Roebuck Alexander had a brown eye and a blue one. When he was worked up and shouting the brown would bulge and the blue would squint. The brown bulged. "If the shoe fits! Wear it!" He was out of the pulpit down in the aisle, pointing his long vein-streaked finger at Spider's nose. "Spider Hornsby! I don't want your kind of trash and commonality in my church!"

He ordered one of the elders to give him back his ten dollars. He said it was blood money, that it had been stolen out of the cribs of babies and the mouths of pregnant mothers, and that either he go down on his knees and swear he was giving up boot-legging or he could leave the church. Someone in the back row coughed. Another said, "Amen."

Spider had hooked his thumbs into his belt loops and standing sideways addressed the congregation. "Well, sir. Seems like you don't give me much choice."

As he took the long walk down the aisle, nodding to his friends and customers, Roebuck had boomed out, "Look at him! I say take a *good* look at him! There's a living, lying, walking lesson for every man jack one of us. There he goes! There goes Spider Harold Hornsby, STRAIGHT TO HELL!"

Outside, Quendolyn Hightower was finishing a solo of "I Need Thee Every Hour." Ruby stopped fanning. "You know something. That old screech owl sounds pretty good."

Quendolyn wasn't the only one in good voice. Roebuck Alexander had climbed up on the third step. "Spider! Spider Hornsby!" The dark house gave him strength. He was louder now, deeper. "This living in wide-open sin is low-rating and corrupting this here neighborhood in the blessed eyes of Jesus. You're mocking everything that sweet man laid down. Everything! What kind of a man are you anyhow?"

Spider threw his Dixie cup at the trash burner, jumped up, and rushed to the porch. He switched on the 200-watter. "Damn you, Roebuck. Get out of my yard."

Roebuck, standing under the yellow light, smiled up and spread his long hands out. They looked green. "Now, Brother Harold."

(14)

Spider's toes gripped the top step. "Don't hand me that Brother Harold crap! Get out of here! And WATCH THOSE PLANTS!"

Roebuck gathered his group in the drain ditch. "All right, Sister Quendolyn, number two hundred and forty-six."

She chorded her guitar.

> "I was sinking deep in sin,
> Far from the peaceful shore . . ."

Spider slammed the heavy-duty screen, stomped back, and plugged the juke back in. He turned it up to full blast and poured a drink. Outside the faint voices held on. . . .

> "Very deeply stained within,
> Sinking to rise no more."

Every porch light on the block was on, and a crowd from Bee Street and Elbow Alley had gathered under the street light on Cherry. Eugene Motes's hounds, after chasing a three-colored cat up past the third climbing iron on the light pole, sat down and with their heads aimed straight up howled at the mixed music. The Washed in the Blood's voices trailed off into the dark. . . .

> "Love lifted me,
> Love lifted me;
> When nothing else could help
> Love lifted me."

Ruby made three fast selections and, woodpeckering her head, snapped her fingers to the fast rising beat. "Don't let that old fool get you down, hon."

He filled a cup with ice. "You still going down there?"

She was pulling Virgil up from the floor. "I already told you I was. Now leave me alone about it."

Virgil was on his feet, finishing his drink. "What's going on?"

She slid into the music. "I'm meeting Agnes so we can rehearse. We're playing out at Stark Street Baptist."

Virgil did a slow, shuffling dance. "Say hello for me."

"O.K." She went into her combination jerk and pony step. "Come on, dead wood, don't just stand there. Move."

(15)

Spider pulled the plug and the juke went off.

She slumped against the wall. "Now what?"

"You know who's out in that mess?"

"My mama?"

"No."

"Who? Come on, Spider, this is really a drag and a half."

"Agnes McCoy."

"Agnes! You gotta be kidding. Spider! You mean it?"

"Right behind Quendolyn."

Ruby's arms flapped down helplessly. "Oh, Lord, now what." Her eyes caught Virgil's. "What in the hell did you do to her?"

"Nothing. Nothing, I swear before God. I didn't do a thing."

Preacher Roebuck Alexander squared his flat black journey-man's hat and touched the miniature Bible in his breast pocket when he saw Ruby legging out of a Yellow cab for the Washed in the Blood's Saturday all-day-singing-and-dinner-on-the-ground so-cial. He crossed the churchyard and smiled down at her. "Miss Ruby Jean Jamison. Now ain't you a picture to behold."

"Thank you, sir." Ruby watched his blue eye dip around her low neckline and his tongue touch his brown teeth. The dress was six inches above her knees, skin tight, and orange.

Roebuck led her back to the tables lined up at the side of the church under the mulberry tree. His long fingers circled her elbow. "Looks to me like you've been to some kind of beauty school or something."

Ruby hadn't worked since she left Southern Bell Telephone three months before and took up with Spider. Since then all she had done was lie around reading movie screen magazines, watch television, and play guitar with Agnes McCoy on weekends. "Yessir, I've been kind of thinking about being a model. They pay you by the hour and all you have to do is just stand there."

"You'd make a dandy model. . . . That's a right nice frock you got on there."

"Thank you, sir." There was almost no back to the bright sateen dress with small white feathers on the short sleeves and tiny rhine-stones on the scooped neckline.

Eugene Motes shouted, "Will you study that!"

Sarah Motes whispered, "Common, that's what it is. That's the lowest kind of trash."

Hooty Hightower crouched up from the long plank table. "Oh, man, if I had me something like that I'd stay broke buying her cookies and taking her to the picture show."

Quendolyn Hightower pulled him down. "Hush your filthy mouth," she hissed. "Look at those shoes." Ruby had on matching orange backless stilts that looked like stilettos. "Them's devil's shoes or I'm not sitting here."

Agnes McCoy took her hands. "Ruby Jean! Just look at you! That's the prettiest thing I ever laid eyes on. Where in the world you get it?"

"Thompson-Ford's."

She circled her, touching the rhinestones and studying the back line. Agnes had been on the high school diving, swimming, and tumbling teams and had won the best posture award her junior and senior years. She pulled Ruby toward the ladies' room, taking five quick steps to her four. "I've just got to try it on."

Ruby skinned the dress off, tucked Agnes's bra straps down, and helped her pull it over her coal-black hair. They wore the same size. "It really fits. Ag, you've got to have one just like it. We'd look wild up on stage."

Agnes stepped in front of the door mirror, fluffing her short bangs straight. "It's like cotton candy." She spun around and pushed up on her toes. "I've never seen anything so pretty. . . . What did it cost?"

"Ninety-six dollars. Eighteen for the shoes. Neat?"

"Nice. Real nice. Spider buy it?"

"You better believe it."

Ruby wiggled back into the dress and nodded at Agnes's hem. "It's crooked, hon. Scootch the back down a little. . . . There, that's it." She stepped into her shoes and standing before the mirror twisted the dress straight and smoothed out the hips. "Ag." She turned to check her back hem. "Spider said you were marching with Roebuck the other night."

Agnes was combing her bangs smooth. "I did, Ruby. I been thinking things over and—"

Ruby interrupted. "And you been listening to Roebuck again. You promised me you'd quit that."

"No, it's not all him. I declare it isn't. I got some plans of my own too."

Ruby rubbed on a second coat of orange lipstick which matched her fingernail polish. "I bet it doesn't have thing one to do with Roebuck. You and Virgil been fighting again, haven't you?"

She wiped the orange trace from her teeth with toilet tissue.

Someone pounded on the door. "Ain't y'all about through in there?"

At the sheet-covered sawhorse table Ruby and Agnes picked up paper plates of meat loaf, egg salad, peas, and cole slaw and sat down. Roebuck slid in next to Ruby and spooned up a mouthful of Crowder peas. "What you two been up to?"

Ruby said, "Nothing, Preacher. Just gossiping. You know how it is."

Roebuck worked the peas up to his front teeth and chewed slowly. "Agnes and me have decided that her voice is the Lord's instrument." He cut his eyes at Ruby. "And I don't want her spoiling it on trash songs. . . . Pass me that catsup."

Ruby saw Agnes's eyes drop and knew she had to move fast. "Preacher you coming out to see us at Stark Street Baptist? We're doing an all-gospel show. Should be a good crowd." Before Roebuck could answer she raised up and looked around. "Lord, it seems like everybody in town's down here today. It's certainly a nice turnout."

Roebuck stabbed his meat loaf. His brown eye swept over her sleeve feathers puffing up in the river breeze. "Did Spider Hornsby buy you that frock?"

Ruby was quick. "No sir! No sir! I swear he didn't. I had me some sick-leave money from Southern Bell. I bought this dress out of my own pocket. Spider doesn't buy me anything."

"Then how come you laying up there at his house?"

"Well, sir, I had me this virus, and you know how crowded we are at my house with Aunt Cassie there." She pushed her cole slaw

(18)

away from the meat-loaf gravy. "Spider's just letting me sleep on his back porch. I do a little cooking and cleaning for him."

"That's all?"

"Yessir, I swear it. He ain't laid hand one on me."

Roebuck splatted catsup on his meat loaf.

"I know it looks pretty fishy and all, but that's the gospel. I declare it."

"All right, I'll take your word. But I'm going to be talking to your mama and I mean to make some changes around here." He pointed the meat loaf dripping with catsup at her. "And I want to be looking out there Sunday morning and seeing you sitting in the congregation. You hear me now?"

"Yessir, I'll be there." Her voice broke. "I'm not missing another service."

"And you be sitting with your mama."

"Yessir."

"And something else. I want you to give Mr. Spider Harold Hornsby a message for me."

"Yessir."

"You tell him the Lord and Roebuck Alexander are going to dog him till he drops."

"Yessir."

"Bullshit! You ain't going down there Sunday and that's final." Spider was sitting in the bathtub smoking a cigar while Ruby scrubbed his back. "Hey, move down a little lower. Yeah, there, that's it."

She rinsed him off and leaned back against the toilet. "I shouldn't have gone there in the first place."

He balanced his cigar on the soap dish. "We all make mistakes. Let's just forget it."

"It ain't me, bonehead, it's Mama. She's going to have a running fit. I'll bet you anything he's down there right this second." She clipped the magnifying mirror on the cold water spigot and worked up a lather in his shaving mug. "Oh, and that stupid Agnes. It makes me want to puke."

(19)

Spider finished shaving and leaned back to soak. "Give me a little more hot water there."

Ruby spotted a blackhead cropping out of the thick matted hair on his chest and moved in. "Hold still, hon. I'll get it while it's soft."

"Make it fast." He gritted his teeth. "God, I hate that."

She squeezed it out on her fingernail and scratched at his thick chest hair. "Lord knows what else's under there."

After Spider dried and Ruby had sprinkled talcum on his stomach and back and poured foot powder in between his toes he put on clean shorts and stretched out on the bed. He pushed the sheet to the foot. "I'm about to roast."

She slid the air-conditioner control from low to high. "That better?"

"That'll do it." He spread out in the whistling breeze. "Call me at four. And keep your eyes peeled, now, hear?"

"O.K., hon."

She folded a cold cloth over his eyes and checked the windows and the doors. The heavy-duty screens were snugged and latched and the back door with its three-by-four timber saddled into cast-iron U joints looked like it would hold wild animals. In the kitchen the red corn whiskey in the industrial mop sink glistened in the two o'clock sun; the level was at forty-four gallons. Underneath the sink a washtub was filled with soaking clothes and laundry soap.

Ruby took a king-sized Dr. Pepper from the refrigerator and with her movie magazine went out on the porch.

She was halfway through an abortion story in *Screenland Scandals* when the four-o'clock whistle sounded at the cotton mill. She called out, "Honey! Honey!"

Spider was a heavy sleeper and she knew he didn't hear her over the air-conditioner noise. She flipped through the story; it was only one more page.

Two paragraphs from the end she looked up. A car had turned the corner at Cooper and was heading down Cherry directly in the sun. She shaded her eyes and squinted.

"HONEY!" She backed through the doorway. "Honey!" She

threw the two three-quarter-inch bolts on the screen. Suddenly her heart was racing and pounding in her throat. "Wake up! For God's sake!" Two hundred yards away the black Ford came barreling out of the sun. She shook Spider, screaming, "Spider! Spider! It's the Law!"

He bounced up. "Jesus Christ! Lock the door! Lock it!"

"I did! I did! Hurry, hon, hurry!"

He raced down the short hall, sidestepped the kitchen table, and knocking over a chair pulled the plug on the whiskey. The four-inch drain with no U trap was straight as an artillery piece, and in twenty seconds the red corn dropped and, with a deep sucking smack, vanished. Spider dumped in the load of soaking laundry to hide the smell and rinsed his hands.

Ruby screamed from the front, "Oh, Lord! Here they come!"

The black Ford had skidded sideways on the clay and stopped with all four doors open. Sheriff Kershaw Miller, his assistant, Maynard Moody, and three deputies came out streaking for the steps.

Spider hollered, "Save that door! Unlock it! Unlock it!"

Maynard, a 270-pound one-eared ex-tackle for the University of South Carolina, led the charge. He tucked his head and thundered up the steps to smash in the screen.

Ruby screamed, "It's open! It's open!"

Maynard came out of his crouch and pulled aside. Kershaw Miller whipped through, flashing the search warrant and heading straight for the kitchen. He stopped at the mop sink and stared down at the soaking socks and underwear.

Spider came out of the bedroom, zipping his fly and yawning. "What's going on here? Hello, Kershaw, Maynard. Didn't hear you boys come in. . . . Give me a cigarette, sugar plum."

Kershaw handed him the search warrant and picked up a pair of soaking overalls. "Spider, you bastard, you been washing this thing out for three months now."

"You're right, Kersh. Maybe I'll have Ruby starch and iron them up. Put some coffee on, doll baby."

The deputies were searching under the house and hammering their five-foot steel stakes into the clay yard. Maynard tap-tapped on the walls and floors and finally knelt down and with his good ear listened to the echo under the gray hearthstone. It sounded hollow. "Sheriff, you want me to tear her up? She's probably loaded."

Kershaw looked at the hearth and then at Spider. "Naw, Maynard, that thing's twenty years old. Call the boys off."

Spider propped the search warrant against the see-no-evil, hear-no-evil, tell-no-evil monkeys on the mantelpiece.

Kershaw said, "Got any iced tea?"

"Should have. Fix him up, baby."

Kershaw nodded at Maynard. "How 'bout checking along the fence?"

"Sure thing, Sheriff."

Spider flagged him. "Careful, Maynard, there's poison ivy towards the back."

Ruby poured coffee for Spider and tea for Kershaw. "I got some fresh cinnamon rolls. Y'all want some?"

Kershaw shook his head.

Spider buttered a roll. "How's Sally?"

"O.K. She said say hello." Kershaw was too tall to sit at the kitchen table and get his knees under. He spun a chair around and straddled it.

"Spider, we're hitting Wateree next week. Stripers are running. Why don't you close up and come along?"

"No, better not. Too much going on around here. Maybe next time."

Kershaw stirred a spoonful of sugar in slowly. "I guess you know old Roebuck's on our ass every day."

Spider bit off half of his roll and buttered the other half.

Kershaw rested his long chin on the top slat of the chair and stretched his legs out. "Election's coming up, old buddy. You just better keep downwind."

"Screw him! I ain't losing any sleep on that sapsucker."

Ruby buttered Spider another cinnamon roll. "I got plenty of coffee, Kershaw. Maybe Maynard wants some?"

"Naw, I don't want him in here." He finished and stood up. "I gotta get on in. . . . Let me know if you change your mind."

(22)

"O.K., horse. Say hello to Sally."

"Take care. And listen, you keep an eye on old Roebuck."

"I'll do that thing."

"So long, Ruby."

"Bye now."

On Friday, Ruby had lunch at the Southern Bell cafeteria with her girl friends from the second shift before her wash, rinse, and set appointment at Dixie-Carolina Coiffures. Later she visited Mary Beth Tyson and Beverly Eppes on the cosmetic counter at Woolworth's, before window-shopping up one side of Main and down the other until the Steve McQueen feature began at the Robert E. Lee. At seven, in Spider's new Oldsmobile with her guitar in the back seat, she picked up Agnes and headed out to the Stark Street Baptist for their eight o'clock show.

There was no backstage at Stark Street, and they tuned their guitars while standing against the wall to keep their blue and yellow Swiss cowgirl "Rose of Sharon" costumes from wrinkling. They were getting eight dollars for the show, and the music was being taped for a later broadcast over WJBD, the 5,000-watt local gospel network.

When the benediction began Ruby ducked her head and through half-closed eyes counted the audience in the low-ceilinged, no-window concrete basement at 124. Sitting straight and tall in the third row with his hat on his lap was Preacher Roebuck Alexander.

After Reverend Wade Wheeler explained how the proceeds from the pie and cake auction would go toward the building fund he suddenly shot his elbows out like Jackie Gleason and, crouching and grinning, waved Ruby and Agnes to the center of the tiny stage as if it were a sixty-foot runway.

Crossing over with a series of fast quarter steps they curtsied twice, thanked him, and, adjusting the mike down, went into their version of Hank Williams's "I Saw the Light."

They played four straight hymns, took a two-minute water break, and tuning up again did three more, finishing with Agnes singing the high part of "When Jesus Washed My Sins Away"

(23)

and Ruby doing the low. The crowd moved in close to shake their hands, and three teen-agers wanted autographs and asked if they had any photographs. While they were spooning up ambrosia in the supper line, a ninety-year-old member printed them out a recipe for sweet potatoes and marshmallows. "Girls, I want you to know that's the finest piece of gospel talent I've heard. It's as pure as spring water."

As they sat at the head of the table and smiled out at the adoring crowd, Agnes whispered, "How'd you sign yours?"

"Same old way. The Rose of Sharon Girls, Ruby Jean Jamison. . . . What's Roebuck doing out there?"

"I invited him."

"I suppose he's taking you home."

"Yes, he is."

Two offers came out of the performance: one to sing at the North Columbia Junior High School Square Dance the next night between the sets for eleven dollars, the other to replace the piano player at the State Street Presbyterian, who was out with a nervous condition. They took the square-dance offer. Ruby wrote out the program, cutting the six hymns down to two. Agnes got mad. "You can't do that. You promised it would be at least three-quarters gospel."

"Oh, for God's sake. That crowd's going to be drinking hard liquor."

"Well, then, you can just get yourself another girl."

"O.K., Agnes, O.K. . . . Four gospel and two c. and w.'s. They're going to love us."

At the junior high school gym the crowd stayed silent and drifted around on the hymns and cheered the country. Ruby cut the last two hymns out and let Agnes finish up with Marty Robbins's "Ribbon of Darkness."

Her voice throbbed and hung in the air and she held the last note high and broke it off perfect. The thin crowd up front loved her and jammed in tight, applauding and shouting their names while they stood center stage, smiling, bowing, and holding hands.

Agnes whispered, "It's like a hymn, you know that? I sang that thing like it was a hymn."

Ruby smiled, curtsied, and blew kisses to the crowd. "Well, from now on that's going to be our finish song."

An old lady trembled forward. "Honey, you there—yes, you. You got a tear in your voice. A natural tear. That's a gift from God."

Agnes's eyes shone. "Thank you, ma'am."

3

Ruby, in her Frederick's of Hollywood mail-order nightgown, lay next to Spider, smoking and watching the shadows cross the ceiling when the cars passed. It was two o'clock. A hotrod with a wide-open muffler squealed rubber as it skidded around the corner and went backfiring out Bee Street toward Sugar Hill. Spider didn't move. He slept perfectly still, flat on his back with his hands folded over his stomach, snoring softly.

Stubbing the cigarette out in the Maxwell House coffee can on the floor, she put her feet up on the bottom rail. She'd read in "Tips the Stars Use for Better Living" that elevating the feet cools and relaxes the body during times of stress. She lay still, waiting for the cooling and the relaxing, but all that came was a sharp pain where the bed rail cut her heels. She folded her pillow over the rail and tried again. It was better, and closing her eyes lightly she began naming five movie stars whose names began with A, and then B, and then C. . . . After E, and Clint Eastwood, she began thinking about Agnes. It was all Roebuck's fault. She had to keep her away from him. If they could only get out of town for a week or so, downstate or over to Georgia. She wasn't the world's smartest girl at Southern Bell pushing Princess sets, but she could sing and play rings around anyone in town. She couldn't afford to lose her. She felt herself getting tense and, pushing Agnes out of her mind, began thinking about Southern Bell. The girls at lunch said if she came back soon she could keep her two years of seniority. She lit another cigarette. She could work hard and be on time and dress sharp. She knew she could pass the supervisor test. She was ten times smarter and better looking than Thelma Jean Hooker, and people liked her more. Everyone had told her that. Yes, that would be it. Ruby Jean Jamison—Supervisor, Room 802. She'd be out of the office pool, into her own office. People would have to knock to see her. . . . It would be hard leaving Spider. What would she tell him? She formed the words silently, carefully emphasizing each one. "But I got to be doing something. I just can't lay here letting the best years of my life go sliding down the drain. . . . One hundred and twenty dollars a week for supervisor wouldn't be too bad, and there would be raises and cost-of-living increases. And there was always something going on at old Bell Tel—bowling, movie parties, dances, picnics, outings. . . . Maybe there would be a fellow who was on his way up. An official's son who was going places and doing apprentice work just to get the feel of things. She shifted her feet up higher on the pillow and pushing the smoke out through her teeth thought about the men: the pole linemen, the riggers, the PBX men, the wirers, the drivers. It was no use. They were all the same. Always double clutching and spinning their wheels and throwing gravel. All they ever wanted to do was square dance till they were soaking wet and then whip off on some dirt road and drag you into the back seat. None of them ever got to wear a dark suit or go to meetings where they served cocktails and had after-dinner speeches. The only things they ever went to were the bowling league and the fish fries or out crazy drunk at the honkytonks. Maybe Southern Bell was dead wrong.

Maybe she would go to the airline hostess school or learn to be a model. She would be a cinch for the airlines. There would be executives flying first class to the big cities, and the pilots were

(28)

always getting divorced and marrying stewardesses. But modeling would be a better future. She would be her own boss and have no one to answer to. Twenty dollars an hour was what the advertisement she had clipped out had said. Twenty dollars an hour for just standing there. Sometimes sitting. And if the job was for a bathing suit company it would be laying there or stretched out on a Hollywood settee glider with all the men rushing around adjusting the lights, patting her face dry, and telling her how gorgeous she was. . . . A freight train rolled by, and the dry chinaberries pinged and rolled down the tin roof.

Ruby Jean Jamison stretched out on her Hollywood settee. She could hear the cameramen around her, feel the lights, and smell the warm California sun outside the studio. She was getting sleepy. She yawned and stretched out and saw herself surrounded by cameramen, agents, light men, and stage managers. A small quiet man with big dark glasses was handing her his card. A whisper had run through the crowd. Talent scout. . . . Maybe a small part at first. Then maybe a western or two. Two would be enough; they wouldn't want to overexpose her. That was what happened to Sandra Dee. No, they would be more careful with her. They would want to protect their investment.

She stared out over Spider's bulk at the tin roofs and TV antennas shining in the moonlight. They had to replace the stars of yesterday with the stars of tomorrow. It was that simple. They weren't fools out there. Look at Joan Crawford and Barbara Stanwyck, they're already playing grandma roles on the TV movies, and a few years ago they were playing young girls coming to town and trying to make it on Broadway. Time marches on. She wondered how old Ann-Margret was. Natalie Wood? Tuesday Weld? One advantage; at least they wouldn't have to change her name. She closed her eyes again. She heard the MGM lion roar and then *Metro Goldwyn Mayer proudly presents the Darling of Two Continents, Ruby Jean Jamison and her magic guitar.* . . .

After another cigarette and a run down the list of songs she would eventually record as her favorite medleys, she pulled the sheet up. Spider farted softly and, as if on signal, stopped snoring. A siren wailed out near Sugar Hill. A coon hound answered. She began drifting off and, after bowing to the 10,000 seated and the 6,000 standing at the Hollywood Bowl and promising she would keep every one of them in her heart and then bowing again and throwing a kiss to each of the eight sections, Ruby smiled and went to sleep.

She got up early, made coffee, and sat at the kitchen table studying the yellow pages. She drank left-handed as she checked the six charm schools listed. And then, remembering from the Southern Bell rate book that the ones in blocked type cost $20 a month extra, she drew a scalloped circle around Hollywood Charm School. Raymond La Mer (formerly of Hollywood and New York City—coach and adviser to international stars, artists, and models) invites you in for a free consultation.

In the back yard the July sun glistened on the broken glass and sardine and oil cans and flashed on the lightning rods out toward the cotton mill. She wondered why Raymond La Mer had chosen to leave the international stars of Hollywood and New York City and come to Columbia, S.C. Maybe he had gotten tired of the pressure and the high living. Maybe he had t.b. or psoriasis and the Carolina weather was good for him. On the top board of the fence, the catalpa caterpillars that had fallen into the milkweed and strangle grass were hunching along, heading back to strip off the last leaves of the mulberry tree. But maybe Raymond La Mer of Hollywood and New York City really knew that the small towns of America were the place to discover the real talent and the true stars of tomorrow. She sipped her coffee and carefully drew a heavy line under the circle around Hollywood Charm School, 1419½ Assembly Street.

Ruby sat against the post at the foot of the bed while Spider drank his coffee and had his first cinnamon roll of the day. "Hon, how'd you like me to go to charm school? They teach you how to walk, talk, have poise. I mean everything."

Spider, in his pajama tops and jockey shorts, bit the roll before the butter dripped. "What do you want to be doing something like that for?"

(30)

"Hon, if I had poise, I could walk into any room I pleased. Any time. And I mean I wouldn't have to be embarrassed about going anywhere."

He wiped the sugar from his fingers on the sheet. "Listen, don't bother me with that now. I gotta get me a driver."

She set his plate on the night stand and wiggled in close beside him. She touched his ear and began worrying his pajama-top buttons. "Love bug, you'd be surprised how much you can learn from a charm school. Betty Anne Brooks only went four months and when she came out of that place—I mean, you didn't even know she was the same girl."

Spider stirred the sugar up from the bottom. "Hell, you got all that going for you now. I don't want any changes."

Ruby's voice dipped low. "Hon, I ain't going to be changing. It's not like that at all. I'm going to improve myself." All the buttons were open and her voice trilled even lower. "Hon, everything I do now I'll just be doing that much better."

She took his coffee cup.

Spider's eyes filmed over. His face relaxed and slowly he let himself slide back down. She blew in his ear and tipped it with her tongue. "That's better. Much better. Now you just relax. Ruby's got a nice surprise for you."

Suddenly he jerked and sat up. "Christ!" He bolted up and snatched on his pants. Barefooted and like a brown bear crossing his cage at feeding time, he rushed to the phone. "I should've been up at dawn." Frantically he began dialing. Dumping the forty-four gallons had cleaned him out. He needed at least fifty to get through the weekend. He dialed and talked, dialed and talked. Five drivers said flat no. The law was too hot. One was down with a broken foot. He kept dialing.

Spider sold a two-ounce shot for 25 cents, a pint for two dollars, a quart for three, and a half gallon for five. A simple one-color label of a black crow sitting on a barbed-wire fence was on every bottle. The caption read Black Crow Whiskey, the Best Made. The bottles came in from a North Carolina glass company and were ridged with a heavy waffle pattern. Spider claimed a man could get a grip on his bottle and drink the fine year-old straight corn even in the rain.

While Spider called, Ruby, in the deep draw of his side of the bed, was spreading her toes with cotton so she could paint the nails and listening to a country and western program from Memphis. She was trying to memorize the words to a new song, but a 50,000-watt Charlotte talk show was crowding it out. She tried the volume, then the station finder. It was no use; Charlotte's 50,000 watts was only 100 miles away, Memphis's 30,000 almost 400. She cut it off and began stroking the bright Love's Blush Red onto her little toe. . . .

Spider leaned on the doorjamb. "Anything to eat around here?"

"Few minutes." She was stretched out reading *Movie Screen Romances* with her cotton-spread feet propped up on the rail. "I'm almost dry. Any luck?"

"I jacked Virgil up to a maybe. . . . Doesn't look too good." He scratched himself where his belt was cutting.

"Listen, hon, I'm still serious about that Hollywood Charm, I swear I am. Think you could see your way clear?"

"Sure, sugar foot. You want to go, you go. . . . Find out how much you need."

She blew him a kiss. "Know something, love bug?"

"What's that?"

"You're much nicer than you're ugly."

He grabbed both ankles in one hand and tickled her feet.

She screamed, "Stop! Stop! I take it back! I take it back! . . . Please! Please! Stop it, crazy! . . . You're *ruining* my pedicure!"

Ruby, clutching her Daytona Beach scarf to her jumbo curlers, stuck her head out the back screen door. "Spider! Spider!" Her voice blew thin in the whistling wind. "Telephone!"

It had been gusting all morning, scattering and plastering the trash up against the chicken-wire fence and grinding the tin roof seams together. Spider didn't hear her. He was cutting the strangle grass and the pokeweed out of his corn patch that grew along the fence. The corn had been planted late in half shade and half sun and sloped off from a high of five feet to a low of two.

(32)

"Spider!"

He saw her waving. "O.K., honey! O.K."

"It's Kershaw."

"Be right in."

Spider sat on the sofa with his feet on the coffee table, nodding and smiling and watching the wind suck the Cherry Street dust up into the chinaberry trees. "Fine with me. . . . Fine. . . . Perfect."

He hung up.

"Stripers are running ten and twelve pounds. Says they could be arrested for assault and battery."

"Great!"

"Sure you don't want to come along?"

"I can't, hon. I'm starting Hollywood Charm. You didn't forget, did you?"

"Oh, yeah, that's right." He twisted around to get at his wallet.

Ruby in her bra and panties stood before the three-view vanity mirror, taking readings on her best angles. She pushed her hair down over one eye and tried looking sleepy, then longing, then sad. She liked the sad view best. She swept her thick hair back and gathered it tight and aiming her chin at the ceiling trim did Noble. Then shaking it out and bunching a soft frame around her face tried Sweet, Thoughtful, Coy, and finally moving in close to watch her eyes completed the eleven suggested expressions recommended by *Screen Fun and Fashion*, going from Brave Happy to Sweet Happy and finally to Joyous, Laughing Happy.

"Hey, hon, look here a minute."

"Yeah."

"Stand right there." She twisted her left arm, tightening her bra, hunched her shoulders forward to deepen the cleavage, and smiled brightly at the ceiling. "What do you think? Tell me the truth, now."

"Christ! Why don't you relax and be natural?"

"This is for the camera, silly. I've got to find my best side."

"Well, I don't like all that straining. You look like you're posing for a constipation ad."

"Bull. You're going to be a big help."

(33)

He flopped down on the bed. "You sure this charm school crowd ain't some kind of hustle? Lot of those moochers work out of orange crates. They suck gals in and get them in all kinds of trouble."

"La Mer must be pretty good size. He's running a three-inch block ad. That's at least sixty-five dollars a month. . . . What kind of trouble you talking about?"

He scratched an armpit and sniffed his fingers. "Naked posing, stag movies, stuff like that. Listen, you see anything fishy you let me know."

"O.K., hon. But don't you worry." She dipped her left shoulder and smiling sleepily moved in close to the mirror. "This is one gal that knows how to take care of herself."

Ruby climbed the double flight of stairs at 1419½ Assembly, went down a short hall, and stood before Hollywood Charm School, Inc., Raymond La Mer, Prop. At the corner of the frosted door glass an embossed card was neatly typed. BACK IN FIF-TEEN MINUTES, Lorlene Tisdale. She lit a cigarette and leaned against the wall, blinking her eyes rapidly to make them shine.

At one-forty a short heavy woman wheezed up and unlocked the door. She patted her chest, catching her breath. "Come in, darling." Handing Ruby a three-by-five application card and a ballpoint, she said Mr. La Mer had an important luncheon at the May-fair Restaurant and would be back at two.

Ruby traced over the "R" in Ruby three times as she studied the form, figuring out her work history record. Skipping the current employment blank and ambitions, she began checking off the facts:

Age: 22
Height: 5 feet 7 inches
Weight: 110
Hair: red
Eyes: blue
Dress size: 8
Bra size: 34 C
Swim suit: 6

(34)

For high school majors, commercial science and home economics; under college and languages, none. Dropping down to chronological employment she listed: curb hop, six months; counter girl, six months; cosmetic sales and demonstrations at Woolworth's, one year; operator and Southern Bell supervisor trainee, two years. For skills: speedwriting, switchboard, and short-order work. Under talents she wrote out singing, guitar, and dancing, and under prizes she carefully printed Columbia High School First Prize for Baton Twirling and Fancy Strutting.

"You finished?"

"Almost." Ruby tapped the current employment blank and filled in None. And finally, across the four lines reserved for ambitions, she capitalized COUNTRY AND WESTERN SINGER.

Lorlene Tisdale, the combination receptionist, secretary and three-line switchboard operator, had small eyes, a small round mouth, and extremely small ears. She spoke carefully, pronouncing every letter in every word, and said she owed her new diction to Raymond La Mer. "I don't have any plans for New York or Hollywood or nothing like that. All I want to do is improve myself." She slid Ruby's application in the Incoming Mail basket. "I always say there's no such thing as being too charming."

"Who else works here?"

"Just me. It's like dog days now. This heat kills this kind of business. People just don't want to do anything. But you wait till the fall comes. We're going to be swamped."

Ruby recrossed her legs to keep from getting a red spot. "What's Mr. La Mer like?"

"You'll just love him. You're sitting right under his picture."

She stood up and stepped back from the 24- by 36-inch soft focus of Raymond La Mer. He was dark and serene-looking; he could be twenty-four or forty-four, five foot two or six foot three. The air conditioner wasn't cooling the room and her dress was sticking to her back. "He is kinda handsome."

"I think he's divine. And Ruby, he's just as humble. He doesn't care where you're from or what you are or anything. He'll just get right down there on your level and make you feel at home. There's an art to that."

(35)

"I guess there is."

"You know what La Mer means? It's French."

"No, don't believe I do."

"The sea. Raymond of the sea. Pretty, ain't it?"

Ruby picked her dress from her shoulders, wishing he would show up.

Lorlene's eyes twinkled. "And you talk about an operator. Why, just this morning he came in and said, 'Lorlene, I gotta go to New York City. Make me a reservation on Eastern.' Just like that. Why, you'd think he was calling a cab or sending out for a sandwich. . . . Oh, darling, you're going to love him. And with your figure and personality there ain't no telling how far you're going."

"You wouldn't happen to know if he knows anyone in the music business. I mean like up in Nashville."

"Raymond knows somebody everywhere. Oh, I just wish I had your figure." She stopped, breathless, and deciding to be confidential leaned forward. "I've been on this H.C. grapefruit and boiled egg diet for three weeks now. I know you can't see the results, but I've gone from a size twenty to an eighteen. That's a lot of weight for a gal my size. But if it wasn't for Raymond I couldn't have done it."

The phone rang. "No, sir, Mr. McNally. Mr. La Mer isn't back yet. . . . Yessir, I understand. I'll tell him the minute he comes in. . . . I know, sir. It's just that he's been so busy." She hung up.

The toilet flushed down the hall. Lorlene shaped her hair in back. "That's probably him now. Oh, I forgot something. If you got any girl friends that want to try H.C., now's the time to bring them. We're giving a flat forty per cent off until August fifteenth."

The door opened and Raymond La Mer came in. He was younger than Ruby had expected, no more than thirty, dressed in sharp yellow Hollywood slacks with a wine-colored long-sleeve shirt and a yellow ascot matching his slacks around his slim brown throat. He had long wavy black hair that covered his ears like Prince Valiant and duck-tailed down over his collar. When he smiled at Lorlene his bright, small teeth flashed. "Grapefruit and egg?"

Lorlene beamed. "Yessir."

He took Ruby's card from the basket and winked at Lorlene.

"That's my girl. . . . Ruby Jean Jamison. Ruby Jean . . . nice sound."

"Thank you." For a minute Ruby thought someone else was speaking. His low disc-jockey voice and careful pronunciation seemed to come from a bigger man with a deeper chest. He took her elbow and pushed open his door.

Raymond's office was over the neon of the ABC Loan Company at 1419 Assembly and looked out toward the Checkerboard Feed Store, the Eat Right Cafe, the tall tower of WJBD and the Congaree River. Pictures of Rock Hudson, Paul Newman, and Barbra Streisand were arranged in a giant horseshoe around one of Mr. La Mer standing at the main gate of Paramount Pictures in Hollywood shaking hands with someone with a cigar that Ruby didn't recognize.

Raymond kept reading the application and glancing at her. He walked to the window. "Ruby, I shall continue looking out this window for another minute. During which time you will prepare yourself for what we call the Hollywood Charm Poise and Assurance Test. Now don't be frightened. It's really very simple."

Ruby felt strangely cool and sure of herself. Something exciting was going to happen.

"I want you to imagine yourself in New York City. You are modeling a twenty-five-thousand-dollar formal evening gown trimmed in seed pearls for nine or ten of the brighter luminaries of Broadway. They are seated around this room. . . . Now you are to walk slowly. You are not to smile or try to sell. You are to radiate confidence, sophistication, and above all"—he kissed his thumb and first finger—"chic. You have ten seconds . . . five . . . O.K., Ruby."

Ruby, following the *Screen Fun and Fashion* instructions for sophisticated entrances, lowered her eyelids until she could see the lashes, sucked her jaw down to highlight her cheek bones, and exhaled. She thought cool thoughts of frozen trees and dripping icicles as she glided out with her toes pointed firm and out, her shoulders down and back, her elbows in. . . . Five steps, six.

"Stop! Don't move!"

He touched her chin to the right and stepped back and cocked

(37)

his head to see her from a lower angle. "Yes. Yes. All right, now, hold it." He vaulted up on top of his desk and crouched toward her, framing his hands like a lens finder tracking across her shoulders, her face, down her body, and then back to her face. He moved in closer as if he were shooting film. "Lovely, lovely. Just a few make-up touches and a little coaching."

He sat on his desk, his Italian buckled shoes swinging, rubbing his manicured hands together as if he were washing them. "I don't know if you want Hollywood Charm. But Ruby Jean Jamison" —he spun the card around—"of 602 Cherry Street, Columbia, South Carolina, Hollywood Charm wants you." There was no ankle flash when he crossed his legs, for his black ribbed stockings were long, and no flapping cuffs, for he had none on his tapered Hollywood slacks.

Ruby smiled. "Hey, great! Mr. La Mer, what I got in mind—"

Raymond frowned and took her hands. His nails were lacquered with a clear polish and the cuticles were half mooned and perfect. "We don't say got."

"Well, anyway, what I'd like to be taking is—"

"No. No." He drew her close and held her elbows. "We say what I'd *like*. Try *like* for me. And let me hear the 'i.'"

Ruby said, "Like." The "i" had an "a" sound and hung in the air too long. "How's that?"

"We'll work on it later." He moved her toward the window light. "Stand here. I want to check something."

Ruby looked at the radio tower and the river in the distance. "What I'd like to put in for is something in Nashville. I can play pretty good and sing a little bit, and that place is a natural showcase for talent . . . I was thinking."

"No. No. I don't want you to do any more thinking. That's what I'm here for." He closed his dark eyes and squeezed her hands. "What I have in mind is the Great White Way. New York City. Broadway, Ruby. Broadway and from there who knows. But the last place on earth we want to have you is that cow town Nashville."

"But—"

"No buts. You're a natural. A natural. There's not a New York

(38)

agent in the business that wouldn't cut my throat to get his hands on a talent like you."

"Natural what?"

"You're a high-fashion model, possibly an actress. Ruby Jean Jamison, you're going to have your picture in every magazine in the country. In six months, with any kind of break, we'll have Hollywood, New York, and Nashville, Tennessee, down on their knees begging for you."

"Three hundred dollars!" Spider sat on the couch flipping playing cards into his felt hat. Six were in the crown, two were balanced on the wide brim, and the rest were scattered across the room as if the wind had caught them. "That's a helluva lot of money for an ante."

"But honey." Ruby squatted in front of him. "Raymond La Mer says I'll make that back in an hour and a half. One hour and a half! You hear that. He wants to take me up to New York City. We're flying up on Eastern. Lord, most of the money is for getting there and expenses."

Spider's chest hair was shining and springing through his tight undershirt. He flipped a card that fell short. "Then why ain't he paying the freight?"

"Oh, Spider, if you had any idea of the way that man's been screwed by Hollywood and New York agents and producers and all. . . . Why, he's got money gone to bed. He just can't lay his hands on it right now, that's all."

"Here, let me see that contract."

Ruby's stockings were straining at the knees. She stood up. "Hon, there's an old fat thing there working for him who is one living mess, and you know he treats that gal like she was Miss Carolina. I swear he does."

Spider sucked in, whistling. "Look at that type. It's like an insurance policy. You need a microscope to read it. . . . Ruby, this fellow's practically your goddamn guardian."

"That's what I've been trying to tell you." She squeezed his hand. "He really takes care of you. You know what, when I told him that I wanted to go to Nashville and try out for the Opry, you know what he did? He put his hand right over my mouth and said, 'Ruby Jean Jamison, you're a high-fashion natural. Every New York agent and photographer is going to break his neck trying to snatch you away from me. I need this contract to protect myself.' Those were his exact words."

"Well, he's sure as hell done that." He slapped the eight-page contract down. "Sugar, he can do *anything* he wants with you."

"Hon, that's what I've been trying to tell you. I'm willing to let him." She bit her bottom lip as tears came to her eyes. She reached for the Kleenex and ran her fingers along the monkeys on the mantelpiece. Her voice began breaking. "I can't be wasting my life lolling around here picking up candy wrappers and dirty socks and reading magazines. . . . I got plans, Spider. I'm going to do something with myself."

He shuffled over in his bedroom slippers. He was an inch shorter than her in her pumps. When he hugged her waist she made no effort to slouch down to him. "Come on, puddin'. Come on, now. Put the coffee on. We'll work something out. You know I can't stand seeing you cry."

"Lord, it's only three hundred dollars, and look what I'd be getting out of it."

"Sugar plum, you know it ain't the money. I'm just worried you're getting in over your head."

"Well, it's my head." She blew her nose and headed for the kitchen. He pushed down on his knees sighing, and rose.

Spider dumped three spoons of sugar in his coffee and slid the bowl across.

"No, thanks."

Ruby sat tall and straight, looking out the window at the summer sparrows dusting themselves in the driveway dirt. "I'm on a diet. I'm losing ten pounds by next week."

"Ten pounds! I suppose that's another one of Mr. Raymond La —whatever you call that New York tap dancer's plans. Now just where in the hell you getting ten pounds to lose?"

She kept watching the sparrows, sniffing through her Kleenex. "He wants my face bones to jut out and be more prominent. He says they'll show up better on camera."

(40)

"Bullshit! You start skipping meals and you're coming down with a virus. Then you'll lose some weight. You look like a forty-cent pullet already."

The hot black coffee stung as she swallowed. She missed the taste of sugar. But then she remembered: twenty-five calories per spoonful eight times a day came to 200. She'd cut out bread, butter, potatoes, salad dressing and dessert, exactly what Raymond had suggested, and it would be another 500. He would be able to relax when he saw he not only had a talent who could wear a bathing suit but one who could follow directions. One who wouldn't have a fit and crack up under the strain of travel or early morning shootings or the grind of personal appearances. . . . She thought of the slender Raymond sitting on his desk swinging his feet and planning her New York debut and cut her eyes to Spider. Every detail of Raymond was reversed in Spider. Where Raymond sat erect and poised, Spider slouched forward in his butter-stained too-tight undershirt with his arm hooked around his cinnamon roll plate. Where Raymond's hands and nails could have been photographed for a magazine advertisement, Spider's were thick with kinky black hair down to the knuckles and black solid rinds of grease under the ragged nails, and where Raymond's long-ribbed stocking and high-gloss shoes kept his legs a secret, Spider's elastic-marked ankles and yellow heel bunions, splayed out and shining like peanut brittle, were barely into his heel-crushed slippers. She bit her tongue and wadded up the Kleenex. "I got me a headache. I'm going to lie down for a while."

He touched her arm. "Slide me those rolls."

"Here you go."

"And hand me my wallet. It's on the bureau."

Ruby salted her beer and lit a cigarette. She and Agnes were sitting at the drugstore counter waiting for the three-ten bus. She watched herself in the back bar mirror, imagining she was on camera and doing a long serious love scene. "Ag, you're just going to die when you meet Raymond."

"What's that last name again? Will you quit doing that!"

"La Mer. Raymond La Mer. It means Raymond of the sea. . . . Doing what?"

"Talking and looking in that mirror like that. You act like you're crazy."

"Let me show you a little something." Ruby tilted her chin and moved the two o'clock shadow that was dividing the store in half to the side of her face. It was a Mia Farrow trick she'd read about in *Movie Life Styles*. "Take a look. See how that shadow juts the jawbone out. That's the look Raymond wants."

Agnes was eating potato chips and drinking a Dr. Pepper. She leaned on her fist. "If you ain't a scandal."

Ruby spun her stool around to look down Elmwood for the bus. She revolved on around. "Ag."

Agnes shook her head. "No lectures, Ruby. You promised."

"O.K., hon. But that man can't be telling you what to do like that. I swear he can't. That's your private life he's messing with. Next thing you know he'll be telling you what kind of sanitary pad to wear. Hey!" She touched Agnes's chin to hers. "You sure that old dog ain't sweet on you?"

"Stop talking like that. That's a man of God. He ain't got no time to be fooling around."

"I bet." Ruby went back to the mirror and the parting-of-the-hero-who-would-never-return expression. "You check your Bible, honey. You check it close. I bet you won't find word one in it about it being a sin to play a few old country and westerns."

"Ruby Jean, you ain't got shake's brains. You just don't understand anything. Roebuck has a different way of reading things. He says there's a lot more there than just the actual words. He says there's words behind the words and words behind those. Why, sometimes he can take just two or three lines and tell you a whole story. Now there's the man with talent. If anyone should be going up to see this Raymond fellow. . . ." She licked the potato chip salt from her fingers. "Ruby, you know the story about Abraham and Isaac?"

"Hush, Ag. I don't want to hear that stuff now. Come on, we got a bus to catch." She paid the bill. "This is on me. Hon, you're just going to love Raymond."

(42)

4

Spider, packing his fishing tackle and gear, was listening to the noon weather report on Channel 2. He whistled as he untangled his hooks and leaders and cut away the dead lines from the old lures. Kershaw Miller and Hooty Hightower were coming by at two. They would be at the Wateree by five.

In the shower Ruby was cream rinsing her hair and throbbing her voice down like Loretta Lynn and singing "Lovesick Blues." She finished and wrapping one towel around her body and two around her hair came dripping into the bedroom, leaving perfect foot marks on the soft wood floor. She sat down, letting her hair fall in front. "Whew! Talk about heavy."

Spider snapped and latched his two-foot-long tackle box. "Sure you won't change your mind?"

"No, hon, you have some fun by yourself. I got plenty to do around here." She began drying. "Hey, guess who talked Agnes back into c. and w.?"

"Raymond La Mer."

"Like butter in his hands." She triangled her hair around her

(43)

eyes. "We're playing Blythewood tomorrow night. Solid c. and w., no gospel."

"Pretty good. Maybe that fellow knows what he's doing after all. . . . What's that do to your New York trip?"

"It's still on. Raymond figures I can use the stage experience. Besides, a little music is always nice to fall back on." She dropped the first wet towel on the floor and started on the second. "He says you never can tell about show business."

Raymond La Mer sat on his desk, swinging his Italian soft-soled shoes. "You ever heard of Jimmy Lee Rideout?"

Ruby shook her head. "Don't believe I have."

" 'San Fernando Rose.' 'The Willow Tree of Love'?"

"Sure, who hasn't. Locklin Matthews does them."

Raymond shot his French cuffs and slicked his creases straight. "Jimmy Lee Rideout wrote them."

"Wait a minute, Raymond. I got the records. It's on Decca."

Raymond breathed in through his teeth. He didn't like being corrected. "Locklin Matthews may be on the label, but Rideout's the man behind the songs. He gave them to him for pushing another single. Locklin Matthews never wrote a song in his life."

"But the record jacket said he did."

"Sure, and they give King James top billing on the Bible." He fitted a filter tip into his gold-trimmed black holder. "Jimmy Lee's in town and he owes me a favor. I told him you girls needed a theme song."

"We sure do. Hey, has he heard of us?"

"Caught you on the radio when he was coming in. . . . Thinks you're going places."

"No lie."

He flicked his lighter on and waited for the flame to settle. "Let's get something straight once and for all. If you make a hundred grand, I make twenty grand. If you make a dollar I make twenty cents."

"I understand."

Ruby shook hands with Jimmy Lee Rideout in the lobby of the Francis Marion Hotel. She felt her skin crawl when he touched her. "You wear those shades all the time?"

"Yeah. Got sore eyes. How 'bout a beer?"

Jimmy Lee Rideout was a thirty-four-year-old albino. He had white hair and eyebrows, bleached skin, and small squinting eyes. Direct sunlight gave him a headache. Even with his dark wrap-around heavy prescriptions, he stayed in the alleys and on the shady side of the street. In the dark bar Jimmy Lee peeled them off, rubbed his eyes, and smiled. "I can tell you don't like me but I'll tell you something else." He talked fast, like a salesman with one foot in the door. There was a two-beat rhythm in his voice, and when he was excited he drummed his fingers in accompaniment. "I ain't going to let it worry me, you hear that? Hear that? And I'm betting fifty bucks, two days from now me and you are going to be just like that." He smiled, holding up two fingers side by side.

"How come you're so nervous?"

He looked around the room as if he were counting the house. A grin flashed. "I'm not nervous. I'm just fast."

Ruby blotted the beer that had run down the glass. "Raymond says you caught us on WJBD."

"Groove. You need a lot of work."

She checked the country and western songs on the juke station. "Everyone else said we were great."

His fast patter sped up. "Everyone else hasn't spend half their lives in Nashville. You need work. You need better music and you need a schtick."

She slid a quarter in the slot and punched down a Loretta Lynn and two by Skeeter Davis. "Listen, mister, you're going to have to simmer down. What in the hell's a schtick?"

"A gimmick. Something to do. Name somebody famous. Name a couple."

"Minnie Pearl. Jim Nabors."

"O.K. Minnie hits them with Miss Ugly. Am I right or wrong?"

"You're right."

"Nabors comes on humble and grateful that he's breathing." Eight fingers were tattooing on the steel table; his lips were barely moving. "Everybody comes on with something. You gals come on earnest as hell, fluttering around, hoping the music is carrying you.

(45)

Well, it won't. You need something. Something new. Different, wild. . . . What's your bra size?"

"Thirty-four C. What the hell difference is that?"

"How about your girl friend?"

"Thirty-six D."

"Great! Small back, all up front. That would do it! No one's done a topless c. and w. in South Carolina. It would be a first. We could call the press and get busted. Now there's something you could run with."

Ruby sipped her beer, watching him twitch and shift in his seat. His eyes shot from hers to the pretzel bowl and up the blue wall to the dark ceiling. His fingers sounded like a stick being dragged down a picket fence.

"What do you say?"

"Bullshit, mister. I ain't going topless for nobody."

"It's up to you, ducky. Just trying to help. The woods are full of hymn bleeders."

"You saying we wouldn't make it in Nashville?"

"You ain't getting out of the Greyhound station with that crap you got. You've got to come up with something new. Let me tell you something, Red. I'm coming down on you hard, but I'm doing you a favor." He peeled a five-dollar bill from his three-inch roll and signaled for two more beers. "Nashville buries sixty duos like 'The Rose of Sharon Girls' a week. They wind up hopping cars or hustling or they get the hell back home where they belong. I'm saving you a lot of grief."

The bartender served the beer. "Hey, mister. That gal on the end wants to know what color's your eyes?"

"Tell her they used to be brown but now they're pink. I ate too much pussy."

Ruby laughed. "Maybe we ought to come on like albinos."

"You'd get a following. One broad heard we carried three balls."

"What'd you tell her?"

"Told her five and they were set up like a revolver and I could fire five times without uncoupling."

"She believe you?"

He laughed once. "They believe anything. . . . Thirty-six D.

(46)

Yowza, Red. If she'd flash those gourds around a guitar neck, we'd really have a package."

"Forget it. What happened to that theme song you told Raymond about?"

"You two need more than a theme."

Ruby's voice was flat, poisonous. "You already said that."

"O.K., your partner sings gospel. Say you come on singing like bad news and she tries to cheer you up."

"Be corny as hell. They'd kill us up North and you know it."

"You ain't going North. You got to put in some time down here." He ran his fingers down the hundred jukebox numbers. "They got ten maybe twelve per cent gospel here. Back in the turpentine you'll get fifty. Hell, I knew a barbecue man who got converted and went hundred per cent. Two hundred hymns. How's that for some dinner music?"

She scratched at her label. "Only trouble is we'd get stuck back in the sticks and we'd never get out. We'd be playing pie parties and dinners on the ground from here on out."

Jimmy Lee's hazel-pink eyes flashed. "No. The minute we get a ripple we head north. Say you're playing Macon. That's a pretty sharp crowd. 'The Rose of Sharon Girls'; I can see it on the billboards now. . . . No, I can't. Lousy name. Grim-oh."

"We had it for six years. Everybody likes it. They voted on it in high school."

"I don't care if it came down in stone from Mt. Sinai. It sounds like a charity group. We'll get you a new one. Anyhow, you're in Macon and your partner—what's her name?"

"Agnes McCoy."

"Agnes! Kiss of death. Anyhow, she's pitching to convert you, only this time you're too wild. Dig? Can you dance? I mean go-go stuff?"

"Sure."

"Fine. O.K., here it goes. She's trying to bring you back into the flock of lambs but this time she ain't getting through. Groove?"

"O.K."

"She gets bugged out there on the straight and narrow. We pull the old switcheroo and you wind up converting her. . . . It'll play.

It'll play wild. I can see it. You're both wailing and pushing it up and telling the crowd about the good life. We can build on that. We can go all the way; it can't miss. There's no way to miss. Get some colored lights spinning around and a strong beat to come down on. . . . If we can't go national with that I'm checking out." He clicked his ballpoint and drew a treble clef and a staff across the beer blotter. Through the bars he printed out HONKYTONK ANGELS. He spun it around. "How's that look?"

"Pretty good."

"Pretty good, hell. It's perfect. It works both ways."

"Yeah, maybe it does. Ruby and Agnes, the Honkytonk Angels."

"Sounds like a bowling team. Agnes has got to go. Need a better sound, something swinging. Wilma Lee or Dotty."

"She's got coal-black hair. How about Mona?"

"Naw, need a better edge. Something you can hear." He snapped his fingers. "Corinne."

"Sounds like a whore. What about Debby or Sandy? How about Candy?"

"Candy. Candy Bar? No, Candy's trouble. I don't mind Robby. It's corny but those long R's look and sound good. Let's see how it settles. . . . Down home all the Rubies are called Ruby Red. Same here?"

"Same here. You from Georgia?"

"Texas."

Ruby sat back, repeating Ruby and Robby, the Honkytonk Angels, while Jimmy Lee scratched furiously on a beer pad.

"Jimmy Lee."

He waved her away, took another blotter, drew more staff lines, and kept writing. He whistled quickly and kept jotting down notes. "Thirty-six D. That's nice. All up front; that's where it counts. How tall is she?"

"We're about the same size."

"Fine. That'll save you a few grand a year and cut down on the luggage." He butted the first and second to a third. "I got something going here. Yeah, yeah, not bad. Not bad at all."

Ruby decided she liked the Honkytonk Angels but wondered what Agnes would say to being called Robby. Jimmy Lee was on his fourth beer pad. Everything was moving fast. A new name, a whole new act, and now maybe a new song. She could see Ruby and Robby, the Honkytonk Angels, on the selection tag in the jukebox station. There was plenty of space for the song. There was no question about it; the pink-eyed albino might be creepy to look at but he was good. Maybe a genius. . . . Still, there was something wrong. There was something crazy about sitting in the dark bar watching his white eyebrows dipping and tightening and frowning over the beer pads. "Jimmy Lee, what's in this for you?"

He ignored her and finished the line. Then patting his left hand on the table and snapping his right while he rocked his head, he ticked it on his teeth. "Listen, Red." He cupped his hands over his ears and closing his eyes la-da-deed a thirty-two-note melody that rose fast, curled back on itself, and left a strong trail. "Try it. . . . Here, I'll do it again."

"Hey, nice. You just write that?"

"Didn't you just see me?"

She grinned. He had to be a genius. "Is that for us?"

"It is when I run some words through it. Great tune, right?"

"Right." She hummed it again. "Great! Hey, how about Oh—we-are-the-Honkytonk-Angels-we're-here-to. . . . You know, something like that?"

"Sounds like a pork sausage jingle. We need something sharp. Sophisticated. Something sneaky they won't forget." He waved for two more beers. "I'll sleep on it. Tomorrow morning I'll have it."

"How do you know you will?"

"Once I get the melody the rest falls in fast. Anybody can write a lyric. You can sing the goddamn phone book against a good tune."

She was excited and wanted to reach over and take his hands. But then from underneath a cool wary pulse began throbbing. "What's your cut in this?"

"I'm Raymond's friend."

"You said that too. What's your other angle?"

He folded the thick beer pads and crammed them in his shirt pocket. He picked up a pretzel and spun it around on his finger. "Yeah, I want something."

(49)

"Well, let's get it out in the open."

Jimmy Lee's rabbit eyes dropped to the table, then rose. "I have trouble getting women."

"That figures."

"This thirty-six D sounds like my ticket to paradise." He spun the pretzel again. "Any chance?"

"She's a gospel girl. Forget it."

"I gotcha." He stopped the pretzel and bit it. "How about you in the meantime?"

"I'm going steady."

"I hear he's over the hill."

She ran her tongue across her teeth. "You heard wrong. Spider Hornsby could buy and sell you and Raymond La Mer out of what he gives to charity."

"Yeah, but the only thing this Spider can do for you in Nashville is get you a seat at the Opry. And then only maybe. . . . You and me and your girl friend are going all the way."

"Sure we are." She poured the last of her beer. "And all I got to do is put out at every crossroad."

"Christ, you make me sound like I'm cutting meat. The song's yours; I promised you that. So's the name, so's the act."

"But we need more than that. We need a coach."

"Groove."

"That's the catch, right?"

"That's your first lesson, Red; there's always a catch. Nobody gives nothing away in this business."

"Don't call me Red."

"O.K. Ruby, anything you say. But what's it going to be?"

"I don't know. . . . I'll have to think it over."

He touched her hand. "See you tomorrow night. I'll have the song finished."

Jimmy Lee's clammy hands looked green in the barlight and his light eyes seemed purple in the neon of the beer sign. She didn't pull away. "You don't work for just straight money, do you?"

He smiled and shook his head. "I don't have to. Tomorrow night. Same time, same station."

(50)

Ruby met Jimmy Lee in the dark corner booth.

"Now, that's what I call a sharp outfit."

She was wearing the tight orange dress and silk shoes that Spider had bought her. She swished into the horseshoe booth and slid around facing him.

"Nice, real nice. Like a beer?"

"Sure."

"Hey, bartender, two Buds. That outfit's all right. You get any ideas for costumes, let's hear them."

"How's the song going?"

"Boffo! Cut the demo this afternoon right here in your fair city." He drank and wiped the foam from his short upper lip. "Finish up and we'll go hear it." He funneled down a handful of pretzel bits and corn curls. "Uh . . . you make up your mind about that thing we were talking about?"

"You don't waste much time, do you?"

"In this business, honey, there ain't much."

Jimmy Lee had all the lights off except one. A bottle of bourbon and a bottle of Scotch reflected in the double-winged dresser mirror flanked by glasses, ice, soda, red- and yellow-shell pistachios and five foil packages of fried pecans. The bed, a red leather-fringed queen size, had a foot-wide control panel on the headboard. From it every three-speed light in the room could be controlled, along with the clock radio, the air conditioner, the color television, and the hotel's advertised summer special, the electric bed vibrator called Magic Fingers.

"Hey, this is a pretty snazzy room."

"It's all they got. Ought to see them on the coast. Sunken tubs, phone in the john, lanai suites, saunas, the works."

"You spend much time out there?"

"Yeah, I can't turn it down. The money's too good. Some guy does a flick he's got to have original music. Otherwise he's paying through the nose to the unions."

"The movies! Which ones you work on, Jimmy Lee?"

"*The Hawk, Blue Tuesday,* a few others."

(51)

"*Blue Tuesday!* Hey, I saw that. Jimmy Lee, you aren't kidding me, are you?"

"No, I did 'em both. They're crap. French horns and violin moods. Crap. It all sounds the same."

"But I remember the *Blue Tuesday* tune, I swear I do. It was good. You shouldn't be low-rating yourself so." She peeled off her dress and hung it in the closet. "I don't want this thing getting wrinkled." She kicked her shoes under the dress and stretched out on the bed in her half slip and bra. "O.K., let's hear the record."

Jimmy Lee had the tape recorder on the night table. He punched the "play" button and turned up the volume. Ruby leaned in close. The driving melody came through stronger than she remembered, and the hard-edged words locked to it like paint on primer.

> "Blue light, green light, red light, whites,
> Just jukebox music and neon nights.
> Oh, there ain't no harps for honkytonk angels,
> There ain't no wings for honkytonk angels;
> Just blue lights, green lights, red lights, whites."

Ruby sat tailor fashion, rocking along with the second verse with her eyes closed and her fingers snapping. She sang it straight through. "Jimmy Lee! I love it. I love the words! Everything. They're wild!"

The music stopped.

"Want to hear it again?"

"Yeah, it's super. Play it louder, Jimmy Lee. It's really great. Lord, you're something else."

He played it again and then again.

"Damn, Jimmy Lee, you really are amazing. I swear you are. That's really a great song."

He smiled with his teeth. His eyes seemed miles away. "I know what I'm doing with music." He shook out a handful of pecans and angled the bourbon at the glass.

"You ain't getting drunk on me, are you? Hey, what's wrong with you anyway?"

"No, I won't get drunk. I can't even feel it." His hands were twitching and he kept wiping the pecan salt on his pants leg. He skinned off his shirt and T shirt and turned on a talk show from New York. He adjusted the contrast. "I get a lot of friends on this one."

The show was in color, and Jimmy Lee, who was as white as upholstery sponge, was picking up the orange tints.

Ruby giggled.

"What's so funny?"

She walked to the end of the bed on her knees. "Hey, wait a sec. Try the blue. Yeah, that's it."

The blue green wavered. "Jimmy Lee, you're like the tropical fish down at Silver Springs." The red came fluttering back on. "Now you're pink again. You're picking up the reds. I'll be dogged. Wonder what's your best color. Maybe you ought to whip in some yellow."

He poured himself another drink and cupped up a handful of pecans.

"Oh, I'm sorry. I've gone and hurt your feelings. I swear, Jimmy Lee, you don't look half bad in that blue light." She giggled. "Put a little more green in it."

"Oh, for God's sake, I ain't standing here all night and crapping around like this. What in the hell you think I am anyway?"

"I'm just trying to have a little fun. I never crawled in bed with an albino before. Make me a drink, Jimmy Lee, you got me all nervous now."

The commercial was on and Ruby pressed the remote control and ran the TV through the channels. She stopped back on New York. "You really like that orange thing, don't you?"

"Yeah, it really jumps. . . ." He pulled it off the hanger and holding it up to his shoulders lisped, "How'th thith, thweetheart?" He vamped around the room with one hand on his hip, twisting and swishing up to the mirror.

Ruby snickered. "Jesus, Jimmy Lee. You ain't got a lick of sense."

He wiggled and holding his hands behind him pointed his foot out in a model's stance. "I muth thay it ith me." He blew the mirror a kiss and hugged himself where his breasts should be.

(53)

Ruby screeched, flopped back, and rolled over. "You're killing me. Stop it, crazy."

He hung the dress up and headed back for the pecans and bourbon. Ruby dried her eyes, watching him. "Why in the world you so nervous?"

"It's always the same. I'm O.K. until I get near the sack. Then it's hello, Bellevue."

"Well, leave that booze alone. You'll get sick as a dog."

"Don't worry about that. I never get drunk. This is my last one, promise."

"No, you've had enough. Come here, Jimmy Lee."

"I'll play the demo again. I want to check that first bridge." He reached for the "play" button.

"No. No more music and no more booze. You come here, Jimmy Lee."

"O.K., Ruby. You sure it's O.K.?"

"It's O.K."

"Ruby."

"Yeah, Jimmy Lee."

"You won't tell Raymond or anyone."

"No, hon. I won't tell anyone."

On Agnes McCoy's front porch Ruby told Agnes about Jimmy Lee, the Francis Marion, the new song, and the new act.

"Lord, Ruby! Lord! I didn't think you'd go that far. Lord!"

"Come on, Ag, grow up. That ain't far when you figure what's at stake. Jimmy Lee Rideout's got more royalties coming in than Carter's got pills. I tell you he wrote the theme for *Blue Tuesday?*"

"Yeah, but a man like that as our coach. I don't know, Ruby. I just don't know about that."

"Well, I do. And I know exactly what we're going to do. Now you just keep your mouth shut and your eyes open. Agnes McCoy, me and you are going to go places . . . and I don't mean no Monck's Corner, South Carolina; I mean Nashville, Tennessee."

5

Roebuck opened two bottles of ginger ale as he and Agnes sat in front of the television set watching Billy Graham preaching from Charlotte. With his handkerchief he carefully began cleaning the bottle top. "No doubt about it, Agnes, that man is gifted."

She started to ask if he was afraid of germs but decided it was the wrong time. "You know something? I'd give just about anything to sing in that choir."

He crossed his legs and looped his arm over her shoulder in one movement. "You'd be right up in front, Agnes, right up alongside him."

His lips tubed around the bottle top and he drank off six of the twelve ounces before lowering it. Then, one-handed, he refolded his handkerchief and patted his mouth dry. "And you'd be a sight to behold." She moved her shoulder into his hand, feeling safe and snug. Virgil had frightened her and she had frightened herself. As she shifted closer to Roebuck, hoping his hand would slide down her arm and pull her closer, she knew she could never love anyone as foul-mouthed and dirty as Virgil Haynes. Roebuck would never be screaming blasphemies at her in front of her own house or clawing at her brassiere or hooking his fingers under her panties. She shifted to set her bottle down, hoping his hand might move. Instead it clung like a clamp to her shoulder while he sat straight and stiff, his long jaw aimed at Billy Graham and his eyes blazing. But the wild fire was all in Roebuck's eyes. None of it touched her. She snuggled closer, hoping for some of the feeling she'd had with Virgil but of a different kind. His leg stiffened against her and his hand gripped tighter, frightening her, while the other clung to the bottle of Canada Dry. Her eyes moved from him to Graham and back to him. He was watching Graham's every motion, every gesture. A trickle of pride ran through her shoulders and down her arms, and she knew he had other things on his mind. Maybe he could go on television. There was no doubt about it, something happened to him when he got in front of the microphone. She had seen him when he delivered the benediction at the American Legion post and had led the big crowd in the Lord's Prayer. Maybe something bigger was waiting if he went in front of the cameras. He was tall and sincere, and forty for a minister wasn't old at all; people trusted him. He didn't have the fancy words and clothes that Billy Graham had, but on colored TV, maybe even on black and white, folks would see the fire burning in his eyes and leaping in his voice. "You know, Roebuck, I believe you got a better voice. It's deeper and I swear if it ain't got more conviction. I don't mean no disrespect, but Billy Graham sounds like he's selling automobiles or wall siding."

"That's the exact thing I was fixing to say. It's wrong, dead wrong, selling the Lord the way you would a piece of side meat. I bet if you cut that sound off he'd look like some New York Jew boy pushing comb and brush sets and integration." He whacked his bottle on the coffee table.

"Well, I wouldn't go that far."

"I declare, Agnes, I think I can out-preach that slicker. I ain't saying I'm better. I'm saying me and him are different. Sounds like to me he's talking over most folks' heads."

"It does, Roebuck, and I don't happen to think he's all that

(56)

good-looking. All prissy-mouthed like that. . . . He looks like an old bleached-out crow to me."

Roebuck rolled the bottle between his hands and reflected. "Of course, you get up in Charlotte and on up North, well, people think a whole lot different than we do down here."

His hand had sweated onto her shoulder. "I'd sure love to see you on a colored channel. I bet you'd give old Billy Graham a fit on the ratings."

"I wouldn't be studying no rating. I wouldn't care a thing about that. There's room for both of us. We're different. My appeal is to a different sort of person. You take some cotton chopper or machine wiper coming home with a backache. What's he want to hear Graham carrying on about elections and what the niggers are doing and seeing the President and all for? Them folks don't care about chin music. They want the hell-fire scared into them and they want uplifting; they ain't interested in any Washington District of Columbia egg roll at Easter time."

"You're right, Roebuck."

He patted her shoulder and, smiling with only his lips, riveted his eyes on Billy Graham storming away from the Astrodome.

Agnes touched the bottle against her teeth thoughtfully. "I bet you could have a big career on radio or television. Roebuck, you ought to go uptown and see Hollywood Charm. There's a fellow up there called Raymond La Mer and—"

He patted her hand. "Later, Agnes, I want to hear this part."

At the Wednesday night worship Roebuck announced there would be no march on Spider's and cut the sermon short. The collection plate was passed during the first verse of "Bringing in the Sheaves," and when he saw it moving into the middle row he signaled Agnes to end at the second.

"Why so fast tonight?"

Roebuck took her elbow. "I got a lot on my mind. Come with me."

In the back room behind the wooden altar Roebuck made instant coffee on the hot plate. "Do I look nervous?"

"Yessir. I mean, yes. Like something's taken hold of you."

(57)

He took her hands and squeezed them. She wanted to pull away but the fire in his eyes held her. She could feel his fingers tremble and sweat.

"I had a vision, Agnes. A vision. I'm afraid to tell anyone but I got to. I just can't hold it back."

"You can tell me."

Tears glistened in his eyes and his lips firmed. He gripped her shoulders. "I knew you'd say that. Agnes, the Lord spoke to me! He spoke to me just as clear as if he was sitting in that ladderback. He said, 'Roebuck Alexander, the load you're carrying is too much for any mortal man. No man can stand up under it. You're going to have to share it with someone.' And you know who he said that someone was?"

Agnes knew. She panicked. His hands were gripping tighter; his eyes were blazing into hers. She felt they were seeing right into the marrow of the bones in her brain. It was like being hyp-notized—even stronger. Her voice cracked and splintered. "Who, Roebuck?"

"You, Agnes McCoy. He wants you to be Mrs. Roebuck Alex-ander. And I do too. What do you say? I can get Hoover Joe Hooks to marry us over in Jasper and we can honeymoon at Stone Mountain. Don't that sound like fun?"

"That's pretty swift."

"Then you're not saying no?"

"Yes . . . I mean no. But I'd like a little bit of time."

His eyes held her like a snake. "Then you're saying yes?"

She looked into the blue eye, then the brown. She didn't know where to look. What to do. What to say.

"I guess. Oh, I mean, I guess so. Yes, I guess I am."

"Oh, Agnes! Sweet, sweet Agnes!" He knocked over the coffee as he cracked down on his knees and buried his face in her lap. His long arms wrapped around her hips. "You've made me the happiest man alive."

She had to say something. "I'm glad, Roebuck. I'm so glad."

His arms tightened. "I've been thinking that there's not much money in straight preaching any more to raise a family, and Ag-nes, I'm figuring on seeing that La Mer man."

"That would be nice, Roebuck." She closed her eyes in confusion. Everything was spinning and she was being sucked toward a strange, dark, greased middle. There was nothing to grab on to, no stairs, no rails, no doors. She didn't know what she was doing or why. She felt Roebuck's head trembling and knew he was crying. "Oh, Roebuck."

Ruby shrieked. "Marry him! Marry Roebuck Alexander! Are you slap out of your mind? He's crazy, Ag. Any fool right off the street will tell you that."

They were sitting on Spider's porch, practicing chord changes.

"You stop talking like that. I happen to love . . . I happen to admire him."

"Listen at you, you can't even say it."

Agnes gripped her guitar neck and stiffened. "Well, it's different than love. It's an understanding. Roebuck says love will come later and that it will be based on mutual trust. It ain't going to be all sex, Ruby."

"Crap! What's gotten into you? What about the Honkytonk Angels? We got a theme song and a manager."

"Roebuck said I got to get shed of all that. He's thinking about trying out for radio. Maybe I'll help him."

"Oh, Agnes, you're so dumb. Here we got the hottest duo in the two Carolinas and you want to toss it off so you can go shake a tambourine for some cornball church."

"Ruby Jean Jamison, you stop talking like that or I'm leaving."

She strummed an F chord and slid into a G seventh. "O.K. Ag, I'm sorry. But, honey, we're throwing away our futures. Raymond and Jimmy Lee swear it's only a matter of days before we're heading for Nashville."

"I don't want it, Ruby. I want peace and security."

"Damn, you're sounding like him already. I never heard you talk like that before. . . . Let me ask you something. You been to bed with that bird yet?"

"I'm still pure, Ruby. You know that."

"Yeah, well, you crawl in with that scutter before you go helling off to Stone Mountain. There's a lot more to living with a man besides doing the Lord's work."

"Oh, Ruby!"

"Don't Oh, Ruby me. I'm telling you what's fact. And what on earth are you going to Stone Mountain for? There ain't a thing there but an old rock sticking up."

"Listen, I ain't going to bed with anyone until I'm married. Me and Roebuck have already discussed it." She walked her fingers down the A string and scratched at a spot on the box. "He told me his father never touched his mother all during the courtship, and from the minute she was pregnant he slept on a pallet on the floor."

"Great."

"And his father taught him that when he saw a woman in an embarrassing position—you know, like climbing out of a car—he was to avert his eyes and go on about his business. Now there's your old-fashioned morality, Ruby. He's just different than most of us."

"He's different, all right. That country son of a bitch is crazy as a hoot owl."

"Stop it, Ruby! Stop it!" She slid her guitar into the black leatherette case. "I'm not hearing any more of this. I'm not."

"I'm sorry, Agnes."

"You keep saying you're sorry and you keep at it. You ain't sorry at all."

"O.K., I apologize. I didn't mean to hurt your feelings."

A red and white dog sniffed the chinaberry trunk, changed his mind, and raised his leg on Spider's Oldsmobile.

"Hon, I hear preachers are the worst. They're so hung up it takes wild, sick, crazy things to get them loose. I saw a story in *True Confessions* last month where this preacher—"

"Hush, Ruby, I don't want to hear any more." She zipped her case. "Roebuck is the kindest, gentlest, sweetest man that ever drew breath. It's just that no one understands him."

"How's he compare to Virgil?"

"You can't compare them. They're too different."

"You bet your ass they're different." She hit a hard G chord and

(60)

tightened her B-string peg. "Virgil can get next to a woman and make her squirm. I bet that Roebuck would bring my period on two weeks ahead of time. I swear, Ag, I don't believe there's money enough in this world to make me face that old brown- and blue-eyed scarecrow under the sheets."

"I ain't hearing any more of this." She was on her feet. "Ruby, I think me and you have made a terrible mistake. I think it's best if we just quit seeing each other for a while."

"Oh, Agnes, don't be silly. Who in the hell you think's going to be the one that stands up for you?"

"Well, I thought—"

"You thought I would. Well, I am. I want to. Hell, Ag, all this is is a little misunderstanding. Everything's going to work out fine. You just wait."

"Well, I know my mind."

"I know you do, Ag."

Ruby told Jimmy Lee how the wedding had been set for Thursday two weeks off at the Jasper, Georgia, Second Baptist, fifty miles north of Atlanta.

"Murder!" He rubbed his eyes and yawned. He'd slept badly. He pushed his eggs and sausage away from his grits. "I told that stupid waitress no grits. What in the hell she call these?" He was eating breakfast at twelve-thirty at the Francis Marion, sitting in the shadiest corner and wearing his sunglasses. "This Roebuck sure as hell ain't going to let her go on the road."

"Road! He ain't letting her out of the house. He wants her singing straight-ass gospel."

"Well, what did you tell her?"

"Nothing, I was listening. . . . Oh, Lord, Jimmy Lee. He's got her all screwed up. She's no brain, but hell—she's never been like this before."

He tore his toast in half and mopped up the egg yolk, steering around the grits.

She stabbed her cigarette out and began sucking on a sugar cube. "Oh, something else. Roebuck's seeing Raymond about radio possibilities."

Jimmy Lee signaled for another coffee and a glazed doughnut. "Me and Raymond will come up with something."

"A real summit meeting, right?"

Jimmy Lee signed the check and circled the tip. "You quit worrying about it, hear?"

"Sure, sure. I've already quit."

"You got to trust me, honey." He took her cigarette and stuck it straight up in the grits. "You couldn't come by tonight, could you?"

"Not a chance. Spider's back in town."

"How about for an hour or so? Say you're catching a flick. Make it around five, and I'll fill you in on what Raymond thinks."

"O.K., Jimmy Lee. What's that number again? I don't want to be hanging around that old lobby."

"Four-ten. Groove?"

"O.K."

6

Roebuck Alexander shook hands with Raymond La Mer and stepped back from the desk two full strides. "I'm pleased to meet you."

Raymond rubbed his glossy fingernails together, looking at the tall, acned man in black standing before him at parade rest. The eyes were not only unmatched, one brown, one blue, they were of different sizes. His long earnest jaw would have to be broken and rebuilt. A photographer's nightmare; there were no good angles.

"Reverend Alexander, Agnes tells me you don't hold with entertainment. I want you to know I respect your opinion."

"Thank you, sir."

Raymond rose and shoving his fingers in his tight pockets faced the Checkerboard Feed Store across the street and the river. His voice was slow, steady. "I recall seeing Oral Roberts in person in Evening Shade, Arkansas, and Reverend, that was one of the most moving events of my entire life. To this day I can recall to the word what that man said."

"Amen to that. That man is blessed."

Raymond spun around, smiling. "Now I know who you remind me of! Reverend Ezra Poole Brothers! Out in Texarkana. Now there's a man who is an inspiration to the entire Baptist community of mid-America. He's up in Des Moines right this minute with his own one-hour radio show. . . . And do you know why?"

"Why, sir?"

"Shut-ins, Reverend Alexander. Shut-ins. The bedridden, the palsied, and the old folk. Why, do you know that man has three full-time secretaries just keeping track of his mail and sending out photographs? Reverend Alexander, while you're straightening out the lives of one hundred or two hundred South Carolinians, Brother Ezra has one million souls down on their knees three days a week on prime-time radio and television."

"Slow down, Mr. La Mer. Slow down. The Lord hasn't told me to reach out for the multitudes. Maybe he will later. Maybe he never will. Right now he wants me to stay here, and I ain't leaving until I get the word. What I was studying was something small, sort of local like."

Raymond La Mer stared at the bridge of Roebuck's nose. He couldn't stand looking at the unmatched eyes. "Sir, your voice has what most announcers spend their lives trying to get. You've got resonance and depth . . . you've got meaning."

"I still don't like things big like that. I'm much better with a smaller group."

"I know you don't, and I'm reasonably sure Billy Graham and Oral Roberts didn't like it at first either. But the way it looks to me—now mind you, this is just my personal observation—is if you take the Lord's word to spread the message I think there's a good chance he meant for you to spread it the best way you could."

"But he never mentioned big-time radio."

"No, sir, and I'll bet he never told Billy Graham to wear single rolled lapels and make friends with the President of the United States. But then maybe we just can't sit back and wait for him to spell out every little detail."

He walked Roebuck over to the plate-glass window overlooking

(64)

the feed store. In the distance the eight-hundred-foot tower of WJBD was catching the sun. Birds were sitting on it.

"Reverend Alexander, that tower doesn't look like much out there, but as far as I'm concerned it's a modern-day miracle. I'm not being blasphemous, sir, but how many more people would have gotten to gaze on that beautiful face if they knew where he was appearing? What I'm saying, sir, and I hope I'm not offending you, is that if radio had been there it would have taken ten thousand Bibles to tell about the miracles and the eyewitness accounts."

Roebuck ran his tongue over his teeth and gazed out at the steel tower and the long shadow it threw to the river.

"And Reverend Alexander . . ." His voice dropped low, slow, steady. "The main thing. The main thing, sir, is the old folks. The shut-ins. The palsied and the spastics. Who's going to pray for them? We should think about them sitting and rocking. Or just lying there watching the wall or the ceiling plaster . . . and waiting." His hand was on Roebuck's tense shoulder as he guided him to the door. "I want you to think about it, sir. Think about it. That's all. There's no hurry."

Roebuck's blue eye narrowed when he shook Raymond's hand. "I'll give it some strong thought."

In the night Roebuck ran the ceiling shadows and the night sounds together, and the Lord told him that local radio was a modern-day miracle and that any vessel should be used to carry forth the salvation message to the world. He awoke triumphant. After praying over his instant coffee and toasted raisin cake he phoned Raymond he would be uptown on the first bus to put himself in Hollywood Charms' hands and sign the three-year twenty-per-cent management, agent, and publisher contract.

Raymond and Jimmy Lee moved fast. At the Disabled Veterans of America Post #68 they drank Seagram's Seven Crown and Seven-Up with the station manager of WJBD, trying to sell him on the idea that a straight-line Baptist fifteen minutes would sell merchandise.

Baily Hutto, a premature bald disc jockey with eyebrows and

(65)

sideburns like pocket combs, who had a voice like controlled thunder on the air and a piercing upper-G nasal riding on a lisp when off, kept shaking his head. "No, fellows. There's no way. No way. We've got a sophisticated crowd going for us. We're out of c. and w. and I'm not screwing it up with some redneck coming down on birth pills and six-packs."

Raymond handled the religious side. "Baily, these crackers are Baptists, Methodists, Church of God . . . you just can't walk off on that."

"Just watch me. Just watch me. Listen, we ran a tricounty poll in April. This crowd wants rock. They want pop. They've had it with the fiddle jumpers."

Jimmy Lee elbowed in. "Running a poll, old buddy, is like going to a whore house: you take what you want. I'll tell you a goddamn poll. A real poll. Cannon County right outside Nashville last year, they put their finger right on it. Half of those shit-kickers were claiming the only thing they heard on the radio was the news of the day and the Bell Telephone Hour. The poll cross-checked them in their cars and they were dog-ass lying. The average redneck pushing a Ford is listening to c. and w. and flipping over to another c. and w. during the commercials. But the minute that ridge runner hits his first red light and thinks somebody's listening he switches over to the pop station. . . . Hell, I've watched them. I've seen it."

Raymond ordered another round of doubles and a plate of pepper sausages. "Baily, check your record shop. Mantovani and his ten thousand strings is picking up dust at a dollar sixty-nine. They can't keep the stock on Nashville country, and at full list, baby."

Baily finished his drink and gnawed on the sausage. "O.K., O.K., maybe you're right on the polls. Flat out, I don't give a damn what they say. If this town thinks they're sophisticated, I'm with them. Put yourself in my shoes. How'd you like to be trapped for twelve hours a day with that fiddle and washboard shit?"

"Yeah, Baily, but if your crowd's not listening then they sure as hell aren't buying."

"I haven't heard any complaints."

(66)

Jimmy Lee snapped his fingers twice. "O.K., Baily, what's the big flour and meal mix around here?"

"Martha White."

Raymond moved back in. "That's Nashville, Louisville, and Atlanta pushing that wagon. Face it, your people are listening to your sophisticated mood music at the crossroads and waiting for the light to change. They aren't buying." He shook his head solemnly. "Baby, big-sell voice or not, with that kind of philosophy going you wouldn't last two weeks in Nashville."

"But it ain't my fault, guys." His voice shot up. "It ain't. It ain't." He rolled the last sausage back and forth. "It's the station. I swear it is."

"We understand." Raymond tapped his arm.

Jimmy Lee closed his eyes. "Groove."

Baily's eyes misted as he lipped his Seagram's. "I'm just going to have to face it. This town's great and all, but for me I guess it's a dead end. You know something, no kidding, I've been kinda thinking about Nashville." He picked up the sausage. "You fellows wouldn't happen to have a couple contacts up that way, would you?"

Raymond's eyes caught Jimmy Lee's and they closed in.

Sunday morning Roebuck announced to the congregation that he would be on the 6:45 Carolina Morning Gospel Show and that Sister Agnes would be at his side to sing "Lead, Kindly Light." Under the pulpit his hand found hers. She blushed when he squeezed it. The congregation sang four verses of "Bringing in the Sheaves" loudly and when the collection plate came slowly up the center aisle it was $22.50 heavier than it had been since the days of Spider Hornsby.

Monday morning at 7:01, one minute after Roebuck's fifteen minutes, the telephone calls began coming in. They came from Ruby, Jimmy Lee, Raymond, Lorlene on Raymond's reception desk, and from the Washed in the Blood of the Lamb congregation. Before the hour was over, Baily Hutto boomed out that if he didn't miss his guess Brother Alexander would be back the next morning.

(67)

Roebuck came back. On the second and third morning his voice went as deep as Baily's and they had to wrap the mike to kill the rumble and the feedback.

On the fourth morning Roebuck Alexander reached inside himself and went even deeper. The words and the pauses, the laughs and the sobs rolled up from some secret lung pit and walked across the room like heavy construction equipment. His tone smoothed out as if eggs and rich cream had been folded in, driving out the bubbles of grit and air, leaving behind only the flowing lava of rich honey, of old bronze, of rose gold. . . . Baily laughed and lisped, "Fantastic, Roebuck! Fantastic! You've got a million-dollar voice. A million dollars!"

The calls poured in for autographs, photographs. Questions burned up the tricounty lines, wanting to know where Roebuck was from. How tall? How old? Could he sing? Why hadn't they used him earlier? Was he married?

By the fifth day Raymond had not only contracted Roebuck to m.c. the Carolina Morning Gospel Show but had agreed to let him do the benediction at the Chamber of Commerce Dinner, open the Water-skiing Festival at Ballantine's Landing on Saturday, and start full-time planning for the big two-week state-wide Pentecostal Jubilee of Prayer Marathon that would be on afternoon radio for a running week. Raymond also advised him it would be best for his image if he would delay his marriage a few weeks until his public got used to the idea. Roebuck agreed.

Raymond wiped mayonnaise from his mouth after biting into a club sandwich at the Market Restaurant. "Jimmy Lee, that crazy son of a bitch is a walking gold mine. I'm going all the way with him . . . one client, all the marbles. Exclusive, baby."

Jimmy Lee slumped back in the horseshoe booth out of the bright light. "Can he carry a tune? Maybe we could get up a package."

"Screw the music, this is Oral Roberts–Billy Graham time. That mother's got a voice like it's coming out of a steel vault. He's a white Father Divine . . . you know Divine came out of these boondocks?"

(68)

"No . . . exclusive. Where does that leave the girls?"

"Nowhere. You can have them." He opened his sandwich and stripped the fat away from the ham. "They're losers, Jimmy Lee. They'll bury you."

"I'll take them."

"You're sleeping with that Red, right?"

"Maybe."

"Any good?"

Jimmy Lee picked up a pickle chip from his grilled cheese, bit it, and grinned. "Like riding a chow dog."

Ground fog covered the Leesville Road on Friday, and Virgil ran in two loads of whiskey before it lifted. He and Spider siphoned 250 gallons into the maple barrel buried six feet down in the back yard, one foot deeper than the Law's five-foot probing stakes. A compressed air feeder hidden in the garage kept the pressure strong enough to push the whiskey up the copper tubing running under the driveway and across the yard into the house. Inside the double floorboarding the tubing snaked up between the studs to a hidden tap behind the industrial sink. The pressure was strong, the tubing was clean and the amber 101-proof corn came through clear and mellow.

Virgil licked his lips. "Smells good, Spider."

Spider drew off a gallon into the steel bucket and inhaled over it. "Yeah. Hey, Ruby, want to crack some ice for us?"

"Sure, hon."

Virgil drank and sighed. "Great stuff. How much age?"

"One year and one month. Smooth, ain't it?" He winked, patted Ruby on her hip, and hooked his head. "Got a nice echo too. Fine. Fine stuff."

Spider cut the TV on and kicking his shoes off sat back, sipping the corn. He flipped the remote control switch and changed channels. Ruby had her transistor radio on the coffee table. "Ain't a thing on now, hon. Come on, cut it off. I got something coming in from Nashville."

He flicked it off. "Virgil, tell me something, boy. You ever think of driving full time?"

(69)

"Not when I'm sober."

Spider sprung his jackknife open and crossing his foot in his lap began squaring off his toenails. "It's getting so any son of a bitch with two hundred pounds of sugar and a car radiator figures he can make whiskey."

Virgil lit a cigarette and whipped the match out. "Now tell me something I don't know."

Spider winced as he cut in too close. "If I had you around where I could find your ass, I'd open another outlet and make us both some money."

"Let me hear something."

He scooped the cut nails into the ashtray. "Two hundred a week plus ten per cent of what you haul. Should go a grand with no strain."

Ruby's Nashville program came on but she turned it down to watch Virgil. He ran his finger down the dust in front of the monkeys on the mantelpiece. "Who'd do the selling?"

"I can get J. D. Flood."

"He could sure as hell do it."

Spider snapped his knife closed, smiling. "Course, I can't be handing out Blue Cross or Social Security benefits."

Virgil looked at the monkeys, then at his cigarette, and then at Spider. "You might just have yourself a deal. J. D. Flood; I'll be damn. That would really be something."

Of the thirty-two years J. D. Flood had been building moonshine stills and running bootleg outlets, he had spent six years and six days watching the muddy waters of the Saluda River from the northeast cell block of the State Penitentiary. J. D. would moonshine three years and then serve a year and a day; moonshine another three and serve another year and a day. Every leap year from 1944 through 1964, J. D. would lean forward on the bar of justice on the charge of manufacturing or possession, or both, and then lean back with a $2,000 fine and a year and a day down the hill. . . . J. D. Flood served his time, every time, in the same way, hunched over *Popular Mechanics*, *Popular Science*, and *Police Gazettes* in the prison library, working up new ways to

(70)

build a new and supersecret still, and each time J. D., a short, intense dark man who could have shaved three times a day, came out of the Gist Street gate it was with a new plan. His first setup was installed in an attic, the second in an outhouse, his third, fourth, and fifth were low-profile ground-hog models hidden four miles back in the Wateree Swamp. The sour mash cooking and slop smell gave away the attic still, the Eleventh Street Methodist reported the outhouse, and the helicopters of the State picked off the swamp rigs by watching the woods for smoke and the streams for slop. In 1967 J. D. built his last still. He had called Spider in to look it over. It was a forty-six-foot galvanized steel bomb shelter sunk down fifteen feet under his tomato plants. The mash slop was vented to the city sewage pipe, and an underground tunnel leading to the basement housed six 500-gallon-capacity mash vats.

Spider had shook his head. "You've put a lot of work in this one, J. D."

"Damn right. Ten thousand dollars buried in this mother, and I mean to make it pay."

"No way, J. D., no way. The heat will kill you."

"I got four tons of air conditioning says you're wrong."

Spider shook his head. "You'd better dress light."

"It'll do it, Spider. It will damn well do it. I put too many hours and dollars in this thing not to."

Spider had put a fatherly arm around his shoulder. "J. D., you can wipe your ass with Reynolds Wrap if you've got your jaw set. . . . But it's going to be painful."

Spider had been right. The air conditioning couldn't touch the fast heat build-up of the Detroit-Burner-fed cooker, and J. D. lost eight pounds running his test run. On the next run another seven pounds melted away and he came out of the Dutch oven heat wild-eyed and crazed, swinging a ball-peen hammer at anything he saw and swearing he had built his last still.

He quit manufacturing and began buying from downstate, across the Georgia border and the local swamps, and watching the quality of the whiskey and his clientele drop lower and lower.

With Spider's proposition of bringing in year-old corn from his own stills and splitting the profits, J. D. stuck his right hand out and slapped him on the shoulder. "Brother, you got yourself a deal."

"O.K., J. D., just as long as you know why."

"Because you can trust me. I appreciate it, Spider. Before God I do. I lost my hat and ass on that last rig. . . . And I'm downright embarrassed selling that crap I've been getting in."

"It'll be the same stuff I'll be selling."

"Fine, Spide. You don't know what this means to me. I'm scared shitless selling that swamp stuff. There isn't a drop of meal in it and God knows what they run it through. . . . You hear about Pete Wilson?"

"No."

"Got in a load of Scotch-flavored 'rub.'"

Spider whistled. "Rough."

"Hell, I'd put your stuff up alongside any store-bought, I swear I would. Ain't nobody going to be getting hit with the vertigo or the blind staggers."

Spider snugged on his baseball cap. "I gotta roll. See you in a few days, J. D."

"O.K., Spider."

Spider headed across town. Heat snakes were rising and drifting over Elm and Sumpter Streets and he could smell the street tar melting. The temperature clock at Liberty Mutual was shading 101 as a strip of lightning flashed and danced in the west. He turned onto North Main and cut the radio on.

Aretha Franklin began screaming something wild from Detroit and he punched WJBD. Preacher Roebuck Alexander was in the last five minutes of his broadcast, but the storm static was chopping it up. Spider wanted to hear it and pulled over to the curb and cut the engine.

"And I'm saying that SIN starts small." Roebuck's thunder voice made the eight-inch speaker buzz and the parking meter change on the dashboard rattle. "Smaller than small. Tiny! TEE-NINY! Way down there when you're in the baby crib and reaching up and shouting Gimme this, Gimme that, Gimme something else. . . . I'm here to tell you that the Lord ain't no gimme, gimme, hurry-up-and-gimme-more Lord. No, he ain't." His voice smoothed down and purred strangely. It trembled on the edge of ecstasy. He whispered, "The Lord takes his own sweet time. He moves at his own speed. . . . He can creep along about the speed of a pea vine and then he can whip around, WOP! Like pure natural lightning."

Spider watched a short beagle trying to mount a tall airedale by a rhododendron bush.

Roebuck paused and began building. "But we ain't got all that time. All we got is three score and ten short rows to hoe. And we got to make every one of them harvest a crop we're proud to take to market. That's why I'm saying that the days and the minutes and the small weeds count. That's why I say the small sins count. That's why I say gum chewing can lead to tobacco, dancing can lead to fornication, white lies to black ones, and black ones to outright crimes of violence on the streets. . . . People tell me, Preacher Alexander, these are modern times out there, 1968. They tell me about the birth control pills and the wild music and how they run bare naked in the grass out in California. They tell me a preacher's a fool to come down on wild music and beer and hard liquor." The radio speaker rattled as he took in a deep breath for his finish. "WELL, FOLKS, meet the biggest fool in the world. Because I'm saying that the adult that allows these noxious sores to fester is in the eyes of the Almighty Heavenly Host the biggest, most horrible sinner of them all, and that sinner, that corrupter, that fouler of flesh shall feel, shall smell, and by everything our sweet blessed savior laid down shall burn in the everlasting hellfire of the wrath of God Almighty. . . . Amen." An organ hit four low chords and held the last one until Baily Hutto moved in, announcing that Roebuck would be appearing at the Township Auditorium on Thursday the fourteenth, the Shriners' the fifteenth, and would pronounce the benediction at the opening of the new Piggly-Wiggly Supermarket at Wales Garden Shopping Center on Saturday the sixteenth. . . . Spider stopped for the light at Gates Street. A city bus pulled along side and Stark Rogers, a steady two-quart-a-week customer, opened his pneumatic doors. "Hello, Spider. How's it going?"

"Hi, Stark. Couldn't be better. How's Bertha?"

"Fine. She's expecting again."

The light turned yellow.

Spider shouted, "You have anything to do with it?"

Stark couldn't come up with anything fast enough and closing his door pulled out into Main.

Spider thought about the ribbing he would get from his passengers and turned down Main. His grin faded as he saw a familiar figure behind a pair of sunglasses as big as Mason jar lids tripping into the Francis Marion lobby. It was Ruby. She was in a hurry.

"Now what in the hell's going on?" He pulled into a parking spot and started to get out. He changed his mind . . . probably something to do with the Hollywood Charm School or a fashion show. There was always something going on at the Francis Marion.

At the house Virgil was sitting on the front steps, reading a Mickey Spillane paperback.

"Been here long?"

"Ten–fifteen minutes. How's J. D.?"

"Perfect. Couldn't be better. Sixty gallons Tuesday, seventy-four last night. It's climbing."

Virgil folded a page down and flopped down on the couch. Spider pulled two cans of beer out of the refrigerator. "You think of any reason for Ruby to be going into the Francis Marion?"

"Maybe getting a beer. It's a hundred out there."

"But she never goes in there."

"Probably using the john."

"Well, I don't like it."

"Forget it. Ruby's straight as they come."

Spider told him how J. D. was forecasting a 700-gallon week.

Virgil creased his beer can. "That is what I call gravy." He bounced up. "Maybe I'll get rid of that sorry-ass Chevy."

Spider popped open two more beers. "You've been talking Cadillac. Go buy one. We're out of the weeds now, boy. We're in the short grass and there ain't nothing stopping us."

Virgil slammed his hand on the mantelpiece. "I could be a rich man." He took a deep pull from his Miller's High Life. "And I ain't letting no hymn-singing bitch go bringing me down."

(74)

Spider touched his can to Virgil's. "Now we're talking. And I'm quitting worrying about Ruby."

But it was all talk. That night Spider slept alone. Ruby had called, saying she was staying at her mother's. . . . He lay awake listening to the dry chinaberry branches brushing the screen and a cat in heat rubbing along the fence trying to give it away. He touched the edge of her pillow and ran his hand from the big dip in his side of the mattress to where she slept without even leaving an impression. It felt warm at first and then seemed to be cooling. One minute he swore he would ask four straight questions, pinning her to the wall, and then beat hell out of her; the next he knew he would ask about her mother and then shut up. He thought of her red hair, her quick smile, and her duck walk when her toes were spread with cotton when she painted her nails. He went for another beer. In the kitchen he pulled out the white bread and peanut butter and dipped in deep. His elbows and arms felt greasy and sticky on the vinyl tablecloth, his feet cold on the yellow linoleum.

The cotton mill clock chimed one and bullbats snickered and flicked around the street light on the corner. A dog was in the garbage; the cat had gone on down the street. And then the phone rang. His heart turned over. It was Ruby. She was whispering. "Mama's in the john. Call me back in five minutes. I'll say you're Agnes and you've got to see me. O.K.?"

"O.K."

"You eating peanut butter?"

"Yeah. Come on home, I miss you."

"I miss you too. She's flushing. . . . Call me back."

Ruby got home at one-thirty. "Lord, I thought she'd talk my arm clean off. Questions. Questions. Questions. You never heard so many questions! Have you been to church? Did you apologize to Preacher? Did you write your uncle? Do you say your prayers? Did you miss your period?"

"She ask you that?"

"Sure, she thinks you got me knocked up."

"Maybe I ought to."

Her eyes met his. "What's that supposed to mean?"

(75)

"I get to worrying about you whipping off to Nashville or New York City with some jew's-harp player or something."

She sensed more. "Honey, you don't think some little baby's crying going to clip my wings, now, do you?"

He was sorry he had brought it up. "Nothing's going to clip your wings, puddin'. That's what I like about you."

"You wouldn't want it any different, would you?"

"No, I wouldn't." But he hadn't said it with any conviction and something was missing in his eyes. She knew he knew something. And opening a beer, she knew he knew she knew. . . . She drank and thought fast. There was too much going on. Her career, the Honkytonk Angels, everything was a mess. Raymond and Jimmy Lee were O.K., but she knew she couldn't trust them as far as she could throw them, and there was no telling what Agnes would do next. No, she couldn't let Spider know anything until things settled down. She needed more time.

In the dark bedroom she stood in front of the mirror. "Hey, hon, watch this." She was naked. She lit her cigarette lighter and holding it out recited the one line she remembered from *Macbeth*. "Is this a dagger which I hold before me . . . ?" She giggled, snapped off the lighter, and jumped into Spider's deep draw.

He was unbuttoning his pajamas.

"Hey, that's my job. From now on I'm going to be taking much, much, much better care of you."

Spider lay back, smiling. Ruby had opened the buttons and he felt her hand under his jockey shorts elastic.

"Ah . . . now, that's better."

7

Hooty Hightower, a nonunion plumber, was stone drunk and soaking wet as he danced with Ruby's friends from Woolworth's. He was doing a heavy clog step, first facing Beverly Eppes and then Mary Beth Tyson, and shouting at Virgil, sitting on the floor. "Come on, Virg. Get your butt up." Virgil was unscrewing the lid on a half-gallon Mason jar of Spider's corn.

"Maybe later, Hooty."

Hooty whooped and came down in his rapid heel-stomp version of a flamenco as the music surged faster, wilder. "How about you, Spider?"

Spider sat on the kitchen table talking with J. D. about mash mixes and condenser coils. "No way, Hoot. Hang in there."

Beverly moved over to Ruby at the juke. "Where'd you learn that one?"

Ruby, with her eyes closed, danced alone. Her hair, combed out straight and long, was flying; her rippling jerks, lightning coils, and rag doll convulsions were locked to the deep Ray Charles beat. "Made it up."

"Wild!"

"Watch this." She splayed her fingers out stiff and rigid and freezing her feet and knees whipped her hips and doubled the rhythm. Beverly tried to match her but gave up and went for the whiskey. Mary Beth moved off with her head back, hitching her elbows and shoulders and popping on the afterbeat.

Hooty, his shirt and hair plastered with sweat, his face flushed with the 101-proof corn, suddenly yodeled a rebel yell, leaped onto a chair, and went into his fast and doomed flamenco. He whooped again and held the electric beat for four bars before losing his balance and slamming against the wall. He slid down by Virgil. "Woooooo, boy. I have had it!"

"Looking good, Hooty boy."

Hooty watched Ruby and Mary Beth. "Where in the hell they learn that stuff?"

"Beats me." He slid him the jar.

Hooty wiped his mouth with the back of his hand. "That stuff doesn't need a chaser. You all put it in an Old Grand Dad bottle and it'll damn well sell for it."

"You're right, Hoot." Virgil jiggled a set of car keys on his rabbit's foot chain. "Know what that fits?"

"Cadillac?"

"Hoot, that son of a bitch will flat out at one twenty-five and you don't even know you're moving."

"How many miles to the gallon?"

"Friend, when you drive a Coupe de Ville you don't worry about crap like that."

Hooty was watching Mary Beth working alone in the corner. He wiped the sweat down with his sleeve. Virgil elbowed him. "You like that?"

"You ain't just whistling Dixie."

Virgil pulled a crumpled ten-dollar bill from his shirt pocket and tossed it down. "Ten says I can fix it up for you."

"The hell you say." He rolled over for his wallet.

Virgil called Mary Beth over. "My buddy here's kinda shy, but what he wants to do is take you up in Spider's room and show you the Northern Lights."

(78)

Mary Beth kept dancing. "You tongue-tied, Hooty?"

Hooty pushed up from the wall. "I hear good things about you Woolworth girls."

Virgil laughed. "He's betting ten bucks he's getting in and bringing back your pants."

"Screw you, Virgil!" Hooty reached for the money but Mary Beth's foot covered the bills.

"Wait a second." She went into the dark front room, came back, and dropped her white-cotton blue-fringed bikini pants with *Friday* stitched on the side on the money. "How's that for love at first sight?"

Hooty scooped up the money and looped his arm around her. "Spider's room's got an air conditioner."

She snapped her fingers with the rhythm. "O.K., tomcat, get a bottle and some Seven-Up."

Ruby danced alone until Spider stopped her with a hug. "Big night, baby."

"You better believe it. You rode in Virgil's wagon?"

"Damn right. . . . And you're getting the next one."

Ruby wound her arms around him and snaked in tight with the new slow music. She kissed him hard and, running her hands around his hips, hooked her thumbs in his back belt loops. "I don't need any old Cadillac. I don't need nothing, hon. Just you—ooo-ooo. I'm going to make some kind of love to you tonight. Don't let me get too drunk."

The heavy beat music and dancing shook the dead chinaberries out of the tin roof seams, and rebel yells, swamp shouts, and three-note yodels rolled down the street toward the river. As a Motown record ended and the changer slid another toward the needle, a new sound came from the front. It was Roebuck Alexander, Agnes McCoy, and the congregation of the Washed in the Blood of the Lamb, singing and marching into position around the geranium beds. Spider had the jukebox volume on high, but Roebuck on the bottom step had a brand new bullhorn.

"Spider! Spider Hornsby! Come out here, Spider! I want these folks to take a good look at capital S.I.N.—Sin."

Spider stomped out. "Get that thing out of here or I'm calling the Law! You're a public nuisance!"

Roebuck laughed into the horn. "I can be the biggest nuisance in the state if I can get shed of the likes of you." He pulled Quendolyn Hightower, a thin, shrill woman with a scarf over her head, out to the center. He boomed into the horn. "Hooty! Hooty Hightower! WE KNOW YOU'RE IN THERE."

Inside Hooty, naked lying next to Mary Beth, crouched on his knees and elbows, peering through the Venetian blind slats.

Mary Beth giggled. "Who's there?"

Hooty in the striped moonlight sucked in, "Oh, my God. It's Quendolyn!"

Roebuck shouted. "Hooty! We know you're in there drinking up that take-home pay and making a fool out of yourself. Come out here! Here's somebody wants to talk to you."

Quendolyn's buzz-saw voice crackled through the bullhorn. "You promised me. You promised on your bended knee! Now look at you! Just look at you!"

Hooty scrambled into his clothes and shoes and stuffed his socks in his pockets.

Roebuck blared, "That's your flesh and blood begging, Hooty!"

Quendolyn was kneeling on the bottom step. "Hooty! Preacher says it ain't too late for salvation. It ain't even too late to be saving our home life."

Roebuck, tired of pleading, screamed into the bullhorn, blasting Hooty against the dark wall. "HOOTY HIGHTOWER! In the name of the Father and the Son and the Holy Ghost I COMMAND YOU!"

Hooty, drunk, exhausted, soaking wet, and petrified, weaved toward the screen door as if hypnotized. On the porch he suddenly lurched forward. He caught himself on the porch rail, then slowly with his head bowed and his shoelaces dragging came down the seven wooden steps. Agnes McCoy hit a ringing F chord and led the congregation into "Love Lifted Me" as Hooty, stumbling like a blind man in a brickyard, staggered into the thin arms of the hair-tearing, screeching Quendolyn.

Roebuck boomed out, "Another black sheep present and ac-

(80)

counted for! Another sinner back from the blackest devil of them all!"

Spider screwed the garden hose connection to the kitchen spigot and unwound the plastic hose to the porch. With no warning he began spraying Roebuck, Agnes, and the whole congregation.

Virgil came out. "Soak 'em, Spider. Sock it to 'em."

Roebuck shouted. His bullhorned voice could be heard two miles downwind and one mile up. "God's water ain't driving us out tonight, Spider Hornsby. That ain't even moving us. . . . We got another message to deliver."

The soaking congregation sang joyously along with Agnes, who had turned to protect her guitar but was singing louder than ever. Spider tapered the nozzle spray and blasted Roebuck in the face. He blocked it with his big hand and aiming his bullhorn at the sky delivered his thunderbolt.

"Ruby! Ruby! Ruby Jean Jamison! Your time has come!"

Ruby slowed her dancing down and stopped. She felt something cold and grainy turn over in her stomach.

"Come out here, Ruby Jean. I want you to be hearing this in front of witnesses and your own best friend."

She listened with her mouth open and her heart thudding in her throat.

Spider came down three steps, as far as the hose would stretch. "If you ain't man enough to insult her in private I'm kicking your slat ass in front of this whole flock of fools."

Roebuck aimed the horn at the front door. "Ruby sleeping with you ain't no private thing." He had backed up. The water was reaching to his waistline. "Laying alongside you at night is only one sin. But sin breeds sin. I knew there was more to be coming. I predicted it." The bullhorn filled the night, and dogs in the distance threw it back. "The bigger sin is selling her body to a Mister Jimmy Lee Rideout, a thirty-four-year-old albino out of Nashville, Tennessee, for a theme song for that God-mocking sacrilegious Honkytonk Angels."

Spider shouted, "That's crap and you know it."

"Would you believe Sister Agnes McCoy?"

(81)

"I wouldn't believe your whole goddamn congregation."

Roebuck pulled Agnes forward. Spider sprayed her. Virgil shouted, "Agnes, damn your ass. This ain't none of your business. Stay out of it!"

Roebuck gave her the horn. "Ruby told me out of her own mouth. She slept with that albino four times for that theme song. That was a week ago. She's probably been with him again." She stepped back, wiping the water from her face. "Maybe three or four times more."

Spider shouted, "Didn't Ruby tell you to keep that quiet?"

Agnes clung to Roebuck's arm. "You can't keep sin quiet. This is the Lord's work."

"This is bullshit work. That's what it is. You sorry little bitch. You deserve this asshole Roebuck. You're both crazy."

Roebuck stepped forward, blocking the water with his hand. "You can't call my future wife that."

Virgil came down the steps. "I'll split that egg-sucking bastard's jaw."

Spider dropped the hose. "You got to get in line." He took one slow step and two fast ones and, sinking his left fist in Roebuck's stomach, winged a long right that landed low on his nose. Roebuck dropped like he was hinged. His nose was streaming blood. Virgil and J. D. held Spider back.

Roebuck looked up smiling through the blood. "I'm not a violent man, Spider Hornsby, and you know that." He drew himself up. "Jesus taught us to turn the other cheek."

J. D. said, "Forget him, Spider. He's crazy as a loon. Leave him alone."

Spider jerked loose. "If you're sap enough to believe that crap." He rolled his full weight behind a stiff right to the sharp point of the jaw. Roebuck went into a slow sitting position in the spreading puddle on the walk. He sat very still as Spider, sucking his bleeding knuckles, shut off the spray at the nozzle and went back inside.

In bed Spider twitched and Ruby cried. He got up four times for beer and twice for peanut butter sandwiches. Ruby smoked.

(82)

"Ruby, let's forget it. Forget the whole mess. It never happened."

"But Mama knows. Everybody knows. Everybody. How can I face you? Oh, and that damn fool Agnes."

He slammed his beer can against the wall. "I don't give a damn! What's done's done. That son of a bitching Roebuck. . . . I ain't through with that bastard yet."

Ruby got up.

"Where you going?"

"You got to get your rest. I'll sleep on the couch."

"No, stay here."

"But I can't sleep."

Spider sat up. "Me neither."

"Please let me. I want to. I'll feel better." He had his arm around her.

"You going to be all right?"

"I'm all right, hon. You go to sleep now. I'll feel better in the morning."

"O.K., puddin', give us a kiss."

In the morning Ruby was gone. There was no note, no explanation. Her orange dress was still hanging on one of her perfumed padded hangers. The orange shoes were on the rack. Her hair dryer and make-up kit, her pink and blue polka-dot toothbrush that hung next to his black one from the two-slot glass holder over the sink, all were gone, and pulling back the bathroom door he saw her douche was missing. Padding around the house barefooted in his pajama bottoms, Spider began to face the hard fact. Ruby was gone. He opened the refrigerator and popped his first beer. By noon he had pyramided seven empty cans on the kitchen table and five between the clock and the monkeys on the mantelpiece. The morning paper lay on the porch where the kid had thrown it; the mail stayed in the box. When the phone rang he let it ring.

Spider was drunk and getting drunker. The idea of being alone scared him, and he thought back over his old girl friends. Who would he call? Joanne had gone to fat; Wilma had a millworker husband and a porchful of screaming kids. . . . The young ones had gone; the old ones had bleached out older, dried up and given up. He remembered a line and smiled and shuddered at the same time. "Too old to fuck, too proud to suck. . . ." He began thinking about them.

Mary Beth Boothe, the carnival barker from Harlan County, Tennessee, had stayed only three days and left in a panel truck with his color television set, five brand-new white-wall tires, and every piece of silver, linen, and small appliance in the house. Letitia Chesterfield, who came from Boston and had a degree in something, swore she had to go home to see her dying mother. He had given her a round-trip ticket, two hundred dollars, and a new winter coat. Letitia wrote a card back saying she'd brought her mother down to New Orleans for some reason he couldn't read. He figured she had written the Mardi Gras card stone drunk, for something had been spilt on the bottom half. It had come postage due. Across the top was the faded impression of Letitia's overpainted lips. Her lips reminded him of Mildred's and Gladys's and then Billy Lou's. They all ran together, all grasping, nagging, late sleepers who'd sweep around a dog and make love to the first snake that slid out of the swamp. He lay across the bed, smoking a cigar. There was no taste in it. He shook his head. He knew he wasn't exactly a bargain, but thinking over the women he'd known he knew that out of the deck of love he'd been dealt some beauts. Women had a way of seeing him coming. Of finding out in seconds that he couldn't say no to anything. He was fresh meat. He didn't understand it. He could do anything he wanted with Virgil, J. D., Kershaw. With men, life, problems, finance was easy; they respected him and always dealt from the top. With women it was different.

But Ruby was honest. He would miss that. He could ask her a straight question and get a straight answer. If he wanted to make love she wasn't ashamed to talk about it. . . . Gladys had been the worst. She couldn't stand the thought. She wanted the lights out and not a word spoken. And she lay as if crucified, rigid, plier-like, pretending it wasn't happening. And then one furious night he'd switched the lights on and slapped her face. "Look! Look, you

(84)

bitch! We're screwing! Fucking! I'm fucking you and you're fucking me. See?" he rared back. "Look, it's me. I'm inside you. Inside, see?"

She screamed in disgust, "No! No! I don't want to know! Cut those lights off! Oh, I can't stand you!"

He had laughed and cocked her head down to see closer. "Look, it's in you. You made it vanish because there's a hole in you." And holding out his hands as if measuring an industrial plumbing connection, shouted, "It's that deep, and big around as an oil can, because every walking tripod in the Carolinas, Georgia, and Tennessee has been there and back."

He stabbed the cigar out and rolled over to Ruby's side. It was higher there, harder, flatter. He wondered how she'd managed to keep from dropping into the deep draw of his side. If she came back he'd get a new mattress, maybe a special one with thicker springs. Maybe he'd lose some weight. She'd like that. His arms and legs were hard and firm. The weight was all gut—potato chips, pork skins, peanut butter, and beer. A pound a day for eighty days would bring him back to his old football weight of 187. He opened another beer and came back to bed. It would be hard losing eighty pounds. Almost impossible. He loved sweets and beer, and at forty-four it's hard to change. He patted and stroked his smooth round stomach. At least it was paid for. . . . And maybe, maybe he wasn't too fat. Some people can carry more weight than others. He had large bones. Billy Lou had said he was just right. Ripe, she'd called it, and he'd believed it. He had believed everything Billy Lou had told him for the first three days. Three days of everything, and then nothing. He'd discovered a rose tattooed as if blooming from her pubic hair and believed her when she said it had been a high school initiation. But she couldn't leave it at one lie; she had to double it and finally tell him that all the girls in class had the same tattoo. He had slept with Janet Osborne, and when he told Billy he was going to phone and check her story, Billy snapped her fingers. "No, all except Janet. She was out with pneumonia." She named the month, the week.

Spider had let the bait trail. "I remember that. I thought it was infantile paralysis?"

(85)

Billy Lou took it. "That's it! That's it! Now I remember, infantile paralysis. Lord, we were all so worried about her. We took up a collection and sent her flowers and candy and the cutest stuffed bear you ever saw." Billy Lou had sailed on. "I believe that poor thing still has a little limp."

They were all lies, harmless lies, but they finally wore him down. He stopped trying to follow anything. There was nothing he could count on. He'd ask for the time and she would shade it five minutes or add ten. If she said she'd been to a John Wayne movie, it could mean anything from getting her hair set to sleeping with the First Street Methodist basketball team at the Blue Light Motel. But despite the lies he still clung to one desperate truth. She insisted, and he believed, he wasn't fat.

It wasn't until he had to buy a new suit for Exeter Crosby's funeral and the clerk had padded him swiftly past the area marked Stylishly Stout and to the end of the rack to Extra Large—Deep Crotch that the light dawned. The clerk held the pants out. Most of the material was crotch, curving the white pinstripe sharply against the dark blue background. At first he thought the long zipper was a mistake, a joke. His hang-up suitcase with the three-side zipper was shorter. It seemed to curve all the way up from the knees. The pants hung from a pinch hanger and the endless fifty-four-inch waistband reinforced with the heavy rubber inner band flapped like a tent.

Spider was firm. "You got to be kidding."

The clerk had had a long day. "'Fraid not, mister." He whipped the yellow tape around Spider's waist and snugged it into the flesh. "You'd split fifty-two inches getting out the door. It's fifty-four inches on the button—or, if you prefer, four feet six, give or take a sixteenth."

"Jesus! I can't believe it!"

"Mister, you want the suit or not? You aren't going to be finding this size just *anywhere*."

"Wrap it up. I'll get my gal to cuff them."

"No one's wearing cuffs these days."

"I am, buster—and no more lip."

But Billy Lou, after measuring a 32-inch inseam and chalking

(86)

it off forty-five minutes before the funeral, cut the pants to a cuffless 27, striking Spider at the top of his socks. It was too late for anything. Finally he hitched the pants low to cover his socks and climbed in the pallbearers' Cadillac. At the funeral the wind was blowing and the deep crotch filled with air, ballooning out and swaying back and forth. Stark Rogers came sniggering over as they lowered Exeter and told him he was looking for a new tailor and asked if he could recommend one.

Spider dropped the empty can to the floor, smiling about the pants, the funeral, and Billy Lou insisting she'd cut them off at 32 inches, claiming there was something wrong with the tape measure or the pants themselves. He laughed and shook his head, wondering what she was doing and what poor bastard was cork-screwing his life around her lies.

He hoped she was still single. But then, as he thought and mellowed with remembering their nights together, he hoped she had found a man. It would be a pity for her to go to waste. With Gladys it was different; she deserved and would be better off alone. But Billy Lou was soft in bed. Sweet. She was willing, eager, and for all her soft brown-eyed innocence knew more about love than any other woman he'd ever known. . . . It would be nice to find her single and available. But if she was happily married it would be nice seeing her again and saying hello. . . . Still, she couldn't hold a candle to Ruby. Ruby, who could touch his ear and make him tremble. Ruby, who could worm her big toe in between his and wake him from the sweetest dream and the soundest sleep, wild to have her. He couldn't stand the idea of thinking of her and padded back to the refrigerator and pulled out three cans of beer.

Ruby, tears streaking her make-up and shadows under her eyes, sat at Jimmy Lee's dresser brushing her hair and crying. Jimmy Lee, in his shorts and dark glasses, was having breakfast in bed. The TV set was on but the vacuum cleaner in the hall was rippling the Morning Movie. It was 9:55. The maid knocked twice and stuck her head in the door. "When you want me making this up?"

Ruby spun around. "Can't you keep her out of here?"

(87)

Jimmy Lee pointed a toast spear at her. "I'll let you know." He bit down. "Next time you knock, you wait till I say come in. O.K.?"

"O.K. with me."

Jimmy Lee said, "Ruby, Ruby, you're going to have to settle down. Everything's O.K. You did the right thing. It had to happen."

She dried her tears with Kleenex and wiped away the running mascara. "I feel awful about it . . . awful."

"Why don't you come crawl in bed. That'll pick you up."

"Go to hell!"

"Suit yourself." He wiped up the egg yolk with his toast and squeezed on marmalade from the small paper cup.

She watched him in the mirror. She gritted her teeth and hissed, "Rotten." Nothing touched him. Nothing hurt him. When she said no he hadn't tried to humor her or coax her across the room or anything. He simply cut off, with his thoughts winging toward some 38-D cup he remembered in New York City or Nashville.

She spoke to the mirror and kept pulling hard on her hair. "Screw this bird. Screw him." Her lips were down and firm and her eyes were narrowed. She recognized the Justifiably Furious attitude from *Screen Fun and Fashion* and wheeling around threw the brush at him.

"Hey, watch that, you little bitch. What do you think this is anyway?"

"Oh, shut up!"

She sat still on the vanity bench, hugging her knees and wishing she were dead. Out of the corner of her eye she saw Jennifer Jones coming toward Joseph Cotten for a big love scene. It was *Portrait of Jennie*; she'd seen it three times before. She remembered the music and Joseph Cotten's soft, beautiful voice and twisted her chair around so she could see better.

Jimmy Lee said, "Want some coffee?"

She liked the way Jennifer Jones wore her hair. Maybe she would fluff hers forward like that. It framed and softened the forehead.

"Come on, Ruby. It's still hot."

(88)

"O.K., Jimmy Lee."

The phone rang and Jimmy Lee clapped his hand over the receiver.

"Know a Virgil Haynes?"

"Yeah, let me talk to him. Hi, Virg. . . . I'm O.K. . . . It's too complicated. . . . I don't know. . . . Listen, come on upstairs. Jimmy Lee doesn't mind. Room four-ten."

She hung up. "Put some clothes on, Jimmy Lee."

Ruby let Virgil in and hugged him. "Oh, Virg, it's really screwed up. I've really done it now."

He looked around the room. "It'll work out, Ruby." He shook Jimmy Lee's hand. "So you're Jimmy Lee Rideout."

"In the flesh."

Virgil was fascinated by the albino. "Heard a lot about you." He half circled him as if he were on display.

Jimmy Lee didn't like it. "Maybe I ought to sell tickets."

Virgil grinned and tapped him on the shoulder. "Sorry there, chief. You're the first one I've seen up close."

"You about finished?"

"Yeah. You always wear those shades?"

"Most of the time. The light, it hurts my eyes."

Virgil nodded at the TV set—"Pretty good color"—and then at the whiskey.

"Help yourself."

Ruby said, "We're out of ice. Is Spider drinking?"

"Plenty. Ruby, you ought to go back before it gets worse."

Jimmy Lee interrupted. "She's staying with me."

Virgil drank the Scotch neat. "Listen, Rideout, don't give me any static."

Ruby poured herself a drink. "Well, what are we going to do? Stand *here* all day?"

Virgil tore open a package of pecans. "How 'bout a swim? It's ninety-nine outside and climbing."

Jimmy Lee had pulled the bottom drawer of the dresser out and was shining his shoes with a hand towel. "I can't go that light. The sun, man, it eats me up."

Ruby chewed on a piece of toast. "Aw, come on, Jimmy Lee.

(89)

We'll park under the trees and you can stay in the shade. It's nice up there, I swear it is."

They drove along the Broad River Road with the top down and the radio on loud. Jimmy Lee had brought along a bottle of Scotch and a bottle of bourbon. At the Pig Trail Inn they stopped for Seven-Up and ice and then, with Jimmy Lee sitting low in the seat dodging the sun and Ruby's hair streaming, Virgil pushed the big red Caddy to 110 heading for Ballantine's Landing.

By four the Scotch was gone and the bourbon was open. They were sitting on the pebbly bank in the pine-tree shade watching the small bass jumping at the shiners around a red and yellow raft. Low rain clouds were hanging at the lake end, but there was no wind. Suddenly Virgil skinned down to his shorts, dove in, and swam out to the raft. He hauled himself up. "Come on, Ruby! It's great out here!"

"I'll ruin my clothes."

"Hell! They'll dry in three minutes. Come on!"

She waded to her waist and then began swimming, her long hair trailing straight behind. He pulled her up and she stretched out on her back, closing her eyes in the bright sun. "Mmmmmm, that is nice."

She called in, "Hey, Jimmy Lee! How 'bout getting us some music!" She breathed in deep. "Lord, am I out of shape. How far is that?"

"Forty–fifty yards. . . . Say, where's that Beverly Eppes live?"

"Over in Olympia. Fun, ain't she?"

"You ain't just talking. She put that Mary Beth in the shade. I'm seeing that number again."

Ruby turned over. Her dress was plastered to her back and clung to the tight scoop of her hips. Virgil propped his jaw on his fists. "You know I've never seen you in a bathing suit?"

"You ain't missed much." She leaned over to watch the flashing minnows.

"Ruby, if you don't go back to Spider, how about you and me teaming up?"

"You mean like keep it in the family?"

(90)

"Something like that. Hell, you could do a lot worse."

"I appreciate it, Virg. But I ain't studying settling down. I got me a career to be thinking about."

"And Mr. Flat White over there's going to turn the trick?"

She dipped her hands deep, watching her fingers foreshorten. "He ain't bad, Virgil. What messed me up was that Agnes. We had a great sound going. I swear we did. Now I got to go and dig me up another partner."

In the distance a Chris-Craft made a wide roaring turn with two water skiers behind splashing up tall V's of spray.

"Virgil, I bet you anything she's dying to see you again."

"The hell with her. Roebuck's got her; he can keep her."

"But she wasn't always like that and you know it. Listen, if I were you I'd—"

"Do me a favor, will you? Let's drop it. I got better things to think about."

They lay still, listening to the water lap under the raft and the music from the car. Two buzzards were circling high above, and from the woods came the low curdling of the brown doves.

Ruby jumped up. "Race you in!" Before Virgil could get up she'd flattened out in a racing dive and was churning toward the bank.

She stretched out on the Cadillac hood and with her hair fanned out in the sun to dry put her feet up on the windshield. "Hey, Virgil, loan me your shirt. I got to watch these damn freckles." She draped it over her face and neck and pushing aside the problems that had been crowding her all morning began feeling smooth and cool and thin. Everything was going to work out fine. She closed her eyes. It was only a matter of time.

Virgil's voice was thick on bourbon. "Know something, Rideout?" They were sitting in the shade on the pine straw. "You're funny looking. No doubt about it. But you ain't too bad a guy."

"You don't give too much away, do you, sport?"

Virgil fanned at the gnats and pointed a steady finger at Jimmy Lee's nose. "I'm telling you something else. . . . You take care of Ruby or your ass is mud."

(91)

8

While Spider and Virgil made, hauled, and sold whiskey and Raymond La Mer pushed Roebuck into state-wide prime-time radio and was thinking of taking him on tour, Ruby and Jimmy Lee polished the third verse of "Honkytonk Angels," arranged three other songs, and made love.

They were lying in bed at the Francis Marion watching daytime television and drinking Scotch. Jimmy Lee scooped up a handful of corn curls and turned the volume down. "Me and you are a pretty good team. You know that?"

"I guess so."

"What say we get married."

Ruby was filing her fingernails. "Are you crazy? I ain't got time to be settling down now."

"Settle down! Hell, that's the last thing on earth you'd be doing with me. We'd be in Dallas one day, Hollywood the next."

She studied her nails and decided they were too soft. "Oh, I don't know, Jimmy Lee. That could be a drag too. Why don't we leave it like it is?"

"Because I want to put some roots down and get married."

"Oh, bull. You just said you'd be gallivanting all over the place. You ain't making *any* sense. . . . Jimmy Lee, where you from in Texas?"

"Big D."

"Funny, you sure don't sound it."

"Groove."

She turned the volume back up and ran the remote dial around until she found a movie.

Jimmy Lee in his Tahitian shorts crossed the room for ice. "Say this Roebuck creep hooks her. I tell you, Ruby, we're just spinning our wheels in this dog town. We ought to be in Nashville."

Ruby watched the movie, thinking about Spider, the future, and her growing suspicions of Raymond La Mer and Jimmy Lee Rideout. She had to have more time. . . . "No, Jimmy Lee. If you want to go on, go on. I'm waiting on Agnes. I just can't be teaming up with any old person."

It was dark when Ruby, Jimmy Lee, and Virgil pulled into Rusty Broome's Drive-Inn with the top down. Red, green, and purple neon spelled out *Rusty's* against the black night and the clouds of flying ants and hard-backed beetles. Car radio music and order pickups on the p.a. system and backfiring came from everywhere. Ruby's spirits were up with the music and the noise and the smell of chicken and French fries. "Big crowd. Hey! There's Junior Rhodes! Hi, Junior!"

"Hi, Ruby. . . . Looking good."

"You still going to that vocational school?"

"Naw, I quit that mess. I'm in the insurance business."

"I'll be dogged."

The food was served, and they lined up the chicken boxes and beer along the deep leather dash.

A Hollywood muffler coughed, rumbled, and chopped down. Another voice sang out. "Ruby! Ruby Red!"

"Hello, Arnold. New car?"

"You better believe it! Three hundred and ninety horses!" He

(94)

spun out double clutching, his muffler roaring and popping, his wide tracks screaming.

Jimmy Lee chewed on a French fry. "Another Leroy Yarborough. . . . You're a popular girl."

"I used to hop cars here."

Jimmy Lee tore into the fried chicken. "Too bad we can't get Agnes back in harness. Four of us would make a great team."

"Virgil could do it if he wasn't so damn lazy."

Virgil poured honey on his hush puppies. "She doesn't want to see me. Let's forget it, O.K.?"

"Oh, fool, she's crazy about you. Lord, you're all she used to talk about." She salted her fries and spread her napkin. "You should have heard her. 'Did you see Virgil? What was he driving? How'd he look? Did he ask about me?' No lie, that's all she had on her brain. You and that Gibson guitar."

He crunched on a leg bone and sucked out the marrow. "Well, it's too late now. I've had it."

She waved at Arnold as he thundered by leaning on his horn. "I bet I could get her out for you."

Virgil drank his beer, remembering the night on Needle Hill. "You hear me, Virgil?"

"I hear you. . . . O.K., I'm listening."

Ruby was ready. "We get some more chicken, some more booze, pick her up, and we go out to the lake. Then you're on your own."

"Think she'll come?"

"It sure as hell won't hurt trying."

Virgil and Jimmy Lee sat in the car while Ruby knocked on Agnes's door.

"Hello, Ruby."

"Hi, Ag."

"You been drinking?"

"A little. Hon, come out; I want to talk to you."

"I don't think I should. Besides, we're just sitting down for supper."

"I'm heading for Nashville, Ag. I just wanted to say good-by and let you know there wasn't any hard feelings."

(95)

Agnes came out. "Let's sit on the swing."

"Ag, me and Jimmy Lee and Virgil are having some chicken and a farewell drink."

"Oh, Ruby, I couldn't."

"I know, hon, but it's my last night in town and I just can't leave cold."

"And you ain't mad at me, Ruby? I acted like such a fool?"

"I just said I wasn't. Come on, hon."

"But I can't face Virgil like this." She touched her hair.

"Get a scarf, we're in his convertible. And tell your folks you're eating with me."

They came down the brick-lined walk arm in arm. Ruby told her that she'd needed a good excuse to leave Spider so she could try Nashville.

"All the same, I'm sorry I told Roebuck. There just wasn't any need for that. Ruby, I want to apologize. I don't know what came over me."

Ruby hugged her waist. "Ag, the way I got it figured, you did me the biggest favor in my life."

"I guess the Lord works in ways we just can't understand until we get back from them."

"Well, I don't know about all that. But things are really looking up. Me and Jimmy Lee are going to turn old Music City upside down."

They were at the car. "Hello, Virgil. Hi, Jimmy Lee."

"Hello, Agnes."

Ruby climbed in the back seat with Jimmy Lee and Agnes slid up front.

Virgil said, "Help yourself to the chicken. We saved you a couple drumsticks."

"Thanks."

Virgil pulled out into Jefferson. "How've you been?"

"Pretty good. . . . You?"

"O.K., I guess."

Ruby elbowed forward. "Hey, Ag, remember that class picnic we went on that old Arnold got sick at?"

Agnes sat sideways. "Sure, second semester, junior."

(96)

"We saw him down at Rusty's. Got him another new car. Hey, you all, listen to this." Virgil slowed down to keep the wind from whistling. "This Arnold Cooper used to never date girls in high school. I mean never. And every time you'd ask him when he was going to start he'd say, 'Well, I'm going to get me a new set of seat covers and then you just watch my smoke.' Then he'd get his seat covers and we'd say, 'How about it now, Arnold? When you taking us to the drive-in?' Know what he needed next?"

Agnes laughed. "Hub caps. I remember that. Then he needed a new paint job. Then—then a hi-fi radio."

Ruby said, "Wound up he never took anyone out. You know who he had with him tonight?"

"No one. Right?"

Ruby pushed her hair out into the breeze. "Right."

Agnes laughed. "Same old Arnold."

At the lake Virgil turned the parking lights off to keep the mosquitoes away. He and Jimmy Lee stripped down and started for the raft in the warm water. Jimmy Lee carried the bourbon and Seven-Up; Virgil swam sidearm with one hand high keeping the cigarettes and matches dry. "Don't slide around, Jimmy Lee. This thing's got splinters gone to bed."

"Gotcha."

In the moonlight his bone-white skin glistened like fox fire. They had a fast drink, then a slow one, and then lighting cigarettes they lay back, watching the black night and the bright star points.

Jimmy Lee said, "Nice."

Virgil sighed. "Fine. . . . Hope old Ruby's having some luck."

The moon, canoe shaped and orange red, was moving up through the pine branches. It reached the top, then, balancing there, seemed to pause before sliding up into the clear night.

"Jimmy Lee, say Agnes doesn't come along. What kind of plans you got?"

"Then we're going alone."

"O.K., one more question and I want a straight answer, good buddy. That Nashville's big-time and tough ass. I want it straight: is Ruby that good?"

(97)

Jimmy Lee held his cigarette above his head and aiming the red ash at the North Star ticked his teeth together. "She's got a lot of natural talent and good energy. Ruby'll make it if anyone can."

Ruby and Agnes with their shoes off sat on the car hood leaning back on the windshield. Ruby had a full Dixie cup of Scotch and a king-sized Pepsi.

"Ag." An owl sailed by against the low moon.

"Yeah, Rube."

"Virgil's still crazy about you." She sipped the Scotch. "I swear he is."

"He's too wild for my taste, Ruby."

She put her arm around her. "But you could settle him down, hon. He's just got a lot of juice in him. Remember how that fool played sixty minutes of football and wasn't even breathing hard? . . . Ag, that man would do anything in the world for you. . . . Want a nip?"

"You know I don't."

"Oh, Lord, you used to take one now and then. Come on, break down. It's my last night."

"I'm sorry, Ruby."

"It's O.K. . . . Listen, you won't get mad if I ask you something, will you?"

Agnes was running her finger up and down the windshield wiper rubber. "No, Ruby, me and Roebuck haven't been in the same bed. Can't you understand, he's a preacher."

"I understand, but what I want to know is do you want to? I mean, like you did with Virgil?"

"I don't want to talk about it. It won't do a lick of good. . . . Maybe I'll try that stuff. Get that Pepsi ready. Ready?"

"Ready."

"Wow! Wow! It burns!" She wiped tears away with the back of her wrist and fanned her mouth. "Lord!" She laughed. "You know something, old crazy, I'm going to miss you."

"Me too, Ag. . . . Honest to God, if I knew Virgil wasn't so hung up on you I'd snaggle him off for myself."

(98)

Agnes took another small drink. "But Roebuck needs me. He really needs me."

"Yeah, but if you're afraid to get in bed with him?"

"I ain't afraid. I tried to but he's different. I've already told you all that, Ruby." The Scotch made her talk faster. "Oh, Ruby, you reckon that fool does? I might as well confess a little something; Roebuck does scare me a little. He's got funny ways."

"Then, hon, you ought to get shed of him."

Agnes sipped again. "I'm in too deep. I've promised. We've set the date and we're already looking at silverware and furniture."

"Tell Virgil you're scared. You know yourself, there's no one takes charge like him when he wants to. I swear there isn't."

"No, Ruby. I've done made up my mind. There's no telling how big a man Roebuck's going to become, and he needs me there beside him. Now let's stop this." She held up the Dixie cup. "Here's good luck in Music City."

"Lord, I wish you were coming along. We'd really have a ball."

"It would have been fun. . . . You're going to write me, aren't you?"

"I'll write. Hey!" Ruby giggled. "Why don't we swim out there and scare hell out of those two idiots? We could come up behind them." She slid down the fender and pulled her dress off.

"We can't go like that."

"They can't see. It's black as pitch out there. Come on, Ag."

"But they'd know. No, Ruby, I just can't."

"Well, I am."

"Maybe I'll come later."

Halfway out Ruby changed her mind and swam straight for the raft. Virgil pulled her up. Ruby had a quick drink and Jimmy Lee lit her a cigarette. She called out, "Ag! Come on out. It's really nice."

"No, I'm all right here."

Virgil said, "She sounds funny."

"She's drinking that Scotch." She told them what Agnes had said. "Jesus!"

Jimmy Lee said, "Maybe we ought to take her on to Nashville. Let her think it over there."

(99)

Virgil flipped his cigarette into the water. "Damn! You sure you ain't lying, Rube?"

"I swear it, Virgil. I swear before God. Hey, hush, I hear something."

"I don't."

"Now it's gone."

Virgil shifted. "Probably a coon."

They lay still, facing the dark shore and listening. Agnes was crying.

Ruby said, "Go see her, Virgil."

Jimmy Lee slapped him on the back. "Now's your chance."

He took a long drink and dove in.

Agnes saw him coming across the pebbles and picking his way through the pine cones. "Hi, Virgil."

"What's the matter, sweet?" He took the whiskey. "You shouldn't be drinking this stuff."

She dried her eyes with her scarf. "I know. Ain't you cold?"

"I'm all right." He took her hand and slid her down from the hood. He hugged her close, and her chin burrowed into his neck. She began sobbing. "Oh, Virgil."

Suddenly she was holding on tight. He tipped her mouth to his. "Honey, I still feel the same way."

Her mouth opened slowly as if she was remembering something but had forgotten how to say it. "Virgil, Virgil."

Her arms arched around him as he pulled her close, kissing her hard. She held on tighter, sobbing and squirming closer. He moved her to the open convertible. They were in the front seat. He turned the switch on and found the seat adjuster trigger. The electric motor whined and the red leather seat rolled back six full inches.

Agnes's mouth was open. She slid it across his throat, up to his ear, and back to his mouth. She moaned and twisted. "Virgil. Oh, Virgil."

"Agnes, you been gone so long." He unbuttoned her blouse and searched for her skirt zipper. She did it for him and raised up to slide it over her hips as he skillfully opened her two-hook bra. Her bra and blouse came off together and he sunk his face between her breasts. Her hands were on him: opening his belt, unzipping

(100)

his fly, pushing his shirt up, his pants down. "Ag, you aren't drunk, are you?"

"Don't talk. Don't talk."

In the dark he touched her eyes. They were closed. For a second he thought he would stop. Maybe she didn't know what she was doing. She would be sorry when the whiskey faded and then hate him forever. She released him and stretching out on the seat opened her arms to him. "You and me, Virgil."

He whispered, "Nobody else, Ag. Nobody else. . . ."

They lay still in each other's arms with the radio on. Virgil spoke. "Tell me what you're thinking about."

"That dumb old wire spark."

He laughed. "Sorry I got so mad."

"You had more sense than I did. Can I have another little drink?"

He reached over the windshield for the bottle on the hood. "Think you'll feel the same when you sober up?"

"I'm crazy about you, Virgil Haynes. Always have been and always will be."

Virgil Hooper Haynes and Agnes Mildred McCoy were married before the Justice of the Peace in Branchville, South Carolina, forty miles from Orangeburg. When the 3 A.M. service ended and after Ruby and Jimmy Lee tossed a box of instant long-grained rice at them between the two-step porch and the red Cadillac, they passed the last bottle around for a wedding toast and then, with the radio on and Agnes and Ruby squealing and sobbing and crisscrossing to kiss everybody, they headed for the dawn and the Quality Courts Motel at the Charleston-Savannah turnoff. Mr. and Mrs. Virgil H. Haynes were given the bridal suite 32A and Jimmy Lee half carried and half dragged the drunk, singing, finger-snapping, laughing, and crying Ruby down the hall to 37A.

Outside, soaped on the Cadillac windows, doors, and hood in Jimmy Lee Rideout's handwriting, were

JUST MARRIED VIRGIL AND AGNES!!!
HOT SPRINGS TONIGHT!!!!!
SOCK IT TO HER VIRGIL!!!!!

Across the trunk a labor of love of six treble clefs and staffs and thirty to forty whole, half, and quarter notes were over, under, and around the beautiful curling script:

GOOD LUCK HONKYTONK ANGELS

And finally Ruby, with Ivory soap that would have to be razor-bladed off of the windshield, had printed in foot-high letters:

LOOK OUT NASHVILLE—HERE WE COME

It was noon in the motel dining room, and as Agnes and Virgil slid into the booth Jimmy Lee raised up and with his left hand on his heart sang out one line, "They-tried-to-tell-us-we're-too-young."

Agnes pretended to slap him and Ruby laughed. "Ah, the newlyweds. How you feel, hon? Lord, you look great."

"I feel fine."

Jimmy stared at her shining eyes. "You sure look different."

Agnes giggled. "Wish you all would quit gawking so. I only had a little bit of that stuff."

Virgil with his arm around her snapped open the menu one-handed. "How about some chow?"

The waitress told them the chef didn't like to cook breakfast after he started serving from the steam table, and Jimmy Lee fingered and tipped his dark glasses. "You tell that cook we ain't eating no triple joyburgers. We want breakfast. If he gives you any trouble bring him out here."

The girl studied his hair and face. "Y'all in show business?"

He nodded.

She wrote out the order. "I'll see that you get it."

"Thatta gal. And how about an order of English muffins."

"You mean those little jobs with icing on them? They ain't called that."

"Forget it. Just hold those grits."

Ruby said, "Hon, I'd love that bacon crisp if you can swing it."

The girl came back with orange juice and coffee. "I squeezed that juice myself. The rest'll be ready in a minute." She hesitated. "Y'all from Nashville?"

Jimmy Lee sipped his coffee. "That's it."

She smiled. "I figured that."

Ruby winked at Agnes.

After breakfast Jimmy Lee tapped his fingers on the Formica table top and ticked out his two-beat rhythm through his teeth. "O.K., here's the spread." He filled them in on how he would call ahead and get bookings in five or six small towns. They would play church socials, junior high schools, and square dances until they got their act set. Then they would hit Augusta, the outskirts of Atlanta and Chattanooga, and be on the road to Nashville.

Virgil shook his head. "I'm losing money hand over fist. I got whiskey to drive."

Ruby said, "All we need is three or four weeks; isn't that right, Jimmy Lee?"

"That'll do it. It'll be like a honeymoon, Virgil. A great chance to see the country."

Virgil spoke slowly. "I already seen that part of the country."

Agnes said, "Please, Virgil. Please. We've got a great act. You ain't even seen it."

He saw no way out. "O.K. If Agnes wants it it's O.K., but three weeks absolute tops. I guess I can fly in and out."

Agnes kissed him, then squeezed Ruby. "Talk about something exciting. This is it!"

Virgil said, "How much these things going to be bringing in?"

Jimmy Lee signaled for more coffee. "We won't even make expenses. But just wait. A few shows behind us and a few notices, and we'll be getting top money up the road. How much you carrying?"

"Two-fifty, three hundred. How about you?"

"Little over a thou. Hell, we can do it easy. I know the swingers in Nashville. They'll back us."

Ruby wrapped her arms around him. "Jimmy Lee! This *is* it. We're going to have a ball."

The Honkytonk Angels' first date was at the Monck's Corner Free Will Presbyterian Square Dance. They were to play during

(103)

the ten-minute breaks for the Free Will Fiddlers. The admission was 50 cents with the members bringing hot covered dishes, biscuits, pies, cakes, and ambrosia. Fruit punch was served, driving the whiskey drinkers outside to their cars or down the hall to the men's room.

The first set ended, and while the fiddlers were drying off and loading up on pork barbecue steeped in Louisiana hot sauce, Ruby stomped her foot three times and led Agnes into "Honkytonk Angels." The younger set crowded down close, beating out the rhythm and urging them to cut loose, but the preacher, the elders, and the entertainment committee looked over suspiciously from the serving table. Jimmy Lee signaled to ease up. They cut it short and moved into "Wildwood Flower." Agnes smiled and Ruby winked at Jimmy Lee as they saw the older members come forward.

When the fiddlers came back the girls jumped down and followed Jimmy Lee and Virgil out to the car. Ruby had Jimmy Lee's hand. "How we doing?"

He squeezed her hips and fingered along her panty line. "A-one. I like the way you follow instructions. You see how that Carter song worked?"

"Damn right. I'm glad you spotted that."

Agnes held on to Virgil. "Honey, it's the nicest crowd I ever saw. I feel so warm and nice up there. It's like they all want to come up there and give us a great big hug."

Virgil poured drinks into paper cups. "How 'bout a toast, Jimmy Lee?"

"Right." He held his cup high. "Our first night. May there be many more. Many, many more."

Agnes drank with them. "I don't know when I've had so much fun."

Ruby held her cup up at the moon. "To Nashville, Tennessee. Music City, U.S.A."

Jimmy Lee leaned on the fender. "Now listen. Give them a couple slow oldies and then go a little upbeat on that Miller piece."

Three breaks later, when the fiddle players were soaking and one had gotten sick out back, Ruby and Agnes did twenty minutes. Toward the end Jimmy Lee gave them the signal to unwind. Ruby went into her go-go number, and the high school crowd started pounding on the stage and frugging in the sawdust. She looked out at Jimmy Lee, who was snapping his fingers and urging her on. Then she saw the m.c. frowning and shaking his head. Jimmy Lee winked and dampened his hands. Ruby eased up and ended the song. The high school kids shouted for more, but Jimmy Lee wasn't taking any chances. Their last two songs were straight waltz time, and after the fiddle players did another straight, hard hour they came back to close the show with a stiff, straight version of "I Saw the Light."

In the car heading out the dark highway Jimmy Lee announced they had cleared $14.03 and all they could eat. "Main thing is you gals can follow instructions. You see them, Virgil?"

Virgil drove with one arm around Agnes. "Damn right. They're great. By God you sure had that crowd pegged."

Jimmy Lee said, "You got to be careful down here in the turpentine. Strange people."

Ruby snuggled into his arm. "Ain't he something, Agnes?"

"Something else."

Jimmy Lee pulled her closer. "What we need is a few more nights like this. Stage presence, a professional attitude; that's the stuff you can't buy."

She kissed his ear and he put his hand on her thigh. "Yessir, a little more polish and hello, Nashville."

Ruby sang, "Hello, Nashville, oh, hello, Nashville," to the tune of "Hello, Dolly!" Agnes joined in. "It's so nice for you—us—to be back home again. Hello, Nashville. Oh, Hello, Nashville. . . ."

"Jimmy Lee, now that's the kind of song you ought to be writing for us."

His hand moved up her leg and he thought of the big double bed that was waiting for them in Kingstree and the nights like this that lay ahead. He squeezed her thigh and then worked his hand up under her blouse. "Ruby Red, that's just what I'm going to be doing."

Ruby pushed his hands away. "Come on, Ag. . . ."

"Hello, Nashville,
Oh, hello, Nashville,
It's so nice for us
To be back home again. . . ."

After four choruses Virgil turned the radio on and flicked his lights up, then down and gunned around a slow-moving watermelon truck and swung onto Route 52, heading north.

The junior high school in Kingstree paid only $12, which covered the gas and the first thousand-mile oil change. Rain canceled the pie party and dinner-on-the-ground-social in Bamberg, and when they arrived in Green Pond the president of the Chamber of Commerce, who owned and operated a Shell gas station, said he didn't know anything about the Honkytonk Angels, the show, or anything. "Maybe you folks want Green Pond, Georgia. Lot of folks get us mixed up with that crowd over there."

The next four nights went better: $16.50 in Sylvania, Georgia; $18.90 in Vidalia; $17.01 in Jesup; and $21.45 in Valdosta. In McRae, Georgia, working their way due north, Agnes played the straight gospel singer and Ruby the wild untamed go-go girl who in the end, seeing the error of her ways through Agnes's songs, came back to the fold to join her in the closing three straight hymns and the finale of "How Great Thou Art." The Episcopalians loved it.

Motels, whiskey, and meals were cutting into the bankroll, and from Swainsboro Virgil phoned Spider for more money.

Ruby asked how Spider sounded.

"Pretty down, Rube. Pretty down. Guess you wouldn't consider changing your mind and heading back?"

"I can't even be thinking about that now. I mean, I'm sorry and all. But Lord, we're red hot, Virgil!"

The church crowd in the small towns loved the show. They wanted encores, curtain calls, and autographs. In return they loaded them down with pies and cakes, smoked hams and four-pound lard buckets of barbecue hash and hopping john. Ruby knew they were on their way. The act was smoother and felt alive and fast, and the friendly smiling faces of the Baptists and Methodists and Free Will Presbyterians made them feel at home. Virgil liked everything. He kept saying "Fantastic!" and picking up words from Jimmy Lee: "Socko . . . boffo . . . out of sight . . . beautiful." He agreed with the girls and Jimmy Lee that the next stop after Nashville, Tennessee, had to be a one-way first-class ticket to Hollywood, California.

9

On the day of the wedding Agnes had called her mother and told her that as of 3 A.M. that morning she was Mrs. Virgil Hooper Haynes and to send her some clothes to Nashville care of the Capri Plaza Motel. Mary McCoy called her husband Fred at work at the Red Ball Trucking and told him the news. Fred was delighted. Despite Mary and her church friends thinking that Roebuck Alexander was the finest person in the Carolinas and Georgia and would make a perfect match for Agnes, Fred had never liked anything about him. All he knew about Virgil was that he was a friend of Spider's and a fast driver.

Fred went into Charley's Delicatessen and, announcing the news, bought cigars and beer for everyone standing around watching the ball game on TV. Charley bought the second round. "This may be out of line, Fred, boy, but I'm sort of glad that Roebuck didn't get her."

Fred said, "Me too. That one gave me the creeps."

Louis Smith, a Sherwin-Williams paint salesman who was having a lunch of pickled eggs and beer and working out an expense

(109)

account on the counter, looked up. "You'll like him, Fred. Pretty good old boy. Might take a drink now and then, but you sure as hell ain't getting no sore neck when he's saying grace."

Mary McCoy reached Roebuck Alexander that evening. Roebuck refused to believe it. Then he did. He saw black; then red; then black with red, yellow, and pale green flashes. He tore the phone cord from the wall, smashed the electric light above his head, ripped the window shades in half and, snatching down the rollers, stomped them until the springs shot out. He jumped onto the coffee table, splintering it and flattening out the four curved legs, and began throwing sofa cushions at the walls and turning over the heavy chairs. He stopped, panting, wild-eyed and frantic; he hadn't touched the television set. His hands were shaking and he plunged them into his pockets, clawing at his legs until they bled. It wasn't Agnes. It was Virgil. Virgil Haynes, the devil that tried to fornicate with her until the Lord stepped in on a streak of lightning. Virgil Haynes, who was clipping around in a red, devil-colored Cadillac with the top down and wild music blaring. He shut his eyes and pounded his fists on the sides of his head. He couldn't stand the idea of Agnes undressing in front of him. The thought of her nude and stretched out on clean white sheets sent him howling and clawing at the rose-and-twining-vine wallpaper. Why had the Lord stepped in on Needle Hill and deserted him now? He had been faithful. He had courted Agnes with no lust in his heart, no desires of the flesh. He had had them but he had stomped on them as he had the window shade roller. Where? Where was the Lord now? Could it be another test? Could Agnes be his Isaac? His sacrifice? He groaned. "I ain't that strong. Me and her were right for each other. IDEAL. She did everything I told her. Everything."

Roebuck stalked back and forth through his five shotgun rooms, slamming the doors, kicking the jambs, and stomping the bare boards in the kitchen. Agnes had said Virgil was working with Spider. Maybe the Lord in his wisdom wanted Spider and Virgil brought down together. Maybe he was using Agnes as part of the over-all scheme. He calmed down and, making a pair of fists so tight the blue veins throbbed, he paced across the back porch, looking up at the night and the full riding moon. Yes, Agnes was his lamb to be slaughtered. Just as Abraham had raised his sword against his only son, Isaac, he was being asked to turn Agnes over to Virgil. But he knew he mustn't try to make everything fit. Too much was missing. The Lord was giving him only a few facts at a time. Agnes was destined to come back to him. Maybe the Lord would strike Virgil Haynes impotent. They would never be married in his eyes. He stopped and gripping his fists to his head squeezed until he saw stars and flashes of light and heard himself shouting. "STOP! STOP! DO SOMETHING! NOW!" He thumbed through his black book to Hightower. . . . "Quendolyn, it's me, Preacher Alexander. I want to see Hooty. . . . No, you stay home. I want to see him alone."

Jimmy Lee told Virgil to pull off onto the shoulder of the road; they had just passed the "resume speed" sign outside Thomson, Georgia. He began dumping pies, cakes, ham, and six kinds of doughnuts into the drain ditch. "We eat this shit and we'll be blowing up like hogs."

Virgil hollered, "Hold on there, Jimmy Lee. Save me that barbecue hash; that stuff ain't too bad."

Jimmy Lee set the hash can on the car hood. As he rolled the cakes and spun the pies into the muddy, froggy water along Route 278, he knew they were in trouble. For $1.00 a head, the church crowd couldn't go wrong. They had to like the Honkytonk Angels. But Augusta was coming up fast. Too fast. After seven shows he was facing the hard fact that what was missing was something the booze and the wild nights with Ruby had been hiding—talent. Even in the motel rehearsal version, with Agnes giving up the gospel and go-going and screaming with Ruby to the end, there was no hard sell, no big wild finish, no nothing. It simply built for an embarrassing thirty-two bars and then flattened out ice cold and stupid. The critics would tear them up. But worst of all the crowd paying $3.50 a head were going to squawk. Something had to be done before Augusta.

"Ruby." They were propped up on pillows eating popcorn.

Jimmy Lee was reading *Variety*; Ruby was watching an old Dan Dailey musical. The reds were orange and the blues green.

"Wait a minute, hon. I'm watching this."

Jimmy Lee rolled his *Variety* into a tube and sighted through it at the Coca-Cola commercial. "We ain't going to make it."

"Me and you or the Angels?"

"The Angels. . . . There's something dead about the act. Something's missing."

She sat up straight. "You're kidding me?"

"I wish I was."

She scrambled around to look in his face. "Why didn't you mention this last week?"

"I had to be sure. Ruby, we're going to bomb in Augusta."

"Jesus, Jimmy Lee." She cut the movie off. "This is serious! What's wrong?"

"It's the act. It flattens out and lays there like a cow turd."

"Jimmy Lee! What's going on? What happened? You said yourself we were great!"

"Guess I was fooling myself. Probably stalling, hoping you'd get hot and see the light."

Ruby was shouting. "What light? What are you talking about? We been doing exactly what you said. What in the hell are we supposed to be SEEING?"

"I'll give it to you straight. Ruby, if you and Agnes don't hit Augusta topless we don't have a prayer."

"TOPLESS!"

Jimmy Lee snapped his *Variety* open and glanced at the "Who's jetting to where" column. "Topless."

At breakfast Virgil hit the ceiling. "Topless! You out of your goddamn gourd? This is my wife you're talking to."

Agnes patted his hand. "Easy, honey. Everybody's doing it these days. I don't mind."

Ruby came in. "Virgil, they got topless pizza and shoeshine places in California. And there ain't no telling what all they're doing in New York City. Ain't that right, Jimmy Lee?"

Virgil's fingers gripped the table edge. "This isn't California or New York City. This is South Carolina and Georgia, and I ain't having it."

Jimmy Lee folded his napkin and chose his words carefully. "The main reason is she's your wife, right?"

"You damn right."

"Well, what if me and Ruby here got married. How would it grab you then? Virgil, we're in big trouble."

"You may be, buster." His eyes narrowed. "Listen, you possum-faced little bastard, what you do with your wife don't cut no ice with me. . . . Ruby, you ain't figuring on marrying this guy, are you?"

She was spooning marmalade onto her biscuit. "I haven't had too many offers lately, Virg."

"Well, you sure as hell can do better than this flat-white pimp."

Ruby said, "Wait a damn minute."

"You wait. I ain't hearing no more of this topless crap. If you want to strip down to your Kotex belt, that's your business. But Agnes is keeping everything on, and I mean *everything*. And if I hear any more of this static I'm slinging her ass in the car and you people can go to hell."

Jimmy Lee took off his glasses, frowning. "I'm sorry, Virgil. Guess I'm used to dealing with a different brand of people. It's my fault. I want to apologize."

Agnes said, "Go on, honey, shake hands."

Ruby sizzled. "What a goddamn bunch."

Jimmy Lee's warning had frightened Ruby, and on stage in Augusta before the dinner crowd of 260 people she clutched. Agnes picked up her nervousness and went stiff and husky-voiced. The back tables could barely hear them. Someone shouted, "Louder!" They tried but they went sharp and sounded scared and terrible. The Honkytonk Angels rambled forward, weak-kneed and strained, stiffening the $3.50 customers and making them shift in their seats. A catcall came from the back of the audience, followed by another. Jimmy Lee from the wings was sweating and pounding his fist into his palm, begging them to turn loose, to relax and get with it. Halfway through they eased up and got better, but it was too late. What little momentum they picked up seemed forced and strained. It wasn't enough and it was dying fast. The people at the front tables had turned away and were talking and laughing. Agnes lost her timing, and when she switched over from gospel to go-go went hoarse. Someone shouted, "Sister, you better stick with Jesus." It was a hard crowd. Jimmy Lee breathed through his teeth. They were dying, looking around wide-eyed and harried for help, the curtain, the end. The microphone went out. Ruby tapped it and counted to three. "Can you hear me in the back of the room?"

The "stick with Jesus" shouter's voice cut through. "It doesn't matter. Ain't you all about through?" Someone sailed a slice of white bread at them. Two Parker House rolls came from the back, a stalk of celery from the front, and then a steady rain of Nabisco soup-pak saltines in red, white, and blue cellophane.

In the motel, Jimmy Lee and Virgil stayed at the bar watching the ball game. They had decided the girls weren't up for Chattanooga and had canceled the date. They were going to push on to Nashville.

"I still think they could make it with a dobro or a bass backing them up. They've got to have that big beat going or people just won't listen."

"You handle it, Jimmy Lee. But make it fast. This thing is running into money."

Upstairs Ruby and Agnes rehearsed in front of the big mirrored dresser. Ruby was topless. She danced, watching her hips and breasts and, shotgunning her guitar straight forward, went back, dipped, and came hitching forward. She nudged Agnes, who suddenly whipped off her blouse and cradling her breasts in the guitar scoop like two cats in a basket wailed into the last verse. She jerked and jiggled, trying them under the guitar, over it, and around the neck while she tried to follow the flying Ruby. She couldn't keep up, and her voice trembled and broke. Ruby pushed her along but she went softer, then faint, then finally faded in the middle of a line. They stopped and as if waiting for applause stood staring into the heart-shaped mirror. Agnes bit her pale lips;

(114)

Ruby's shoulders sagged. Then, dropping their guitars on the bed, they hugged each other, crying.

"We're lousy, Ruby. Lousy."

"Maybe we are. . . . No, we ain't, Agnes. We're just tired and scared; that miserable crowd scared us." She dried her eyes on the inside of her arm. "That's what happened. We're going to be all right. All we need is some decent songs. . . . Just wait, Agnes. Just wait till Nashville. We're going to be fine then." Tears flooded her face, streaking her eye liner. "We're going to be fine."

It was raining when they hit the Nashville city limits, and the low road from Chattanooga was under three inches of water. Virgil drove slow, keeping the spark plugs and the distributor points from getting splashed. "Which motel, Jimmy Lee?"

"Capri Plaza. Stay in the right lane. Should be seeing it pretty soon."

Agnes said, "I'm about to starve. Let's eat."

He pulled in under the awning at Shoney's Big Boy Hamburgers. "Might as well keep dry."

Inside they ate cheeseburgers, French fries, and cole slaw. Virgil spiked the Seven-Ups from a fifth of Jim Beam he had in a brown bag. Ruby and Agnes checked the juke.

"Look at that. Solid c. and w. Only one Dean Martin. Count the gospels."

Agnes was counting. "Four—only five gospels out of two hundred and forty. This is some town."

Ruby had her arm around her shoulder. "That's what I've been telling you. This is it, duck. Music City, U.S.A."

Back on the Murfreesboro Pike the rain slackened and stopped. In the gutters cigarette packs, hamburger wraps, and Dixie cups were piling up at the crossroads. Traffic was heavy and slow in the right lane. Virgil squinted through the moisture. "Damn. They sure got enough signs around here."

"Careful now," Jimmy Lee said. "Other side of that McDonald's."

At the Capri Plaza, the turnip-shaped pool ten feet from the road was filled with skinny kids diving from the one-meter board and playing tag around the slick corners and the flooded grass. Two pale men with red necks, wrists, and ankles were sitting on the side drinking beer, with their feet in the shallow end; lounging on a vinyl chaise, a blonde with bruises on her leg and shoulder was reading a 20-cent astrology book. One of the men had a black eye. Ruby paired him with the blonde. "Friendly looking spot, isn't it?"

They checked into two adjoining rooms. Ruby bounced on a bed and tossed the pillows back against the headboard. "Not bad, not bad." Two double beds with a three-pronged gooseneck lamp on the night table faced a color TV and a gold-spackled vanity with rosebud drawer pulls beneath an eight-foot mirror. The room was salmon pink with blue trim and a deep red fireproof rug. Above the TV an Indian brave on black velvet was searching down a dark and threatening canyon. His maiden, with a fawn nosing in the moss, was on the next wall, combing her hair in a sylvan pool. The decorator artist had ended the pageant between the headboards with the couple in a profile embrace by a moonlit waterfall.

Ruby went into the bathroom and tried the shower pressure. "Hey! They sure give you plenty towels. This place is O.K. . . . Jimmy Lee, reckon we can get some wooden hangers? These wire jobs ruin my things."

"No sweat. Anything else we need, just holler." He unplugged a standing lamp and slid it over to the vanity. "I can work here."

"Won't that mirror be bothering you? It would drive me crazy."

"When I'm working nothing bothers me."

He began making phone calls, setting up appointments for the afternoon, as Ruby stripped down to put on her bathing suit. "Aren't you coming in?"

"No. I got work to do."

The phone had a twenty-foot cord, and he looped it over one of the vinyl chairs facing each other to form the conversational area and punched "supercool" on the Philco. A loose compressor bearing thumped under the room-wide Venetian blinds, and he stepped the big two-horse unit down to "medium."

Agnes pounded on the thin wall. "Ready, Ruby!"

(116)

"Be there in a second." She rubbed herself down with vanilla extract provided by the motel to keep the black flies off. "You using that vanilla stuff, Ag?"

"Yeah, Virgil says put plenty on. These Tennessee flies will eat you alive."

The sky was clear, crisp. Over the Southern Bread and McDonald signs, fresh white clouds came sliding in from the west, as the big Diesels and Trailways buses headed down the Murfreesboro Pike into Nashville and southeast to Chattanooga and Atlanta. They trotted down the walk barefooted and with Virgil leading the way dropped their towels and dove in. . . . After swimming, showering, and changing clothes, Virgil drove them downtown to see the sights, leaving Jimmy Lee behind to meet with his song-writer contacts.

Each song plugger came in telling Jimmy Lee almost the same story. How great things had been going for them. How everything they'd been writing had been selling. How lucky he was in reaching them. Two said they were catching Delta to Hollywood that night. Both had big confidential offers from the coast, but since Jimmy Lee was an old friend they could trust they would play him their demos. Between five o'clock and seven he listened to eleven disasters. One song pitched as a sure-fire Carolina-Georgia smash was a five-year-old girl crying out about her dead mother. Jimmy Lee closed his eyes sinking as he heard the lyrics.

> "Who will make my little dresses,
> Who will see that I am fed?
> Please, sir, let me kiss her lips once more,
> Please, sir, before they close the lid."

The plugger, Marvin Clarke, a pale tight-faced bleeder with a nose like a new moon, sold hard. "It's got to hit, Jimmy Lee. No way for it to miss."

"You got anything else?"

"Come on, Jimmy Lee, one of your gals can fake the voice. This ain't no kid singer headache. This is another 'Rudolph the Red-Nosed Reindeer.' Church crowds will swamp you."

(117)

"Maybe you, Marvin, not me."

"You got a closed mind, Jimmy Lee."

"I'm tired, Marvin. Anything else around town?"

"That's all I got. I got a buddy that's got a few hot ones."

"Who's that?"

"Buddy Bolton."

"I thought he was dead. Forget him. . . . I need a hit, Marvin. Something hot. No more talking miseries or Vietnam-and-Mom stuff. I need something different. Something wild."

"Want me to level with you?"

"Not if it'll give you a hernia."

"You ain't finding it here. Everybody's copying. Everything sounds the same. Some cat told Grandpa Jones he'd just written a new hit. Know what Grandpa said?"

"I'll bite."

"Said, 'What's it the tune to?' "

Jimmy Lee laughed as he opened the door for Marvin. "That's why my 'Before They Close the Lid' is going to make it."

"Keep swinging, Marvin." He held up a flat palm as if he was stopping traffic. "No Buddy Bolton, O.K.?"

"O.K., Jimmy Lee."

He cupped his hands under two imaginary breasts. "Any big ones around?"

"Next door at the Twilight Zone: forty-four or forty-six double D. She serves beer and sandwiches on them."

"Sandwiches! They sound like eggplants."

"Take along a tape measure. She ain't shy. Same old Jimmy Lee."

"Thanks for coming by. If I find you a buyer I'll give you a ring."

"Take care, now."

(118)

10

     For five days and five nights after Ruby left, Spider was drunk. The jukebox, the radio, the TV and all the lights stayed on. Five days of mail were unopened, and the morning *States* and the evening *Records* lay on the porch where the boy had thrown them. He didn't shave or bathe, and every dish, cup, and glass in the house was stacked in the flooded and dripping sink. The phone kept ringing. He let it ring as he drank beer and ate Crowder peas from the can and spread his peanut butter with his pocket knife.

On the sixth morning he cut the jukebox off and decided he wanted some eggs. He fried them in butter and slid them out of the pan onto the cover of *Life* magazine. After mopping up the egg yolk with white bread, he balled the cover up and threw it at the sink. And then he answered the phone.

It was J. D. Flood. "Where in the hell you been?"

"Never mind that, what's on your mind?"

"Everything! Everything! I'm out of whiskey. Cold-assed out!"

"You ain't seen Virgil, have you?"

"That's why I've been trying to get you. He and Agnes ran off together. Got married some damn place. They're out on the road with Ruby and a Rideout fellow. He's been calling here all week trying to find you. I'll give you his number. . . . You been drinking, Spider?"

"I had a few. Give me that number. I'll get back to you."

Spider called Virgil and arranged for him to bring in a truckload from the Augusta still.

"Be sure you rent something solid. I don't want that thing limping in here on some half-assed trailer. They're going to be looking for overloads."

"O.K., I'll take care of it. Spider, we're running low on cash. Can you send me four or five hundred?"

"Sure. It'll be at Western Union in a couple of hours. Oh, congratulations! From what I hear you moved pretty fast."

"Thanks. I'm a happy man; there's nothing like it."

"How's Ruby?"

"Seems O.K. . . . You were drinking pretty hard, there, weren't you?"

"I'm O.K. now. She still with that albino?"

"Afraid so. But I ain't sure she's sticking with him. . . . Want me to say hello?"

Spider thought a minute. "Yeah, might as well. Tell her I said take care of herself . . . and if she needs anything, just holler. Wait a minute. I'll send her two hundred and fifty in your money order. I don't want that albino paying for every damn piece of soap. When you getting back?"

"I'll leave tonight. Get J. D. ready. Guess I'll leave the Caddy here and fly down."

"Well, hell, how long you planning on being up there?"

"Spider, I really screwed up. I promised Ag I'd give it three weeks. I'll just have to go back and forth. Real honeymoon, right?"

"We're all crazy."

Three blocks away, Roebuck Alexander opened the screen door. "Hello, Hooty."

Hooty Hightower, in a fresh-starched, razor-creased Cub Scout

(120)

leader uniform, folded his cap in half and slid it under his web belt. His crew-cut hair was flat on top and tapered high in back.

"You're looking splendid. How're you feeling?"

Hooty squeezed his hand hard. "Never better, Preacher. Practically a new man."

"How about some iced tea? Just made it."

"Yes, sir, I'd like that." He followed Roebuck back to the kitchen with his new, fast-chopping, businesslike step. His mirror-glass shoes had metal heel and toe plates. "You know something? I actually taste things these days. Take tea. I used to swill it by the gallon and didn't no more know what it tasted like than a flea —no sugar, please. . . . Now it's wonderful. Wonderful. And beans, tomatoes, okra, corn—you name it, Preacher, everything. It's a whole new way of life."

Roebuck touched his glass to his. His gums curled back from his long teeth in a joking smile. "Let's drink to that."

"Why, I even eat light bread and get a kick out of it. I figure all that whiskey I was taking in was paralyzing my taste organs."

"It paralyzes everything it touches, Hooty. Everything. It either burns it out or rots it out. One way or another it brings you down. Far as I'm concerned, you're a modern-day Lazarus. You stop by the public library and take a look at what whiskey does to the brain. They got colored photographs of just exactly how it breaks down."

"Wonder how they got them?"

Hooty sat opposite Roebuck at the kitchen table, looking him straight in the eye and following his every move. As far as he was concerned, Roebuck singlehandedly had snatched him from the grave. He knew he wanted something: probably money. The conversation would soon start sliding over to the building fund or something for the old folks. He was trying to figure out how much. He had added up his $708 in the savings account, the $800 value in his Ford, and the $6,500 equity in his $11,000 house. . . . A flat ten-per-cent Catholic-type tithe which he knew had gotten popular in some of the fancy Episcopal and Free Will churches would be perfect, but two or three thousand would mean cashing

(121)

in everything and reborrowing on the house. Whatever it was, he had sworn to Quendolyn he would do it.

Roebuck began slowly, explaining how the kind of courage Hooty had was a rare commodity on today's market. "Preacher, you're right. I know this fellow out in Blythewood. You talk about a problem with drinking! Why, that rascal can't even put the cork back in. That stuff sits on his night table and—"

Roebuck held up his long hand. "I don't want to cut you short, Hooty, but I got to be up to the station pretty soon. There's a lot I want you and me to be going over."

He apologized, sipped his tea, and leaned in on his elbows. Life's problems to Hooty Hightower had always been like watching the windows in a slot machine. Eventually everything made sense: things lined up, or they didn't. It was that simple. With his fingernail he traced a square within a square on the red-checked oilcloth, figuring the money pitch was beginning.

"The source, Hooty, the source. The Lord always went to the source. Take your moneylenders, your Red Sea; take your walls of Jericho. The Lord didn't mess around with explaining, diagnosing, or waiting for some city council to sit down and get together. 'I am a vengeful Lord. . . . My wrath shall be felt and all that stand before it shall fall.' Hooty, if he saw a cancer, he snatched it out or tore it down. When it's evil, it's evil. And evil begets evil."

"That's exactly what you said, Preacher." His mind kept watching the small windows. Bells, bars, cherries, and lemons kept rolling by, but nothing was lining up. It would come soon. He dreaded another mortgage loan, another seventy-two months of perforated onion-skin coupons that never seemed to get smaller. But evil didn't sound like money. It sounded like work. Like a sacrifice. A warm feeling gathered in his stomach. It couldn't be money or he would have been talking about it or toward it. It had to be a sacrifice, something to do. His feet felt light on the floor. He could feel each of his toes through his high-gloss shoes and his new white socks. He would do anything, and now that it wasn't going to cost anything he would do it twice, three times.

"Now, a lot of your so-called liberals will tell you that this here or that there's a sickness, and it can be isolated and treated; all

(122)

you got to do is isolate it and then get rid of it. Well, I say evil is like a basket of rotten peaches. You take off one layer and there's another one even rottener staring you in the face. Not to mention the blowflies, the ripworms, and the maggots. The basket's even rotten. Leave it there long enough and it'll take out your floor boards. Any farmer worth his salt will pitch out the whole mess."

Hooty knew it was a testimonial; it wasn't going to cost him a dime. He was dying to tell him cases he knew that would back up his logic. "You're right, Preacher. You're dead right. Why, I know myself—"

Again Roebuck's hand was raised. "I'm leading up to something, Hooty."

"I figured that."

"I'm leading up to whiskey, Hooty."

Hooty felt solid. No Home Loan, no H.F.C., no Beneficial Finance. It had to be a testimonial. Maybe he would be on the radio. He rehearsed one in his mind, recalling how deep in sin and drink he'd fallen, the night he was lying naked with Mary Beth Tyson.

Roebuck ran his finger around the rim of the thin iced-tea glass, and a shrill note rose and held in the kitchen. "I'm talking about moonshine whiskey at the source, Hooty."

Hooty swallowed fast. "Back up to the sugar bill. That's source enough. If they can't get sugar they're wiped out."

"They'll find a way."

Hooty nodded. He would agree with anything now. "They can bring it in from Georgia. You can buy anything there. Fireworks any day you want and venereal disease cures right off the sidewalk."

Roebuck crossed the room for the tea pitcher. He set it between them. "It's not sugar, Hooty. It's the moonshiner and the bootlegger. It's your Jasper Deeks, your Frank Lancasters and your Frazier Foleys. It's your Spider Hornsbys." He slid the lemon wedges across the table. No shadow passed over Hooty's bright eyes. Roebuck watched them carefully.

"These men must be *made* to stop selling."

Hooty shook his head from experience. "Folks will just go up-town and buy it at the package store."

Roebuck pulled a pad from his jacket pocket and spun it around. He read it upside down and tapped the top left figure with his ballpoint. "Eighty-four dollars. That's your average weekly take-home pay of the people in the Bottom. Here's your rent, food, clothes, utilities, and two picture shows. Here's what you got left." Four dollars and forty cents was circled.

Hooty studied the figures carefully: $84 seemed high but he knew the mill hands, the shirt-factory workers, and the $4-an-hour mechanics pulled up the rock-bottom wages of the house cleaners, the ones on unemployment, and the river rats who didn't even draw unemployment.

"City Council figures. They're within twenty-five cents of ex-actly how the four thousand and fifty people in the Bottom live."

Hooty nodded. "You can't argue with fact."

"All right, now, how much whiskey does four dollars and forty cents buy uptown at the package store?"

"Depends on what you get."

"Your cheapest busthead. Gin or something like that."

"It'll get you a fifth. Maybe a shade more."

"And how much corn liquor will Spider sell you for four dollars and fifty cents?"

"Almost a half gallon."

"So." He laid his hands flat on the miserable mathematics on the ruled paper. "If the bootlegger is gone, our heavy drinkers—our Bevo Mitchallburgers, our Bootsie Boyds and Dennis Dysons—are down from almost three fifths to one. Am I correct?"

"I guess so."

"Figures don't lie. There they are." His long hands seemed flatter on the table. "Now if that ain't getting to the source, I ain't sitting here."

Hooty kept looking at the circled figures. "It makes sense on paper."

"It makes sense period."

"Yeah, but how do you get rid of people like this?" As the word sounded in the raw pine and linoleum room, two jackpot black bars began lining up and he thought he knew why Roebuck had sent for him. A cool chill trickled down his spine, and the blond hair on his freckled hands stiffened and rose.

Roebuck watched his eyes darken and the sunburned skin around his throat tighten. "This ain't no ordinary request, Hooty. It ain't even mine." His long arm moved out and his reassuring hand settled on his shoulder. "I'M not asking you, Hooty. I'm just carrying a message to you from someone else."

Hooty started to ask who, but then the last jackpot black bar joined the other two. Everything was clear.

Roebuck's eyes were blazing. "I'm just his miserable vessel. I'm just telling you what he told me has to be done. . . . He's singled you out, Hooty." He gripped his shoulder tight. "Hooty Hightower, you are a living proof of a miracle. Think! Think, man! Think how bad off you were, puking home every night at midnight with your payroll gone and the bills stacked up a foot high. Think of Quendolyn's tears and Blanche and little Hooty, Junior. . . . Look how far you've come. Why, man, you're tasting okra and beans and the living bread of God's love." His voice rose, pulling Hooty through the rough rocks of his consciousness toward God's sunny shoals. "I can't no more tell the Lord you're ungrateful and refuse to help him than I can command you to fly up to the drugstore and bring me back a six-pack of Pepsi-Colas."

His voice dipped and rushing water pounded in Hooty's ears. He was in a dark ocean cave lighted by strange, living rocks. Weird shadows were moving. He was alone. Roebuck's voice was the surf breaking, pounding and shaking the very stone.

"I can't tell him, Hooty . . . and I ain't." He was up and crossing the room. His voice went low, lower, powerful. "If you want him told, you go home and get in a dark closet. Get in there with the door closed and get close to him." He whirled, pointing, shouting. "AND THEN YOU TELL HIM YOURSELF. Tell him you're grateful for him saving you and your family. Tell him you appreciate his services. Then you explain why it is you're too busy or too selfish or too infernal lazy watching the TV and eating fried chicken to do a little good on this dunghill of evil."

Hooty's trembling hands came together. All eight knuckles were stretched tight and white. His voice broke in two parts . . . three. He coughed, swallowed, stared at the red and white calico pattern, and cleared his throat. "What's it he wants me to do?"

Roebuck told him.

Hooty groaned. "Spider's my buddy. I only got a couple left. We went through school together. Please, Preacher. Please. Ain't there something else? I could help pay for someone to do it. I swear I can lay my hands on some money."

"I'm afraid not. That's what HE wants done."

"Damn. Pardon me, Preacher. Can't he find some other way? Looks to me like he'd know plenty ways."

"I guess he figures he wants you to work with him. . . . You've been chosen, Hooty. Just like Isaac. Just like Daniel."

Hooty wheezed. "I guess I should be grateful. But Lord, this hurts. This really hurts."

Roebuck caught his eyes and held him like a snake. "Course, if you want to get in that closet and tell him you're too busy enjoying his fruits. . . ."

"Naw, that ain't no good. . . . Oh, Jesus, I really hate this."

"Does that mean I can tell him he can count on you?"

"I guess so."

"He doesn't want any guessing."

"Tell him I'll do it. . . . But tell him I don't like it."

"He'll understand."

"Yeah, I guess he will."

Roebuck Alexander flipped the pink copy of *Police Gazette* he was leafing through on the waiting room table when Assistant Sheriff Maynard Moody opened his door, grinning. "Pretty hot stuff, eh, Preacher?"

"Absolute filth! I don't know why the United States Government puts up with it. . . . Come on, I ain't got time to waste."

Maynard circled his desk, fingered his good ear, and slumped down in his Posturepedic chair.

"O.K., Preach. Let's have it again. We're spinning our wheels."

Roebuck's brown eye narrowed as he hunched forward until his head seemed to be coming out of the Outgoing Mail basket.

"Moody, if you pull in Spider and Kershaw Miller ain't in on it, you're the next sheriff."

Moody checked his watch. "That's precisely how I got it figured."

"Ain't no figuring to it. It's fact."

Moody leaned forward. "I need information, Preach. I can get men, time, money. I can get dogs, cars, and dynamite, but I gotta have something to go on."

"How'd you like a pimp?"

"You got one?"

"Hooty Hightower."

"Hooty! You're kidding!"

"Took the pledge the other night." Roebuck stabbed his long right finger into his left palm. "That's right where I got him. Anything I want him to do, he'll do."

"Damn, Preach, I just can't believe it. Old Hooty. You sure he ain't sick or something?"

"The Holy Ghost's got him by the scruff of the neck. He's healthier than you and me put together."

"But he's Spider's buddy. You sure he ain't picked up a cancer or something? Talk about something hard to swallow."

"You want to call his wife?"

"No, I'll take your word for it."

"Then you'll set me a trap?"

"No one's told Kershaw?"

"No one knows anything except us. It was a private salvation." The noon whistle at the cotton mill sounded, and the girls from Southern Bell began switching across State Street heading for the S and G Cafeteria. Moody swung around in his chair and watched them until his view was cut off by the rhododendron. From Sheriff Kershaw Miller's corner office, the view was unobstructed. "O.K., Preach, you got yourself a deal."

Roebuck squared his flat journeyman's hat. "And you figure he'll get three years?"

"At least, podner. At least."

11

Ruby and Agnes were trying to get Jimmy Lee to come along with them on the Nashville Tour of the Stars Homes. "No way, girls. I've been that route. Go on, it's fun. They use to stop by a recording studio."

Ruby pulled at his elbow. "They still do. Come on, Jimmy Lee. It won't be the same without you."

"Better not. I got to get some work done. I'm on to something good."

Agnes said, "We better leave him alone then."

Ruby kissed his cheek. "Stay with it."

The Nashville Tour bus left Broadway from in front of Ernest Tubbs's, which was featuring a lighted oil painting on glass of the younger Ernest slowly revolving up Broadway and across Clark. A recording of him singing "Slipping Around" was miked out to the street, and customers were three deep at the record racks. As the bus started off, Agnes unfolded a map of Nashville and began tracing the route they were taking. Ruby leaned against the window, listening to her transistor radio and watching the Nashville skyline.

The tour guide, a short, pretty freshman from Vanderbilt, introduced herself as Maybelle Frick. She tapped her microphone. "You folks hear me in the back?" The bus was packed.

"Loud and clear, little bird."

Maybelle's sweet but nasal voice carried easily. "Well, O.K., then. Now, for the first thing I want us all to get acquainted. So when I count to three I want everyone to shout 'Hey, you all!' and reach across the aisle and introduce yourself to your neighbors. O.K., now, everyone ready. *One, two,* and *three! Hey, you all!!!!!*"

Ruby and Agnes met Merle and Betty Tyler of Indian Springs, Indiana, who were in Nashville for their fifteenth wedding anniversary. Merle, a red-faced druggist with camera and light-meter straps cutting across him like an ammunition bearer, was checking his shutter speeds. "We been here fifteen times. Haven't missed a year yet."

Betty leaned over Merle. "I practically know this route by heart." She had clip-on sunglasses over her heavy prescriptions.

Ruby said, "How come you keep taking it?"

She hinged her sunglasses up. "Things keep changing so. Now take Brenda Lee. That little sweetheart's been married four years now and has two little kids. We follow them pretty close in the magazines. Feels like we sort of grew up with them."

Merle snugged a strap tight and crowded Betty out. "I got pictures of all three places she lived. I even got the spot where Jim Reeves went down in that airplane crash. I'll show it to you when we go by. It's pretty much all growed up now. Houses all over the place."

Agnes twisted so she could talk without turning.

Maybelle announced they were coming into the residential area. "Now, you all watch out on the right. That white house set way back there. That's it, that one with the black dog. Well that belongs to one of your favorites, Mr. Carl Smith." The bus stopped. "Anyone that wants to take a picture can get out."

Merle was out like a shot, squinting through his light meter and setting up his aluminum tripod. Four Instamatic camera fans shot and then gathered around as Merle crouched over his Yashica, adjusting the balance and resetting the lens speed.

Betty moved into his seat so she could talk easier to Agnes. "That man lives and breathes photography. You ought to see our house. It's just covered with shots. Opry folks, that's his specialty. You name one, he's got him."

Ruby couldn't stand her singsong voice and felt a numb feeling coming over her as Agnes said, "That's nice. It's nice having a hobby like that."

She changed radio stations and tried to pick up the words to a Loretta Lynn song. There was too much static, and Betty's tin-lined voice was grinding on. "It keeps them out of trouble. Lot of men run off and get on bowling teams and golf and all that. Indian Springs is full of that. I like my Merle at home where I can keep an eye on him. Fellow like that can get in an awful lot of trouble if you don't watch him."

Ruby hoped Agnes wouldn't ask any questions. . . . Agnes pursed her lips, looking at Merle outside. "He looks like he could take pretty good care of himself."

Betty Tyler's lips puckered as if to whistle and she looked stretch-eyed.

"That's because he's got that camera. If he didn't have it, folks wouldn't give him the time of day. You wouldn't think to look at him how bewildered he is most of the time. Heavens! I even buy that man's shirts and shorts for him. You put him in a store, and the first salesgirl that gets to him could sell him the whole place. I just had to put my foot down. Easygoing is one thing, but when folks take advantage that's another."

"Yeah, he does look kinda easygoing."

Merle crowded back into Betty's window seat as they wound out Old Hickory Boulevard toward the Governor's mansion.

Ruby leaned over Agnes. "That's quite an outfit. What did it cost?"

"Five hundred and fifty. And that's only the camera. The rest set me back another thousand. Took it all to Europe last year."

Maybelle announced, "On your left, folks, is the home of one of our all-time greats, Mr. Eddy Arnold." Again the bus stopped and Merle got out, set up, and shot away.

Ruby cut her radio back on.

Agnes nudged her. "What's the matter, Rube? Ain't you enjoying this?"

"I'm not interested in where all these people live. That ad said we were going by a recording studio."

Betty leaned over, offering a piece of divinity fudge. "Darling, we'll hit Holiday Records on the way back. Don't worry."

Merle was changing film. "You ought to of seen us in Europe. I shot about a hundred and twenty-three rolls of film and every shot a knockout."

Agnes said, "Where'd you go?"

He laughed. "More like where didn't we go. Man, we made tracks. We saw it all, everything. I even took shots lying flat on my back. Tell her about it, Betty."

"At the Sistine Chapel. That's in Rome, Italy. You all heard of it?"

Agnes said, "I saw the movie. *The Agony and the Ecstasy*. It was all about that place. . . . Charlton Heston."

Merle beamed. "You did! Well, I'll be dog! We saw that thing three times getting ready for the trip. It paid off too. The second that American Express bus set his brakes I knew exactly what I was going to do. Took fourteen rolls of pictures. Man, I wish you could come up to Indian Springs; I'd show you some stuff that would knock your eyes out."

Maybelle announced, "Now, folks, if you'll look out to the left you'll see the home of Mrs. Audrey Williams. She's the widow of Hank Williams, and I know you've all heard about him. Hank used to call her 'Miss Audrey,' and that's what we all call her in Nashville. . . . Miss Audrey still keeps the green nineteen fifty-three Cadillac that Hank Williams had his famous heart attack in in the garage. That isn't open to the public, but we're hoping that one day it will be. . . . Is there anyone here that knows what 'Miss Audrey' has in her living room?"

Merle winked at Agnes and Ruby but didn't raise his hand.

"Black satin drapes from floor to ceiling. And written on those drapes are the words to Hank Williams's greatest hit, 'Your Cheatin' Heart.'"

Agnes said, "How about that."

Ruby thought about it.

The bus moved up another fifty feet and stopped. "Right here, folks, almost directly in front of the Williamses' home, is the exact spot where Governor Frank Clements got killed in a head-on collision! I guess I don't have to tell you how famous Nashville is for its traffic and plane accidents. The reason is that so many of our stars and their families are on the road so many nights of the year, going from show to show. Roy Acuff used to average over two hundred and fifty thousand miles a year. You put that in on Tennessee roads, and brother, that's driving."

At the Governor's mansion next door to Minnie Pearl's residence, Merle moved in as close to the fence as he could get. Betty said, "Look at him. Ain't he a scandal?"

The bus wound down a series of snake curves under big oak and hickory trees and stopped in front of a white gravel driveway. "Folks, back in there behind those hedges is the home of Webb Pierce. Now, you all know his picking and singing and song-writing reputation, but I bet none of you know that he's the first man in Nashville to have a guitar-shaped swimming pool."

Someone from the back cracked, "How does he dive?"

"I never heard of Mr. Pierce doing too much diving. . . . Our next stop, ladies and gentlemen, will be at the Holiday Recording Studio."

Ruby said, "I never heard of that one."

Merle said, "It's brand new. One of the biggest."

At Holiday, Ruby crowded into the front row to watch and listen close as the recording man explained how eight-track stereo worked. He played "Wildwood Flower" on two tapes, then four, and then ran in four more. The music surrounded them. Agnes looked around. "It's coming from every which a way."

Ruby hugged her elbows in tight. "What a sound. Lord, listen at it."

The recording man asked if there were any questions, and her hand shot up.

(133)

"How about new talent coming to Nashville. Where do they start off?"

He looked her over. "No special way. I guess your best bet is to get discovered by a star or a good agent." He smiled. "You just get in town?"

Ruby blushed. "Well, yessir, matter of fact we did."

"Well, the main thing is not to get discouraged. Play anywhere you can and meet all the people you can. Little girl, you never know who's going to be up next and who can give you a helping hand. . . . Folks, I'm telling this little redhead cutie down front here about how to get into the music business. The main thing is not to get discouraged. It's tough, but if you're good and you stick it out you'll get there. Nashville's a great town and there's a lot of great people here. People just dying to give new talent a helping hand. So, Red, you work hard, meet people, be nice, and you're going to score. . . . Now, folks, as a 'Welcome to Music City' special, we're offering everyone on the tour a thirty-five per cent discount on any record you see on the shelves. Normally they are marked at six ninety-eight, but today the thirty-five per cent off is going to bring that price right down to something you can fit in your pocketbook."

During the rest of the trip, while Agnes talked to the Tylers, Ruby folded the *Nashville Banner* in her lap and went through the help wanted columns in the classified ads.

She circled three ads and put a star by

"Shugin Enterprises. Wanted: two sincere and attractive girls to sing and put on small shows five hours a day. We furnish uniforms. If you are not willing to work do not apply."

Agnes elbowed her. "Look, look."

"What? Where?"

"There's a car with a South Carolina plate. Wonder where they're from."

Ruby tore the ad out. "Probably Green Pond."

Merle smiled over. "Y'all seeing the show tonight?"

"If we can get tickets."

"Well, get in line early. It's going to be a good one."

(134)

The long line of Louisiana and Alabama farmers, and clerks, Wisconsin dairymen, and Iowa corn and hog men ran from the Opry ticket office on Clark Street to Broadway, where it turned the corner for another two hundred feet, passing Tennessee Novelties, Broadway Better Clothing—No Money Down, and the Roy Acuff Hobby Museum.

Ruby was fanning herself with a copy of *Hoedown*. "Lord, I've never seen so many people." They were thirty feet from the end of the line.

Virgil spat in the gutter. "And I had to wear this goddamn wash and wear underwear. This heat's wiping me out."

Agnes kissed his cheek. "It won't be much longer, honey."

Ruby blew her hair out of her eyes. "Listen at this. 'The Grand Ole Opry has one of the most remarkable histories ever recorded in Tennessee history.'" She folded the article flat. "Listen, Virg, it ain't but a little bit. . . . 'In 1898, Captain John Ryman docked his Cumberland two-stack sidewheeler at the Nashville pier and after visiting an unreported number of saloons led his drunk and shouting crew up the hill to where the Reverend Samuel P. Jones was preaching to an audience of Davidson County Tennesseans. Reverend Jones, who had heard the unruly gang coming up Broadway, switched his sermon from salvation to his favorite one on Mother. On entering the tent, Captain Ryman stopped and, remembering his own dear dead mother, sank to his knees and began weeping. He stayed on his knees, begging forgiveness and promising through his tears that from that day on he was through with gambling, drinking, and the Cumberland River. He also swore he was going to build a brick tabernacle on the site of the canvas tent where Jones had saved him. It was John Ryman's last night as a captain. He stopped drinking, tore off his captain's braids, and never rode the Cumberland again. Ryman was true to his word. He raised the money and built the Ryman Tabernacle, which today we call the home of the Grand Ole Opry.'" Ruby whistled. "Now, ain't that something."

Agnes said, "That is some story. I say we save that thing."

Through the two-story skyline they could see the top roof lights go on. Ruby pulled Agnes out. "Come on, I want to see it all lighted up." They trotted out into Clark Street. The big stone and brick building with its tapered gospel windows was before them, and the white lights framing the eaves and the fancy fluting reflected the red and green neon of Nashville against the low hot clouds. She squeezed Agnes's hand. "Tell me the truth now. Ain't it pretty?"

"It is, Ruby. It's beautiful."

They got back in line. Agnes hugged Virgil's waist.

"Oh, it's beautiful, Virgil. It's really beautiful."

Virgil's undershirt was soaking wet and his shorts were riding up. "Hope we get seats. Where in the hell is that Jimmy Lee?"

Ruby checked her hair in the plate-glass window. "He'll be here. . . . Oh, I'm so excited I could pee."

A man ahead of them had his shirt off and was reading a Steve Canyon comic book. He was saving the transparent yellow and black short-sleever for inside. A few feet farther up an identical pair of thirty-year-old twins dressed in knee-length Bermudas, tennis shoes, and matching Hawaiian shirts were watching an eighty-year-old man in overalls and an undershirt eating chicken. On his arms were faded and wizened World War I Field Artillery panthers. The twins shook their heads together, as if joined by a connecting rod. One did all the talking. He had a choirboy's voice and spoke to the line at large. "Never seen chicken ate like that before." He pointed with his thumb. "He don't have a tooth in his head."

The old artillery man smiled red and wiped his rubbery mouth. "Gums, son. Gums. Hard as steel." He fingered back his upper lip and thumped it with his knuckle. It sounded like wood. "Got me a ninety-six-year-old brother up in Harlan County that can open up a can of Vy-eena sausages." He broke a hush puppy in half and waited for a reaction. None came. "The scutter can eat roasting ears as fast as you can butter them."

The twins' eyes narrowed and they whispered. The second one fanned himself with a Martha White fan. The first one spoke. "I just don't happen to believe that one. My brother here don't either."

The old man was examining a chicken wing, looking for an

(136)

opening. "I don't care what you look-alikes believe. I'm telling you what's fact."

Ruby giggled. "Let's look in Roy Acuff's. O.K., Virgil?"

"Sure, sure. Bring me back a beer. I'm about to dehydrate."

They went back down the line to Roy Acuff's Hobby Museum. Agnes looked over the kewpie dolls, the ash trays, and the funny postcards. "I got to send something to Mama. She just loves Roy."

Ruby picked up a five-color plate. "How's this?" Agnes was reading the religious inscription on a silken pillow cover with roses and crosses at the corner. Ruby said, "You don't want that thing. Here, take a look. I'm getting one for Ma."

The gray dinner plate telling the Roy Acuff story was on sale for 49 cents. At the top "The Great Speckled Bird," was flying toward a fleecy pink cloud heaven carrying a Bible in its curved beak. "The Precious Jewel" was pictured at the bottom in the form of a fist-sized diamond throwing off sparks and rays of hope, and "The Wabash Cannonball," Roy's most famous song, was painted along the side, climbing a steep Tennessee mountain. Scattered in the background was a rocking chair on the porch of Roy's humble boyhood cabin, Noah's ark, an olive branch, and the Bible opened at Jeremiah. In the center of the gray fired china, framed by short bars of music, was a picture of Roy himself, with red lips and blue eyes, smiling up and singing his heart out.

Agnes said, "Ma will love it. I think I'll get her two. They make a nice pair."

"Me too. One for each end of the mantelpiece. Oh, she's going to die when she gets these."

Jimmy Lee, with three beers in one hand and popcorn in the other, came hotfooting down the line.

Ruby saw him first. "Hey! Jimmy Lee!"

"Ruby! Hi, Virgil, Agnes."

Ruby hugged his waist. "I don't know when I've been so excited. . . . Will you study this crowd? Must be two thousand."

Jimmy Lee looked up and down the long line. Everyone in range was staring at him in his white cowboy suit, black-edged cattleman's shirt with arrow pockets, and Hollywood 180-degree curved sunglasses. The twins began whispering.

He popped his beer open. "Hot! Jesus! I've never seen such heat." He took a long drink. "How long y'all been here?"

"'Bout an hour." She took a handful of corn. "Man back there said it wasn't air conditioned."

"The man's right." He drank again and handed her the beer and the popcorn. "Listen, wait here. I can't go this route. I'll get us backstage."

Virgil said, "I'm coming along. I gotta take a leak."

Agnes sat on the curb, taking off the green silk stilts she'd bought that morning. "These things sure ain't built for standing around."

Ruby slipped off her mica-flecked backless Springalators. "These neither. They're cutting my toes to pieces."

"Reckon Jimmy Lee can get us backstage?"

"If he can't nobody can. I can guarantee that."

The twins were peering down Agnes's low neckline. Ruby flared up. "What in the hell you creeps looking at?"

They backed off, rereading their programs.

In ten minutes Jimmy Lee came back. "It's all set."

Ruby nudged Agnes. "What'd I tell you?"

He led them down the alley and across the street to Rosie's Bar and Grill. Virgil was at a table with the chairs cocked in facing four beers and four bags of boiled peanuts. Stars of the Opry, dancers, and back-up men dressed in ruby- and rhinestone-studded cowboy suits and vinyl-finished high-gloss boots were jammed to the bar, having a last drink before going onstage.

Jimmy Lee shouted, "Hey, John!"

Big John Harmon looked over. Ruby grabbed Agnes's wrist. "It's Big John Harmon. Lord!"

Big John pushed his lampshade-sized hat back on its leather thong and came over. "Jimmy Lee Rideout! Boy, now if you ain't a sight for sore eyes. Where in the hell you been?"

"Been busy, John. Like you to meet some friends." He introduced him around, and Big John spun a chair and straddled it.

(138)

He was a tall heavy-voiced Louisianan with the biggest hands Ruby had ever seen.

Jimmy Lee said, "John, how 'bout introducing the girls to a few stars."

"It'll be a pleasure."

He raised up and looked over the crowded bar. He called out, "Marty! Marty Robbins!" Someone shouted back that he had left. Big John shook his head. "Bill Anderson and Hank Snow's gone on in. Hell, there ain't nobody else here worth talking to. I'll take you backstage. Anyone you want to meet, just sing out." He winked at Ruby and called out to the bartender. "Hey, Jeb! Jeb! Let's have another round over here."

Ruby said, "Lord, I never thought I'd be meeting you."

John wrapped a big arm around her. "No reason why not. I'm just a plain old plow jockey. Ain't that right, Jimmy Lee?"

Ruby's words ran together. "You really know Marty Robbins?"

Big John smiled. "If we were any closer we'd be married." His eyes were small and set in narrow slits but had the sharp flash of a man who was in charge. He hugged Jimmy Lee left-handed and frogged him with his right. "Man, I'm telling you it's good to see you. You been gone a long time, long. Something on the coast, right?" John took a long knowing drink and winked at Ruby. "This guy's a character and a half and I want you to know it. Anything he wants in Nashville, he gets. And any time I can do him a favor, I'm doing it, you hear?"

Ruby wanted to ask a hundred questions. "Where's Merle Travis?"

"Down in Dallas. Probably fishing. Sent me a crazy postcard from Baton Rouge last week. That's my home."

"I know that. I read it in the magazines. You know Roy Acuff?"

"Ruby." He laid his big hand over hers. "He's been like a father to me, a father."

"Really?"

"Really, Red. We're just like one big old happy family down here. Everybody knows everybody."

"Then you must know Loretta Lynn?"

He held up two fingers side by side. "The greatest. Me and her

(139)

are like brother and sister. You know something? I really love that gal. I guess I don't have to tell you she sings a song every once in a while?"

Ruby felt warm and tingling, getting in on the joke. The air conditioning, the cool beer, the wild clothes and colors, and Big John's big inside voice made her dizzy. She wanted to ask more questions, but his act was coming up and she didn't want to take his mind off his music. . . . He was older and heavier than he looked on his record jackets, but as he laughed and joked with Jimmy Lee with his arm around her she felt drawn to his deep voice and easygoing manner. She had autographs of Skeeter Davis and Billy Walker, but John Harmon was the first star she'd ever really met to talk to. She figured his hat cost over a hundred dollars, and his custom suit with red and green stones spelling out *Big John* over a semi truck with yellow flashes of lightning on the sleeves and front panels must have set him back close to five hundred. She couldn't help herself. "Mr. Harmon?"

"John's the name, Ruby." He moved in tight, pressing his leg against hers.

"John." She almost forgot what she wanted to ask. . . . "How about Minnie Pearl? What's she like?"

John pulled the long lobe on his right ear. "A living, breathing angel. That gal has done for me more than I can ever hope to repay. . . . You know, if I had to describe her, you know what I'd say?"

"What's that?"

"I'd say she was all heart. All heart."

She shifted away from him, smiling. "I heard she can't do enough for the churches and the cripple children and everything."

"You heard right. And you talk about someone being humble. You'd have to go a long way to beat old Minnie."

Big John's hand, that was big enough to stretch over five frets or hold three steins of beer, covered hers. He patted it twice until their eyes met. He seemed to be looking for something. "You stick around, Red. This is the greatest town on this here earth and some of the finest people in the world. Ain't that right, Jimmy Lee?"

(140)

Jimmy Lee opened a boiled peanut. "You took the words right out of my mouth."

A fiddle player from the Sugar Mountain Boys spotted John and hurried over. "Come on, John. We're on in fifteen minutes. We don't know what we're even playing."

Big John waved him away. "Well, I do. Lemme alone!"

"But you said you'd lay off the brew. You promised."

"Just simmer down, Leonard. Everything's A-O.K. We're talking business."

Leonard wouldn't budge. "What songs you want?"

Big John raised one finger as if testing the wind. "I'll let you know on stage. Give me a call when we're down to five."

"But, John—"

"But hell. Now get your ass back inside." Big John shook his head at Jimmy Lee. "All those monkeys do is pack out rhythm. Hell, it all sounds the same."

Jimmy Lee tilted his beer. "Play 'Flight of the Bumblebee.' That'll shake 'em up."

John Harmon laughed and hugged Jimmy Lee to him. "Folks, this little fellow kills my natural soul. If I had him managing me and writing my songs I'd be another goddamn Roy Rogers— younger version, that is. . . . Come on, Jimmy Lee, ain't you got something for me? I'm dying for a new single."

Jimmy Lee shook his head. "Nothing, John. Not a line. I'm drying up worrying about my girls here. What happened to that Wilson number you cut?"

"Shot up to ninety-eighth and died."

"Rough."

Virgil drank beer and ate peanuts and watched John moving in on Ruby. He wondered what Ruby was up to and put his arm around Agnes and drank left-handed.

John kept talking. " 'Truck Driver's Blues,' 'Mississippi Gravel,' 'Truck-Driving Fool.' My three big ones. And you know who wrote those mothers? That sweet little son of a bitch sitting right there."

Ruby sat dumbfounded. She'd never dreamed Jimmy Lee was that good.

(141)

Jimmy Lee told John about the girls and how he needed three or four new hot specialty songs in a hurry. Big John rolled his heavy lips into a tube and closed his eyes. His flat features and small black eyes gave him a strange Eskimo quality.

"It's been thin lately, Jimmy Lee. Mostly patriotic crap. Too many words in the lines to get your mouth around. I been sticking with the old ones." He looked the girls over. "You need something with a big tune for gals like this. Something fresh with a big melody line. Something like 'King of the Road.'"

Ruby said, "Now you're talking." Suddenly she wanted to sit closer to John to make Jimmy Lee sweat; instead, she filled John's glass and then her own.

Big John took her hand. "Stick around, Red. We'll find you something."

Jimmy Lee flicked his cigarette lighter on. "Like what, John?"

"Like Baumgarten's got a couple hot ones, that's what. Wait a minute! Wait a damn minute. I got it. Marvin Clarke's got something really way out."

"Why ain't you singing it?"

"Ain't my style. Listen, Jimmy Lee, it's sad. A real weeper, but it's great. I mean great. Loretta may have grabbed it up by now." His hand gripped Ruby's. "With a dobro, a couple Fenders, and a bass, these gals could really break 'em up. It's crying for the charts. Call up Marvin. You tell him I sent you."

"I already heard it."

"Then your troubles are over." He rocked back, drinking. He wiped his mouth. "Great, wasn't it?"

"It was shit."

John's face went crimson. "Well, I sure as hell didn't think so."

Ruby grabbed his arm. She didn't want to miss out on going backstage. "John, what's it really like out there?"

He paused, looking Jimmy Lee over. Then he laughed and pounded the table. "Jimmy Lee, damn your Texas ass. I don't know why I even try arguing with you. You got your ideas of what's good and I got mine."

"That's the music business, John. . . . Just don't be telling me that Marvin Clarke's another Hank Williams."

(142)

"O.K., Jimmy Lee. But I'll clue you; if Loretta cuts it, it's starting off in the top ten."

John looked at Ruby. "Honey." Leonard was rushing over, pointing at his watch. "I'll tell you what it's like out there. It's hot, sisters and brothers. It's HOT!" He tossed a ten-dollar bill down. "Bring your beers, folks, you're the guests of Big John Harmon."

He led them through the side door. Outside under the sputtering Budweiser neon a drunk was sleeping face down on a stack of crates. Beer bottles, cans, Dixie cups, and fried chicken boxes were everywhere, and green and clear-winged flying ants and beetles were swarming over the door light, the screen door, and the sleeper.

Ruby fanned her face. "Damn, they're getting in my hair."

John took her waist. "Somebody ought to call the sanitation men about this mess. Watch this gully." She felt his big hand spread down to her hip.

In the dark by the parked Lincolns and Cadillacs and the long Oldsmobiles of the Opry stars a man was screaming at his wife. "You think I ain't got eyes?" He shook her. "You sorry little bitch! The next time—the next time I'm taking a twelve-gauge to *both* your asses."

A side man in a cowhide jacket with the matching chaps had his Stetson on a white Cadillac hood and was arched over the front fender with the dry heaves. In the back seat a man and woman were coiled together like they were going down in a plane crash. On up the alley, five musicians dressed in white suits and red ten-gallon hats were clustered around a brown-bagged bottle. One was whining, "Dammit, Cordell! Don't drink it *all!*"

Most of the car radios were tuned to the Opry broadcast on WSM. Roy Acuff had just finished his act and was introducing Bill Anderson and his Po' Boys.

Big John said, "Now, we sure as hell don't want you to be missing them."

"You hear that, Agnes?"

"I hear it. Come on, hurry up."

Big John slapped the door guard on his back. "Eugene, you old dog. How's she going?"

(143)

"Pretty good, John. These folks with you?"

"Yeah, look out for them if they get lost. I'd appreciate it. How's the foot?"

"O.K., John. . . . Hot, ain't it?"

John whistled one long note and a short one and led them up a short flight of stairs. They turned a corner and squeezed through a crowded narrow hall. The men's room door was open, and five men were lined up at the galvanized trough. Passing a thick canvas backdrop curtain and a tangle of prop ropes, Ruby was suddenly blinded by the flood, floor, and key lights. She couldn't see anything and then she saw it all. Every seat on the main floor and the high arched balcony backed up with red, green, yellow, and blue gospel tapered windows was filled and three thousand pairs of eyes were watching Bill Anderson, dressed in gold and white, sweat soaked, and rolling into "Orange Blossom Special." Goose-flesh tingled up her bare arms and tears were in her eyes. She hugged Agnes. "God Almighty, Ag. This is something!"

"I can't take it all in, Ruby. I declare I can't."

There was no backstage; everything and everybody, singers, dancers, banjo players, agents, and subpoena servers, were in the wings, opening and closing deals, rehearsing, trying out new songs and new materials, swapping hunting and fishing lies, waving to the audience, and waiting for the moment when the m.c. announced their act.

Big John bent over Ruby. "You can't hear unless you go out front. Want me to find you a spot?"

"No. I'm staying right here. When you going on?"

"We're next. Any requests?"

"How about 'Tennessee Tiger?' "

He winked and squeezed her. "You sure you ain't trying to tell me something?"

"Hurry up and tell Leonard. I'm so nervous I'm about to jump out of my skin."

Bill Anderson's act ended, and as the Po' Boys stepped back, playing softer, Anderson tapped and cleared the mike. "All right, folks. Now, all the way from Baton Rouge, Louisiana, let's have a hand for Big John Harmon and his Sugar Mountain Boys. . . . Take it, John!"

(144)

John came on, rolling his shoulders and grinning and pounding his guitar into his Jimmy Lee Rideout theme song. . . .

> "I'm a truck-driving fool,
> Never been to school,
> I'm mean as dirt and stubborn
> as a mule. . . .
> Roll on, roll on."

He chorded down and shouted, "Howdy, sisters! Howdy, brothers!"

The Instamatic camera fans rushed forward, squatting, angling, shifting, their flash bulbs popping while they called out, "This way, John! Over here, John! Hold that guitar down! Point it at me, John!" Dead center in the pack, his tripod spread and leveled, his fingers flying over his Yashica adjustments and light-meter readings, was Merle Tyler from the tour bus. The crowd was on its feet applauding. One shouted, "Big John is our boy!" Another, "How's the weather up there, John?"

"Sisters and brothers, it's HOT. . . . Got a request here from a little Carolina redhead. Come on out here, Ruby, let's let the good folks take a look at you."

Ruby froze. Agnes pushed her into Big John's outstretched arms. "Here she is, sisters and brothers. Let's hear it for Ruby Red."

Ruby tried to pull away but John held her firm as the audience clapped and whistled. "You Nashville supper-club folks might be getting lucky next week. Come out here, Robby." Agnes stepped forward. "Here's the other half of the Honkytonk Angels. Watch your papers, now, and get out to see them." He plugged his yellow Fender into the amplifier and shook the cord free. "And now, for Ruby Red and Robby, the Honkytonk Angels, I'd like to dedicate an old favorite of mine"—his voice dropped to set up a hard raw chord—"and I hope yours . . . 'Tennessee Tiger.' "

At midnight Ruby called her mother to find out if she had heard her introduced on the Opry. Mrs. Jamison had missed it but Mary McCoy, who kept a pencil by the radio and TV for recipes, had not only heard it but had written down every word. The social reporter for the *State* had called and said they heard it too late for the morning edition but would give it a nice write-up in the afternoon.

"Ruby, he wanted to know if you were married to that Jimmy Lee fellow. You ain't, are you?"

"Mama, I'm not studying getting married."

"When you coming back?"

"I don't know that either. Hey, listen, get a dozen of those write-ups . . . more if you can get them. We can put them up in plastic. They'll make nice Christmas cards. And I want you to send me a few things."

"O.K., hold on. I'll get a pencil."

Long forty-foot semis heading north for Louisville and west for Memphis rumbled by, down-shifting on the upgrade and back-firing on the down. Out in the parking strip a bottle broke, and in the distance two police sirens began wailing. Ruby was smoking with her feet propped up on a cushion from the chair and a folded pillow. The ash tray was on her stomach. "Busy night."

They were sleeping nude with the chenille bedspread pushed down to the bottom and draped over the luggage rack. Through the thin walls they could hear Agnes moaning. "Virgil, Virgil."

Jimmy Lee elbowed up and lit a cigarette. "God, they really go at it."

Ruby studied the hot coal of his cigarette. "Jimmy Lee, I still don't like the way you locked horns with Big John like that. I swear I don't. That man really wants to help us out."

Jimmy Lee spoke slowly, the words sounding like lyrics he was planning for a song. "That man really wants me to give him some songs. And he really wants his own show. And he really wants a job in Hollywood, with Vegas on the weekends. But most of all, right now, tonight, tomorrow, and as long as we're in this town, what that man really wants is to get in your pants."

"That's where you and I started, Flash."

He sat up quickly. "That mean you'd sleep with that sap?"

"I slept with you for a goddamn song and a hayride."

"What in the hell's getting into you? We just got here!"

(146)

"I'm saying, Mr. Know-it-all, that John Harmon can be used for something. You can't mark him off because he wants to lay me."

"No, but I sure as hell ain't handing him the room key and a hand towel."

"Jimmy Lee, what if he decides to make us part of his show and we do a couple numbers?"

"Ruby, ain't you got eyes? Big John does fifteen minutes here; how's he fitting you in? This ain't no Ted Mack Amateur Hour. . . . Listen, you watch that snake."

"I hear you talking, Jimmy Lee."

"O.K., Ruby, you got eyes for John Harmon you go with him. Only take your clothes along. He'll let you lay him for about two weeks, and then you can get in line behind the three ex-wives he's paying off."

"Three?"

"Three! He's in so deep he'll never get out."

Next door Agnes moaned, "Virgil, Virgil."

Jimmy Lee sighed and faced the thumping air conditioner. "What in the hell am I in for."

12

Jimmy Lee decided there were no good songs in Nashville for the Angels. He gave up on a bass or an electric dobro backing them up, figuring high-voltage amplification with six-foot booster speakers would only make it worse. They had to have music, good original music, and he hadn't been able to write it. He thought again about Ruby going topless but knew the crowd wouldn't buy it. Once they saw her they'd want to see Agnes, and she couldn't keep her mouth shut. And then Virgil would loosen every tooth in his head and snatch her back to Columbia. Still, there had to be a way to get them started. Maybe the right crowd, the right place on the right night, might do it. He made phone calls, argued, threatened, pleaded, traded. Finally, after promising to plug the Harlequin Club on the next talk show he or any of his friends were on, he made a date for the Angels to sing on Friday. They were to follow Leroy Cotton, a red-hot country comic who could get the audience ready for anything and carry them through ten minutes of their programed fifteen.

Ruby and Agnes went shopping and, spending over a hundred

dollars apiece, came back with matching blue and white mini-skirted cowgirl suits with fringed hems, leather tasseled sleeves, white boots, and white hats. They rehearsed three hours straight, then did fifteen minutes in their new outfits. Every word, chord, and move was where they wanted it.

"We're going to kill them, Ag."

Agnes kept turning in the mirror, checking her suit. "I love these outfits. I just can't wait for Virgil to see us. That hat sets your hair off so nice."

"Yours too. God, don't you just love the boots?"

At eight o'clock at the Harlequin Club, a long windowless concrete-block house with red and green neon scalloping the outside and bad acoustics inside, Jimmy Lee introduced them to the owner-manager and m.c., Fletcher Riddle. Fletcher, a slim, carefully tailored, and tanned man who looked like he had stomach trouble, barely glanced at the girls as he took Jimmy Lee aside. "Catastrophe, Jimmy Lee! Absolute and total. I'm sold out to a hardware convention, four hundred and fifty men. Every seat in the house." He opened his office door. "And LOOK! Look at him!"

Leroy Cotton, a red-faced heavyweight, was sitting on the floor against the wall sweating. Sweat was beading on his forehead, running down his face, and dripping from his nose and finger tips. His eyes were closed; his lower lip and left hand were twitching.

"Jesus!"

Ruby knelt down. Even his lapels were wet. "He's going to die! He's having a stroke!"

"Naw, it's pills. Doc said let him sweat it out."

She dried his head with her handkerchief and fanned him. "He's sure doing that."

Agnes touched his forehead. "He's a hundred and four easy. This is serious."

Fletcher backed to the wall and spread his arms in surrender. "My best night all year. I had it made."

Jimmy Lee slumped in Fletcher's chair, facing the soaking

(150)

Leroy. "You dumb bastard." Then, to Fletcher, "Who do the kids follow?"

He hiked himself on the desk corner, fingered his program, and glanced at Leroy. "A trampoline act."

"Hello, it's Ed Sullivan time. Come off it, Fletch. Where you getting ceiling room for that crap?"

"Midgets, Jimmy Lee." His voice shredded and went faint as if the wind were taking it. "Three of them. Just hit town from the coast."

Agnes said, "That sounds cute."

"Shut up!" Jimmy Lee didn't look around. "Couldn't you get a toy poodle act? That's pretty cute, too. Those drummers are going to eat you alive. Who's the other pallbearers?"

His voice came back. "Baton twirler from Mississippi. She dips them in pitch and lights them. She's young and she came cheap, but she looks good, Jimmy Lee. I wouldn't kid you."

"Piss!"

Ruby tried to pull Jimmy Lee aside but he shrugged her off. "Fletch, you sure this moron can't shape up? Let's load him up on coffee or dunk his ass in ice water."

"Doc says no shocks. High blood pressure. He could drop for good; then where in the hell would I be?"

"Well, I got a news flash, cousin. My girls ain't following that other crap."

Ruby spun the program around. "We could open the show, Jimmy Lee."

"I'll handle this. Listen, you two, sit down and look at a magazine. And don't go near that guy. He could be carrying something."

"Come on, Jimmy Lee. I'm on the spot."

"And what the fuck you think I'm on? Boy, when this hits the trade your ass is mud. O.K., who's the stripper?"

"Blaze Fury."

"Blaze. . . . You better have a good man on the lights. I thought she quit the business. O.K., we'll follow her."

"Can't. She's got top billing. She closes the show. No food, no drinks served while she's on."

"It's your house, Fletch. Move her."

Leroy made a gargling sound and blinked his eyes.

Fletcher patted his shoulder. "Easy, boy . . . She'll hit the ceiling. I can't, Jimmy Lee. I just can't."

"Come on, girls. We got other fish to fry."

"Hold it, Jimmy Lee. O.K., I'll talk to her." He pulled Leroy up. "Doc says I should keep him moving. . . . Come on, boy. Easy. Watch your feet now. It's me, Fletcher." He led him out the door and down the hall.

Ruby said, "Damn, Jimmy Lee, we can't follow no stripper."

"You can this one. A real rummy. It's the only spot. That twirler and midget routine are going to MACE the place. At least we'll have them in their seats."

Agnes whispered, "I've never even seen one."

Jimmy Lee ripped the program in half. "Comics! Craziest goddamn people in the world."

Jimmy Lee was right about the trampoline act and the baton twirler. The crowd watched the midgets for a minute and then began table hopping, telling jokes, and going to the toilet. The applause was weak and scattered.

Fletcher pleaded for more as the midgets bowed and grinned and backed off, but nothing happened.

Halfway through the baton twirling act they began shouting, "BLAZE! BLAZE FURY! WE WANT BLAZE!"

The twirler panicked in the dark and rushed to her full-split act end before her flames had died. The house lights came on. With her head touching the floor and her batons still burning, she waited for the applause. It came from the help at the back of the room and Fletcher and Ruby and Agnes in the wings. The rest of the crowd was shouting for drinks and beer, talking stock cars and whore houses, while she smothered her fires.

Ruby hissed, "Dumb bastards. She's only a kid."

Fletcher came out, pounding his hands together. "Come on, fellows. Let's hear it for Sherry Stevens of Tupelo, Mississippi. Come on, give her a break." A small shower of applause rose, but not enough to keep Sherry from leaving the stage in goose flesh and tears.

(152)

Ruby hugged her. "You were great."

Sherry had on contact lenses that bulged her eyes when she cried and bad skin. "But they didn't like me."

"What do those morons know? You got a TV act."

"You reckon?"

"I'm positive. You ought to try it. Put something on, hon, you're going to catch a chill. How old are you, anyway?"

"Going on sixteen."

"Lord, you'll get there. Won't she, Ag?"

Agnes took her arm. "Ruby's right. You listen to her. And, darling, you get yourself a can of Dr. Wendell Lewis Skin Conditioner. I had this gal friend back in Irmo that had it about like you, and that stuff really cleared it up."

"I'll write that down. Dr. Wendell Lewis?"

"That's it. It's a salve."

"And you really think I'm good?"

Ruby had her arm around her waist. "We do, hon, talent's something you don't kid around about."

"Well, thanks, y'all. Bye."

"Take care of yourself." Ruby watched her go. "Pretty little thing, isn't she?"

Blaze came on, quivering and twitching fast. Wasting no time during the opening applause, her breakaway evening gown was off and sailing to the wings. She was down to a rhinestone G string and pink tasseled pasties as she reached the mike. "Hello, boys."

"Hello, Blaze."

She ground one deep rolling dip for leverage and pile-drived forward on the drum beat. "Getting much?"

The three-piece amplified bass, drum, and dobro went into an all-rhythm riff as the calls came in. "Me, Blaze! Hey, Blaze, two hundred dollars tax free!"

"Hey, Blaze. I got a cabin on the lake!"

"I'll cook and sew and wash the damn dishes!"

The music slowed, slurred, and then worked with her as her G string and pasties dropped and she rolled and ground up against an imaginary male dancer.

Ruby was trying to figure out how old she was. "That gal's no spring chicken! She's tough, I'll say that for her."

Blaze's fingers worked an invisible zipper down and then pulled at a pair of pants and shorts. The guitar began building an anticipatory mood as she reached out and with both hands convinced the salesmen that it was three inches across, cast-iron hard, and two feet long.

A cry from the back. "You can handle it, Blaze!"

"In the head, Blaze. In the head!"

Ruby sprung her hip out and leaned on her guitar. "What a bunch of assholes."

Blaze, blinking her eyes like a schoolgirl, went from embarrassment to interest and then, as the music changed keys and the drummer went to brushes, she smiled wickedly. With her legs spread, she scooped her hips onto it and, twitching in pain, then disbelief, and finally wonder, trembled to her knees in a back hairpin. The phantom two feet had passed her kidneys and was moving up into the back of her throat.

Agnes said weakly, "Ruby. . . ."

Ruby gripped the guitar neck tight. "This is the end. We can't follow that bitch. We'll go down like the *Titanic*. I'm for walking off."

"Me too . . . only . . . you never can tell about crowds. I swear you can't. Maybe it's good experience."

Blaze, eyes closed, her legs and arms in a crucifixion as the tough flesh on her stomach slithered and crawled like a lizard, was on the floor humping two full feet straight up with the crowd on its feet pounding out the rhythm.

Ruby smiled. "You remember when Mary Lou said that old Powell girl was hung like a doughnut?" She pointed out, giggling. "There's a prune Danish."

Agnes laughed. Suddenly she took Ruby's arm. "Let's go on. All they can do is boo, and then we can just walk right off."

"Hell, I'm game. You swear you won't let them get to you?"

"I wouldn't give them the satisfaction."

Ruby smoothed her blouse tight. "How's my liner?"

"Here, I'll fix it."

(154)

"Christ, she's coming seven times. Where does she go from there?"

"This must be it."

Blaze's hips bounced and jiggled as she thrust faster, twisting and snapping at the top with the bass drum beat. Her purple-highlighted eyes, lashes, brows, and lids were closed in rapture as she levered into her invisible lover, clutched him tight in a five-thousand-volt spasm running from her finger tips to her toenails, and pierced the crowd with one C-sharp, final, and ultimate "YEAH!" She rolled over fast, bowed quickly, and bounced off.

Fletcher Riddle came loping out, red-faced and screaming. "Let's hear it! Let's hear it for the sweetest little gal from the Red River Valley, way out yonder in West Texas, U. S. A., Miss Blaze Fury."

The house collapsed, rose from the ashes and screaming, shouting, and begging for more pounded on the tables and the floors. "Blaze! Blaze! More! More!"

They wouldn't sit down, stop applauding, or shouting. "We want Blaze! We want Blaze!" A bottle broke and then another. A table went over. "We want Blaze!"

Blaze stuck her head out and croaked, "Sorry, boys. That's all I got."

Agnes pinched color into Ruby's cheeks, Ruby cocked Agnes's hat. "You ain't scared, now. You promised."

"Don't worry about me."

"Hold it! Hold it!" It was Jimmy Lee, running up the hallway. "You ain't going out there."

Ruby pushed him back. "We want the experience."

He held her tight. "If you don't let a kangaroo screw you out there they're going to smash the place."

Ruby hit a G chord and tightened the string. "We can take it."

"Ruby! They want tit and ass. Listen at them. . . . Johnny Cash couldn't face that crowd."

Fletcher came trotting over. "Forget the girls! Forget them! Listen at them! They want blood! You see that Blaze work? She's never been that wild, never!"

Jimmy Lee wiped sweat from his face. "What's she on?"

"Some little green job. Had an 'L' or a 'W' on it. Same thing they caught Leroy with."

"You better buy a case." He told Ruby and Agnes to pack their guitars. "No business like show business."

Jimmy Lee pounded on the thin wall. "Dammit, Ruby! Turn it down!" She had moved in with Agnes while Virgil was gone.

She shouted back, "I'm listening at it."

He slammed out of his room and into theirs. Ruby bounced up from the bed.

"Listen to me, Jimmy Lee Rideout, you ain't barging in here like that." She pointed. "That's a door, pinhead! You knock, you hear me?"

"Blow it out, you little bitch. I want that goddamn radio cut down. I can't work like this."

Agnes was in the bathroom, drying down from a shower. He tried to get a look in the dresser mirror's reflection but the steam was too thick. She stuck her head out. "Hi, Jimmy Lee. What's all the racket?"

"This radio freak's trying to drown me out. I can't work that way. I can't."

Ruby laughed through her nose. "Work, my ass. Maybe you're all washed up, Mr. J. L. R." She bit each initial off, like jagged glass.

His face went tight and pinched. "You bastard."

Agnes wrapped on her red terrycloth robe. "Stop it! Y'all stop it! Lord, it is loud, Ruby."

"I don't care. I want to hear it."

Jimmy Lee hooked his thumbs in his belt loops and dropped down on the luggage rack. "That ain't music. All you're getting is feedback and overload."

"How in the hell would you know what music was?"

"Listen, Red—"

Agnes shouted, "Stop now! Stop! I'm getting a sick headache."

Ruby snapped it off. "How about getting out of here. She wants to change. Or maybe you want a sack of popcorn?"

(156)

"When I want to see Agnes undress I don't want your loud mouth around." He winked at Agnes. "How you stand living with this bitch?"

"She's O.K., Jimmy Lee. Guess we're all getting jumpy. You having any luck?"

"Don't even ask that peckerhead."

"I got four that feel good. Be ready tomorrow."

Agnes tightened her robe. "Can we hear them?"

"Forget him, he's just sucking you along. He's got nothing going but that big mouth. Agnes, I think me and you've been taken for a hayride."

Agnes touched her shoulder. "Ease up, Ruby. He's doing the best he can. I swear he is."

"Talk to her, Agnes. Must be her time of the month. I'll have the demos in the morning."

Ruby laughed once. "O.K. Music City, we'll be here."

That night Jimmy Lee rented a sound room and piano, hired a lead guitar, a bass, and a dobro man. They recorded each of his four new songs three times. Each time a different tempo, trying out softer, harder, fuller rhythms and richer counterpoints. They taped until two. After the side man left, Jimmy Lee played each demo back twice, then stopped the machine. He knew he was in trouble. Deep trouble.

The songs were thin, tired. They sounded stolen and reworked. A theme would etch itself out to where it had to commit to a popular tune and then change key, blur, and turn to mush. He couldn't believe he had written them. It was like B-movie mood music. Worse. It was tuneless. It wasn't that one was bad or even two, but four out of four was too much to take in. He walked around the block on Printer's Alley, chain smoking and spitting. Finally he came back, convinced he could find some of the old Jimmy Lee Rideout buried underneath the tired, lukewarm surfaces. He listened close for something original, a progression, a phrase, a line. . . . Nothing rose from the ashes but the gray taste of something old and used and sour. They were as dead as yesterday's fish. He sat back stunned, his face blurred as if freeze photographed. His hands were shaking and his tongue moved over his dry lips, tasting salt sweat and the copper rust of fear.

Back at the Plaza he paced the floor, snapping his fingers, popping his hands, and ticking out his two-beat rhythm through his teeth. He rolled his shoulders and fanned his hands to kill the tension. He had to keep moving, moving. If he stopped and thought about it he would choke. In front of the triple-view mirror, ducking and bobbing and shooting lefts like a middleweight, he reached for a line, a riff, a beat, anything. Anything to break the ice. In one corner of his mind he kept looking for the opening of blue he needed; in the rest he promised and swore he would never listen to another TV show or radio commercial or read another cereal box back or candy wrap. He had to get back to the old Jimmy Lee. The old loose and free and grooving Jimmy Lee who at twenty-three had held the number-one spot on B.M.I. and Cashbox for seventeen running weeks with "Blue Tuesday" and "Angel Love." The Jimmy Lee who dead drunk had written "Swamp Devil" and "Moondog" back to back on a paper napkin at Ruth Rossi's Honkytonk Heaven, and whose early songs had been thick enough to weed out two or three others. Where had it gone? Where? He stopped weaving and bobbing and dropped his hands. The mirror threw back his white hair and eyebrows, his pink face and dark glasses. It came slowly. Without his music and success he would be squeezed back into the water-cooler, coffee-break, nine-to-five world of his old clerk-typist job. Back into the white hot sun and the blinding streets, with cars stopping and slowing down so the kids could point and the old folks could shake their heads and grind him down about brothers sleeping with sisters, and cousins with cousins. He had to come back. He peeled his glasses off and looked into his bloodshot and red-rimmed eyes. A thin chill trickled down his spine, and as the hair on his hands rose and trembled tears formed and fell. Where had it gone? How would he get it back? Work in the morning? Night? He pounded and twisted his fist in his palm. It wasn't scheduling. It was Ruby. He had to get rid of her. He had enough of his own problems. It was dumb to keep her alive and hoping. He would

(158)

tell her the truth. Two girls in Nashville trying to make it without talent or music would barely make it as hookers.

He drank from the bottle and paced the floor. He had to get rid of them. He had to get clean and fresh, free his head and loosen up. He'd been lying for weeks, using up his juices keeping the lies straight and the enthusiasm up. And all for a piece of redheaded tail that now he wasn't even getting. It would be a break for Agnes. She'd go home and raise a yard full of kids and keep Virgil fat and happy on barbecued pork and Miller's High Life. But what would happen to Ruby? He wondered if he still liked her. No, she was too tough, too smart, and getting smarter every day. He liked his women a little fuzzy, a little off center, not honed in tight on everything he said or did, remembering his every fart and port-folioing feedback questions he couldn't answer. He wanted respect, admiration, and he wanted to be alone. Ruby picked up on things too fast. Eventually she would be a threat. "The hell with her! I'm using up juice just thinking about her." He pushed and crowded her out of his mind and dropped across the bed with his head and feet dangling. He had to relax. He whistled through his teeth and studying a cigarette burn in the carpet began thinking about green trees and blue lakes. He closed his eyes. A swan drifted by. A canoe followed and then a tune. It held for a second, then two, then three. He didn't crowd it or try to block it in. He let it drift, coming naturally, smoothly, as it did in the old days. It came with a fresh clear tune and a French horn back-up and hooked into two bars, four, six. He blanked his mind and kept it soft and open. It came again with the last two bars curling into a solid twelve-note bridge that was as intricate as the theme. "Nice, Jimmy Lee. Nice. Easy, now. Don't push it, baby." His neck was relaxed and smooth, his pulse rate was down. He smiled and closed his eyes luxuriously. It was a start. Maybe more. Maybe a whole song had come at once, the way "Blue Tuesday" and the old ones did. He let it wash over him again. It came completely scored and arranged. It was set on his blue lake, the canoe was there, a willow tree trailed in the water, then a girl's hand, a girl, a swan, a boy. . . . "SHIT! SHIT!" He whirled and leaped up, slammed the pillow to the floor, and kicked the headboard, screaming. "SHIT FIRE!" It was the Salem commercial.

From the other side, Agnes hollered, "Anything wrong, Jimmy Lee?"

"Leave me alone! Leave me alone! Goddammit, leave me alone!"

13

Ruby fished in her purse and came up with the clipping she'd torn from the *Nashville Banner*. "Know something, Ag? If we sit around and wait for the Right song from Mr. Wrong next door we could sprout leaves. No lie, he could flip any day now."

She phoned. A meeting was set up for the afternoon with Mr. Moses Shugin of Shugin Enterprises. He was in the franchise business and seemed vague about his connections with show business. He didn't want to discuss it on the phone.

In two hours they were crossing the thick padded lobby of Shugin Enterprises on the twentieth floor of the Davis-Dalton building. Ruby gave the switchboard operator their names. "Hey, hon, how does this fellow pronounce that name?"

The girl cocked her head and squinted. "Shugin like in sugar. No, like in shoe: Shugin. Y'all go on in, he's expecting you."

Moses Shugin was ancient. He beamed at them as if they were long-lost friends. "Come in. Come in." For a short shrunken man, five foot one or two, he had a long stride and quick, sure movements. He spun a pair of matching red leather wing-backed chairs toward his own behind his big kidney-shaped glass-topped desk. "Sit here, girls. Sit here. Very comfortable."

Ruby figured him for eighty. He insisted on being called Moses. "Well, girls, here we are. Ruby Jean Jamison and Agnes McCoy, right?"

"Yessir."

He tapped his nose with a single finger. His head torpedoed to an almost blunt point; the only hair on it curled from his long leathery ears. "I'll be eighty-four next month and I've got a mind like a bear trap."

A big window overlooked the green campus of Vanderbilt and on the walls were pictures of him shaking hands with smiling mayors and aldermen during various ground-breaking ceremonies. A bronze plaque reading BITE QUIK hung at his left. Underneath, a blue and white flag with red letters spelled out BITE QUIK, EVERYTHING FRESH, NOTHING FROZEN. Left-handed he hitchhiked his thumb at the plaque without looking back. "I own it. Own it outright. . . . These other franchisers are on paper. Banks got them by the throat. Me, I own every frying pan, every drop of grease, every slice of tomato." He laughed and quickly wiped his eyes.

Ruby, wondering what he was laughing at, said there were two in Columbia and she remembered a couple more in Charleston. "We see them all over Nashville."

He pointed at a map studded with red, black, and gold markers. "Four hundred and fifty. If you don't believe me, count them."

"I'll take your word. What's the gold ones?"

"They gross over two hundred and fifty thousand, the red over one twenty-five, and the black a hundred. If they don't go to red in six months, I put them on wheels and relocate. . . . Bite Quik, the first mobile hamburger franchise in the country. These other outfits locate you in the swamp and you die there." He laughed again as if some invisible man were whispering jokes in his ear. "Times are changing, you got to change with them. This is the Now Generation."

Ruby asked him what he had in mind and he doubled over,

(162)

laughing. She cut her eyes at Agnes and shooting a look at the ceiling whispered, "Oh, boy."

Moses had his handkerchief out. The slightest laughter brought floods of tears. "I'm sorry, girls. It's just that my competition is going to have a cardiac arrest when he sees you two." His eyes narrowed, his lips thinned. "There's two things I still love. One's competition. The other's driving the bastards to the wall."

Ruby tried laughing with him but couldn't.

Moses straightened up and leaned forward, carefully touching the long fingers of each hand together as if he were testing blisters. He smiled and then fighting it down turned solemn.

He directed his question at Ruby. "You ever read *The Restaurateur?*"

"No, we don't get that one."

"A joker. . . . Good, a sense of humor will go a long way in this field." He flipped a copy before them. On the cover was Moses Shugin with one hand on a brand new Bite Quik door and the other inviting an unseen audience to come in. "That's this month's. . . . Look behind you."

On the wall Moses beamed out from two others.

"I've been 'Restaurateur of the Month' three times. Julie Birnbaum, two; he owns 'Sonny Boy.' My ambition is to be on five. With two good lookers like you, I'll get my fourth, and then I'm going for 'Restaurateur of the Year' for number five. . . . I'm not getting any younger."

Ruby swished her legs crossed and lit a cigarette. The ash tray before her, a plastic reproduction of the 29-cent Bite Quik double cheeseburger, was cut on the bias to show the meat, onion, lettuce, tomato, and the two thick slices of bright yellow cheese. She knew it was the curb. Singing curb girls. "Mr. Shugin, we aren't hopping no cars. We've done shows. We're not exactly starving."

Moses laughed. "My God, my God." Again the handkerchief. "Hopping cars! No, no, nothing like that." He was on his feet and at his map, tapping his finger on the heavy concentration of Bite Quiks in the Nashville area. "One hundred and fifty stores right here within a hundred miles."

The plan was for Ruby and Agnes to do what Moses referred

(163)

to as Bite Quik mini-shows. A car would be at their disposal with a driver and a p.a. system; in between Bite Quiks they would sing over the p.a. system.

Ruby leaned forward. "Sounds fine, but maybe you ought to have tapes for the road shows. That gets pretty hard, picking and singing when the car's moving."

"No. . . . I want live entertainment. I want everything live." He spun his chair and pointed at the red, white, and blue banner on the wall blazing out: BITE QUIK, EVERYTHING FRESH, NOTHING FROZEN. "I have that on four hundred and fifty store fronts, over twenty-five thousand feet of neon. No, everything's live and everything ties in. What do you girls call yourselves?"

Agnes said, "The Honkytonk Angels."

"The Bite Quik Honkytonk Angels. I like that. It's catchy. Girls, I'm offering each of you, in addition to the usual benefits, a company car and a flat salary of two hundred and twenty dollars a week. Hours are eleven to four, five days a week. That'll be for one month, so we can feel one another out."

Ruby said, "I guess we aren't the first ones, right?"

Moses's eyes, set in deep folds of gill-like flesh, twinkled. "I've had bad luck with some of my girls." A brown-toothed, gray-gummed smile eased across his face. "Frankly, I have to be careful of hookers. They use my Bite Quiks as pick-up spots."

He was on his feet, addressing the Vanderbilt campus.

"Now, down to business. . . . You do three songs per shop, maybe an encore or a request if you got a big crowd, and then you're on your way. Bite Quiks are three to twenty miles apart, so that lets you hit two or three before noon and maybe six after. Some days you'll do more, some days less. My research team tells me that a big percentage of people eat two meals a day at Bite Quik. . . . Now, I don't see this as any Pied Piper of Hamelin routine." He started to laugh but stopped. "I'm saying a lot of these two-mealers, when they see you're appearing at another place around suppertime—well, maybe they're tailoring their day to catch you. People are crazy. Especially the buying public. There's no telling what might happen."

(164)

Agnes said, "How do we come on?"

"Good question. Simple, you have the counter boy cut the Muzak and the jukebox off. Then you go into your little act. I don't allow any pinball, and the stools are backless, so you won't be hitting too many loungers. If you have trouble from the help get the badge number and call me up."

They signed a one-month's contract with a pick-up clause if all parties were satisfied and shook hands. Moses broke out a bottle of brandy, and they toasted the new partnership and the Bite Quik Honkytonk Angels. The uniforms were micro-miniskirts of blue leatherette and tight three-button red and white blouses with blue piping on the short sleeves, collars, and pockets. *Bite Quik* was sewn over the pocket, on the side of the skirt, and the back of the blouse. Blue and white calf-high boots stamped B.Q. and plastic blue cowgirl hats completed the outfit. They could keep the Bite Quik Ford Galaxie 500 at night and on weekends; Shugin Enterprises covered the gas, oil, and all insurance.

The Bite Quik driver, Cecil Drake, a fifty-nine-year-old black, arrived at ten-thirty in a red, white, and blue Galaxie 500 with only eighty-eight miles on the indicator. On the front seat was the public address system, fourteen comic books, a Gideon Bible, a lunch of sausage sandwiches and cold sweet potatoes, and *An Introduction to Spanish*. Cecil was in night school and said he would get his high school diploma exactly one day before he turned sixty. When he was younger he had been a Western Union messenger and claimed he still knew every street and alley in town. As they headed down the Dickenson Pike for their first Bite Quik, he pointed out how a cloverleaf junction had wiped out the section where he was born. "See that Spur station? My house would be right under where that car wash is set up."

Cecil had been working for Moses Shugin for over thirty years as a handyman and chauffeur and said he was probably the best-paid driver in the Southeast. From the back seat, Ruby elbowed up. "Cecil, no disrespect, but don't you think old Moses is a little off in the head? You know, crazy?"

Cecil's neck creases deepened in thought. "Crazy like a fox.

(165)

Girls, that man's forgot more about business and world history and current events than the three of us here put together. Right this minute he can still carry on in five languages."

"You're kidding."

"God as my witness." He tooled the long tricolor car through the traffic and pointed at a new store front. "Another franchise. Hank Williams, Jr. Barbecue. Lord, they're trying everything. I hear a couple fellows are selling stock in a Bobby Layne chain of pancake stores. People done forgot all about Bobby Layne."

"I never heard of him. You, Ruby?"

"Seems like I have but I can't place him."

Cecil stopped for a light. "Texas football player. One of the greatest. But people don't keep track like they used to."

Ruby kept her elbows up. "Tell me something. Moses have many of these harebrained ideas—I mean, like serenading people like this?"

He swerved to miss a tailpipe section. "Moses tried those little Ferris wheels and merry-go-rounds; tried dog and pony acts, a few seals. He even ran in a gang of clowns handing out balloons and whirlybirds. Everyone's doing that now; they all copy him." He slowed down. "I remember once in Statesburg, Sonny Boy opened up right across the street from him. They carry about the same merchandise we do, only it ain't as good. . . . Well, sir, Sonny Boy moves in and begins putting two pats of meat between the buns and dropping the price from seventeen cents to fifteen. You know what Moses Shugin did?"

"Went to fourteen?"

"No, sir, went to a penny. One cent. One cent for a Bite Quik doubleburger; that's the job with everything on but the cheese. Doublecheeses were crossing the counter at two cents. Julie Birnbaum, that's Mr. Sonny Boy, flew in, raising Cain and shouting he was going to sue us for one million dollars. I was standing right there when he said it." Cecil pulled the car into the parking lot behind the first Bite Quik. "Then Moses Shugin tells Mr. Birnbaum that he is going to teach him a very expensive lesson. He was going to keep on selling Bite Quik doubleburgers for one cent and doublecheeses for two until Sonny Boy put up the closing boards."

"He do it?"

"Mighty right. Julie Birnbaum left here on a jet plane to Atlanta and went straight into a hospital with an ulcer big around as a baseball."

"Damn."

Cecil cut the engine. "Well, girls, here's your first stop. Don't look like there's much of a crowd." He picked up a funny book, then laid it down and opened his *Introduction to Spanish*. "Good luck, now."

Agnes buckled her guitar strap. "Ready, Ruby?"

"Let's hit it."

They slung their guitars and crunched across the white pea gravel. Two couples were sitting at the low red and blue tables, hunched over hamburgers, milk shakes, and fried onion rings. A tall high school boy with an order in was spread-eagled over the jukebox, flipping selection cards, while soft strains of Muzak flooded the bright white room with a violin, accordion, and harp instrumental of "The Yellow Rose of Texas."

Ruby paused in the door. Agnes pushed her. "Go on, tell 'em who we are."

An acne-faced clerk in a Drink B.Q. Cola paper-boat hat had his ballpoint ready. "May I help you?"

"Mr. Moses Shugin sent us."

"Are you ordering or not?"

"We're the Bite Quik Honkytonk Angels. Didn't you get a notice about us?"

He struck his forehead with the heel of his hand. "Damn, I'm sorry. Got it yesterday." He reached up and flicked off the accordion solo. "God Almighty—you're six hundred per cent better than those last dogs they turned loose. Anybody ever tell you you were cute?"

Ruby winked. "Just you, sweetheart."

He called to the back, and two hamburger boys and a short pretty girl from the deep-fry pots and the taco rack came up. "This is the new Bite Quik team. Not bad, hey?"

(167)

One whistled through headgear-braced teeth. The girl smiled. "Y'all want something to eat or drink? You get it free, you know."

"I'll try that B.Q. Cola. Agnes?"

"Me too, and a couple of those onion rings. They look good."

The two couples were wiping their mouths and getting ready to leave. The clerk called out, "Hey, y'all keep your seats. Got a floor show coming up." He was reading the flyer. "The Bite Quik Honkytonk Angels."

One man stuffed a thick wad of napkins in his back pocket. "Well, how about that."

The deep-fry girl slid the drinks and onion rings out. "Y'all from out of town?"

Agnes nodded as she sipped.

"But you ain't from Hollywood, are you?"

Ruby squared her shoulder strap. "Sure, honey, we're just here cutting an album. We're doing this as a favor for a friend. Ready, Ag?"

She finished an onion ring and wiped her fingers. "Give me a G." She ducked three times and came in on the upbeat of "Honkytonk Angels." Ruby, backing her up on bass, sang harmony. Their voices wouldn't blend in the stainless steel and white-tiled room and bounced around, metallic and shrill. Ruby went lower to kill the echo but the glass-hard tile threw it back, raw-edged and tinny. The crowd applauded at the finish, and three more customers came in and leaned on the long steel counter.

Ruby nodded at the clerk. "Can you open the window? Everything's bouncing around."

He pushed the door and stepped on the front lock. "Window's permanent. Can't move it."

"O.K., that'll help." They stood in the door doing "King of the Road" to let the breeze dampen the sound. Eleven more customers came in, and they went into "Midnight Special," with Agnes stretching out the high notes and Ruby stabbing and bobbing her guitar neck and grinding into a big freewheeling finish.

The crowd applauded and the clerk began taking orders. Ruby whispered, "No encores."

"Suits me."

(168)

The taco girl came out, wiping grease from her hands. "Reckon you could play a tune for me when you come out again?"

Ruby said, "Sure, honey, what is it?"

"Well, it's kind of silly but I like it. It's 'Billy Broke My Heart at Walgreen's and I Cried All the Way to Sears.' You know it?"

"Not offhand. Tell you what, we'll look it up."

Cecil folded the corner of the page down. "¿Cómo está usted?"

Ruby sat with her eyes closed and her fists clenched. "You can knock that off."

"I asked you how you did."

"Well, ask it in English." She didn't open her eyes. "It's stupid. Stupid. We can't sing in those places. We sound like we're in a pay toilet or a goddamn trash can."

"It was kind of harsh, like."

Cecil backed up. "It's that tile. It gives everybody trouble."

Agnes said, "Well, maybe the other places won't be so bad."

"Bull . . . they're all the same. Right, Cecil?"

"Afraid so." He pulled out of the center lane and slowed down to twenty. "You girls should be singing now, shouldn't you?"

"Oh, that. Yeah. . . ."

Agnes chorded into "Honkytonk Angels." Ruby sighed. "Boy, we're going to get sick of this one."

They went through four refrains. Agnes said, "How about 'Pink Carnations'?"

"O.K. Hey, Cecil, come on; you're just creeping. Kick this thing."

"Moses said for me to take it real easy down in through here. This is sort of a depressed area."

Ruby glanced out the back, fingering an F chord. "Guess he figures some customers might be following us."

Cecil laughed once and the speedometer rose slowly from twenty to twenty-five.

At the Chickamauga turnoff Bite Quik on Interstate 40, their third stop, two couples waiting for service complained that all the music was doing was delaying the orders and letting the grease set. "We can hear all that mess on the car radio." They didn't applaud. Except for them the small crowds liked them, applauded,

(169)

and wanted to know where they were going and when they would return. Three subteen girls and a boy of seven wanted autographs and one couple in their sixties, after requesting "Tennessee Waltz," joined in and sang along with them to the finish.

The last stop of the day, except for a journeyman preacher trying to interest the help in salvation, was bare. They listened for a while and then interrupted.

"Mister, could that wait a few minutes? We got a show to do." He ignored them and pointing to the Bible went on about redemption.

The clerk hit his order bell. "Sorry, Reverend, you're going to have to knock it off. These gals are on the payroll."

The man scooped his Bible and literature from the steel counter and stepped back toward the door.

Ruby said, "Thanks."

"Don't mention it. You know 'Boots'?"

"Sure."

They played it fast, moving around, trying to see where it sounded best. The only place was by the door. As the number ended, the clerk speared a bent cigarette out of his shirt pocket. A hamburger boy lit it.

"Tough room to work, isn't it, Red?"

"It's the tile. It makes everything bounce around so."

"Lucky you ain't electric. You'd break every glass in the house."

The taco girl fished for a cigarette in his pocket. "I don't care what it does, it sure beats the Muzak. . . . I get so tired of that stuff I could puke."

The route ended at four. At five they were floating in the twelve-foot end of the Capri Plaza pool, holding onto a green Sinclair plastic dinosaur that Virgil had gotten free with a twenty-gallon fill-up and oil change. Diesel smoke from the semis wasn't rising or blowing away and they could stare straight at the sun without squinting. Ruby ducked under and came up with her hair straight back and smooth. "It's really a breeze when you stop and figure how little we're actually doing."

Agnes had her chin hooked over the green ridged-backed neck. "Mama doesn't make that kind of money in eighty hours. Rube, there's no telling who all's hearing us from the car. We could be playing to nine or ten thousand people without even knowing it."

"Something's going to happen out of this, Ag. I just know it."

Through the sheet-rock wallboard Jimmy Lee could hear Ruby and Agnes rehearsing their Bite Quik songs, laughing and giggling and flipping from talk show to movie, to nonstop hours of c. and w. from WJBD. The bad night at the recording studio was still fresh and sour in his mouth, and trying to avoid his worried face in the eight-foot mirror he worked furiously to sketch out a melody or surprise himself with a decent lyric. He felt himself getting tense and beginning to sweat, and he reached for the bottle of Scotch. He stopped and reminded himself that it wasn't good to be alone this much. He needed a change of scene. And then, remembering Marvin Clarke's description of the bartender at the Twilight Zone Club, he tore the polyethylene dry-cleaning sleeve from his white western suit and pulled his white boots from the shelf.

Jimmy Lee walked along the muddy shoulder of the road. It had rained earlier and the pot holes and runoffs were still full. Everything was going down: his music, his lyrics, his royalties, and now his love life. He kicked at the loose cement; a grease or road-tar stain on his suit would be the end. As he moved into the drain ditch to keep out of the way of a fast-moving furniture van splashing up the road he wondered if this was the beginning of "falling action."

At the Twilight Zone he sat at the service end of the bar where he could watch the girl work. She was wide-shouldered and pretty and her breasts in a rhinestone-studded open-nipple bra were all that Marvin had said. They were perfect beehive formations, miraculously straight out, with bright red nipples. Up close, he saw each had a pair of eyes, lashes and brows on top and a mouth beneath. One face was comedy, the mouth turned up; the other tragedy, the mouth down. "Who's the choreographer?"

"Say again?" Her Clinch Mountain accent sounded like it was coming through cellophane.

Jimmy Lee nodded. "Who did the art work?"

"Oh, me. You like it?"

"Boffo. Great."

"Enough to buy me a drink?" There were four customers on the bar, slowly drinking beer and avoiding each other.

"Name it." They had boilermakers.

"You been sick? How come you're so pale?"

Jimmy Lee explained. From the explanation he moved on to who he was, what he did, and what he was doing in Nashville. The girl's name was Alice Eubanks from Blossom, Tennessee, and her favorite singer, male or female, was L. J. Whipple. "He used to come in here every night. And funny, that fellow would keep you in stitches."

Jimmy Lee counted eight pinball machines stretched across the lobby end of the room. "And he never touched a drop."

She laughed. "Never touched it, but he sure as hell drank it."

"Like another?"

"Sure."

She slid two beers on the counter and centered two shots on her breasts. "Help yourself."

"That's what I call service." He palmed the top, smoothly hooking his little fingers cleverly around the nipples.

"Slick, ain't you?"

He winked.

She drank the whiskey neat and sipped the beer. "You're a song writer, all right; you're all nuts. Another guy comes in here once in a while. He's more like weird, though. Keeps telling me how great he is and rattling off a string of songs I never heard of. I don't think they made the charts. Marvin Clarke. You know him?"

"Yeah, I know Marvin."

The place had been reserved for an insurance company executive party, and easy-to-dance-to music pumped out of the six-foot-wide gold, black, and red Seeburg in the dance pit. Two couples were dancing.

"This place always like this?"

"Bread and butter night. The worst."

(172)

At ten a rhythm and blues trio of guitar, bass, and vibes came on with shoulder-length hair, finger-tip Nehrus, and a thousand dollars' worth of electronics. But as Jimmy Lee listened he knew nothing was going to happen. They reached their peak almost by accident, stayed there ten seconds, and faded off to where they were comfortable. Alice did a tight pony on the duckboards but stopped when the music dropped. Jimmy Lee liked the way her hard body held and real muscle rippled in her thighs. "You dance much?"

"Not with those creeps. Come here tomorrow night. . . . You know what I'd just love to do? Topless go-go."

"Hell, do it. You got the gear."

"Money, friend; this thing pays."

"I gotcha."

The more he watched Alice serving drinks, scooping ice for set-ups, and doing her pony work when the beat picked up, the better he liked her. He loved her breasts and body and her simple straightforward ambitions. All she wanted was topless go-go work. No New York City or Hollywood or string of gold and silver records and first on the charts. Just a good dancer with a good body who wanted to have fun with it and show it off. It was a relief being around someone practical. Someone who could actually do something well and didn't need the world to stop turning so everyone in Alaska, China, and Paris had to see her at the same time. . . . Why in hell couldn't Ruby get smart and be like that?

"You know something, Alice? You ain't bad."

"Another round?"

"Anything you say. . . . What time you cutting out of here?"

"Four, but you better save your strength. I got a date."

"Next time?"

"You never can tell."

14

Ruby wheeled the Bite Quik Galaxie across the motel gravel and pulled up in front of the Coke machine and the manager's office. Agnes checked the mail. A postcard had come from Virgil, showing four people in line at an outhouse. Each was dancing in constipated pain at a closed door while a smiling face beamed out from a roofless one-holer. The caption in South Georgia Day-Glo read, "A Full House Beats Four of a Kind." Agnes kissed the signature. "Ain't he a crazy something?"

"He's crazy enough." She cut on the air conditioner and TV, sipped her Coke, and began undressing. "Lord, this uniform is beginning to stink."

"Mine too. It must be a hundred out there." Two weeks of Bite Quik work had brought in nothing but their payroll checks, minus withholding tax and social security.

Ruby swam four lengths and then floated one. She pulled out at the metal steps and stretched out, watching the traffic heading down the Murfreesboro. She was trying to remember from her

Hollywood magazines how the old movie stars had been discovered. Kim Novak had been riding a bike, Raquel Welch was sitting in a drugstore. Tuesday Weld and Debbie Reynolds had been Miss America or Miss Something and Jose Iturbi had discovered Mario Lanza singing in a garage; no, that had been a Late Show movie. "Ag, you remember how any of the old actors or singers got their break?"

"Can't say that I do."

"Me neither."

Agnes stretched out by her. "I saw an old movie about this cowboy. I forget his name now. Anyhow, he comes into this night club where everyone's dancing and he's carrying his guitar. . . . He just went right over to the juke and pulled the plug and—"

Ruby shot into a sitting position. "Hey! I saw that. Yeah! One of those old jobs."

"It wasn't Roy Rogers, was it? No, that wasn't him. That's one singer I never could stand. Always so prissy and squinty-like and doing funny things with his mouth and all. I got him right on the tip of my tongue. Tall, good-looking fellow with curly hair. And there was a girl there."

"Yeah, a little bitty black-eyed thing. I can see her just as clear. She had her hair up and her eyebrows plucked down to almost nothing. Now who in the hell was that?"

"And it was in color. That old funny orangey stuff where their lips looked smeared—sepio, sepia, something like that. This cowboy came in and sang, got the girl, the job, and a trip to Hollywood. I remember crying, it worked out so nice and all."

Ruby stood up to dive. "Ag, old girl, you're a genius."

Later they talked and planned, listed songs, and began checking the yellow pages under "night clubs." Finally Ruby slapped on the wall. "Hey, Jimmy Lee! Come see us!"

"Be right over! Yeah, right over!"

Agnes tucked her blouse in. "Sounds like he's drinking."

He came in with a half-empty bottle of Scotch and a glass. "Hello, girls."

Ruby said, "What's the occasion?"

"Just wrote a great tune. Listen." He conducted a whistling overture in the mirror as if he were Bernstein at Carnegie Hall.

Ruby's eyebrows creased flat as she dropped ice in his drink. "That's the Salem commercial."

He finished his drink and quickly poured another, leaving the cap off. His eyes were glassy and he kept licking his lips as if he was tasting something. "That represents three weeks' work."

Agnes said, "You O.K., Jimmy Lee?"

He seemed not to hear her. "I'm telling you girls something straight. I'm cutting it all off! All of it! The TV, the radio, everything. . . . And if you can't keep that Jap radio down I'm moving out. Out! You hear?"

Ruby was smoothing on her eye liner. "No need to shout."

"I'm brainwashed!" His face flushed red with strange white spots. "You hear me? Brain-Goddamn-white-ass-washed! WIPED OUT! PLOWED UNDER!"

Ruby clipped her Maybelline box shut. "You're drunk."

"Irregardless, as of today, August fourth, nineteen sixty-eight, I, Jimmy Lee Rideout, am disengaging myself from the services of the Honkytonk Angels."

Ruby's fresh Maybelline eyes nailed him. "Well, good luck, cowboy. You just keep cranking out those Salem jobs and you'll be back in the top ten before you know it."

Agnes scooted up on the bed pillows against the headboard. "Jimmy Lee, Ruby and me got this great idea."

He finished his drink, smacked his lips, and poured another. "O.K., long as it isn't out of my skin."

Ruby said, "You better watch that juice." She explained how they planned to hit the first big night club they could find, pull the jukebox plug, and start in singing.

He rattled his ice cubes. "We saw the same movie. Art Demone in *Rambling Rose*."

Ruby snapped her fingers. "That's it! Hey, who was the little black-haired gal he was running with?"

"Millie Stevenson. Come on, let's hear the rest."

"That's it."

"You'll need a peddler's license."

Ruby glared. "Listen, you son of a bitch, we ain't asking you for thing one."

His fingers twitched and trembled as he pulled out a curved cigarette from his crushed package. "You got to have a rehearsal. We'll hit the Twilight Zone."

Ruby figured that under the salt was meat and lit his trembling cigarette.

"You could do six or seven a night and pick up some nice change."

"No, Jimmy Lee. No six and seven and no hat passing. We want one good place where we can showcase." She checked herself in the mirror and she smiled with one corner of her mouth. "Some place where the two-bit all-mouth agents can't afford the cover."

He exhaled and studied the broken cigarette. "How about the men's room at the Andrew Jackson?"

Agnes slapped her hand on the dresser. "Will y'all stop. You're both so nasty and hateful it's crazy. Ruby, he's right. We got to start somewhere. I'm for trying it. Maybe we can wear our new outfits."

Jimmy Lee had broken off the cigarette and relit it. He seemed calmer. "Not at the Twilight Zone. They see those San Fernando outfits and they're figuring you're the Campfire Girls selling cookies. Wear the wildest thing you've got. Something heavy." He smiled and making a soft fist tapped Ruby's shoulder. "We still buddies?"

"Still buddies."

At the Twilight Zone Dine and Dance Club Jimmy Lee introduced Ruby and Agnes to Alice Eubanks behind the bar and checked their guitars with the hat-check girls. "Let's have a knock. Three Scotch on the rocks, Gorgeous."

They sat with their backs to the padded bar. On a stepped-up velvet-flocked platform the three-piece combo was wailing away, going nowhere. A raised go-go turntable in the center of the sunken floor was decorated in red and gold foil, with mica flecks throwing back the bright colors of the side lights.

Ruby chewed on her swizzle stick. "They could fight dogs in

that pit." The band finished their mood piece and two of the three couples drifted back to their tables. The third, a late forties couple, bounced into a slow version of "Tico-Tico." They minced out in a wide arms-extended break, and while the man stood still, tapping his foot and snapping his right fingers on the beat, he flicked his left wrist, sending his wife twirling left, then right. Finally, dizzy and soaked, she moved in to finish the long number in her tried and true 1943 defense-plant box step.

Ruby sipped. "Pretty sad bunch."

Jimmy Lee called Alice down. "Where'd the embalmers come from?"

"Beats me, lover, I only work here."

"They breaking soon?"

"Couple more minutes. Then all hell breaks loose. How 'bout buying a fellow a drink for old times' sake?"

"Put it on the tab." He elbowed Ruby. "This ain't no country and western crowd. There's a lot of hair out there. I'm checking the juke."

"I thought you'd been here."

"Wrong night. Maybe I had a few too many."

"You and Miss Torpedo, right?"

"Right. Hung, ain't she?"

"That's the word. Turn 'em loose and you'd need a shovel."

"Don't hand me that. How do you think she balances a sixteen-ounce beer?"

"It's called support, shithead."

Agnes was getting nervous. "I think we got the wrong night."

Jimmy Lee drifted over. The standard three-pronged electric plug was four feet down the baseboard and easy to reach. But the crowd was wrong; leather, granny glasses, micro-minis, bushed hair, and headbands; it looked like Sunset Strip. As he was checking the selections and counting ten rocks for every c. and w., the band broke. A silence came over the room. He looked around as a rising hum started, as if bees were swarming in dry cane. A solenoid tripped and clicked and, as a record slid onto the turntable, flashing psychedelic lights leaped out from the walls and down

(179)

from the ceiling. Before he could run down the song number, he was blasted by the sound.

It came like the moving van whipping by him on the highway and backed him up with his mouth open. He'd never heard such volume. It came from the ceiling, from the walls, from the rim of the dance pit, and from the six-foot Seeburg, booming, backing, and pulsing strong enough to shake foil, peel paint, or push leaves. The dancers began pouring into the pit. He pushed through to the bar. "Jeee-sus! What a mob!"

Agnes watched spellbound. "They really go at it."

Ruby couldn't believe it. She'd heard the record on her transistor and danced to it at Spider's, but she'd never heard it on multiple stereos. "I gotta try this one."

"You'll get stomped. Wait till it clears a little."

Jimmy Lee jammed his elbows in the bar padding. "Well, I ain't going down there. You'll get killed in that hole."

She finished her drink. "Order me a beer. Miller's if they got it."

"Have fun."

She worked her way to the floor. It was jammed at the edges of the pit, but the turntable center reserved for the go-go girl was empty. The music was on fire and popping her hands she jumped up into the flashing, whirling, red, green, and yellow lights.

A tall fellow in a seersucker suit, high on hash or up on bennies, stepped up. "Move it, Red." He closed his small eyes and did a clogging twist with his long hands and feet flapping. Ruby turned sideways so she wouldn't have to watch and began a snapping frug to the blinding beat. A motorcycle rider in black vinyl with *Mother of Pearl* across the front pulled the seersucker down.

"Leave her alone, farmer. That's a rocket. Short fuse and low roof. Right, Red?"

"Right, Blacky!" Ruby snapped her fingers and crawled over the music.

The music slowed, coiling down to its foundation, getting ready to build, and she cranked down with it. She cut the rhythm in half, and in half again, and splaying her fingers stiff to feel the slow back beat jammed her elbows in tight. The music leaped and

(180)

she rode it, rippling into the electric convulsions of a rag doll. Some of the dancers stopped to watch. Jimmy Lee had climbed a chair to see and was shouting, "Go, Ruby! Go!"

Her pony tail whipped and snapped, her shoulders jacked and jerked in an insane seizure, as she glued her green silk shoes to the floor to hold the flying fulcrum of her blinding hips. The music rose, sped up, doubled up, and began building even higher. Ruby gripped it with her eyes closed, her head back, and her fingers stiff and tight, grooving on the after beat and driving the crowd crazy. "Go, Red, go! Look at her go!"

And Jimmy Lee. "Ruby! Ruby! Ruby Red!"

She was sailing, skimming, diving, flying. No one could touch her, feel her, follow her. She was out by herself in the sweet convulsions of her own lonesome madness and could stay as long as the music held, knowing the only way back was to work her way through the fires she'd left behind. French horns, trombones, and three juiced-up Fenders struck and blazed into the last thirty-six bars, and she pushed herself to the peak she needed and came in soaking wet, delirious, supercharged on top and in a dead heat into the incredible end. The screaming, whistling, and rebel-yelling crowd parted as she worked her way back to the bar. Jimmy Lee cupped his hand over her ear. "Where in hell you learn all that?"

"Around." She took the beer and his handkerchief and, raising her hair, wiped down the sweat. "I want to try that one again."

She had a beer during one song and then went into the pit for the next. A short hippie with a Buffalo Bill hairdo, moccasins, and leather fringe and Indian beads trailing from his suede bounced up, pony dancing with her on the turntable. He snaked down, bobbing until it was right, then with his eyes closed, his hands straight out and rigid, he blasted into a blinding jackknife.

Ruby shouted. "Hey! You're O.K. California?"

"Pismo Beach."

"Cra-zy!"

After three numbers with the hippie she pushed her way back to the bar. A tall man in a white hard-creased suit and dark glasses stopped her. "Hello, Ruby. Name's Mungo. Mitch Mungo. I'm the owner." He took off his glasses. "Caught your name from your friend." He had dark eyes, long dark sideburns, and bushy eyebrows.

"Pleased to meet you."

"You dance for a living?"

"Well, I play and sing a little too."

"You move around like you know something. New York?"

She shook her head—"South Carolina"—and waved to Agnes. "That's my partner in that green thing."

"I've seen her. She's O.K. too, but I've been watching you. Listen, I'll start you at two bills a week for a couple of hours of that. And I'm not looking for any withholding tax."

She dried her hands on a paper napkin. "I appreciate your offer. But me and Agnes got a great country sound going. Hey, how about auditioning for you?"

"Sorry, Red. This place is going all rock. Hard rock, acid rock. Nothing else."

"Well . . . I'd like to sort of keep our act together."

"Dance here a week and feel your way around. All the contacts stick their heads in."

She looked at Agnes, laughing and talking to Jimmy Lee. "No, I can't do it. We got something good going."

"Well, you think it over and give me a ring. Here's my card."

Jimmy Lee watched Ruby switching through the crowd. Her tight hips and sweat-plastered breasts glistened in the flashing lights. She was holding her hair high to cool her neck, picking up the red, the yellow, and the spinning green. He had never seen her so intense. Her eyes were wide, shining as if she were drugged, and four years had slid from her face, leaving her a creamy eighteen.

He looped his hand around her waist. "You looked great, Ruby. Great! Absolutely wild!"

Agnes said, "Who was that talking to you?"

"Mitch Mungo. Funny name, isn't it? He owns the place. Says no on auditioning; he's going all rock."

"Say anything else?"

(182)

She cocked a leg on the brass rail and sprung her hip out. "Offered me a go-go job."

"What'd you tell him?"

"Told him to buzz off."

Jimmy Lee slid his arm around her shoulder. "Are you hot! Forget him. Jobs like this are a dime a dozen."

"Don't lay it on too thick. It beats that Bite Quik route."

Jimmy Lee said, "Maybe. . . . Let's try another club."

"No, not now. That little hippie is showing me something. You watching us, Ag?"

"You looked wonderful, Ruby. Wonderful. I didn't know you were that good. Everybody's watching."

"We're trying out a few new things. That kid knows some California moves."

Jimmy Lee ticked his tongue on his teeth. "I bet I know one of them."

As Ruby danced, she knew she wanted a man for the night. Jimmy Lee had looked and touched her like he wanted her, but she was tired of him. She wanted something different. The hippie was available, and Mitch Mungo was standing in the shadows watching like a hawk. She could take her choice. The hippie could move, he was young, elastic, and probably on a trip. They could try some things out, and if they didn't work they could try something else. But Mitch would be the pro. He would know what to do and how, and when it was over, she knew she would feel she'd been appreciated. The hippie told her he lived in a bus with three others. There was plenty of room. But she knew in the morning, when the light came in, the four years between them now would seem like ten. No, Mitch would be the one for tonight. But the morning would come there, too. He'd be telling her the job was hers as she was snapping her bra or scratching around for a shoe, but the understanding she was his when he wanted her would be heavy in the air. Still, he was tall and strong and when he came she knew he wouldn't flip on the Late Late or roll over and start snoring.

High on the dancing and the spinning lights skimming over the ceiling and bouncing off the walls, she closed her eyes, listen-

(183)

ing only to the driving electric beat and the flying Buffalo Bill. "Yeah, Ruby, yeah." She followed the zigzagging white light as it slowed down, turning the corner, and then exploded in the bar mirror. "Yeah, yeah." The fast yellow light, breaking out of the slow green, knifed through the crowd. She saw Mitch's teeth flash as the strobe lit his face like a skull. He was waiting for her, knowing the dance was ending and she was coming back his way. The circling lights flashed red on him, then blue. She watched as the white light skimmed him and the green, yellow, and orange, bleeding together, striped him like a barber pole. He scared her and she loved it. He would be a mastermind in bed. She wanted something new; she waved and Mitch smiled.

She smiled back, wondering if he had leather straps dangling from the bedposts, and then laughed out loud. "Jesus! Too many sex-fiend books." The music ended. "God, he's going to be insane." She pushed through. He took her elbow lightly.

"Why don't you tell your friends you'll be along later. I have some iced champagne upstairs." Something had peaked and flattened out, and she was scared.

"You know who you remind me of? He's an old-time movie star?"

He waited.

"George Raft. All he had to do was stand there with his Wildroot shining and the gals broke their backs jumping in his sack."

"That means we're having that champagne?"

"Means I'm having beer with my friends."

"I'm sorry. I'd looked forward to spending some time with you." Nothing seemed to rattle him. "Maybe some other evening."

"Maybe."

"You'll keep my card?"

"I'll keep your card."

Jimmy Lee lay naked under the sheet, waiting. "Come on, Ruby. Please! I'm dying."

"Oh, Jesus, listen to him. Casanova, the greatest lover in the Carolinas. What's it going to be tonight, Cas, the big twenty seconds or are you going for the full thirty?"

(184)

"Aw, come on, Ruby." He rattled the ice in his drink to let her know he was finished. "Don't tease me, Rube. I'm really in pain."

She crawled in by him in her bra and pants. "Now just take it easy."

"I will, I will." He was crawling all over her, kneeing and elbowing her, trying to unsnap her bra and take off her pants.

Ruby bolted up. "Dammit. Slow down! You slow down or I'm sleeping with Agnes. You're whacking me up and getting me all nervous. I should have gone with that Mungo."

"Aw, Ruby, don't say that."

"Can you say anything but aw, Ruby?"

"I'm sorry, Rube. I guess I was rushing you."

"Jimmy Lee, why don't you take a cold shower? Then when you come back I'll be all calm and smooth again."

"No, I don't need any shower. I'll be O.K. now." He pulled her bra off and hung it over the goosenecked lamp. He lay back, smiling. "How about holding it?"

"You'd be off in five seconds."

He laughed quickly and carefully began taking off her pants. Suddenly he jumped up.

"I'll put on some good music. That'll slow me down."

"O.K. Hey! Get me another drink."

The only thing on the radio was talk shows, a country gospel hour, and a Bach sonata.

"Leave that funeral piece on."

"Bach. You like?"

"It's O.K., I guess. Kinda serious. How come you know it?"

"We studied it in school."

They made love with the moonlight and the red and green Capri Plaza neon lighting the room through the Venetian blinds and the ten-year-old air conditioner on "medium." Jimmy Lee was slow, thoughtful, almost in time with the haunting music, and Ruby rocked beneath him. As the music curled and twined over them, she thought he was someone else, even Mungo. He had learned something or found out something. He was good and she told him so. The music changed key and dipped into a cool icy

(185)

region where frost hung and ground fog slid along moss banks and trailing Spanish moss.

Then something snapped in Jimmy Lee. "Oh, my God! Oh, my God!"

He leaped and pounded on her as if he'd stepped on a snake and was trying to stomp it. She pinched him and tried to hit him. "Dammit, stop! Stop!"

"I can't! I can't!" He fluttered and shook in a four-beat convulsion. "I'm coming, coming! Ruby! Oh, Ruby!"

"And all by yourself. . . ."

They lay back smoking and watching the ceiling. The music reminded her of death and her father's funeral. She remembered the flower-filled small front room and the people filing in and out the door and the long table of uneaten cakes and pies and barbecue that the neighbors had brought in. But most of all she remembered standing in the hard clay yard watching the six pallbearers balancing the cheap heavy casket down the narrow pine steps and out the gate to the black Cadillac.

"Tell me something, lover. What do you have against women?"

"Nothing, Rube. Guess I'm just used to a different kind."

"No offense, Jimmy Lee, but I know a hog farmer down in Lower Richland that's got his bo-hog trained to hump against a saddle stump so he can catch the sperm and freeze it."

"Maybe I could take a pill of some kind."

"Well, you better take something. No woman's going to live like that."

His voice tightened. "Well, maybe I ain't had the experience you had."

"You've been getting it, Flash—you've been getting it steady. But I'm going to tell you a little something. If I were you I wouldn't be making any long-range plans."

15

For the next three nights, after the Bite Quik route, Ruby and Agnes marched in, unplugged the jukebox, and wailed into "Honkytonk Angels" at seven different supper clubs. In Bill and Leslie's Green Rabbit they were thrown out before they'd finished twelve bars. At Murphy's Hide-Away they were deep into the first bridge when big Al jacked the Muzak up to full volume and came smiling across the fresh-waxed floor, shaking his head and pointing to the red EXIT sign. Two clubs let them finish before the manager snaked them between the kitchen grills and the sandwich boards and out the back way, and at Sandy's Silver Slipper Sandy himself led them down the steam tables and fry pots out through the garbage-can maze all the way back to the parking lot.

It was Saturday night, and after tuning their guitars in the car to save time inside they rushed into Gus Gillespie's Tip Toe Inn near the Chickamauga interchange, skipped across the empty floor facing the bar, and played all the way through their theme. The crowd applauded, and they sailed into "Midnight Special."

(187)

Two drunk women at the front table kept saying "Wonderful. Wonderful." The men at the bar applauded, yelling "More! More!" One small man with a withered face, a Panama straw hat at a sharp angle, and a carnation in his lapel licked his lips and making a tunnel around his mouth shouted, "If that ain't nice, grits ain't groceries, chicken ain't poultry, and Mona Lisa was a *man!*"

Ruby winked and wiggled at him. "You tell 'em, sport. Want some more?"

"Hell, yeah! Cut loose, we love it."

After two more full numbers, Gus Gillespie came yawning and limping from the back. He looked weary and hung over and had a breath like wet shoes. "How long you two been here?"

Ruby smiled. "We did four numbers. I'm Ruby; this is Robby McCoy."

Agnes moved in. "And they want more."

Gus looked over his thin crowd. "People in hell want ice water, too. You passing the hat or you doing this for fun?"

Ruby slicked her guitar back and with both hands near the pegs, like Johnny Cash, sprung her hip out. "Well, we were sort of looking for jobs."

Gus shook out five Bufferins from a plastic bottle he kept in the black cardigan he wore over a blue serge vest. "See that?" His hand was flat. "Eat 'em like candy. Know why? This place, this business. Look at it! Saturday night, and I got twenty-six beer and maybe five whiskey drinkers. See that sign from the fire department?"

"No sir."

"Well, it reads maximum people I'm allowed is six hundred and forty. That's how many I can serve. Look what I got."

Ruby stood close, wading through the sour breath. "Maybe we could help. We got a nice following. They'd all come out here to see us."

Gus sat down at an empty table. "You girls play country and western?"

"We sure do."

"Well, this town's down on it. Tell you the truth, I don't know

(188)

what they want any more. Used to think I knew something about the night club trade, but everything changed so sudden-like I got lost in the shuffle." He looked around sadly. "First thing I did when I bought this hole was turn it into solid country, just like the big radio shows were doing. Had little outhouses painted in the johns, square and round dancing, chicken in the basket, barbecue, and catfish stews on Friday nights." He belched and rubbed his eyes. "Had a three-fiddle, bass, and washboard square-dance band and five or six cloggers to keep them stirred up." He slapped his gray hand on the table. "Nothing worked. Nothing. Don't ask me why. All I know is I'm going broke hand over fist. . . . But come December and that cold-ass rain sets in, your old daddy's clearing out of this Tennessee mess and high-stepping onto that Trailways to Tallahassee. I'm selling every stick in this place, right down to the toilet paper rollers and the Tampax machine."

Agnes said, "Maybe me and Ruby could run it for you."

His eyebrows bunched together in a gray strained V, and a glint of light touched his eyes. He nodded three slow times. "No, girls. Tell you the gospel, if I wasn't a scrupulous fellow I'd take a percentage of the profits and saddle you up with the old Tip Toe Inn and high-tail out of here. But I was raised better than that. No, I'm going to do you the biggest favor I know. I'm kicking you out and I'm giving you a piece of advice." He rattled his Bufferins and set them on the table like salt. "Stay out of this field. It's dog eat dog and the devil take the hindmost. It's a plain-out death sentence." He grabbed Ruby's right hand and Agnes's left. "You're both young and sweet right now, but a couple years pounding the duckboards and putting up with customer sass and you're turning hard. Hard. You ever look a lady pro golfer or a roller derby queen flush in the face? That's the kind of hard I'm talking about. Gut-bucket, spitting-between-the-teeth, cussing-like-a-man, and drinking-out-of-the-bottle hard. Damn women look more like men than men. Like lizards, old strung-out lizards, thimble-titted and hanging by their garter belts and popping gin and every pill they bottle. Hell, I've seen them tattooed and wearing men's drawers. You babies don't want that, I declare you don't. Get yourself a nine-to-five someplace where you can go the the pic-

(189)

ture shows in the evening instead of pushing sawdust around and sweating out subpoena servers. Pick out a stud you can live with. Hell, I'm talking too much. Come on, pack up them fiddles and clear out of here. You ever hit Tallahassee, I'm in the phone book. Gillespie's the name, Gus Gillespie."

"Thank you, Mr. Gillespie." Ruby looked around at the thin crowd and the dusty square-dance posters. But Gus wasn't through.

"Something else, don't let any of these smooth-talking cabbies talk you into hooking, you hear me now?"

"Yessir, and thanks."

"O.K. I'll buy you a drink. You earned it listening to that sermon on the mount." He crouched up. "Hey, Maurice! Maurice! That's my son, ain't worth a shit. Maurice! Fix these gals a double something on the house."

Cecil had taken the car to go to a lodge meeting, and Ruby and Agnes were in a cab heading for The Black Tulip. It was the seventeenth club on their list. The cabbie, a one-armed Cherokee who smelled of port wine, drove sideways watching them. "I've been listening to your accent and I'm saying you're from down around Gainesville, Florida. Am I right?"

Ruby shook her head. "Wrong. Tacoma, Washington."

He slowed and swung around. "Well, somebody in your family's from down in there. I ain't ever been that far off." Stove-black clouds were sliding in from the west and the wind was whistling. "Let me hear you say ice cream."

Ruby leaned forward. "Ice cream. Think you could goose this wagon? We don't want these suits getting wet."

He moved out into the fast lane and began picking up speed. "Tacoma, whew, that's really out there. Well, you gals got to see one thing before you pull out of this old town. It's our Parthenon. I believe the original is one of the Seven Wonders of the World."

The rain began and Agnes groaned. "Here it comes."

He switched the wipers on slow speed. "Look at that: rain and shine at the same time. Now there's Nashville for you." He slowed and pulled off on the shoulder. "This won't take but a second.

I want you to look out here at that capitol." The wet dome was shining in the sun. "Now that right there is my favorite sight around here, bar none. People that have been around say that when the sun hits that dude like that it looks like Athens."

Ruby was watching the gutters fill and the black clouds rolling in. "Athens, Georgia?"

His eyes narrowed in the rearview mirror as he gunned the engine, skidding and fishtailing the end around. "Come off it, sister. Italy."

At the Black Tulip they sat outside waiting for the storm to stop. Agnes sunk wearily back in the seat. "Oh, Rube, we're going to ruin our suits. Mine's coming apart already."

Ruby, checking the ticking meter with one eye and the big drops bouncing on the black top with the other, touched her sleeve. "It'll be over soon."

"You sound tired too."

"Guess I am. We're running out of spots." She had planned the campaign from the yellow pages the same way she'd picked out Hollywood Charm. Figuring that clubs advertising in eight-point type were beer licenses and hamburger stops, she had listed only twenty-one clubs in Nashville that featured dining and dancing.

The cabbie hooked his stump over the seat back. "Girls, I can't get any closer. Why don't you make a dash for it?"

Ruby watched a clogged downspout overflow. "Just hold your horses. You're getting paid."

"I'm trying to save you some money. . . . You girls ain't *playing* here tonight, are you?"

Agnes said, "Hope so. We're trying to break in." She told him about their act.

He flipped his meter arm up.

Agnes said, "That's nice of you. Thanks."

"You're going to need it. This place is all names. Last week Marty Robbins. Week before, Billy Walker."

"Who's on tonight?"

"Dunno, but it'll be somebody hot . . . sit tight."

He came back with an umbrella and escorted them in. "Good luck now."

Ruby kissed two fingers and touched his cheek. "We're from South Carolina."

Inside, a cowhide-decorated bar with saddles for seats ran the entire seventy- to eighty-foot length of the long room. Centered against the opposite wall, a small but exact version of the Grand Ole Opry stage and the famous barn doors stretched to the ceiling, complete with advertisements for Martha White flour, J. P. Stevens overalls and Trailblazer dog food. On stage a leaping, spinning, hand-popping comic was into his big last joke.

Ruby said, "Want a drink?"

"Sure. Ruby, we can't play here, there's no juke."

"Guess this is what Jimmy Lee would call a class place."

The m.c. came bouncing out of the wings, grinning and squeezing the applause out of the crowd and pounding the sweating, red-faced comic on the back. "O.K., O.K., let's hear it, folks. Let's hear it for Otis Whitworth from a hundred and ten miles right down the road, from Chattanooga, Tenn—essee."

Otis bowed and sweated, waved at a friend in the front row, and backed off. "And now, ladies and gentlemen, without further adieu and with the shortest introduction I know, because this is one old boy that don't need one, here's"—he waved to the wings—"Big John Harmon and the Sugar Mountain Boys!"

Agnes jerked and turned her drink over. "Ruby!"

The bartender wiped the bar down quickly.

"Sorry."

"It's O.K., honey. It's on the house. Scotch, right?"

"Yessir."

"Give me your names. I'll make sure he knows you're out here."

John sang two truck-driving songs back to back and brought the house down. He read off three birthdays and one anniversary, and after announcing that Country Music Heaven had just received a fresh shipment of all of his records at a new low price he sang a five-chorus lovesick ballad and a room-shaking railroad blues.

At the bar he squeezed Ruby and Agnes together in a big bear hug. "Lord, looka here. Looka here. Now if you two ain't a sight to behold. Ruby Red and Agnes, right?"

"Right. Only it's Robby. That's my stage name."

"Robby it is. What you doing in these outfits?"

Ruby told him everything.

John finished two double Wild Turkeys while she talked and slid his glass back for another. "So Jimmy Lee's still dry. That's mean. It'll happen though, captain. It'll damn well happen."

He bought another round and told the bartender to put their bill on his. "We got to figure some way to fix you gals up. Seventeen places. Christ, you must be seeing double."

Agnes said, "We're about ready to go home."

"Hush up, Agnes. The hell we are. We're just getting started."

John lipped his drink and closed his eyes. "Well, I ain't having any more of you playing at feed stores. I'll let you do a couple numbers tonight. Then we'll sort of play it by ear."

"Thanks, John." Ruby squeezed his arm. "We really appreciate this. Jimmy Lee said there might be a couple producers here."

"You never can tell. Now when you're out there put some backspin on it and move around. This crowd gets go-go stuff and they get tough. So show 'em you can move."

"We'll move, John. Just watch us."

He slid his empty glass back for a refill and squeezed Ruby's waist. "I don't want to crowd you, but if there's any chance of coming on topless let me know."

Ruby shook her head. "No way, John. We're making it with our clothes on or we're heading back to the wagon."

"O.K., but come on strong. I'll be right behind you."

They followed John backstage. Agnes whispered, "Thanks, honey. Virgil would have killed me."

"Wasn't all you, Ag. I've got my mind made up. If it's all tits I'm checking out."

"You sure I'm not holding you back?"

"Will you hush? Anyone right off the street can shuck off a bra and shake around and get these grass eaters clapping. Doesn't have thing one to do with talent."

"You're right, Ruby. You're really right."

"Damn right I am. . . . O.K., now, let's wail."

With Big John coaxing and shouting, the audience whooped and shouted for an encore to "Honkytonk Angels." They dipped and bobbed their guitars for three beats and went into a hyped-up version of "Midnight Special" with Agnes riding the high notes like she was strapped to them and Ruby dancing around the music the way she did at the Twilight Zone. The crowd didn't know whether to listen to Agnes or watch Ruby. They did both. They applauded them into a second encore as Big John grinned and waved in the applause. "O.K., take 'em again. Great going, Ruby. Beautiful, Robby. Beautiful."

The last number was "King of the Road." Agnes never sang better and Ruby had never been wilder. The audience loved them as John joined them on the last chorus and into a standing ovation. Ruby beamed. "Ag. I think we got it! We're going to hit! We're doing something right. Listen at them."

Big John pulled the microphone from the stand and leaned out over the first row. "O.K., now, come on out there. I want someone to step right up here and sign up Ruby and Robby—the Honkytonk Angels. If you don't like their act they'll do anything you want. Ain't that right, girls?"

Agnes smiled. Ruby hit a G chord and then an F.

After the show a tall blonde in heavy make-up and a silver fish-scale micro skirt slid a chair in next to John. She took his left hand as he ate a club sandwich with his right. He put his sandwich arm around Ruby's shoulder and swallowed. "This is Irene Cash. No relation to Johnny but one helluva guitar player. . . . Ruby, Agnes."

Agnes shook her hand. "Pleased to meet you."

Ruby asked her where she worked.

Irene was picking at John's lettuce. "The Red Glove out on Memphis Bristol." She had green eyes that were tapered back like a panther's with blue and silver eye liner. "You know it?"

" 'Fraid not. c. and w.?"

"Rock. I dance in the cage. You got to come out. Got some wild sounds."

John snugged her close. "She's the best. Got more moves than

(194)

the law allows." He poured water into his napkin and mopped his face down. "Damn, I can't cool off. Ruby, call me tomorrow." He scratched his phone number on a matchbook cover. "I'll probably have some leads for you."

"Hey, great. Any chance of an autographed picture for my mother?"

"I'll even give her a stack of records." He laughed and stood up. "Beats hell out of trying to sell them." He pulled Irene's chair out. "You kids hold 'em in the road now."

Irene said, "Bye now."

Ruby looked Irene over as they crossed the floor. "Talk about a tall one, look at that."

Agnes said, "She's nice though, I declare she is."

John and Irene stopped at a table near the door and shook hands with two men who looked like twins except one was bald and one had bushy black hair. He waved back, signaling with one finger straight up that they were all right and wanted to see them.

The men introduced themselves as Myron and Henry Gladstone. They were in the motion picture business and were old friends of John's. Henry had the hair. Myron did most of the talking. He handed them a card each. "Myron Gladstone, President of Magna Gladstone Films, Inc., Ltd, Hollywood, New York, Nashville, Mexico City."

Henry was drinking vodka and tonic and gouging out pistachio nut meats with a silver knife. Myron was all business. "You girls looked good up there. A little rough on the edges but good."

Ruby asked, "What do you film in Mexico?"

"Lots of things. It's great for locations. Spectaculars."

She watched Henry lining up six nut meats side by side. On the seventh he ate them. "Name me a couple shows you've done. Maybe I've seen them."

Henry spoke, pointing his knife at his finger. "You see *Seven Brides of Mazatlan?*"

She shook her head.

"*War of Guadalupe? Mexican Hat Dance?*"

"I've never heard of them. Must be drive-in jobs."

"No, no drive-in." Myron was back in charge. "International, they go all over the world. We dub in different languages. Hell, we got them playing in Japan."

Henry had five more nut meats lined up. Myron said, "Shot *Mazatlan* and *Mexican Hat* near Acapulco. Great weather. Didn't miss a day. You try shooting around this nuthouse and you go crazy sweating out the rain. Take like today, like now. You know what happens? If you'll pardon the expression, you lose your ass."

Ruby didn't like Myron's sudden familiarity, and Henry looked like trouble. She had to flush them out fast. If there were other contacts in the room, they wouldn't come over until the Gladstone brothers left.

"You made any name features? I mean something I would have seen?"

Myron sucked a back tooth and examined her eyes. "We got three features being cut right now. One's got Cliff Robertson in it. Henry wrote the script; I directed. Correct, Henry?"

He cracked a nut. "Correct."

"You're kidding."

"I never kid about business."

"Me neither. Now tell me about the Mexico City setup. I mean outside of the multi-million-dollar spectaculars."

"So what's to tell?"

"Do you do nudies?"

"Nudies. Nudies." He raised his eyes to the ceiling. "You give Sam Goldwyn three million and tell him to shoot you a nudie and he's shooting. Sweetie, everyone's doing nudies, and sweetie, everyone's got a price."

"The name's Ruby. I want to know if you do nudies for a living?"

He clasped his hands together as if praying. "I'll level with you. That way you don't waste any time, that way I don't waste any time. That's the business we're all in, time. . . . You understand what I'm saying?"

"I understand."

"So we make a few skins? The country's swinging now. It's getting more liberal every day. One year it's skin, pornos, Mickey Mousers . . . the next year it's art. Look at your Andy Warhol. You don't think he's got brains? You think he's not a merchant?

(196)

O.K., O.K., Honkytonk Angels, I like the way you move and I like your style. I'm willing to take a chance with you. But in this business chances cost money, big money. I pay you good money and you in turn give me your cooperation. . . . So we make a nudie. We make a couple down in Mexico. It's like a vacation down there. No rain, no snow, all the grass you want."

Henry added, "And no unions."

"We shoot in twenty days, on the outside thirty-six. While we're cutting and dubbing you're in Acapulco. And when we distribute, you're in for fifteen per cent of the net plus all expenses."

Henry had finished his nuts. "On expense account money, the government doesn't get a dime."

Ruby said, "I ain't making no nude movies."

Myron stayed with her. "O.K., I wanted to hear it from your own mouth. I told Henry you'd be tough but I figured I had to try. You can't kill a guy for trying. . . . Listen so there's absolutely no mistake. I'm telling you you could make a fortune. You think most of your Hollywood and Vegas stars are coming out of drama classes and Miss East Tennessee Cotton pageants? I happen to know exactly how many are discovered out of the art films or nudies or whatever you want to call them."

Henry said flatly, "We call them money. You know how May Taylor got her start?"

"All right, I know all about that. The answer's no. I'm not screwing on camera for no money. Leave us alone. We're expecting someone."

Myron wouldn't give up. "Wait a second. Listen, lady, I understand, I understand. We have that problem with a few of our big names. They don't like to be seen in an embarrassing position so we cut to a stand-in on the tight shots. We shoot in close of you in an embrace, then cut to the other girl who doesn't mind the exposure."

Henry cracked a nut. "Loose shots for faces and bodies and tights on muff and ass work. My brother's right; no one gets hurt."

"I'll handle this, Henry. You're making them nervous."

"You damn right you are."

Agnes cleared her throat. "I suppose the only thing you got shooting right now is in Mexico."

"Yes, that's all there is right now. But we have a great one ready to roll. Henry just finished the script."

Ruby spun her ice cubes with her finger, "You mean there's lines?"

"Lines? There's songs, exteriors, process shots, mob scenes, everything. What in the hell you think we are, some eight-millimeter Tinker Toy? We even carry our own cutting room along. This is big business. Big. . . . Something else, little lady. Every casting director in Hollywood and New York City is breaking his hump screening our stuff for new actresses. . . . We got an international reputation. If I was to tell you the actresses that got a start with us you'd fall down."

Ruby looked around the room to see if anyone else wanted to see them.

Henry said, "Forget it, Myron."

Myron wheezed, "O.K., O.K."

The Gladstone brothers tuned out as they slid their chairs back. Myron spoke to Henry.

"You get that Irene's number?"

"Yeah, I'm calling in the morning. Looks good. Good bones."

"What's she like?"

"Perfect if we can get her. She'll fuck mud."

16

On Friday, the only thing higher than the twenty-three-star general who hung around the Andrew Jackson men's room was the Mississippi heat wave that had hit Nashville in the night. By ten it was 98 degrees and climbing. Jimmy Lee, who had spent $38 drinking boilermakers and eating pigs' feet with Alice Eubanks until 4 A.M., only to watch her go home with a steel guitar player, had made it across the Capri Plaza gravel only as far as the pool. Here he had passed out on the vinyl chaise facing due east and the uninterrupted sun. By ten-thirty the damage was done. His wrists and hands were fire red and swollen and the sun slashes around his collar and the top of his socks looked like open wounds.

A cabbie who had stopped to use the men's room in the lobby shook him. "Mister! Mister! You're about to burn up!"

Jimmy Lee didn't budge. He tried again, gave up, and told Rudolph the manager about it.

Ruby shook him. "Come on, Jimmy Lee. You look terrible. Come on now."

He sat on the tile floor, his chin resting inside the toilet rim, watching the green-yellow liquid swirl as he retched and heaved. Ruby flushed it down. She held a wet towel to the back of his neck. "Come on, get it up. You'll feel better. Give me those glasses before you break them. . . . Jesus!" The snow-white circles and glasses-frame outlines looked like they'd been painted on. "This is serious!"

The doctor told Jimmy Lee he was lucky he hadn't ruined his eyes, and after giving him a sedative and a shot of antibiotic and larding him down with yellow salve he told him to stay in bed for at least a week.

Jimmy Lee winced hard. "Doc, I got too much on the fire. How about if I cruise around at night?"

"Sorry, fellow. You need all the sleep you can get." He wrote out a prescription. "Now you'll feel rocky for a few days, maybe nauseous, but that shot should take care of things. If you get any dizzy spells or a big depression call me up. I'd lay off the booze and the fried foods for a while."

"Groove."

After telling him what bad luck he'd had with Capri Plaza checks, the doctor took $25 in cash and snugged his card into the edge of the dresser mirror.

"Good luck, now. And call me if you get in trouble."

"O.K., doc. Thanks for coming."

On Saturday and Sunday Ruby sat with Jimmy Lee, checking his temperature and reading him back issues of *Variety* and *Billboard*. Monday after the Bite Quik route she and Agnes brought him fresh fruit and homemade ice cream and stayed until the Johnny Carson show ended at one; Tuesday they did the same. Wednesday afternoon, after the route, Ruby told him that Big John Harmon wanted them to do two numbers on his show at Cumberland Furnace, Tennessee. "It ain't Nashville, Jimmy Lee, but John said they'll be some wheels there from the Opry."

He sat at the window, watching the kids doing cartwheels down the grass and into the pool. "It'll be good experience. Say hello for me."

"Jimmy Lee, you sound so down."

"I'll be O.K. You give them hell now."

She kissed his cheek. "We will, hon."

The show began with Big John and his Sugar Mountain Boys singing two truck-driving songs and one mule train. He moved on to a ballad and then back for another loud double-clutcher about the Memphis–Chattanooga run. Local jokes were fed in between the numbers, and when he wasn't shouting out to special friends and announcing birthdays and his road schedule he was plugging a North Georgia potato chip company's new line of flash-fried pork skins.

Halfway through, after promising he'd do "The Face in the Windshield" and had the crowd where he wanted them, he swept his Fort Worth hat off and mopped down. "But folks, first I got a fireball surprise that just can't wait." His glycerine eyes sparkled, his teeth flashed, and with his guitar slung on his back he waved Ruby and Agnes half-stepping in a fast prance across the sixty-foot Georgia-pine stage. He bear-hugged them together. "Now, ain't this something else?"

The crowd applauded and laughed.

John said, "Tell 'em about it, girls."

They did fourteen bars of "Honkytonk Angels" before Agnes chorded down. "I'm Robby McCoy." She stepped back, smiling and picking light, as Ruby slid in tight to the twin mikes. "And I'm Ruby Red."

The applause peaked, and moving in close they slid into "Ribbon of Darkness." Ruby sang the low part, Agnes the high, as they aimed their key pegs at the ceiling, the back of the hall, and then the floor. Then, crisscrossing one another into the first strong bridge, they dropped back together on the refrain. Ruby felt cool and warm and right and stomping her left foot twice began weaving in and out of the mikes, the way they'd practiced at the Capri Plaza, setting Agnes up for her soaring, long, last notes. As they were bowing and smiling to the applause, Ruby saw that Big John's long arms and hands were wringing it out of the crowd. It wasn't enough for an encore. Something had gone wrong; they wanted Big John back.

(201)

In the wings during the break Leonard grinned around a missing front tooth. "You were carried, you dumb broad. One more number and you'd have died out there."

Ruby, getting as many teeth in her smile as she could, said sweetly, "Go to hell, you fish-eyed bastard."

When the show ended, Big John made Leonard take Agnes back to the Capri Plaza. He and Ruby had a drink in his Airstream trailer. "Well, honey, I'll give it to you straight because that's the kind of guy I am." He poured another and drank it fast. "These people know 'Ribbon of Darkness' belongs to Marty Robbins. That's his song and they don't want just anyone messing with it."

"But I told you we were doing it. You could have said something."

"Sorry, baby, guess I got too much on my mind." He thumbed her chin and patted her cheek. "That crowd really dug you at first. I bet if you'd had a different song you'd still be doing encores." He snapped down another two ounces of Wild Turkey. "Whew! That's a long show. Really takes it out of you. Any chance you giving me a back rub? I'm in about ninety-seven knots."

"O.K. I guess so."

"You don't have to unless you want to."

"No, I'd like to do it." He unzipped his Naugahyde jacket and let her help him take it off. "Hey, this thing weighs a ton. How much something like this cost?"

"Seven–eight hundred."

"Including the pants?"

"Yeah. Nice, though, ain't it?" He held the red and yellow jacket at arm's length. "That semi and forked lightning was my idea. I got an artist to draw it up." He skinned out of his T shirt, and his yellow flesh shook down over his wide belt. "You and Agnes ought to think up something special. Say a honkytonk and a halo. I can have this artist put it on paper; then we can see about getting it made up."

"That's not a bad idea."

He stretched out on his double bed and hung his arms to the floor. He seemed to fill the room.

"Where do I start?"

"The neck. That's where it gets me. . . . There, that's it. Say, you got strong hands. Nice. You keep that up and you might get yourself a steady job."

Ruby worked his muscleless back. The meat was so thick she couldn't feel his backbone or his ribcage. He kept sighing and groaning. She kneaded and rubbed, stopping only to dry her hands on his T shirt, which smelled like a sour dishrag. She hoped he was going to sleep and wasn't going to give her any trouble. But then he rolled over and through half-closed eyes glanced at the pillow.

"Come on, honey, kick your shoes off. You must be beat too."

Ruby knew he didn't mean sleep. She sipped her drink. "No, John, I'll just sit here."

His eyes wouldn't leave her. "Come on, sweet. I'm all tense inside. I can't tell you how much I need you."

"It's my time of the month, John, and I got these cramps. Maybe that's why we were off tonight."

The betrayed look in his eyes changed to a questioning one. Wasn't there something else she could do for him? He didn't speak, only looked. At forty-six Big John Harmon, despite his six feet four inches and 250 pounds, still played the deprived kid with women. Coasting on his reputation, he made them take the 180-degree turn and see that underneath the forked lightning and the sixteen-wheel diesels was a small boy wanting to be loved.

"Sorry, John. Maybe some other time."

Big John nodded reassuringly. "It's O.K., Ruby. I just want it understood you ain't under no obligation to me."

"I understand."

She poured him another drink and he nodded at a stack of mail. "Hand me that mess."

He leafed through the envelopes, looking for familiar names. Except for a red envelope from Internal Revenue there was none. "Bastards!" He slung it aside and unsnapped his silver belt buckle with a relief carving of a lightning-lit semi.

Ruby almost shouted. "Hey, this is all fan mail. Let me read you some."

"O.K., if you want to." His eyes were closed; dark half circles lined them underneath.

(203)

She unfolded a yellow-lined sheet of tablet paper. The message was printed carefully, skipping every other line.

Ruby read:

"Dear Big John Harmon:

You have brought real happiness to me and my wife and our children for a long time. Next month on the 12th it is our 25th wedding anniversary. Would you please play and sing 'Georgia Morning, Tennessee Night' for us. That is the first song we danced to back in 1942. May God Bless you and your family and all your wonderful musicians. A faithful Atlanta, Georgia, listener,

Turner Dixon, Jr.

P.S. My wife's name is Alma and our children are Floyd, Toby, Robert, and Effie. I am enclosing a photograph which was taken last year. You don't have to send it back."

She checked the calendar on the wall. "The twelfth is Saturday. Lord, wouldn't they be happy if you announced that anniversary on the Opry. Twenty-five years, now isn't that something?" She filled in the twelfth square with *Turner and Alma Dixon 25th anniversary* and listed the children. "And doesn't he sound like a sweet old duck. John I want you to promise me . . ." Big John was snoring. She wrote in "Georgia Morning, Tennessee Night." The second letter began:

Dear Big John,

I first heard your "Truck Driver's Blues" in 1958 when I was in the Women's Marine Corps at Cherry Point, N.C. . . . Me and my girl friend were in the day room and I remember we played that thing five times before we turned it over. On the flip side was "So Long Mama. . . ."

She read another dozen letters. Everyone loved him and wanted their songs played for a birthday, a wedding, or an anniversary. Three came from the Tennessee State Prison. Many enclosed checks for autographed records. Some sent recipes for everything from pecan pie and hopping john to family guarded secret banana-cream-pie recipes and barbecue sauces, and one said when she last saw him in Tip Top, Kentucky, he looked like he had bad color and gave him directions for making a brew of Lipton tea, willow roots, and turnip tops.

One letter that had been mimeographed on yellow legal pad paper was rubber stamped CHANG MOONG AND CO., SONG WRITERS, FRESNO, CALIF. Above the lyrics was typed: "This song can be played to any slow tune you want or in any key you desire." The one-chorus lyrics covered the whole page:

> When jet planes freeze in the sky,
> And the air is sucked up from the earth,
> And plagues and lice and fire and mice
> Blot out the moon,
> Then, my darling, I'll come to you with
> Jesus' hand in mine.

Ruby put it aside and began going through his stereo records. One was all truck-driving songs, and John was pictured leaning on the front bumper of a big twenty-four-headlighted rig. On his gospel song jacket he was in a dark suit with his hands folded in front and his eyes glowing in a strange blue light coming from a simple candlelit cross.

The back of the truck-driving jacket told the Big John story.

In 1956 Big John Harmon, a hard-fisted, iron-jawed truck driver, rolled out of Mobile with an oversized load of I-beam steel. Somewhere between Baton Rouge and Dallas he decided that someone big, someone with muscle, and someone who knew the truck driver's story should tell it to the world in song. In a diner outside Shreveport on the back of a menu Big John wrote his first two songs, "A Truck-Driving Fool" and "Truck Driver's Blues." Two months later they were number one and two on the charts and were riding hard. Which is what Big John Harmon with his unique genius and knowledge of the big diesels that roll across our country at night keeps on doing. He says, "Man, it's tough out there. But you got to be tougher. Sisters and brothers, I've been there and back."

Ruby sniggered. Both songs were Jimmy Lee's; the only truck in John Harmon's life was the diaper-service panel he used to push around South Jackson, Louisiana.

Big John slept until midnight. He sat up. "Jesus, I really went out." He washed his face in the small sink and sprayed his armpits with deodorant. "Pour me a couple inches. You been sitting here all this time?"

(205)

"I didn't mind. I've been reading your fan mail and doing a little thinking."

He tucked in a dark blue cowboy shirt with white scalloped pockets and, inhaling deep, tightened his belt. He knocked the whiskey down and combed his hair. "Hungry?"

"Little bit."

"How 'bout a steak?"

"Suits me."

In the big Lincoln John tried all of the selector buttons before he found Hank Williams, Jr., singing "Lonesome Me."

He flicked his turn signal on and gunned around two slow-moving cars. "Nice kid. I'll let you meet him." The song ended, and as the announcer began talking about a new weed killer he cut it off. "Now tell me about all this thinking you were doing."

Ruby had her shoes off and was sitting curled up in the corner. He sounded as if he thought it was about him.

"Well, I figure maybe I ought to be getting some advice from you."

"It's simple. You got the talent but you got to have the right songs. And I don't mean recitations. I mean music, something with some backspin and bite to it."

"How come you quit writing them?"

"Went dry. It's tricky business, sweetie. That thing you just heard, 'Lonesome Me.' Hell, I bet half of old Hank's songs are about being cold and lonely and locked out: 'Cold, Cold Heart,' 'Lovesick Blues,' 'Your Cheatin' Heart.' I can name ten just like it. Him and Jimmie Rodgers had a bad time with women and they put it to music." He laughed. "Guess my hot streak ruined my writing. . . . Way I see it, you've got to be a genius or in so much trouble it just pours out."

"I guess you put your genius in your singing and playing."

"Thank you, honey." He pulled into the Mr. Ribs Barbecue and Steak House parking lot. While they were drinking beer and waiting for the steaks she asked about Chang Moong and Co.

John salted the back of his hand and licked it. "Jesus, that pest. Three songs a week, every week. He's got this town flooded. He's got to be a retard."

(206)

"How about Marvin Clarke?"

John sat sideways and put his feet out in the aisle. "Marvin's his own worst enemy. He doesn't want stars singing his stuff. He wants the songs to make the star. A real bullshit way of looking at things, if you ask me."

"But say someone like Johnny Cash or Marty Robbins wanted to do something. You ain't telling me he's turning them down for some unknown?"

"No, he'd be glad to write for Johnny or Marty. It's just that by the time he gets a song ready the word gets out and his drinking buddies move in. Best thing for Marvin would be to shack up someplace for a month or so and then come back." John speared up five chick-peas from his salad and leveled them at Ruby. "Now there's an idea."

"Live with him?"

"Hell, yes, then you get first crack at everything he puts out. Say you're gone a month. That'll bring you into Nashville with nine or ten good ones."

Ruby chewed her steak. For filet mignon it tasted like the dollar-ten special at Otto's. "So I live with Jimmy Lee to get a manager. Then I crawl over to you to get some experience, then with Marvin Clarke to get some songs. How 'bout if I moved in with that rhinestone suit man we're going to be needing? Jesus Christ, where am I supposed to set up my hair dryer?"

"Don't get sore at me. I'm just giving you the facts of life."

"I knew the facts of life when I was twelve but there's nothing in that list about having to sleep with every son of a bitch I buy a pack of cigarettes from."

"Don't get so excited."

Her voice leveled. "I'm not turning myself into any Welcome Wagon." She paused and picked at the foil on her baked potato. "Maybe I'd live with someone like old Jimmie Rodgers if he was alive and I had the chance. I like his stuff. Chances are I'd like him, but I'm sure as hell not getting myself zipped up in a sleeping bag with some Marvin Clarke. I've never heard of song one of his."

Big John was through with his steak and was scraping the potato down. "You know 'Sweet Monday Morning,' 'Big Stella.' "

"Sure, and I know they had nothing to do with Marvin Clarke."

"Wrong."

"You mean they were stole from him?"

He mopped his Texas toast over his tipped platter. "That's what I mean."

"How in God's name can a man have everything stolen from him like that?"

"He drinks."

"Sure. So do I." She sat back, chewing the tough meat.

"Not like Marvin. He drinks down to the bone. He did four months as a carnival geek. He'd take a chicken and bite the head off slow and—"

"Stop it! I don't want to hear any more."

"He's clean as a whistle now. I tell you, Ruby, as a friend, if Marvin Clarke had a month with you cooking flapjacks and keeping him working, you'd be coming back to Davidson County with a dozen songs."

"Say I did. What's in this for you?"

"I need material myself. Why do you think I was so nice to that albino bastard? Songs are scarce these days. Everyone's writing poems or love letters or telling L.B.J. what to do in the Congo. All junk. I need a song I can hear, something I can get my teeth in, something with a melody." He flipped a cigarette out for her and lit it with his truck-embossed lighter. "Coffee?"

"No, I want some sleep. I got to work tomorrow."

"What say I set up a meeting with you girls and Marvin after you get off? He'll play you some tapes."

"Maybe."

"I got to know now."

"O.K., set it up. I'll phone you."

"Tell you what. I'm playing Ophelia next Wednesday. It's sixty miles out. Maybe I can bring you and Agnes in for a couple of numbers."

"Hey, great. We'd love it."

"But no Marty Robbins stuff, O.K.?"

(208)

"O.K."

"And you reckon you'll be over your little problem about then?"
She patted his hand. "I'll be O.K. You be sweet."

Jimmy Lee was feeling better. His eyes were clear, and at night
he watched TV through his dark glasses. He didn't call the doctor out about his depression; he knew it was from his music and
Ruby. A couple of good songs was what he needed to hold her,
but the harder he tried the worse they sounded. She was drifting
off with Big John, and it was only a matter of time before she
stopped coming home at all. He tossed over, pounded his pillow,
and reached for the face lotion. After oiling his face he checked
TV Guide. There was nothing on worth seeing. A car crunched
into the gravel and he heard the girls saying good night to John
Harmon.

Ruby unloaded a box of assorted candy, the New York Variety,
Billboard, five men's magazines, and three pounds of green grapes.
She told him how they'd been out to Marvin Clarke's house. Agnes interrupted. "Jimmy Lee, he must really be some kind of genius. He does gospel, go-go, mule train stuff—I mean everything."

Jimmy Lee slid into his loafers and looked over the grapes.
"Marvin reads a lot. How was the casket lid song?"

Her eyes shone. "I thought it was really beautiful, and like he
said, if it was backed up with a lot of strings and maybe a harp,
it would be something else. He calls it a novelty song."

"It's that, all right."

Ruby pushed her shoes off and flopped across the bed. "It's
sorta morbid if you take it wrong, but I bet it would be a seller.
Jimmy Lee, it's the kind of song you don't forget."

"I'll buy that. What would you follow it with?"

"I don't know. John says he'll give us a hand on programing.
He says that's the trickiest part of doing a show."

"How about washing some of those grapes for me?"

"Sure thing."

Agnes stripped the cellophane from the candy box and picked
out two chocolate-covered Brazil nuts. "We're doing 'Way Out
on the Mountain' and 'Tennessee Rose' at the Ophelia show. John

figures everybody loves Jimmie Rodgers, and 'Tennessee Rose' is so old it's got whiskers."

Ruby lit a cigarette and thumbed through Jimmy Lee's sheets of music. Margins of corkscrewing doodles, small x's, and heavy blacked-over lines surrounded the big X's scratching out whole pages. "Not going too good, is it?"

"My head isn't right. I keep hearing TV jingles. Every damn tune I start turns into one."

Agnes picked out a miniature praline. "That's the same way I am. I'll get about a dozen notes going and they'll just go on and on and there's no way of getting rid of them. Seems like the harder you try to shake them the faster they play." She scratched in her purse for her key. "Listen, y'all go on and talk. I got to call Virgil and wash my hair. I'm about to go crazy, it's so dirty."

Ruby hugged her knees in tight and rested her chin on top. "Jimmy Lee, I can't follow all this crap. How come John's record jacket claims he wrote 'Truck-Driver's Blues' on the back of a menu?"

"That's PR. Hell, they bill this place like another Stratford-on-the-Avon, with Rosie's coming up like the Mermaid Tavern . . . Shape up, Ruby. I let him sign them when we were both down. We figured he could build his image up and move records. It's all dollars and cents."

"That figures." She rolled her cheek on her knees and looked in the mirror, trying out her blank and staring expression. And then, shaking out her hair and remembering it was the way Spider liked it, she wondered what he was doing and if she missed him. She decided she did.

Jimmy Lee laughed. "Can't you see folks going home at midnight remembering a five-year-old singing that casket song?"

She was in no mood to be laughed at. "You got room to talk. You been scratching around here like a chicken with the pip for a solid month. That casket song, Mr. Jimmy Lee Rideout, is *all* we got. Hell, we don't even have that."

"Sorry, kid. Do me a favor, though, so we can put it to bed. Try whistling that thing."

"Oh, crazy, you're such a pain in the ass. That kind of song has feeling. It's all in the words. It doesn't need any tune."

"Let's not argue. Ruby, there's something bugging me, and we might as well lay it out right here and now."

"Me and John?"

"That's only part of it."

From next door they could hear Agnes in the shower singing "Engine Engine Number Nine."

He made her a drink and himself an ice water. "Ruby, there's a seventy-year-old ASCAP pensioner running around town in a World War One uniform. Calls himself Uncle Bone Driggers. He comes on doing hoot owl imitations and tree toads, then he moves up to crows calling across a cornfield, and finishes up with four or five hogs being slopped. The absolute worst. That horse's ass couldn't do twenty seconds on the Ted Mack show without getting the hook, but when John Harmon or Junior DeLoache sandwiches him in between two big numbers he really works. He can do three great minutes, but every time he does four—forget it."

"You saying John's sandwiching us?"

"I'm not saying it's bad. Honey, all I'm saying is don't let it set you up."

Ruby closed the Venetian blinds to keep the neon out. "Jimmy Lee, we're so green it's pitiful. You aren't going to stand there and tell me we can't learn anything from John Harmon. Because I'm not going to swallow that one."

"You can learn plenty." He popped three grapes in his mouth. "Take a look at the back-up men. Watch their faces when they go on and when they come off. You know what you'll see? Nothing, because nothing happens to them. They're just out there playing four or five chord changes and making a living. Then you look at Big John. That moron really burns it up; that's why for all his crap he's a star. He comes off that stage like he's on a horse and ready to puke from putting out. Those back-up men could go out and lay brick if they had a union card."

She watched him over her drink. He was flushed and talking fast. He meant what he said.

(211)

"The minute that bastard's in the light or near that mike he's on. You kids been coasting on charm and being earnest. It'll work for gospel down in the turpentine but not here. You got to jump out there and shake hell out of that crowd. And don't be blushing and carrying on like you're some kind of charity case. Smile at the son of a bitch and go along with his lard-ass jokes, but then move in and take that mike over and cut loose." He rolled in more grapes and spoke around them. "I bet you haven't listened to a single thing I said."

"Yes I did, Jimmy Lee. I declare I did. I'm going to watch him."

"And you're going to be careful?"

She watched her lips in the mirror and spoke slowly. "I'm going to be very careful."

At the high school gymnasium in Ophelia, Tennessee, the basketball bleachers were up and filled around three walls, and out on the double court twelve hundred seats were lined up from $1.25 to $3 each. Pronto pups, homemade barbecue, and beer were sold in the big hallway, and soft drinks, ice cream, boiled peanuts, and popcorn were hustled in the aisles by kids picking up twenty cents on the dollar. Tables at every exit were covered with autographed 8 by 10s of Big John, his paperback biography, and a foot-high stack of each of his eleven albums. At 7:50 the Muzak was cut off. Last-minute beers were bought and mothers began clucking in their broods. Someone dragged a whining dog out the side door.

The m.c. introduced the Baptist minister, who blessed the crowd in a record-breaking one minute flat and waved on the president of the Shriners, who asked for a round of applause for the sponsoring lodge, standing up with their red felt hats across their hearts. He then reminded everyone that the profits for the night, which included the Big John albums marked down from $6.69 to $4.99 plus an autographed picture, were going to the crippled children's hospital. He picked up a cue from the wings. "Well, you people didn't fight that parking lot and pay out good money to hear me run on." And smiling and waving at his family and fellow Shriners, he moved offstage. The house lights dimmed. The crowd shifted, quieted, and then sighed as the stage went dark. Then against the black backdrop a blue key light picked up John Harmon shoulder-rolling, and swaying in out of the wings.

> "I'm a truck-driving fool,
> Never been to school,
> I'm mean as dirt and stubborn
> as a mule. . . .
> Roll on, roll on."

His long slow stride was timed to the big bass back-up and he wheeled around, shotgunning his guitar neck at each bleacher and then straight out over the mike battery down the middle. He slicked the guitar back, working high up on the neck during the second bridge, then slid it forward, with one smooth motion backhanding the box into the rising twenty-four bar refrain. The crowd went wild, and the steel-reinforced concrete-with-glass basketball backboards and a forty-foot-high ceiling rocked with the big electric echo. Ruby, in the wings with both hands squeezing her guitar neck, forgot her stage fright as she watched him burning, sweating, pounding, and pouring it on. Singing "Truck-Driving Fool" like that made it his. When he sang it it stayed sung and was his because no one could touch it. Her mouth was dry, her knees and elbows trembled as she watched him hunched over his scooped yellow Fender, coiling the electric cord out like a bull whip. He was a born entertainer. He was exactly what Jimmy Lee had called him: he was a star.

She hugged Agnes. "Isn't he wonderful?"

Agnes's eyes were closed as she snapped her fingers and whispered the words along with him. "I've never seen such talent. They really love him."

The crowd wouldn't let him talk. He kept raising his hands, throwing kisses to the women and grinning and muscling out soft six-inch punches at the men. Still they wouldn't stop. He chorded hard, and aiming his Fender at Leonard and at Horace, the dobro man, he thumped hard into "The Mobile Run."

The audience settled fast and hung on every word and run that boomed over the four shoulder-high hundred-watt amplifiers. Someone shouted, "Play that thing, Big John!"

He grinned around a fast progression, talking to them through it. "Watch out, now. Watch out! *Got it!*" He flung his hands up as if he'd calf-roped a bull. The back-up men moved in to fill the hole as the crowd cheered and stomped, and a full five seconds of music was lost in the noise. John stepped back in for the finish, whipped off his hat, pushed his black hair back, and rubbed his face down with his red bandanna. He crouched over the mike. "Sisters and brothers, where'd you get the heat?"

They laughed back, and a front-row old-timer cupped his hands over his toothless mouth. "Should have been here last week, Big John. Hotter'n a mail-order stove."

He aimed a pistol finger at the old man. "That's hot, old trooper. That *is* hot." He wheeled around. "Leonard here gets the hives, but Horace don't feel a thing. Right, boys?"

It was their introduction. They smiled foolishly and hooked over, pretended to be tuning up. Big John spun his hat and cocked it low over one eye. "What y'all want to hear?"

Forty songs were shouted out.

"Whoa, now! Whoa! Let me think. Tell you what. Maybe we'll whomp up a big nine-song medley."

The applause rose again.

"But as the old man says, while I'm cogitating let's hear from a couple of the sweetest little gals in the sunny state of Tennessee, singing a great song of our old buddy, the Mississippi Blue Yodeler, Mr. Jimmie Rodgers." He slung his guitar back on its rhinestone-studded strap. "Folks, let's hear it for the Honkytonk Angels, Robby McCoy and Ruby Red!"

They pranced out, smiling and bowing, and took John's hands. "Sisters and brothers, this one under my left arm is Robby." They applauded. "And this cute little redhead powder puff is Ruby Red. Robby, tell the good folks what they're going to hear."

She pointed her chin at the tall microphone. "We're going to try—"

Big John laughed. "Sorry, honey." He telescoped it down.

"We're going to try 'Way Out on the Mountain.' "

(214)

"You do that thing now, you hear. Sit back, sisters and brothers. This here is *talent.*"

It was a simple straightforward arrangement right off the old Jimmie Rodgers record. It was perfect for them, and the audience was ready. Ruby backed off at the high parts and Agnes, her fingers sliding over the frets like they were walking, cocked her head and sang the old song right. A hush came over the crowd. The old-timer up front loved it and across the floodlights curiosity mixed with pleasure moved into his wary eyes. The applause was strong enough for John to hold them on and insist, with the audience cheering, that they do "Tennessee Rose."

Again they sang and again the crowd shouted and whistled. This time it wasn't as strong, and a voice knifed through. "We want Big John."

But it wasn't picked up and it didn't spoil the two minutes of solid applause as they smiled, bowing and backing from the stage. Ruby jabbed at Leonard with her guitar neck. "How 'bout that, fish face?"

"Drop dead!"

During Big John's next song Virgil came tiptoeing up behind Agnes with his fingers hushed to his lips for Ruby. He grinned and spoke bass. "O.K., you two. You're under arrest."

Agnes's mouth dropped. She wheeled around. "Virgil! Virgil, you crazy fool." She hugged him. "Where'd you come from?"

He kissed her hard and then hugging her with one arm brought Ruby in with the other. "You all were great. Check those hands. I almost wore them out clapping. That crowd solid ate you up."

Ruby said, "You mean it?"

"Damn right."

Agnes held on. "But when'd you get in town, fool?"

"About an hour ago. Jimmy Lee told me how to get here." He pulled back, shaking his head and laughing. "Lord, I wish you could have seen your face."

Virgil stayed until the show ended, said hello to Big John, and took Agnes back to the Capri Plaza.

(215)

Ruby sloshed rubbing alcohol on John's back and began chopping away at his neck and shoulders with the heel of her hands.

"Ow! Ow! Jesus, that hurts . . . no, don't stop."

"How's that?"

"Yeah, that's it . . . yeah."

She pulled his shoes and socks off. "Hunch up, hon, I'll get that belt off." She reached under and unfastened the buckle and went back to kneading his neck and spine.

"Mmm, mmm, lovely. Lovely. Don't let me go to sleep. Me and you got a date."

"I'm not going anywhere. Just take it easy now."

"Maybe I will. . . . Mmm, oh-you-are-so-nice."

She watched his wrists and arms relax and heard his breathing go deep and slow. His eyes fluttered and closed and she kept on rubbing.

She stood up, flexing her hands and pinching her shoulders to straighten her back. A stack of photographs were on the dresser, and kicking off her shoes she stretched out in the contour chair to go through them. One shot of John was on a porch step of a pillared mansion, another at a sweeping ranch house, another balancing on a split-rail fence, smoking and looking out over a herd of cattle. She wondered how much he was worth. Shots of him and Opry stars ranged from soft-focus 8 by 10s with Merle Cummins to Tennessee State Fair candid shots with Junior De-Loache or the Glipper Brothers and Snuffy. The older, yellower ones showed him thinner in his tapered form-fitting pink shirt with black piping. The newer ones caught him in baggy sweaters and loose Levi jackets. In Hawaii, shaking hands on the first tee at Mauna Kea, he was at his heaviest, with his extra-large, extra-long Tahitian print coming down six inches below his waist. He had lost some weight since then, but he still used the last notch on his big belt.

John slept for two and a half hours. He mumbled something about a gold record but she couldn't make it out. He awoke bright-eyed and thirsty. He had a fast double knocker of Wild Turkey and reached for her. Ruby offered little resistance and John liked it that way. He took her like he did his whiskey—

straight and fast. It was over before Ruby had even gotten ready. Under him, stroking his neck and back and lying to him, saying how wonderful he was, she made plans to make some changes.

Ruby stayed with John all night. In the morning they made love again. She kept whispering, "Slow down, slow down," and stretched his two minutes to five. When he finished she nimble-fingered down his neck and backbone and slapped him on the tail. She got up and made coffee.

John was up on one elbow watching her. "You know something? You'd make a damn good wife. You know exactly what a man needs."

"Not for you, hot shot. You don't know thing one about me."

"I know if you'd sail out of here I'd miss hell out of you."

"You could say that about a cocker spaniel."

"I'm serious. Listen, Ruby. I know what I'm talking about. You're my kind of woman. We're cut out of the same bolt of cloth. Everything about us matches up."

She poured the coffee. "Sugar?"

"Yeah, two. Look how you took hold in here. I tell you, you're exactly what I need."

She blew on her coffee and sipped at the edge. "And what do I need?"

He grinned. "Ruby Red, I wouldn't want to put words in your mouth, but you need John Harmon."

"Sorry, John, I'd need a lot of convincing on that one."

"Well, I'm the boy that can do it." He checked his watch. "I gotta be at Cherokee Records cutting a single. Want to come along?"

"Love to. Let me take a shower first."

He held her to him. His big hands were on her tail, cupping it to him. Her hands were in his back pockets. He kissed her nose, then her forehead. "What's that the preacher says? Cleanliness comes right after Godliness?"

She raised her lips to his. "Something like that."

At the Cherokee Records 17th Street studio, John introduced Ruby to the six-piece studio group looking over a new song called "Mississippi Morgan" about a gambler who had it all and threw

(217)

it away for love. The artists and repertoires man, Eutah Davis, who had chosen both Big John for the record and the studio back-up men for the music, adjusted John's microphone.

"How's that?" Eutah had on a striped T shirt with the sleeves ripped out at the armpits and a Coca-Cola in his back pocket.

"O.K. with me. How's your daddy?"

"O.K. That thing healed right back up. Can't even tell he had it."

"You say hello for me, hear."

Eutah slid a knee-high mike in close to Mule Owens, the lead guitar, pulled one back from the dobro man, and hurried across to the control room and his tape decks. His voice came out over the speaker. "O.K., Chauncey. Let's hear those drums."

Chauncey did a riff and banged the bass three times.

"No! No! Hell, that won't get it. They sound muddy. Check 'em, Chaunce. Check 'em out. . . . O.K., Miller, run down those vibes. . . .

"That's it, doctor. O.K., Chaunce, now you got it. Now hold it right there. Mule, dammit, put that sandwich down till the break! Ready, John?"

"Ready, Eutah."

"O.K., gentlemen, a one and a two and a three. . . ."

John, with his foot on a chair, winked at Ruby and dried his left hand on his pants. The rhythm slammed into the song and built for twenty-four bars, setting it up. Then the dobro and the drums softened and slid back. John moved in and climbed on top of the first verse fast. His morning voice was deeper than it was at night and the rich grain was right for the riverboat song. His strong lead pulled Chauncey, Mule, and the others in tight and he cocked his head at Eutah in the booth. Eutah flagged a circle with his thumb and finger as he worked the tape deck and sipped his Coke.

John came in on the second chorus for twelve bars before he suddenly stopped. "Dammit! I hit it wrong. That bass messed me up."

Chauncey said, "I'm sorry, John."

"It wasn't your fault. I forgot the damn words."

(218)

Eutah came on. "O.K., let's hear that demo again. Gentlemen, let's listen this time."

John handed Ruby two dimes and four nickels. "Get me an orange or a grape. And something sweet. Something with some chocolate."

Outside the sound stage Ruby was sliding dimes and nickels into the soft drink and snack machines. Around her agents, musicians, hangers-on, and drifters were drinking R.C. Colas and eating peanut butter and cheese crackers and watching the session through the plate glass. A short fellow in tight seersucker and meshed shoes was frowning. "I had me this doggone headache all day. That damn Molly had the TV on till two damn thirty."

No one was listening. A moon-faced stammerer stuttered, "L-L-Look at old M-M-Mule in there chomping down on that sandwich. He just finished breakfast. No wonder that fool's so f-f-fat."

Eutah's voice crackled. "Got it, John?"

"Got it, Eutah. O.K., sisters and brothers, let's make a record."

Eutah flipped a toggle switch. "Knock hell out of it, Chaunce. One and two and a three. . . ."

The seersucker fellow with the headache hooked his head. "That John's a pro's pro. Man, would I love to work with him."

"You and m-m-me both."

Eutah came on. "On the nail. Right on it. Gentlemen, we have ourselves a song. O.K., one more for insurance and we'll wrap."

Big John drank his grape and wiped his purple mouth. "This your first session?"

Ruby was so excited she gave up trying to pour peanuts into her Dr. Pepper. "How does that Eutah fellow keep track of everything? Lord, looks like he'd go crazy with so much going on."

John kissed her forehead and patted her tail. "I'll let him give you a rundown on what all's going on. He can explain it a helluva lot better than me." He slapped Mule on the back. "Nice going, Mule. How've you been?"

"No complaint, Big John. You hear I went and got married?"

"No, I sure as hell didn't. Who's the lucky gal?"

"Owen Perkins's daughter Thelma. We hollered at you one

night over at O. J.'s. You probably don't remember. You were with old Marvin."

"The hell I don't. Blonde gal, right? Kinda tall?"

Mule smiled.

Big John shook his head. "Well, congratulations. Now that's what I call a fine-looking gal. Mule, boy, you're a lucky man."

Mule stared at the horseshoe of crust he had left. "Damn right I am."

17

Agnes was hitching on her bathing suit top. "Here, do me."

Ruby buckled the back. "Hey, you're putting on weight. I swear it. It's those damn onion rings."

She turned, smiling. "Want to hear a little secret?"

A cold fist clamped down in Ruby's stomach. "You're preg."

"How'd you know? How'd you know, Ruby?"

"Oh, Jesus! What in the hell's wrong with you! I didn't drag you to Nashville for that. How in God's name are we going to get bookings? Ag, you got to get rid of it."

"Rid of it! Are you crazy? What do you think I am anyway?"

Ruby dropped down on the luggage rack. "This is the living end. Just when things were rolling for us."

"Ruby, it won't show for another month or so. We still got plenty of time. And I read where a lot of the stars were raised in guitar cases. Now where did I see that? It was somebody big. Oh, wouldn't that be cute. If it was a boy I could line the case in blue. And if it was a girl I'd do it in pink with little white ruffles."

"Agnes McCoy, you ain't got snake's brains. Why in the hell couldn't you all wait?"

"It was an accident, Ruby. We didn't plan it. I swear we didn't."

She looked at her own tight face in the mirror and then at Agnes's unblinking eyes staring at her. "Oh, Ag, you're such a moron."

Jimmy Lee whispered painfully, "Agnes is pregnant and John Harmon wants to marry you." He was sitting in the window chair eating potted meat out of a can and drinking an Orange Crush. The blinds were up and the sun was blasting in like mortar fire. "You sure there's nothing else? I mean like the doc told you to spring something on me when you figured I could take it?"

"No, that's it. How you feeling?"

"Don't change the subject. Ruby, I hope you ain't taking that creep serious. Move your clothes and magazines in, get knocked up if you have to perpetuate the Harmon dynasty, but, honey, use your head."

"Oh, fool, I'm just thinking about it. He swears he needs me. Hell, maybe I need him."

Jimmy Lee scraped the can. "What John Harmon needs is two gold records back to back and two months at Vegas."

"You don't know what you're talking about. You should have seen that crowd in Ophelia. He must have sold four hundred records. That place was jammed."

He ticked his fingers on the empty can. "If John played Ophelia three times a week for a solid year from here on out he'd go broke."

"Bull!"

"I mean it. He probably grossed four thousand. Take off half from the top for side men and expenses and you're down to two. Then there's John's old buddy Uncle Sam waiting on him with his April fifteenth hand out."

Her voice jumped. "He's got other things going. He cut a single yesterday at Cherokee Records. I was there when he did it."

"Honey, I don't want to sound like the messenger of doom on everything, but every cent John makes at Cherokee goes straight to the I.R.S. He doesn't even see it. And every first of the month he owes three ex-wives two thousand each. You think he's living in that Airstream because he likes it? That old boy is six foot three or four. You realize how crowded it's going to be with you in there with him?"

"I said I was just thinking about it. I wish you'd hush up."

Jimmy Lee tossed the can and the Orange Crush bottle in the wastebasket. "Tell you what. I'll phone Ruth Ellen and run you out there. I got to see her anyway. She's one of John's ex's. Maybe she can clue you in on him."

"Why in the hell should I go out there?"

"You might can see what you'd be getting in for. I'm surprised it wasn't part of that bus tour. John Harmon's three houses, wives, kids, and dogs are a regular Nashville institution."

"Well, I'm not going out to see any old ex-wife. Jimmy Lee, you're crazy."

"You remember 'One Man, One Gal'?"

"Sure, Ag and I sang it. She didn't record that?"

"Wrote it."

"You're kidding. I really like that thing. Jimmy Lee, if you're lying—"

"I swear I'm not. O.K. I'll set it up for tomorrow. We won't mention you and John. Maybe she's got some music for us."

A six-foot-high hurricane fence glistened in the two-o'clock sun circling the long brown and white aluminum-sided ranch house like a concentration camp barrier. A kid was swinging in a tire swing, another was screaming. Two coon hounds came wagging out and drooling. It was the ranch house that Ruby had seen in the photograph at John's. But since the time of that picture the place had changed. The red geraniums that had sparkled along the porch rail were gone; so were the green lawn and rose bed that John had been smiling over. The grass had burned, and bald spots of iron-hard clay looking like bathtub rings had taken over.

Ruth Ellen, with a two-year-old nose wiper at her side, pushed open the screen. "Hello, Jimmy Lee." She was barefoot. Her black hair was straight and tied in a clumsy doughnut. She could have been a wiper at the cotton mill.

"Hi, Ruth Ellen. You haven't changed a lick. This is Ruby Jamison."

Ruth Ellen's large dark eyes met hers openly. They didn't search or pry. "Hello, Ruby. . . . Well, you're certainly pretty enough."

Ruby liked her. "Thank you."

Her face was tired and strained but strong Cherokee Indian bones had saved her mouth and eye sockets from lining. Raymond La Mer would love her. If he photographed her from under her jaw, she would look like a Mexican queen or one of the old gravure pictures she had seen of Dolores Del Rio. Ruth Ellen smiled. Her teeth were large and blue white. "What's wrong, honey?"

"Didn't I see you in the magazines? Some advertisement or something?"

"Not lately. But thanks, anyway." She aimed the kid and patted him out the rear door. "O.K., Rhett, go play now."

She shaped and powdered her store biscuits and checked the oven heat. "Jimmy Lee, look in the icebox. Should be some beer on that bottom shelf." She laughed. "Unless you'd rather have Hawaiian Punch."

"What happened to your lawn?"

"I cut the water off and it burned up. Kids were driving me crazy with that hose. Look at that hallway."

In the hall two pieces of long flooring had humped up three inches and the quarter molding was curved out, gapping from the wall.

"They ran the hose in under the door. Ruined my wall-to-wall."

In the yard the screamer screamed, "Lemme alone! Lemme alone!"

"Where's Leo?"

"Fishing. He'll catch 'em, too. God, I hate frying that stuff in this heat."

A rubber ball began slamming against the kitchen wall. Another kid shouted, "God damn you, Lance! I'm going to fix your ass!"

Ruth Ellen was at the back screen. "O.K., O.K., let's hold that racket down." Four boys and two girls were leaping and swinging

(224)

on a hammock and climbing over the barbecue table. Rhett was at the side, delicately examining a large load in his diapers.

Jimmy Lee asked, "Which ones 're yours?"

"You saw Rhett. Oh, hell! Look at him. And those two on the table and that girl in the peach tree. Nice quiet bunch."

She shoved her self-rising biscuits in the 400-degree oven. "Y'all excuse me."

Ruby said, "She's really beautiful. How old is she anyway?"

"Thirty-six, thirty-seven. Ain't she, though?"

"What's Leo?"

"Big dumb stud. Picks at a guitar and just hangs around. He used to super at the Girard-Savoy."

Ruth Ellen washed and changed Rhett. "Sorry things aren't a little more organized around here. . . . You two going steady?"

"Off and on."

She smiled. "Same old Jimmy Lee. When you going to straighten out and fly right?"

"You never can tell. Those other kids John's?"

"Yeah, me and Darlene swap them back and forth and Louella sends hers over. She hasn't been feeling too well. How about giving her a ring, Jimmy Lee? She'd love to hear from you."

"I'll do that."

"How's John doing?"

"Looks good to me. Alimony coming through?"

"I'd have some help if it was. You know he stuck me with three of his coon dogs? I got a sixty-dollar-a-month dog-food bill."

"Well, he'll be hitting it pretty soon. He's overdue."

"Hope so. . . . Ruby, where you from and how'd you get in this rat race?"

Ruby sketched in her history and told her about the Honkytonk Angels. "Jimmy Lee told me you wrote 'One Man, One Gal.' It's one of my all-time favorites."

"Well, thank you, darling. Now ain't that sweet." Ruth Ellen looked over her beer. "John still hitting those truck-driving songs?"

He nodded. "And still going strong."

She traced her finger around the top of her can. "I'm glad he's got something he can hit fifty on. I hate seeing the old fat ones girdling up and bopping along on the moon and the June and the young love crap."

Ruby's heart sank and she felt herself shiver.

Ruth Ellen was at the window, watching the kids. "What happens when the public gets tired of all this wide track and double-clutching?"

"Damned if I know. You writing anything?"

A faint smile touched her lips and flashed in her Indian eyes.

He snapped his fingers. "I knew it! By God, I knew it. I figured you were up to something. You been quiet too damn long. Come on, Ruth Ellen. My girls are starving for something."

Her eyes tracked over to Ruby and back to Jimmy Lee.

He took her hands. "You can trust Ruby."

She pulled out three more beers, a new package of Kruncheeze and a cream cheese dip. "John ships this crap out by the case. The kids love it. O.K., Jimmy Lee, let me tell you about these songs." She explained how she and Darlene and Louella met for beer and exchanged kids. How at first no one trusted the other but how it all faded when they discovered they were all getting the same money each month or not getting it. "Then one night Darlene said she wondered what would John do if some new hotshot rolled in and pushed him off the truck-driving throne. Anyhow, we got to thinking about that. You should have seen us, Jimmy Lee. Three ex-wives sitting around in print dresses half stoned on beer and barefoot, with the kids running around the room like it was a monkey jungle. I think it rained for a solid week. . . . We went down the gospel lines, the old-time favorites, the new rock, everything."

"Groove."

"Anyhow, we figured John was too old for rock and too set to do experimental stuff and too big and slow to get on that Simon and Garfunkel route. The gospel show could have been good if he teamed up with a good preacher. But that cuts the money in half and they'd nail him the minute he took his first fifteen-year-old into that trailer. It looked like a dead end."

Ruby was beginning to hate her. The idea of the three blood-sucking leeches sitting around trying to wring money out of him made her want to slap her, stomp out, and flag a cab back to town.

"Then all of a sudden something hit me. A whole new thing. A brand new career with forty songs just waiting for that old bottom feeder."

It was all Ruby could do to keep a straight face and her lip from curling back over her eye teeth.

Jimmy Lee was tap-tapping his fingernails on the Kruncheeze box. "Come on, Ruth Ellen. Spill it."

"Big John simply plays himself." Her voice was flying. "He's funny, sad, appealing, a whore hopper, a son of a bitch, everything. He does stuff on his marriages, his kids, trying to marry us off, alimony, nut houses, visitation, our boy friends, the works. Everything, Jimmy Lee."

"Straight?"

"Absolutely. No message, no moral. Nothing but the straight facts and how it all happened."

"You might be on to something. Let's see the songs."

She hurried out of the room. Ruby whispered, "I hate her guts. Who in the hell does she thinks she is, anyway?"

"Keep your shirt on. We'll have a look."

Ruth Ellen dumped a stack of music on the table. "You read script, Ruby?"

"Little bit."

Jimmy Lee laid the first sheet flat and tapped out the rhythm to a hand-printed title, "Alimony Jail." Ruby looked over his shoulder at the nine key changes and the chord clusters that looked more like Concord grapes at the supermarket than the simple C and G scale music she had been practicing on. "How's it go, Jimmy Lee?"

"It goes great!" He ticked out a tune behind his teeth, skimming the four sheets fast. He backed up. "It's O.K. . . . O.K." He bobbed his head and in a small high voice sang

> "Down on the corner of Hoover and Dale
> There's a brick house called Alimony Jail. . . .

"Not only good. Damn good. Nice going, Ruth Ellen."

The second song was titled "Please Tell the Kids I Won't Be Out Today." The third, "Lost in the Mail," was about a post-dated check that had bounced three times.

Jimmy Lee kept flipping through, scanning the scores and repeating the lyrics. "You got some great stuff here, Ruth Ellen. Great!" He scanned a fifth score. " 'I'm on the Long End of Leaving and You're on the Short.' You're really cutting across some nerve endings."

"I want you to polish them, Jimmy Lee. I think I need a little bridge help."

"Maybe a shade." He made a fist and in slow motion softly punched her arm. "You got a gold mine here."

The kids were fighting in the back. "Oh, those goddamn kids." She went to the door. "Hush up out there or it's no TV tonight! AND THAT'S FINAL!" The kids kept screaming. "Y'all go sit in the den. I'll be right back."

They went down the water-spotted floor-sprung hallway to the den, which had been converted to a kids' room. Toys, blocks, jigsaw puzzles and foot-high wind-up monsters were on the tables, the chairs, and the window sills. The piano was covered with sweaters, socks, Pepsi-Cola cans, and popsicle sticks. Small handprints in chocolate had walked down the keyboard.

"Jimmy Lee, I can't stand her squeezing John nine ways like that."

"Ruby." He cupped his hands under her breasts. "If these were only brains." He touched one finger to her cheek. "That's an old music joke. You don't know the half of it."

"What's up?"

He rolled the twenty-eight pages of scores into a tube and sighted on the kids in the peach tree. "Not a prayer." And then, wearily, "They're all recitations."

"But all those chord changes?"

"Gravy. The stuff is nowhere."

"But you stood there and told her you loved them."

"What in the hell could I do with her breathing down my goddamn neck?"

"Well, do one. Let me hear how it goes."

(228)

"Sure." He brushed the keyboard off and played through thirty-six bars of "Alimony Jail." "That's it. From here on in it repeats. Groove?"

"Damn, Jimmy Lee, you can't just waltz in there and tell her they're lousy. Lord, I bet she put some time on those things, too."

"You bet your ass she did."

Outside two kids were still in the peach tree. One was spitting down on Rhett, who was rubbing it in his hair and laughing.

"I'll tell her they got possibilities."

"Bull! And then what?"

"Then comes the problem."

"Ruth Ellen Harmon, you are a genius!" He took her shoulders and staring into her brown eyes smiled. "They're great, honey. Great! Absolutely great."

She searched his face, looking for the lie, but couldn't find it. "You wouldn't kid an old doll, would you, Jimmy Lee?"

"No way, Ruth Ellen. You're sitting on six hits or I ain't standing here."

Ruby found herself smiling and agreeing. "That's what he told me, Ruth Ellen. I swear it."

Jimmy Lee went on raving and repeating the lyrics he remembered. "They're top of the charts, Ruth Ellen, the top. How about letting me move them for you?"

"That's just what I was fixing to ask you. Maybe they need a little polishing. We'll split it down the middle fifty-fifty."

"No, Ruth Ellen, you've done the work. I'll take twenty per cent and that'll be outright stealing."

"But they need some work and it's worth more than that to you. I insist, Jimmy Lee."

"O.K. We'll split."

"And you'll rework some of them?"

"O.K. I'll take a look. Won't take more than fifteen minutes. You've really done it, Ruth Ellen."

She dried her eyes. "Oh, Jimmy Lee, I'm so damn happy. I guess I got so close I couldn't tell what they were." She smiled. "There's a bottle of Wild Turkey around here somewhere." She was squatting

(229)

down to look in the cabinet under the sink. "I've got to keep it away from Leo. That fool will knock down shaving lotion if I let him. Here it is. Let's see what we can do to this."

Suddenly a bolt of lightning forked and danced out of the west, splitting a tall pine tree on the hill toward town. Thunder clapped and shook the house as Ruth Ellen went to the window. "All right, you kids! Get in here this instant!" The coon hounds began their long air-horn howls as the thunderstorm swept in from Kentucky and Missouri.

18

The storm pounding Nashville headed for Chatta-
nooga, picking up speed. By the time it cut the Carolina-Georgia
corner it was traveling sixty miles an hour and flash flooding every
river bottom, small creek, and fish pond. Billboards split; drain
pipes and downspouts were twisted and torn off, and telephone
lines whipped and snapped, popping off insulators all the way to
Savannah.

In Columbia the Congaree flooded the basement of the Pacific
Cotton Mill, and the driving wind smashed down Elroy Dixon's
$8,000 neon barbecue sign. In Spider's yard the water was up to
the first step and white rapids tumbled tin cans and Dixie cups
down the brick-lined drain. Spider lay stretched out on the couch,
drinking beer and watching the news. Virgil, his shoes off and his
pants rolled up to his knees, was at the door watching a twenty-
gallon garbage can pounding down the ditch. "Look! Look at
this!"

Spider raised up. "Jeee-sus. . . . Hey, see if you can get that
picture clearer."

Virgil worked the fine tuner. "Wind's slapping the antenna around."

"That's what I figured. Boy, call up Sandy's; they'll deliver."

"No. I got my jaw set. I ain't eating that crap any more. I want me some barbecue." He folded two newspapers together. "I'm hitting it."

"You damn fool, you're going to drown."

Virgil sloshed through the yard and jumped the ditch. The Cadillac started fast. He switched on the radio and windshield wipers and dried his face with his sleeve. He cut his twin stereo speakers on loud as Johnny Cash and June Carter doing "Jackson" came in from Charlotte, and making a skidding, mud-flying U turn up Cherry he headed for the Pig and Whistle House of Barbecue.

Johnny Cash's heavy beat flew down Cherry past the shuddering Coca-Cola sign in front of Preston's store on the corner and whistled over Maynard Moody's police car.

Maynard had the same station on. "I really love this song. Listen here when June Carter comes in."

Hooty Hightower, sweating in the back seat and looking through the streaking windshield at Spider's, thought he had to say something. "They're married, ain't they?"

Roebuck Alexander, sitting tall in the low Ford, had his hat in his lap. "Cut that trash off. We got work to do."

Maynard pushed his hand from the radio switch. "Hold your horses, Preach. I gotta hear this." His stubby fingers patted out the rhythm on the steering wheel into the finale. "Now that's what I call music." He cut it off and squared his garrison hat. "O.K. Spider's by himself. It shouldn't be a lick of trouble. . . . You ready, Hoot?"

Roebuck reached over and gripped his knee. "Tell Maynard you're ready, Hooty."

"Yessir, I guess so. Only thing is"—his voice trailed off into a whisper—"I feel like that dirty little coward who shot John Howard."

Maynard turned his lights on, then off, then on and off again.

(232)

Another car blinked twice and pulled up the street and parked. Hooty said, "Why can't we wait till it stops?"

Roebuck held his knee. "You got an umbrella. A little water won't hurt you."

Maynard sped his windshield wipers up. "Go on and get wet. That'll make it more convincing."

Roebuck's long hand moved from Hooty's knee to his shoulder. "Look me in the eye, Hooty."

Hooty raised his eyes.

Roebuck's blazed with righteousness until Hooty's dropped, glazed and beaten. "He's ready now."

Maynard slowed his wipers down. "O.K., Hoot, take a drink with him if you have to. Then buy a pint with that five-dollar bill I gave you. We'll do the rest."

Roebuck's voice was low. "And Hooty. . . ."

"Yessir."

"This is going to do wonders for you and your relation with the Lord."

Hooty stood dripping in Spider's doorway. His umbrella was ruined, the steel shafts sticking straight out, the black cloth flapping. Spider unbolted the door and unlatched the screen. "Hoot! What the hell you doing out in this mess?"

Hooty slicked the water from his smooth crew cut. "It's really coming down."

"I'll get you a towel."

As Hooty dried, Spider dipped him a drink from the bucket. "Wagon or no wagon, you're heading for pneumonia."

Hooty held the glass. He was shaking. "You know why I came by?"

"Save it. Come on, pop it."

He drank quickly and handed the glass back. "Hit me again. Reason is, I'm off the wagon."

Spider poured another. "You could have phoned me. Quendolyn know about it?"

"I'm telling her today." He spoke his rehearsed lines as if he were reading them from a card. "I can't be spending my life doing

(233)

only what she thinks is right. The way I figure it, Spider, I got my own life to live."

"Whatever you say, Hoot. Sit down, sit down. How's the plumbing business?"

He was eager to talk to cover his nervousness. "Pretty good. Pretty good. Put in fifty-four hours last week; that's fourteen overtime and every bit of it installation. You know I ain't been on a repair job since June? Everything's installation these days. I bet I ain't wiped a seam in nine months." They watched the television in silence. A used car salesman in Greenville with a trained English sheepdog who jumped from car hood to car hood during the sales talks was pitching his September clear-out sale.

Spider said, "Wonder where that dog would squat on a Volkswagen."

"Probably get up on the roof."

"Maybe he's got him trained to stand on his hind legs and sort of lean on the doorjamb."

"I wouldn't mind seeing that. It's really something how they can train dogs to do things like that." He looked around the room and sucked his teeth. "Wasn't that Virgil barreling out of here a minute ago?"

"There's his shoes. Fool's gone for barbecue. Stick around; they'll be plenty."

"No, I got to get on in." He pulled out a roll of bills and peeled off the top five. "Better let me have a quart."

"I'll give you two pints. Be easier to carry. Drinks are on the house." He gave Hooty two dollars back.

Hooty pushed a dollar back. "No, Spider, you got overhead and things."

"Forget it, Hoot. Old times' sake." He tucked the bill in his shirt pocket. "What's new down at old Washed in the Blood?"

"Oh, nothing, I guess, except Roebuck's show on the radio. You ever catch him?"

"Not when I can help it. Tell you what, you see old Mary Beth, you give her a pinch for me."

Hooty grinned strangely as he worked the bottles into his back pocket. The rain was coming down in sheets.

(234)

"Stick around till Virgil gets back. He'll carry you home."

"No, I gotta get on in. Besides"—he squeezed his umbrella spokes together—"I can't get much wetter."

"Well, get some dry clothes on—you look like you're coming down with something."

"O.K., Spider."

"Be good, Hooty."

Spider jumped when he saw the camera bulb flash. He rushed to the window and wiped away the moisture. Hooty was wading through the drain ditch and holding both bottles out to Moody as another police Ford pulled up.

He whispered, "Son of a bitch."

Maynard saw Spider looking and tossed him a soft salute. Hooty Hightower, sitting low in the back seat, slumped down below the level of the glass.

Spider unlatched the door, unhooked the screen, and, after punching three rhythm and blues selections on the juke, dialed AL 2-1600. He told the secretary to put him through to his lawyer, H. K. Jarvis.

Ruby, curled up behind John, watched the moon lighting the chrome edging on the table and the ceiling trim. An air freight to Memphis whistled by, rattling the glasses and bottles in the bar, and near the lake, where John had parked the Airstream, bull frogs and peepers kept hammering away at the night. She felt lost and drifting, and now with Agnes pregnant she knew it was only a matter of days before she was really alone. She traced her finger lightly across the seam in John's pajamas. Suddenly he jerked and thrashed out, making her scurry into the corner. He had gotten in the habit of sleeping in a sprint position across two thirds of the bed, with one leg straight out, the other tucked up tight. From the ceiling he looked like he was going over a low hurdle. She lit a cigarette and hunched down close to the ash tray as John, through a strangled snore, began counting off wives, kids, and dogs. He seemed to be matching them up, as if they were shifting and he had to get them straight. The names trailed out every two or three breaths, and buzzing underneath like faint riffs of a drum brush

(235)

was the mumbling accounting of incoming earnings and the arithmetic of three alimonies and two revolving never-ending bank loans. Suddenly he gagged. "NO! DAMMIT, NO!"

Ruby shoved him. "John! Wake up, hon! You're having a bad dream."

"What? What's that?"

She hoped he would stay awake and talk to her.

"Oh!" He slung himself sideways and was back asleep in seconds, snoring low and steady.

Ruby tipped her ash, wondering how he kept it all straight. Why it didn't drive him crazy. In his dreams he probably saw himself in a swamp of I.O.U.s and a three-view screen, each with a different wife and litter of kids, all wearing worn and torn clothes to make him look bad in the judge's eyes. All screaming, spitting, and sassing him, with their long hands out trying to claw and pull him down from the bright lights of the Grand Ole Opry. Poor John. Pressing her hands to the back of his thick neck, she felt him pulsing and tingling with the dates and due bill amounts that filled his dreams and drove him to the bed edge gasping for the floor air.

She mashed her cigarette out. If anyone ever needed anyone, John Harmon needed her. She imagined herself alone on stage. Her jaw was set and she swung around angrily, her hair swinging behind her. "If I'm sleeping and cooking for him I might as well be married. . . . You just don't understand anything. None of you do. A man who's been burned three times—hell, you can't expect him to turn on a dime and straighten out. He'll need time!" Her voice hushed and went deep for her final line. "The hell with all of you. It's going to work out fine."

Ruby sat on the contour chair, watching the red and green neon in the distance.

"Time." She repeated it. "Time." The record jackets were holding John at thirty-nine, but Ruth Ellen had said he was pushing fifty. He couldn't be fifty. But if he was, in ten years he'd be as old as Roy Acuff or Ernest Tubbs, the grand old men of the Opry. She remembered feeling embarrassed when Tubbs or Acuff sang of dashed hopes and young loves. Their strained and withered faces cocked up at the key light had nothing to do with the words and the thoughts behind the songs. It was O.K. for them to sing "The Wabash Cannonball" or gospel, but the love and crawling-into-bed-with-a-stranger songs should be left to Johnny Cash and Marty Robbins. She wondered what John would sing when he was sixty. . . . Still, he was better than nothing, and nothing was what she had. There would be the nights on the road, and the trips and the towns would all be exciting. Each night a different place, a different crowd with a new battery of flash bulbs aimed up at John on the microphone-stacked stage, long-striding and raring back and singing his heart out. She would meet the stars and their families. They would all be friends. Porter Waggoner would phone from Hollywood; Marty Robbins and Kitty Welles would come to dinner. Merle Travis would stop by with a string of fish. . . . Maybe she would work with John on stage. Bringing on the guests and making them feel at home, fixing the mike and holding the guitar while he talked or played mouth harp. They could be a team and wear matching cowboy and cowgirl suits. He would write and dedicate songs to her, and through his voice and guitar she would become famous and be written up in the country music books. . . .

She paused and whispered "Jesus!" And holding her knees tight she whispered, "You are out of your goddamn mind. That boa constrictor will wrap round you fourteen times and suck every drop of blood you got, then shuck you off like new skin in the springtime. Haven't you got enough troubles?" She opened a beer and tipped it at the moon. "Ruby, old girl, you better get with it." She reached for her purse and taking out her plastic reminder kit took a birth control pill for Sept. fifteenth.

With Agnes having trouble getting into her Bite Quik skirt and talking more about being with Virgil, Ruby knew that marrying John Harmon made more and more sense. She would be near the stars and producers and maybe get the break she needed, and if John got too rough she knew she could get a Mississippi divorce in a matter of hours. Fearing she might cool off and change her mind before he proposed again, she took the plunge at Mr. T Bone

(237)

while they were eating the chef's Surf and Turf special. The individual jukebox speaker in their booth was playing mood music from famous movies and John was splatting catsup over his double order of shoestring potatoes.

Ruby traced her finger around her wooden salad bowl. "O.K., John Harmon, you're on."

"On what?"

"Mr. and Mrs. John Harmon, fool. I'm saying yes. That is, if the offer's still open."

His left hand shot out and grabbed her right. "On! On! Did you say on? Lord, it's on now stronger than ever. Oh, Ruby, you swear you mean it?"

She nodded.

The neon reflected in his surprised eyes. "Oh, Ruby! Ruby! You really make me feel so—so—well, so doggone grateful. Damn, this is wonderful!"

She squeezed his hand. "You really are pleased, aren't you?"

"Am I? Am I? I don't know what to say." His eyes were glowing but his face didn't crease. All the attention and affection was in the eyes. He troweled up a mouthful of cole slaw. "I don't know when I've been so happy."

His back gold teeth flashed as he forked in the slaw and reached for the fries.

For a minute Ruby followed the Hollywood mood music, wishing she was in Nome, Alaska, and standing on the last rock looking out to sea, or down on the tip of the Cape of Good Hope, lying on the sand watching the strange South American birds diving for fish; anywhere away from John Harmon and his double order of fries and the catsup dripping down his chin. Then the next minute she was back, reaching over and wiping it off. "Oh, John, you're such a mess. You shouldn't take such mouthfuls."

He was chewing and making plans fast. "Hey, we gotta be buying you a wedding dress."

"Oh, I don't care so much about that. Tell you what I'd really like, though."

"You name it."

"John, I want to get married in Hollywood. I'd love that."

"Then that's where it's going to be. Now let's pick out a day."

(238)

He spread open his black date book. "Today's the eighteenth. Let's see now. . . . I can get out of here on the twenty-third. . . . I'll make old Cedric get us some bookings and we'll stretch it out for a couple weeks."

"John, you ever been married there?"

"Just once. Me and Darlene." He pushed away his greasy plate and held her hands on the map-shaped place setting showing how many Mr. T Boneses were located in Tennessee and Alabama. "It was out in the Valley, honey. You can't actually call that Hollywood. Me and you will do it right. Hollywood Roosevelt Hotel. Right on Hollywood Boulevard. Now by God, that's about as Hollywood as you can get."

Three heavy knocks sounded on John's door. He raised up. "Don't answer it."

It came again, six loud shots and then eight, followed by a strange scratchy voice. "I know you're in there, John Harmon, and I aim to see you. I traveled too many miles to give up now."

John threw open the door and slapped a bottle of Wild Turkey in his palm. "O.K., no closer. Let's hear it from there."

He was tall and wore a dirty white suit, a plastic modified Western hat, and a psychedelic necktie tied short and hanging long. His face was like the handkerchief and thumb characters that ventriloquists talk through. A thin smile touched his lips and his crazy eyes burned. "I've been trying to get at you for two years now. . . . You been setting on one hundred and forty of our songs and I aim to know what you intend doing with them."

Ruby whispered, "It's that Chinese name. You know—the yellow pages."

John said, "Our songs? I only read one name. Moong, right? Chang Moong. Why'd your mother slap that name on you?"

"My mother's been long gone to glory. She wasn't studying that name." He looked Ruby over carefully and then, sucking in his boneless face, took two long steps forward. "I had me a name change out on Route One-o-one. California Route One-o-one." His hat was tilted forward, and he craned his neck back to see better as he looked over the trailer and the empty lot behind him. "'Bout this kind of day. 'Bout this kind of light. I was a Bob

Whiter, that's trade for a potato chip and pretzel route. I was coming down the grade just out of Salinas, heading for Fresno, when the Lord spoke to me. Told me to pull off the shoulder of the road. I whupped that Dodge Dart off like he said and I sat there a trembling. I thought it was the Judgment Day. 'Drew,' he said—that was my name back then, 'Drew Horne—I've had my eye on you and I've decided that me and you are going in the song-writing field together.'"

Ruby looked around to see what Chang Moong was driving. There were no cars around. Hamburger and candy wrappers were caught and fluttering in the hog-wire fencing, and a long, short-legged dog moved along the hedge shade.

"The Lord said the first thing I had to do was change my name. That's where Chang Moong came from. It's not so local, like, and you don't forget it. Drew Horne looks like a tombstone name; it just sort of vanishes. Mr. Harmon, Mrs. Harmon, right there on that spot I made a solemn promise that out of my own pocket I'd buy a mimeograph machine and we'd write and mail out one hundred songs a week. I'm here to say I haven't missed a time. As of last month we're over nine thousand."

John sat on the stoop. "Brother Moong, the gospel field's been rough lately. Too many old ones around that they just keep re-releasing. It's tough sliding in a new one."

"Well, I didn't figure it would be easy when I took on the load. I just want it clear you people ain't turning me down, you're turning down the Lord's work. . . . Reckon you could spread that around?"

"Sure. Be glad to. Better still, you go down to Acuff-Rose. Tell Roy I sent you. That rascal's been looking for some good gospel and he'd be a natural for it."

"Oh, he would be wonderful, Mr. Harmon. Wonderful. I been sending him stuff steady." His hat came off and he stuck his hand out. "We appreciate this. You won't be forgotten, Mr. Harmon. I know exactly where I can find Roy Acuff, exactly."

"And you say hello for me."

"Yessir, I'll do that." He backed off, then turning suddenly began double-timing across the open lot.

19

"Listen, Ag." Ruby had borrowed Jimmy Lee's electric shaver and was crouched on the luggage rack, trimming back the pubic hair that stuck out of her bikini. "John's promised we can do two songs on every show he does. You realize what kind of exposure that is?"

"Ruby, you're going to itch like crazy when that starts growing out."

"The hell with it. I'm tired of looking like an orangoutang. . . . You hear what I said about John?"

"I heard. Crazy, you aren't marrying him for that, are you?"

"No, I kinda like that fool. He needs somebody steady like me around. No lie, this thing might really work out."

"I don't know, Rube. All that alimony and kids and all. Jimmy Lee says he owes everybody breathing."

"Jimmy Lee better stick with his typewriter. Hon, he doesn't know thing one."

On the twentieth and twenty-first John made no mention of plane tickets or reservations at the Hollywood Roosevelt, and

Ruby began feeling relieved. But on the night of the twenty-second, when she couldn't sleep and sat by the window, watching the razor-edged moon slicing through the clouds and listening to John's whistling snore, she wanted to look around and see their luggage packed and ready for California. She felt cheated, as if something had been taken away, something she knew she would never have again. She felt old and fragile, as if she didn't fit anywhere or belong to anyone. A chill touched her neck and a strange weariness came over her. Part of it was her period coming on, but most of it was a strange and heavy feeling of loss.

The twenty-third came and John said nothing about Hollywood until she brought it up. He took her shoulders lightly and shook his head. "It's no go, honey. Something's come up. Hell, I might as well let you have it straight from the shoulder. Because that's the way it's going to be between us from now on. I'm behind on alimony and we're going to try and work something out."

"How much?"

"Not much. Eight thousand dollars. I've told Cedric to make me some fast dates around here. Honey, I don't know when we're going to be able to go to the coast."

"Well, don't worry about it now. Does that pay everything?"

"Afraid not. That's arrears. There's seven thousand current, and the goddamn bank is squawking for forty-five hundred on a note I signed."

"Jesus, John!"

"No big deal. I'll play a few dates and resign the note. It'll work out. Nothing to worry about. What I really need is a couple of hot singles." He hooked his thumbs in his belt loops and, rolling his lips, sucked his front teeth. "Maybe I'll buzz out and see Marvin."

Ruby didn't want to ask the next question.

"John, how soon we getting married?"

He flipped through his book. "I'll need a week to get this legal junk out of the way. Then another two to do the shows. . . . Three and a half, say four weeks." He held her shoulders again and pulled her to him. "Then it's California, here we come."

Ruby stayed close to him, burying her chin in his throat. "What

(242)

if I said I wanted to get married here in Nashville? It doesn't matter that much. We can always go to Hollywood."

He kissed her forehead, then her nose, and tilted her chin up. "Honey, I just thought it would be better for both of us if we had a little time to relax after the ceremony. If we get married here it's going to be between sets with all kinds of crap going on. But Ruby Red, if you want Nashville that's what it's going to be."

"I don't unless you do, hon."

"I want us off on the right foot. If we can fly out to the coast and buy a couple of things and maybe stretch out on the beach a few days, it sure would be nice. Hell, we might find us some songs out there."

"O.K., John. I can wait."

Agnes was singing "Detroit City" and washing out her bras and underwear and hanging them on the shower bar. "Know what, Rube? That's a song we could use. It's got a nice beat and I ain't heard a soul singing it lately."

"O.K. We'll try it in the morning." She lit a cigarette.

From the rear Agnes looked like she'd gained ten pounds and it had all settled in her hips. Her back zipper was wide open on her Bite Quik skirt. "Lord, Ag, you're really putting it on. You sure Virgil doesn't expect something?"

"So far, so good. You're right, though; nothing fits me. Maybe I can lose some before he comes back."

"Fat chance."

She hung up her last pair of panties and dried her hands. "Come on now, what's cutting you up so? Is it John?"

She nodded, "It's sick, Ag. Sick. The more I can't have that rat-running son of a bitch, the more I want him. I ain't ever been like that. I swear I haven't."

"Maybe you ought to go home for a while and think it over."

"Bull, that's the last thing I'm doing."

"Well, at least he's not slapping you around."

"He wouldn't hurt a flea. It's just, dammit, I keep getting the feeling we aren't getting married."

"Maybe you're better off."

(243)

"That's where it's all so crazy. The minute I know it's off I want him. Then, when it's on, I don't. I'm cracking up, Agnes." She mashed out her cigarette and checked her eyes in the mirror. They were red-rimmed and bloodshot. "I'm taking me a nap. I look like I've been strangled."

Big John, dressed in his red and black polka-dot dressing gown, stood before his mirror, fingering his guitar and practicing the introduction to "So Long Mama." He smiled broadly.

"Now, folks, here's an old one and one of my absolute favorites." He creased his face in concentration and hit the big G seventh. Cocking his head and easing the grin off his two black molars, he held the guitar box up close to his ear as if listening to something far away and delicate. He'd picked up the trick from Lester Flatt, but where Flatt was listening Big John was acting. He knew it looked good; as if he was pouring his life and soul into his rhinestone-studded Martin D-28. Ruby sat on the sofa, flipping through a stack of old *Lifes* and *Looks*.

"New trick, John?"

"Like it?"

"Looks like Chet Atkins."

"Look a hell of a lot better if I had some decent songs."

"I know it, sugar. Wish I could help out, I swear I do."

He talked on as if he hadn't heard her. "If something doesn't break soon, the sheriff's going to be the next one knocking on that door."

"I didn't know it was that bad."

"Well, you know me. I like to take a pretty hopeful view of things and—well, hell, I just don't like talking about my problems."

She stacked the magazines and put them in the rack. "I still bet anything old Jimmy Lee can do something. Lord, I saw him write one in about four minutes one night. No lie. I was sitting there watching him."

"He's dry. Forget him." He dropped into the contour chair. "Hand me a beer."

(244)

She opened the icebox. "I don't believe in that dry-period crap. Most of the time it's plain-out-laziness."

"It's like sex, dumpling."

"Well, you sure as hell ain't dry on that."

"Was until you came along."

She jumped on him, tickling him until he thumped down on the floor and rolled out, bellowing, "No more! No more!"

She crawled after him, pinching and tickling until he collapsed in the corner, laughing and pleading.

"Stop it! Stop it! Please, honey, please! I can't stand it."

She sat on his lap and blew in his ear and poised her fingers over his ribs.

"No. No. Please! Ruby Red, you really kill my soul."

"Now tell me you can't live without me." Her fingers inched up his ribs.

"No. No! Stop it! I can't live without you," he shouted. "I can't."

"Now say it like you mean it."

"I just did."

She tickled him.

"No! No!"

"Say it again."

"No! No!" He held her hands. "I can't live without you. Now for God's sake stop it. I'm going to have a stroke." She nibbled his throat and he cupped her face in both hands. "Ruby, I ain't never going to let you go. You hear me?"

She snuggled in close. "Hon, there must be something someone can do about some songs. You sure you been trying around? I mean, really trying?"

"Everybody's sitting back waiting to see which way the wind's blowing. I gotta find a girl for Marvin." He barked a two-note laugh. "Great, isn't it? Only gal who could swing it and the only gal I'd trust with him is the gal I'm fixing to marry. Funny, isn't it?"

"Funny as strangling to death." Her blue eyes went hard as she cut the radio on. "It's hilarious."

(245)

"Oh, Ruby, for God's sake. You don't think I'd send you out with that wing-ding just to get some lousy songs?"

"No, John, I guess not." She patted his shoulder. "Wonder what it would be like with a creep like that for a month? Probably couldn't get it up more than twice." She laughed. "I'd get more rest than I do around here. Hell, maybe he can cook."

"Don't joke about it, honey. Drop it. Just drop it. Let's catch a movie."

"O.K."

A thin chill ran along her arms and legs as she combed her hair and clamped on her beret. "Anything good around?"

"We'll find something."

In the Lincoln, heading downtown against the six o'clock traffic, Ruby kept changing stations, dodging commercials and listening to the country and westerns that crowded the dial. She knew she couldn't push John, but something hard in her egged her on.

"I just did a little mathematics. Say Marvin comes up with six songs and they're worth thirty thousand each. I mean, long term, if they're hits. . . . That's almost two hundred thousand."

"Will you please drop it." He sounded straight, but something told her he wasn't really telling her to stop.

"I ain't exactly going to wear out. That's still a lot of money."

"You saying you're considering it?"

She caught the way he was holding his voice firm. "I'm thinking about it."

"Damn, Ruby, I don't want you doing something like that. What do you think I am anyway? Jesus, what would people say?"

"They'd say we were damn smart if we pulled it off, and damn fools if we didn't. But how do we know Marvin can produce?" She saw his eyes in the rearview mirror darting up and down and read him like a magazine ad. She could almost call the words and where the cough would come.

"Ruby, I don't want to be talking about this."

"John, I got a lot at stake here."

"I've said it once, I'll say it again. This is my problem."

"It's our problem. Now face it. I sleep with Marvin for a few

(246)

nights and, well"—she baited the trap and cocked the spring—"it won't be the first one."

He cleared his throat and walked in cold. "But it will sure as hell be the last." He pulled off onto the shoulder and held her. "Ruby, I'll take an oath and swear before God Almighty, if you do this for me—for us, I mean—we're getting married the minute you come back. And I'll tell you something else: we're getting married with or without songs. Hell, I'd even marry you before you go."

She wanted to tell him that the mountaintop month with Marvin would make a fine honeymoon, but all that came out was "O.K., John, something's got to be done." His arms around her were squeezing too hard; his voice was whining, pleading. It was a side of John she had known was there, but now she was sorry she'd seen it. He had waited for her to suggest it, then backed off until she insisted, and then nailed her. He kissed her hard and held her tight as the Nashville-to-Chattanooga traffic whined down the Interstate and the big semis rocked the car as they thundered by. He was a real pro. She hated him.

After the movie and dinner, Ruby watched John as he bowed and waved and smiled in the mirror, rehearsing his number. Nothing was natural with him. Not one line was ad lib, not one gesture hadn't been planned, and she knew if she had to hear another of his "Howdy, sisters, and howdy, brothers" she would throw up. "John, you ought to try something new."

"Like what?"

"Why don't you try being yourself?"

In the mirror he was practicing his finish and walk-off on "Loving and Lying." "Wouldn't know where to begin."

"You could start by being a prick. Then you could work your way up."

He chorded a G seventh and ran his tongue over his teeth. "How'd you like a fat lip?"

She was stuffing her things into her Delta Airlines zipper bag. "You're really a pretty amazing character when you get right down to it. Too bad you missed your calling. You'd have made a great pimp."

(247)

He held the door open. "Come on, Red. Clear the hell out of here till you feel better."

Outside Ruby set her purse and bag on the ground, picked up a brickbat in both hands, and slammed it against the door. "You rotten pimp son-of-a-bitching bastard. As far as I'm concerned you can—you can go to hell!"

She started across the oil-spotted gravel, sniffing, crying, and cursing, holding both bags and trying to blow the hair out of her face. A heel broke and she squatted down to put her shoes in her bag. And then, sitting down in the damp grass, she spat back at the big chrome Airstream. "You son of a bitch. You stupid son of a bitch."

Ruby was at the vanity, working on a Hollywood "Name the Stars" crossword puzzle. Agnes was lying flat on her back with her hands on her stomach, listening and feeling for movements.

"Ruby Jean, you sure you didn't work on his nerves? A fellow like that with all those pressures is liable to say anything."

"Come off it, Ag. This ain't no Sunday school class. The hell with him." She hitchhiked her thumb at the wall. "Anything new with that fool?"

"He's been whistling and beating time. Maybe he's got something going; he's just as nice as pie."

Ruby chewed on her ballpoint. "Guess he figures I'll be breaking down his door now to get in bed with him." Her voice caught and when she looked up her eyes went large and she bit her bottom lip.

"Ruby, who you like best, Byron or Duane?"

"Who you talking about?"

"Names. I'm getting up some boy names."

"Oh, bull."

"Ruby, what in the world's the matter?"

"It's my birthday and nobody gives a good goddamn but my dumb old mother."

Agnes sat up. "Why didn't you say something? I'd of gone out and bought you some little silly or something."

"It doesn't matter."

(248)

"Sure it does. I'd be hurt if it was me." She stood behind her with her hands on her shoulders. "I declare, no one would ever think you were twenty-three." She caught her eyes in the mirror. "How about that guy at the Zombie Club—he didn't even think you were eighteen."

"Oh, they always pull that crap. It sets you up."

"You're such a dope. That fellow works the floor; he doesn't make a dime for doing that. You're just low. Let's go for a walk someplace."

"Like down the road shoulder? Every truck driver in town will think we're hustling." She creased her thumbnail down her cheek and watched the mark fade. "You know when you get old it takes hours for the red to go like that. Oh, Agnes, I can't stand the idea of getting old. I'm so light. I'm going to age so fast it'll be pitiful. You ever see a redheaded old lady? They look like dried-up little old nothings."

"We're the same age, fool."

"Yeah, but you're dark and you got Virgil and security and a baby coming and all. All I've got is me. Nothing." Tears were in her eyes. "How'd I get so old so fast? Seems like it was last week when I was messing around the bus stop and wondering what happened to nineteen sixty. That was eight years ago. It's scary, Agnes, it doesn't seem that long ago. I swear it doesn't."

"You're just low. Come on, put your suit on. At least we can sit by the pool."

"O.K., maybe I'll get lucky and drown."

At the pool they stretched out on the chaises, watching two ten-year-old boys silently skinning the cat under the one-meter board. The rest of the pool was empty. Twenty yards away the semis, flat beds, and Greyhounds rumbled by on the slabbed concrete, heading north toward Chicago and west to Kansas City. They lay still, watching the heat exhaust foreshortening the used car lots and the deep-fry franchise shops lining the Murfreesboro Pike into Nashville. Above it was light blue; farther up, dark. Seashell clouds with sun catching ice edges were sliding in from the north, and the slow thin plume of a 707 was holding tight as it scribed itself west across Davidson County, Tennessee.

(249)

"Ag, you ever been to Lookout Mountain?"

"No, but I aim to one of these days. We could go from here. It's only a hundred miles."

"Spider took me there once. It was so clear and nice. You could see all the states they advertised. Seems like it was five. Then we took in Rock City and Ruby Falls. He let me buy all kinds of kewpie dolls and Smokey Bears and crazy things. We really had a good time. You know, I'm getting so I kind of miss that old fool. Wonder who's cooking for him?"

"Probably no one."

"No, he's got someone. He can't stand living alone. Gals would line up to get a deal like that."

A red-faced truck driver shifted down and tapped out three notes on his air horn. "Hey! Hey! Looka there! Looka there!"

Ruby smiled and waved. She laughed. "That'll keep him charged up till the Late Show."

Agnes sat up, examining her toenails as if she were reading directions. "Ruby, you think you still like Spider?"

"I don't know. You know what he gave me for my birthday last year? A big four-hundred-dollar Zenith. I could get Hawaii and the Scandinavian stations on that thing. And on top of that a three-foot-high koala bear. And talk about cute . . . that thing wouldn't quit. Wonder why he doesn't even send me a card?"

"Probably slipped his mind."

"Probably the new gal put her foot down." She stood up. "I'm hitting it." She dove in, swam across the pool and back twice, and then, diving straight down until the water was too cold and her ears began thumping, came up. Pushing her hair back, she climbed out and stretched out on the chaise. A wet newspaper lay under her, opened at the entertainment section. She read through the movies and the TV schedule and then, carefully turning the page so it wouldn't tear, scanned the night club news. Marty Robbins, Merle Travis, Bobby Gentry, and Mel Tillis were all in town. Roger Miller was still packing them in in Vegas. A picture in the bottom right corner caught her attention. Two women in their heavy forties with big doughy faces were smiling out, showing every available tooth, their small eyes so bright and merry they seemed painted in. "The Happy Two," Ruth and Ellen Sawyer, were celebrating their twentieth year on their 6 A.M. radio show and were thanking the Nashville area for their acceptance and many cards and letters. "Take a look at these two." Ruby's voice went high and nasal. "'Our prayers and thanks go winging out to you in radio land.' Jesus, how's that for inspiration?"

Agnes knelt down. "They're so plain looking. Poor old things."

"Been eating those self-rising biscuits so long they're beginning to look like them."

Agnes laughed. "That Ruth's got to be a size twenty."

Ruby lit a cigarette. "The Happy Two—wonder who sponsors them?"

"Some breakfast something or other. Probably a bacon or sausage factory. Those gals cooking for the mill hands and the sawmill crowd are the only ones up that early."

Ruby giggled. "I guess the Happy Two hit the sack pretty early." She bit the inside of her lip. "You know something? That's the exact way a lot of stars get their start. I mean it, Ag. They do these jerky morning shows, pick up a following, and the next thing you know they're doing solo stuff on the Opry and got their own show on TV. Now how in the hell you reckon a pair of plain old dogs like that got their foot in the door?"

"I thought those shows were all records."

"Naw, lot of them want that personal touch. You remember that idiot in Columbia on the piano. Always laughing and carrying on with his 'Oh, What a Beautiful Morning.'"

"Rube, if we had us a morning show I could take the kid along with me. Lord, we wouldn't have any trouble at all."

"Oh, yeah, you and that kid."

Agnes checked her watch. "It's three o'clock. I gotta take my medicine." A minute later, she stuck her head out the door. "Hey, Ruby! Long distance!"

Ruby clutched her top close as she trotted up the sidewalk. Another air horn and wolf whistle came from the highway. "Hey, Red! Let it all hang out!"

She hipped the door open. Suddenly it seemed the room was on fire. She gasped, jumping back, almost dropping her bra. A big

(251)

red and white cake sat before the triple-view mirror and sticking straight up were twenty-three foot-long sparklers, hissing, sputtering, and lighting up bottles of champagne, ice, glasses, and presents. She wheeled around as Jimmy Lee, Virgil, and Agnes, who were standing on the bed, jumped down shouting, "SURPRISE! SURPRISE!" They sang:

"Happy birthday to you,
Happy birthday to you,
Happy birthday, dear Ruby,
Happy birthday to you."

The big square cake was white with the outline of a red guitar across the middle. Under it in three-inch-high letters was Ruby Red. Ruby held her bra up with both hands as they kissed and hugged her and spun her around. "Oh! Oh! Wow! Tie me up, Agnes! Y'all scared me to death! It was like an explosion. Virgil, where'd you come from? I thought y'all didn't know. Oh, Jesus, I'm going to cry."

Virgil was pouring champagne and passing out the glasses. He raised his. "To Ruby, the best-looking redhead that ever came out of the Carolinas and the best goddamn singer in the world." They drank.

Jimmy Lee leaped up on the bed. "To Ruby—the grooviest gal that South Carolina ever put on the market, and the best thing that's ever happened to Nashville, Tennessee." He pulled Agnes up. "Your turn, honey."

Agnes was in tears. "Oh, Ruby. I had something ready, I swear I did. My mind's blank. . . . God bless you. Oh, Ruby, ain't it nice?"

Ruby was crying and holding on to Agnes. "Oh, it is, Ag! It is!"

They drank, poured and toasted, and drank again. Agnes had bought her a pink sweater trimmed in seed pearls with a mink collar. She put it on over her bikini and wouldn't take it off. Jimmy Lee produced three dozen American Beauty long-stemmed roses out of the bathroom and Virgil a white velvet-lined mirrored box with brushes and three combs. Everything was pink trimmed in

(252)

white, and on each piece was a big R under a thick raised rose. He gave her an envelope. *For Ruby, Happy Birthday, Love, Spider.* Enclosed was a check for $1,000.

"Wow! A thousand dollars! Look, Agnes, Jimmy Lee. Look at that! Oh, Lord, this is too much. Wow! That crazy old Spider!"

Jimmy Lee put his arm around her. "And now I'm taking you all out to dinner. And I don't mean no Tennessee deep-fry. I mean dinner with meat and a salad and dessert *à la flambée.*"

Agnes giggled and hugged Virgil. "Listen at him."

Jimmy Lee raised his glass. "And maybe a little more champagne." His lips thinned and broke into a grin. "As a matter of cold fact, I have another little present here in my pocket." He held out a typed note, announcing in a deep disc-jockey voice, "Ruby Jamison and Robby McCoy, eleven-thirty A.M., Saturday, September twenty-eight, Seventeen-sixteen Tenth Street, Nashville, Tennessee. I wonder what it is? I can't seem to make it out."

Ruby snatched it from his hand. "Oh, my God! Ag! We're auditioning at Holiday Records! Holiday! Wow!" She flung her arms around Jimmy Lee and kissed him. "You little scamp. You planned all this, didn't you?"

"We all did."

"But why so much at one time? No one's been this nice to me. I can't take it all in." She pulled out a Kleenex and brushed her hair back from her eyes. "Why? Why'd you do it?"

Agnes pushed Ruby's hair back. "Because we love you, fool. Ain't that reason enough?"

At the Continental Cafe, featuring French, Chinese, and American cooking, Agnes buttered a hot cross bun. "This is a great place. We ought to come here more often."

Virgil sat back, sipping his whiskey. "This one's on me, Jimmy Lee. Me and old Spider have immortally been coining it these days." His eyebrows flattened. "Honey, you look different. You putting on weight?"

Ruby's heart sank. She spoke quickly. "You better talk to her, Virgil. She's been eating candy and fried foods hand over fist."

Agnes smiled. "Tomorrow morning I'm going on a crash diet."

After the Bite Quik route they rehearsed "Honkytonk Angels" and "Midnight Special" until their fingers were raw. Jimmy Lee sat in on Thursday. "Ruby, you're pushing too hard. Listen at Agnes. You get way the hell off by yourself. The stuff's got to cook together or it just lays there."

Ruby sang softer and concentrated on blending with Agnes. It felt better and when she checked Jimmy Lee he touched his finger to his forehead. "Better, much better."

Agnes's eyes went hard. "Better? Is that all?"

"I guess I'm getting too close to it. I only heard it five thousand times now."

Ruby dropped her guitar on the bed. "Let's take a break. My fingers are about to bleed."

Agnes propped her guitar up in the corner. "Wouldn't it be wild if we really hit?"

He peeled off his glasses and began polishing them. "It's been known to happen. And once you do, the club dates will bury you."

Ruby arched her back and stretched. "I'd love that. Oh, I'd love to be buried like that."

Agnes yawned. "I just pray we're going to be good."

20

It was Friday night and Ruby was too nervous to sleep. Jimmy Lee made her take a hot bath and then rubbed her down with alcohol while she watched the Late Late Show. "Jimmy Lee, I'm 'bout to jump right out of my skin. You reckon Agnes is sleeping?"

"Must be. I don't hear 'em screwing."

"But what if we ain't no good tomorrow? What happens then? Jimmy Lee, I don't want to be a Bite Quik girl or have to go back to Southern Bell. I swear I don't."

"Doll baby, three months ago you never dreamed you'd be in Nashville, let alone auditioning for a record company. Now isn't that a fact?"

"It is, but it doesn't help. I'm scared to death."

"Wait'll you hit that first G."

"Yeah, I'm going to throw up right in the goddamn box."

"Oh, be still and loosen up. My hands are tired."

"Hey, right there. Keep rubbing in there. There, that's better."

He leaned in with both hands and worked the small of her back and the top of her tail. "Nice?"

"Mmm, nice. . . . Ooooooh. You been taking lessons someplace. . . . Oooooh, do some more."

He rubbed in silence for a while. Ruby sighed and wiggled. "Jimmy Lee, you can make love to me if you want to."

"You sure it's O.K.?"

"What do you mean?"

"I mean, you're all bathed and everything."

"God, you're a moron. Come on and turn that fool set off."

At eleven o'clock Saturday, Ruby, Agnes, Virgil and Jimmy Lee arrived at Holiday Records on Tenth Street. Ruby and Agnes combed over every picture in the lobby showing the stars of Holiday and the glass cases of gold records they had produced there. They read the Grammy plaques out loud.

Jimmy Lee bought everyone Cokes and when Billy Hargrove, the artists and repertoires man, came out he introduced him around. Billy was fat with a wide hog nose and combed his hair straight forward to hide his high hairline. He and Jimmy Lee were old friends and had worked together on sessions for nine or ten years.

Ruby was so frightened she couldn't taste the Coke. She thought she had to go to the bathroom, but once there and seated she knew it was a false alarm. She felt she had a fever and checked her eyes and tongue in the mirror but knew it was cold, simple unadulterated fear. Agnes had been right about her pubic hair. She had scratched it raw at the edges. It was itching now.

Agnes was smiling. "Isn't it complicated, though. Look at that thing. Wonder what it does?"

"I don't know and I don't care. You ain't nervous at all, are you?"

"I guess not. And I thought I'd be sick as a dog."

Billy was positioning three mikes around them.

Ruby was dying to ask how and when they were to start. She opened her mouth but Billy spoke first, smiling and calming her. "It's simple, girls. Simple as one, two, three. You just start playing

(256)

and I'll be back there with Jimmy Lee and your other buddy. Now, warm up just as long as you want; we got all day. Then just give me a nod. I'll do the rest."

Ruby asked, "That's all there is to it?"

"That's it. You're in charge of this show; nothing gets taped until you say so. Understand?"

Agnes said, "Yessir."

Ruby nodded and began tuning. "Let me hear your E, Ag."

"How's that?"

"Got it." She chorded a G and tightened the A peg. "Hey! I'm O.K. I'm not nervous at all. Ain't Billy nice, though. Jimmy Lee says that scutter knows more about this business than any man breathing. He handles all the stars."

Their guitars were ready and Ruby adjusted her strap. "O.K., now whoever gets set first winks. Then the other signals. O.K.?"

"O.K."

The playback box buzzed and squawked. Billy's voice came on. "Testing, one and a two and a three and a four and a five. . . . O.K. O.K., Honkytonk Angels testing. Take one when you're ready." His smooth, reassuring voice flowed like syrup. "O.K., girls, this is nice and easy. No pressure. No hurry. We got all day. Ain't that right, Jimmy Lee?"

Jimmy Lee waved and leaned into the mike. "Nice and easy, girls. Nice and easy."

Virgil joined in. "Give 'em hell."

Billy laughed and cut in. "O.K. out there?"

"Yessir."

"All right, now. Pick around a little and let me know when you're ready."

Agnes gave Ruby the beat and they came in together on four. Ruby smiled. She was loose and free and her voice came out where she wanted. She heard herself blending and folding in under Agnes's strong lead and knew they had never sounded better. It was the way Jimmy Lee said it would be when they were right. Agnes climbed up fast and, bobbing her guitar every two beats, cocked her head at the mike as if she'd been there a thousand

(257)

times. In thirty-six bars they were right and Agnes winked. Ruby wanted to giggle, it all felt so right.

"We're ready when you are." She winked at Jimmy Lee. He grinned and saluted back with his Coke. They finished the refrain and came in at the top of "Honkytonk Angels," strong and smooth, and stayed on top with no holes or cold spots.

Jimmy Lee laughed. "All right, girls, kick it."

After two takes on "Honkytonk Angels" and two of "Midnight Special" Jimmy Lee and Virgil came clicking across the high-gloss floor. Jimmy Lee was snapping his fingers and popping his hands. "Great, kids! Great!"

Virgil kissed Agnes and put his arm around Ruby. "You're a lead-pipe cinch. Christ, you're going to be multimillionaires before you know it."

Jimmy Lee was wiping his brown and white shoes like a charging bull. "This is it! Damn if I can't smell contracts. Ruby, you were a smash."

"And wasn't Agnes cool? You see her?"

"A pro. A pro. Billy wants to see you a minute. We'll meet you in the lobby. Come on, Virgil, let's me and you find a beer."

In Billy's office the thin green hall carpet changed to a thick-pile maroon. The walls were covered with 8 by 10 glossies of Nashville stars shaking hands and hugging Billy or smiling out from under big white Stetsons and diamond tiaras. He sat them down in deep leather chairs with matching ottomans and flicked the blinds, throwing the sun stripes to the floor. "Good session. You kids know what you're doing." The tape was in the center of the glass-topped desk. "I'll play it for you." Agnes looked at Ruby, and Ruby winked. She watched Billy mount the tape on a built-in recorder. He didn't seem pleased or displeased. He didn't seem anything. He threw a switch and looked up smiling, waiting for the music to come on. It was too loud and he jacked it down and balanced the bass. Closing his eyes, he listened with his hand cupped over his left ear. He gazed hypnotized at the top corner of the room molding, tapping the rhythm with his fingernails and lipping the words to the refrain. "Midnight Special" ended and he smiled broadly. "Nice, very nice." He rolled his head from side to

(258)

side as if he had an earache, but Ruby knew it meant nothing. He was still deciding. She wondered if she should wink at him or smile. It wouldn't do any good. He wasn't after her. She felt off balance, as if the muscles in her body were going one way, the bones the other. She smiled and he smiled back. But it was a strange mouth smile, with little light in the eyes and the dry skin around them remaining stiff and dry.

Finally he spoke. "You like it?"

Agnes brightened. "Sounded fine to me. That's a nice recorder."

He looked at Ruby, but she could do no more than meet his gaze and force a smile. She had nothing to say. He pulled out the drawer and propping his feet leaned back in his chair. He looked straight up at the ceiling, showing Ruby his throat, his chin, and the red lining in his wide nose. "Girls," he began slowly. "I'm going to tell you a story."

Ruby's legs flashed; the nylon crossing sounded like paper tearing.

"We had this baseball pitcher up in Minnesota—that's where I'm from, Minneapolis, Minnesota." Ruby wet her top lip and watched his nose hair. She dug her fingernail into her thumb. "This guy had everything. Height, range, speed, heart—he had it all, in spades. Pitched four no-hit games and had a string of shutouts as long as your arm."

Ruby knew that the Minnesota pitcher hadn't made it and the story would soon turn over and it would be the Honkytonk Angels. His eyes were still on the ceiling. His nostrils dilated as he spoke.

"This guy was so fast you couldn't even see the ball." He tipped his seat down and leaned forward. "Then one day a Chicago Cubs scout came up to look him over. He watched our boy work an inning or two, and when the coach asked him what he thought you know what he said?"

Ruby sighed. "I got an idea."

He went on as if addressing a third party sitting between them. "Said the kid was good, very good, maybe even great. And then he said that great wasn't good enough. He said we need to get them when they're sensational. That way we have something to start with. In other words, something they can build on."

Ruby sat back. "I knew that fellow wasn't going to make it."

Billy smiled quickly and continued. "And that's what I'm going to tell you girls. You're good, you're damn good, but you aren't sensational, and that's what we need. You got to be sensational just to get in the line-up around here. Now, girls, I don't want to hurt your feelings or get you discouraged." He leaned forward as far as he could and looked at Ruby, then Agnes, and back to Ruby. "But facts are facts. I'm not saying you can't make it in Nashville or out in the San Fernando Valley or that you won't record some day. All I want made absolutely clear is that in my opinion—and mind you, it's only my opinion—you just aren't quite ready for recording at Holiday."

Jimmy Lee shaded the sides of his eyes from the bouncing sun. "Screw, I really thought we had it. You sounded great. Great!"

Agnes's jaw was set firm. She kept kneading Virgil's right hand as he drove. "Oh, Lord, I don't know. I just don't know. We sounded so good to me I couldn't believe it. I swear we did. Lord, I'd hate thinking we don't have enough talent."

Virgil squeezed her knee. "You got more talent than the whole goddamn studio back there. Ain't that right, Jimmy Lee?"

"Right, and Billy Hargrove isn't the only A and R man in this goddamn town." He looped his arm around Ruby. "That's what I'm doing, honey. I'm lining some more up. This is crazy business; you can't go on what just one man says. Hell, they used to kick Hank Williams out on the street and hope a car would hit him. Boy, if someone wanted to write a real book that would be the place to start."

"Thanks, Jimmy Lee." Ruby was watching the wind kicking over the colored plastic spinners announcing two cents off on Texaco. "Funny, I liked that moron at first, then I really started in to hating him. He didn't have to draw things out like that and give us that static about the Minnesota pitcher."

Jimmy Lee said, "What was that all about?"

(260)

"It doesn't matter. . . . I'll bet that jerk really hates women. Is he married, Jimmy Lee?"

"Yeah, since high school. Three kids."

"That's it, then. She's cut him off and he's pissed at anything with a pair of legs."

"Could be, Rube. Yeah, it could be. He kind of keeps her in the background."

Agnes turned around and sat backwards. "What are we going to do, Ruby?"

"Let's me and you go buy a couple of new outfits. Something different, something flashy. Maybe a coral or a wild green."

Virgil slapped on the dashboard. "Good damn idea! It'll take your mind off that Billy Hargrove or whatever he calls himself. I'm a good mind to whip back there and give him an ass full of foot."

Ruby shoved her shuffleboard disc, but a kid had been doing cannonballs from the board all morning and had soaked the court; it stopped short. "Hell, this isn't fair. You're twice as strong as me."

Virgil crouched, aiming. "Quit bitching. I'll spot you five points."

Agnes was floating in the pool on her plastic dinosaur. For three days Virgil had stayed in town, trying to talk her into coming home. She had promised she would give Nashville only two more weeks. She hadn't told him she was pregnant.

Ruby pushed harder. "Virgil, I been calling Spider all week and no answer. He isn't out of town, is he?"

"Probably in Augusta."

"Well, give me that number. I got to thank him for that birthday money."

"Why don't you write him a card?"

"I want to talk to him, that's why. He ain't sick or something, is he?"

Her black disc nudged his red out of the five-point square. She took his jaw and moved in front of him. "Look me in the eye, Virgil Haynes."

He jerked around. "Dammit, stop that."

"I didn't hurt you."

"Well, I don't like being handled like that."

"Virgil, there's something you ain't telling me."

"Oh, Jesus, what a pain in the ass. I've told you nothing's wrong. Now come on, play the game."

"Spider's in trouble, ain't he? Otherwise he'd of been here for my birthday or called or wired or something. Come on, Virgil, you might as well cough it up or I'm going to make some phone calls."

"O.K., Ruby." He hung his stick in the rack and took hers.

She was pale. "He's O.K., isn't he? You weren't lying about that, were you?"

"He's all right physically. . . . O.K., Rube. Moody caught him and Judge Wheeler gave him a year and a day. He's in the pen."

"A year! A year! Oh, my God! That'll kill him! Virgil, you got to be kidding."

"I wish I was."

"But why in the world didn't you tell me? I could of been down there seeing him and taking him food and things."

"He wants you to have a shot at Nashville without worrying about him. Those were his exact words. I swear they were."

"But you should have known better. You could of told me. Oh, you men are the living end."

They sat at the pool edge as Agnes breast-stroked toward them. He pulled her up. "Jesus, you're getting heavy."

"I know, ain't it awful. What's wrong?"

"Ruby knows about Spider."

She shook out her hair. "Honey, Virg says he's O.K. They're treating him real nice down there."

"Yeah, I'll believe that when I see it. Oh, I just hate this. Here he is sending me money and that poor sap's lining up with a tin plate and living behind that ninety-foot wall."

Virgil stretched out, leaning on his elbows. "Kershaw's getting him out on weekends. Rube, he's even got a corner cell all by himself."

(262)

"Great. That food's going to kill him. Spider can't live like that."

"He's got a hot plate and those little boil-in-the-bag jobs. It's one helluva lot better than that mule shit they throw at you in that chow line, I'll damn well clue you on that."

Agnes said, "Tell her how he got caught."

"Hooty Hightower pimped."

"Hooty!"

"Bought a bottle with marked money. Moody met him in the drain ditch with our old buddy Roebuck. Short and sweet."

Ruby rolled her lips and bit them. "He didn't have a chance. I'd of sold Hooty anything. Oh, poor Spider, that's the end."

"Guess who the first visitor was with a Smithfield ham and a watermelon? Came down in tears."

"You wait till I see that miserable son of a bitch."

"Could have been worse. That trial been next month he would have been looking up at Judge Stackpool. Been three years easy."

"Oh, damn, I can't stand it."

"Well, there isn't a thing you can do about it."

"I can sure as hell go see him."

"You ride it out here and get a good spot singing someplace. Then when he gets out you'll have something to show for it. You go back there and mope around, and it'll just bring him down. I tell you, Ruby, all he talks about is how you're up in Nashville and how you're going to be a star."

"Well, I got to see Mama anyway. Who'd Spider move in when I left?"

"Something called Billy Lou or Billy Lee. I never got it straight. Won some tabacco or canteloupe festival about fifteen years ago. A real zero. Sits around all day listening to talk shows. And lie—Jesus, you never heard so many lies in your life. She parlayed that canteloupe crown into runner-up for Miss Universe."

Ruby sat forward, hugging her knees. "I remember her. Short little frizzy blonde with a funny squinched-up mouth?"

"She's blonde, all right. Mouth sounds like her. Looks like a cat's ass. And talk—Jesus! Didn't matter what you were talking about, she's squirreling in how some congressman or governor told her how beautiful she was and what a fool she was not to get out of South Carolina and go up North where she could make money on her great beauty. . . . I used to call her Scarlett O'Hara. That really pissed her."

"She still there?"

"Spider gave her a few hundred and ran her out. I drove her up to the Greyhound. Said she was heading west."

"Who came in after her?"

"Nobody, that was it."

"Come on, Spider ain't going to be alone without a woman for no two months."

"Well, I guess he got to looking in at Cora's. Listen, don't you be telling him I told you all this. We got enough troubles."

"I'll say I got it from Mama. What time's that flight on Friday?"

21

Ruby left at noon on the southbound Delta. The airlines were busy shuttling infantrymen between Fort Jackson and
Macon Training, and she was ticketed only to Atlanta with a
stand-by on Piedmont to Columbia. After three hours of reading
movie magazines, brushing her hair, and writing postcards, she
decided to take the Southern Railroad the 280 miles home. The
train left at seven-thirty.

She stamped the card to Agnes and looked it over.

Dear Ag,
   I bet everything's groovy at the old C. Plaza. Do you miss me yet?
At least now you get first shot at the big towels. This card will probably
get to you before I get home. Couldn't get a plane to Col. so am
taking the train. Keep on top of J. L. about the music and out from
under V. (ha ha).

She clicked her ballpoint down and underlined the ha ha and,
drawing a stick figure of herself dancing, signed it "Me."

Her mother's panoramic view of "Seven Flags over Georgia" was
written large to cover the big card.

Dear Ma,
This card will probably get to you before I get there. Couldn't get a plane to Columbia and I am taking the train. I'll tell you all about Nashville when I see you. I hope you are feeling O.K. and everything is all right.

Love,
Ruby.

She decided not to underline "all about Nashville."

Spider's card of two bathing beauties with forty-inch breasts pointed sideways, holding peaches and locks of cotton and looking out at Stone Mountain in the distance, was too big for a six-cent stamp. She put on two and addressed it to the State Penitentiary, 1501 Gist Street, Columbia, South Carolina.

Dear Honey,
Mother told me everything on the phone and I am on my way to see you now. You're crazy keeping this a secret from me, but I guess you know that's not exactly the hottest news in the world. I'll buy you some things that I'm sure they don't put on that menu down there. In the meantime, write me up a list of everything you need or want to read. . . . Guess this is a good chance for you to go on that diet (ha ha). . . . How do you like the pin-up girls? There's some great ones of Raquel Welch but I'm not going to give you one of those. I can't stand the competition. Or can I?

Love,
Ruby.

In the club car, Ruby watched copies of *Playboy* and the *Atlanta Constitution* lower as she legged through to the bar in her white vinyl micro skirt, jack boots, and her Hollywood wraparounds. One man sucked in and whistled a long single note. She loved the sound and felt it running down her spine and clenched her teeth to keep from smiling. She molded her hair in the back bar mirror and ordered a Miller's High Life and a pack of Tom's peanuts. She had washed it that morning, and in the slant sun rays it was shining the way she liked it. Swaying through the footrests, the magazine racks, and the combination ash trays and serving tables, she took the last seat in the car.

The sun had softened as it sank over the tracks, heading west,

(266)

and streaks of purple, red, and gold lay across the Atlanta skyline. She took off her sun glasses and arching her back shook her
hair free and stretched out with the heel of her left boot on the
toe of her right. She wouldn't think about tomorrow or the next
day or the day after that. She wouldn't think about anything except
which one of the men had whistled at her and what was on the
supper menu.

As the train slowed down for its first stop, a man sat next to her.
"Whew! Mind if I join you?"

"Not at all."

"Damn porter told me the bar was in the back, but he sure
didn't say twenty-seven cars." He had a singsong in his voice, a
rhythm, almost as if every line was a sales pitch. He spoke rapidly,
running his words together, and she had to listen close to hear
everything. "That's some walk, you know that?"

Ruby said, "Didn't know the train was that long."

"Longer, they got two engines pulling her. Where you heading?"

"Columbia."

"Is that a fact? I got a good friend on Rosewood out near the
drive-in, Elgin Simmons. He's in the mattress renovating business. That's a sharp outfit you got on. A real knockout."

"Thanks. I know a Veda Simmons. Sets hair out at the Forest
Lake shopping center." She knew there would be no getting rid of
him and decided she might as well save her money. "Want to buy
me a beer?"

"Delighted. That's what I like, someone that speaks up. Name's
C. C. Blackwing. I'm in sales."

"I'm Ruby Jean Jamison. I've been working up in Nashville."

"Music?"

She smiled. "How'd you tell?"

"I got ways. You just feel like show business."

"Well, tell me what you sell. Maybe I'll buy something off you."

He crossed his hairless ankles. "Too bad I left my samples in
my room." He laughed once. "No, I'm just fooling around. I sell
manufacturers . . . polyethylene, that's my game. You know,
sweater bags, vegetable bags, bread bags, things like that. Georgia-
Carolina Plastics. We cover Dixie like the dew. That's our motto."

(267)

The porter filled her glass and thanked C. C. Blackwing for the dollar tip. Outside, a mixed flight of sparrows and doves were perching together on a stretch of four-strand power lines, looking like whole notes and quarter notes. "Want to hear a little secret? I never fly. You want to know why?" He didn't need an answer. "Guess I'm like old Will Rogers; he's before your time. He used to say he never met a fellow he didn't like."

Ruby started to say she'd bet Will Rogers had kept out of Nashville.

"You know something, little lady? Everybody's got a story. You agree with that?"

She licked beer foam from her lips. "You can say that again."

"And that's something you just don't get when you're flying. Hell, no. First of all you're sweating too much on that take-off. You realize that ninety per cent of your crashes take place at take-off? That's a fact; you can run that one down."

"I read that someplace. That's where that Cincinnati crowd got it."

C. C. nodded. "And O.K., so you get up in the air. Next thing you know here comes the stewardess throwing food and pillows and magazines at you and plugging you into those happy, no-crash tunes on Muzak so fast you don't have a chance to even look around. You ever see anybody change seats in a plane? Hell, no, they just sit there like bumps, praying they're getting down safe." He laughed and clipped down three-fourths of his bourbon. "Once in a while you wind up sitting next to someone you think might have something to say, but nine times out of ten you're wedged to the wall by some harelip trying to load you up on mutual funds." His hand shot up for the porter. "That's why you find this old roscoe traveling on the Pullmans. I like to move around and pick and choose who I'm going to talk to." He ordered another round. "Take a looker like you on a plane. How's a chump like me going to meet you if you're jammed in between some piece-goods salesman and a Bible College student? Only chance I got is to catch you going to the john."

Ruby was smiling into her beer and watching the tracks shining as the last slice of sun vanished. The long rows of September

(268)

cotton were pink in the red light. "O.K., C. C., now you got me. You seen any good movies lately?"

"Honey, I've seen them all." He recrossed his legs and tugged up on his short flesh-colored socks. "I can't go that honkytonk routine. So every night after supper I catch me a movie. Then when I get home on Saturday I generally take the wife and kids to a drive-in. Movies are my middle name. That Hollywood crowd can't crank 'em out fast enough. Tell you what, you name one and if I ain't seen it I'll give you a dollar. If I have, you give me a dime."

"O.K. . . . *Barefoot in the Park.*"

"Saw it in Valdosta."

"Owe you a dime. . . . *Cincinnati Kid.*"

"Twice, once in Augusta, once in Tallahassee. Want me to tell you about it?"

"No. . . . Hey, you really move around, don't you?"

"Florida, Georgia, and both Carolinas. A hundred thousand miles on a new Olds Ninety-eight every year plus all this train traveling. Come on, give me some more."

"You're too good on that one. Name me five male stars that begin with B."

He reeled off without thinking. "Bogart, Beatty, Belafonte, Bridges, and Bill Boyd."

"Never heard of him."

"Cassidy. Hopalong Cassidy. Guess that's a few years back. O.K., make it Bogarde, Dirk Bogarde; now there's a fellow that can act."

"Jesus, you flew through them. You must have a photographic mind. O.K., try me."

"All right, female stars beginning with H."

"Audrey Hepburn, Katherine Hepburn, Kim Hunter, Olivia de Havilland, and—and—and . . . Oh, I can't think. H. H. . . ."

"Want a clue?"

"No. Hayworth. Rita Hayworth. I saw her on the Late Show. I didn't know she could dance like that. No wonder all those rajahs and oil tycoons were sniffing around."

C. C. drank. "One of the all-time greats."

They went through the Rs, the Ws, and the Ts. C. C. didn't

know that Warren Beatty and Shirley MacLaine were brother and sister or that Connie Stevens had divorced Eddie Fisher. Ruby didn't know that John Wayne had actually played football or that Joan Greenwood was born near Atlanta and was Miss Peach Festival one year.

C. C. drank four more bourbons to Ruby's two beers. He told her how good business was since the bread industry had gone all out for polyethylene bags and about the big scare in '64 when polyethylene hula hoops died off. He said then there was too much around; now there wasn't enough. Today it was a seller's market. Prices were up and holding, and a salesman didn't have to come in with his hat in his hand to get an order. Purchasing agents had been forced into being human beings. The last streaks of light went from dark blue to purple and the tracks vanished. C. C. went on about how he had spent a year and a half out in Kansas working on a dog-food account. "You know, some people eat that stuff. I'm not putting you on. They slice it up and add onions and—"

Ruby didn't want to hear about it and interrupted, telling him the movie *In Cold Blood* was shot in Kansas. "Did you see that one?"

"See it! See it! I visited the doggone house out near Garden City. Used to drive by it every day. Course I never knew the Clutters; that's the family Perry Smith and Richard Hickock murdered. I think he was in the farm machinery field."

"You really went in there after the murder?"

"Damn right. You had to get in line for that one. Man, now talk about an experience. . . . Ruby, you could see the actual blood and hairs. People came from everywhere. . . . I even read the book. The movie didn't even touch it." He pulled out a black book and clicked his ballpoint. "You give me your address and I'll mail it to you. That's what I call a great piece of writing. A classic. You really felt like you were there. And you talk about your descriptions, that fellow Capote can't be touched. Tell you one thing, that thing sure cured me of picking up hitchhikers. . . . I bought another of his books, *The Other Voices and the Other Rooms,* but I couldn't cut that one. Too fancy for my taste. Sorta prissy."

(270)

"So you really saw the house. Lord, I can still picture that place in my mind with those big old trees swaying in the wind. That must have really been something."

"Wait till you read the book. It's all there, every speck. The movie doesn't hold a candle to it. The wife and kids are through with it, and it just sits there picking up dust. . . . Wait a minute." He rolled over on his hip. "Let me show you something." He riffled through his Diner's Card, American Express, Carte Blanche, three oil companies, and Blue Cross and came to a series of family pictures. He laid it out on his hand. His wife, a flat-mouthed, large-eared girl with sad small eyes, was holding a bridal corsage and smiling at the camera while C. C., much slimmer and in the arrow pointed lapels of the forties, was cutting a big wedding cake. "Now there's the little woman." He snapped the back of his fingers against the plastic as if he were laying down four aces. "Vital! Absolutely vital! And kids . . . take a look at this trio."

Three dark-haired boys with C. C.'s eyes and his wife's mouth were standing stiffly in front of a mantelpiece. Above the mantel was an oil painting of the wedding picture. C. C. fingered the oldest. "Wayne. All A's in everything and never cracks a book. Hell, I can't even pronounce the stuff he reads. A genius. The principal said he was a natural genius. He'll probably wind up being a research physicist or something like that." He tapped number two. "Anthony, we call him Tony. Plays anything you give him: piano, accordion, mouth harp. He's the musician in the family. You talk about kids, I got 'em. . . . This is Wyatt. Coach says he's the best all-round athlete he's ever laid eyes on. Quite a group, isn't it?"

"They're real nice. You must be mighty proud."

The porter sounded three notes on a hand xylophone and announced dinner. C. C. kept staring at his wife and him on one side of the flap and the three boys on the other. His voice broke and went husky. "Greatest kids in the world. Greatest little woman." He snapped it shut. "O.K., no more family, no more business. . . . I'm buying you the highest-priced thing on the menu and the best goddamn bottle of wine they serve on the Southern. Tonight you're eating on Georgia-Carolina Plastics."

"We cover Dixie like the dew?"

"We cover Dixie like the dew."

The steward seated them with a couple in their seventies who had gone in half-stepping ahead of them, holding on to one another to keep their balance. The lady, short and stooped but with bright nearsighted eyes and a fresh blue hair rinse, read the menu out loud to her husband, who had on a hearing aid. He kept looking around behind him.

"George, for heaven's sake, listen."

"I'm listening." He focused on Ruby and C. C. and in a voice that was almost a shout said, "You see a lady with a little blue dog back there?"

Ruby said, "Yessir, a little poodle. Cute, wasn't he? They call them teacup poodles. You talk about something expensive. . . ." She touched C. C.'s hand with her butter knife. "That's the kind of dog Mia Farrow loves so."

George slapped his battery at his belt and shouted, "They ain't letting it eat in here, are they?"

His wife touched his lips. "You're too loud, George. Now hush up about that dog. It ain't none of your business."

C. C. spoke clearly, emphasizing every syllable. "No sir, they don't let dogs in a dining car. There's a Board of Health ruling on that."

Ruby watched George. There was no telling by his concerned eyes how much he heard.

The wife zeroed in on Ruby. "My name's Ethel. This is George."

Ruby said, "I'm Ruby." She nodded to her left. "C. C. Blackwing."

Ethel hooked in over the table as if to spring across. "I've never seen a blue one before. I bet you anything that woman dyed it, and you see her wearing those strap shoes and all that make-up. I wouldn't put it past her for a second."

Ruby was reading the menu. "I've never heard of someone dyeing a dog. I think they come like that."

C. C. said slowly, "It's not exactly blue. It's sort of gray."

George heard part of it and nodded. "Never did like those little

(272)

yippity ones. Always nervous and looking like they're getting ready to puke." Everyone in the car stopped eating to listen. Suddenly he picked up volume as if he'd been shoved. "Give me a bird dog or a coon hound or a bloodhound, or a foxhound." The veins in his neck were like ropes. His face was purple as he screamed. "Give me a goddamn-dog-that-can-do-something!"

The steward rushed over. "Madam, you'll have to keep him a little quieter."

"See there, George, I told you." She shook a finger in his face.

He slapped it away. "Dammit, I heard him." He whacked his hearing aid. "Bastard keeps cutting in and out."

Ruby laughed and salted her celery. "Those little teacup poodles really cost the money."

Ethel winked at Ruby, trying to hedge her into a private conversation. "I bet you anything that gal thinks she's the Queen of the May. I just know she's not from around here."

George stuffed his napkin under his chin and smoothed the corners into the armholes in his vest. "Write down chicken for me, only don't let 'em pour any of that damn sauce over it. And I want some potatoes and some greens. None of that sour cream mess; I want butter. . . . And get me a beer in a can." He slid his long ropy hands on the table as if a meeting were beginning and smiled broadly. His mouth seemed to stretch to his ears. "Where you folks heading?"

Ruby started to speak but his thin arm reached out and grabbed a passing porter by the sleeve.

"Yessir."

"You know that lady couple cars back with that little dog?"

"Yessir, that's my car."

"I know that. What I want to know is where she takes that little thing to the toilet."

The porter knew he was in trouble and leaned in, trying to keep his voice down. Ruby elbowed C. C. and bit into a bun to keep from laughing.

"Well, sir, she gets off at stops and she walks him."

"Hell, any fool knows that." He held on to his sleeve. "How

about at night. A little high-strung skinner like that can't hold it for no eight and ten hours."

His voice was gaining in volume again. The porter whispered, "Not so loud, sir."

"Don't you fellows have some little something for him then?"

"Yessir, they got a box with some shavings in it. . . . Sir, I've got to get back. Will you excuse me?"

"Not until I'm through with you, young fellow." He gripped tighter as his voice rose. "I seen a fellow up in New York City hold his dog right out of the window so he could take a leak. Must have been up five or six floors. Damnedest thing I ever saw in my life."

Ruby bit down hard on her napkin. C. C. had invented a combination laugh and cough and was shaking all over.

Ethel leaned over George and pointed up with her sharp nose and salad fork. "We both saw it. On the New York Central Railroad coming right down the very center of that town. And I mean that fellow was as white as me and George here put together."

George's hearing aid must have died. He boomed out, filling the car. "Hee-hee-hee! I guess that's New York City for you. I'll just be goddamn if I see how people live like that."

The porter shook his head and pulled away, drying his eyes.

The train was running fast and smooth over the flat piedmont, and the rising moon threw the club car shadow far out into the tall corn.

C. C. stayed with bourbon on the rocks after dinner. Ruby switched to Scotch. A one-filling-station town slid by, and a kid in pajamas waved from a lighted window. Ruby waved back. "Look! Ain't he cute? I used to do that. I used to wave at everything. . . . You ever live near the tracks?"

"No, we grew up in town. On top of a service station. I can still smell the hydraulic fluid."

"I used to watch the waiters and try to figure out what they were serving and try to see what the women were wearing."

"Right by the tracks?"

"About as close as you can get. And you talk about something

(274)

shaking, that little old dog trot almost came off its brickbats. We couldn't keep windows in it for nothing. And you know when the freights came through, the furniture would start crossing the floors."

"No kidding."

"I mean it. We used to have to push all the drinking glasses to the back of the shelves." She touched her glass to her teeth. "It would just break Mama's heart. She had her this little glass collection, you know giraffes and ballet dancers and birds, mostly birds, and about every three or four days one would slide off the chifforobe or bump up against something. Lord, they were so thin and tiny almost anything would break them."

"My aunt used to keep them. They were thin. I think she had swans and some angels. Seems like they were smiling."

"Funny, that's about all I remember about that place. I mean, that and watching and waving. I thought everybody on a Pullman was really going big places and doing big things."

C. C. rattled his ice cubes. "Another Scotch?"

"Yeah, thanks. You know, it's nice sitting here talking with you, C. C." Suddenly she laughed. "Wasn't that George and Ethel couple a mess?"

"She was on you like a duck on a June bug."

"You see how I kept talking to everybody so I didn't get trapped with her?"

"I never laughed so much with my mouth shut in my life. And that poor damn porter, he didn't know which way to go." He pulled the tear tape on a fresh pack of Camels and shook two out. "Are you really in show business?"

"Sure. . . . Well, I'm not exactly what you call a headliner. But we've done a few shows. We probably played some of these towns in through here."

He tipped a tobacco fleck from his tongue. "That must be the toughest field in the world to break in."

"Brother, you can say that again." She told him about Jimmy Lee and John Harmon, the seventeen tryouts, and the recording session at Holiday.

"Well, I'll sure as hell give you credit for hanging in there."

(275)

"If I knew then what I know now I wouldn't have even tried."

"Come on, don't kid me. You'd of gone to Nashville if you had to walk."

"Say, why'd you say that?"

He touched his fresh bourbon to her Scotch. "Let's just say I'm a good judge of human nature."

She frowned over her drink. "You don't believe in that astrology stuff or read hands?"

"No, I just figure no one's going to slow a gal like you down for too long. Seventeen places! Damn, I like that. Most gals would have gone home crying to Mama after three or four, or married the first thick wallet that put his arm around her. . . . You know something, Ruby Jean? You're O.K. in my book. . . . Yessir, O.K."

The warm wings inside her turned cool and brushed a tender area. It was getting late. He had invested a dinner and seven or eight drinks; he would make his move soon. She felt him shift and stiffened as his hand came to her knee. But it wasn't soft and tentative; it was friendly, firm, innocent.

"You're going to be all right, kid. It's like sales, you can't let them get you down." He was like an old friend, an older brother, almost a father.

She told him about how Jimmy Lee and John Harmon and Spider all wanted to marry her but none of them felt right. Then, switching around in the seat and crossing her legs Indian style, she folded her arms. "What would you do if you were me?" She smiled. "Come on, say you were me, C. C."

He slumped down on his spine and closed his eyes. "O.K. I'm Ruby Jean Jamison and I'm riding east to see an old boy friend who's doing a year. Let's see now." He paused. A strange note broke in his voice as he gazed out at the night. "I know exactly what I'd do. I'd make C. C. Blackwing clean out his bank account and I'd run off with him to Key West, Florida." He smiled but kept looking down the tracks. Ruby felt trapped and cheated. She knew behind the smile he meant every word. "Then I'd talk him into marrying me and buying a little motel or an orange grove

(276)

and then just sit back and fish a few trotlines and sunbathe and tell the world to go to hell."

"You shouldn't talk like that. You got a happy family and a wife who loves you and a house to take care of and everything."

He avoided her eyes and kept watching the tracks shining red in the trailing lights. They were in the low rolls of the Blue Ridge Mountains, and the moon was dipping into the valleys and vanishing behind the hills. "I ain't slept with my wife in two and a half years."

Ruby mashed out her cigarette, snapping it. "Oh, Christ, here it comes. I knew this was too good to last."

His voice was low and husky. The bourbon was hitting him. "I just discovered something. Don't laugh. . . . The only people you can talk to is strangers."

"You heard that in some damn movie. Now stop it! Crap, C. C." She jammed her boots into the window ledge. "Now you've gone and spoiled everything."

He spoke innocently, openly, and for a minute she was listening. "You know that spiel about why I don't fly?"

She nodded, knowing there was no stopping him now.

"All horseshit. The only thrill I get any more is taking off and landing. You heard the ad about getting there is half the fun? Well, with me it's all the fun. . . . Ruby, and this is the God's truth, I ride the trains because I don't want to get where I'm going and I don't want to get back."

"Oh, C. C., what in the hell's gotten into you? You must have a jillion friends. You got a great job and you're practically your own boss. Hell, you got more than enough. You shouldn't talk like that."

His eyes were hard and set. They reflected none of Ruby's hopefulness. "But when a man and wife ain't sleeping together, none of it's worth a dime."

Her boots squeaked together as she crossed them. "Well, I just don't happen to believe that one, Buster. You're trying it out to see how it sounds. I sure figured you could do better than that."

"No, kid, this is no line, I swear it isn't."

He talked on about his troubles with his branch manager, his

(277)

wife, his kids and in-laws, and how life had sold him short and how stupid he'd been. Ruby quit listening and kept looking out beyond where the tracks were shining in the dark. Out beyond she knew Jimmy Lee, Spider, and maybe John Harmon were waiting. C. C. wound down and was silent for a while. Then he looked at her. "Ruby, which one is the truck-driving singer?"

"John Harmon."

"Sounds like trouble. So does the albino. Why don't you tell me about the other one?"

"Why don't you leave me alone. I'm not telling you anything about anything."

"Want me to go away?"

"No."

C. C.'s voice picked up his old singsong. "Kid, forget everything I told you and put this one thing in your brain and turn it over. You need someone that'll know how special you are. Anyone else is wrong, dead wrong."

"But you'd be just right."

"Naw, I'm too old. You don't want to be stuck in some orange grove sweating out kill frosts. You need a stud that'll take you honkytonking and be able to keep up with you."

"I'm sorry you've been so unhappy, C. C."

"Nobody's fault but mine. I knew a gal back in school like you. Funny and wild and full of juice. I was crazy about her, too, but I was too stupid to marry her." He stopped and thought about it. He finished his drink and waved to the porter.

Ruby sat low on her backbone, supporting her chin with the heels of her hands. She felt her jaw work as she spoke. "You're right. I shouldn't marry any of them."

"Of course I am. Hell, twenty-three isn't a thing to a looker like you. You'll be the same twenty years from now."

"Thanks." She took the fresh Scotch without changing her position and sipped it smoothly to keep from spilling. They wound through a thick stand of Georgia pines, and she watched the moon popping in and out of the quick openings. Then the trees fell away, the curve flattened, and the *click-click-click* of the wheels on the rail cracks sped up.

(278)

The porter came back again. "It's one o'clock, folks. Last call for drinks."

C. C. ordered another round and three minis of Scotch and three of bourbon. "We can always drink them for breakfast." The train was stopping. Outside, halos of fog ghosted around a station and the street lights of a small town.

Ruby turned up her jacket collar. "Spooky, isn't it?" No one was on the street. There were no cars on the road, no window lights. The orange-green eyes of a cat flashed, fixed, and then vanished.

C. C. said slowly, "Looks like it's a hundred years old."

A cold whispering fear ran over her arms and shoulders, making her feel lonely and scared as if time were speeding up. When she woke in the morning she would be thirty—forty—fifty. She drew her knees in under her. "It gives me the creeps."

The train pulled out. They finished the drinks and began skinning off the cap closures on the mini-bottles.

She touched his hand. "C. C."

"Yeah, Ruby."

"I don't want to be alone tonight. I wouldn't mind sleeping with you."

His hand rested on her knee. "Ruby, I'd like to be with you, too."

22

Ruby and her mother sat on the combination swing-glider watching the lightning bugs rising out of the Johnson grass and the bullbats swooping at the street light on Cooper. Across the street the chrome bumpers, headlights, and dashboard trims in Crawford's junk yard glistened in the moonlight. Ruby had her shoes off and her feet up on the porch rail. The hair between her legs, where she had shaved to keep from showing in her bathing suit, had grown back and no longer itched.

Her mother seemed to have asked a thousand questions. "Why? Why, Ruby? What I want to know is why?"

"Mama, I already told you."

"You don't have to get snippity. I just don't understand why you have to go traipsing all the way up to Nashville, Tennessee, to sing a few old songs. You were doing fine right around here. People liked you. There ain't a soul up there that's even heard of Ruby Jean Jamison."

"There are now, Mama." She had to get her off the subject. "You been going to church?"

"Yes. And you know who I've been praying for."

"Mama, we're doing all right up there. It's just like any other town. Lord, it's smaller than Columbia. And you know yourself how much you like the Opry."

The river breeze was up and cool but Mrs. Jamison fluttered her funeral parlor fan as if it was a hundred. It stopped. "I don't suppose you saw Tennessee Ernie Ford?"

"No, ma'am. He's out in California. Saw Grandpa Jones and Skeeter Davis, though."

"Skeeter Davis? Oh, I do love to hear her sing. You meet her?"

"Just to shake hands."

"What's she like?"

"Oh, she wears her hair a little like Mary Lou Tyler, you know, straight across, and her face is kinda long. But she's just as pretty and nice to talk to. . . . You know what she does when she records?"

"What's that?"

"Comes in barefoot. John Harmon told me that. And you talk about someone that goes to church regular, that Skeeter Davis is it."

"Well that's nice to hear. . . . I understand there's a lot of drinking and carrying on going on up there."

"Mama, folks are so busy working they just don't have time for raising a lot of hell."

Mrs. Jamison took off her glasses and squeezed the bridge of her nose. "All right, but just don't be trying to make it sound like you've been on retreat someplace."

Ruby laughed. "Oh, Ma, you kill me."

A black and tan coon hound crossed the clay yard. He looked up twice to see if there was any food, then went on about his business.

"Hey, who took old Roebuck's place?"

Mrs. Jamison's fan fluttered. "Reverend Ferlin Stover Peterson. Arno Peterson's kin. He's up from Yemassee. Ruby, I'm going to tell you something, but I don't want it getting off this porch."

"Yes, ma'am."

"A lot of us like Reverend Peterson a sight better than we do Roebuck Alexander."

"You're kidding!"

"No, I'm not. . . . It got so all Roebuck would do is shout at us."

"But he always did that."

"No, but then he'd ease up and preach a sermon. Now he just keeps on bellowing. Got so bad I had to move to the back. It ruined the choir. Just ruined it. That radio and TV turned his mind. He got the taste of getting up in front of a big crowd, and then when he looked out and just saw a few of us old biddies from up the block he got mad."

"Guess that figures."

"We're asking the council if we can have Reverend Peterson instead of Roebuck."

She whistled. "That is something."

"Now you keep it quiet, you hear?"

She crossed her heart. "You got my word."

"Ruby, you work all week in that loom room noise and you want something you can sit still and sort of enjoy on Sundays. I'm getting too old to be shouted at. . . . I guess I just don't have the education to sit there and be quiet."

Ruby flipped her cigarette onto the hard clay pan. "I never did understand how preachers get the call from one church to another."

"It comes from the council. Wherever they send you, you got to go. . . . It's just called 'getting the call.' It might have been different in the olden times, but I guess now it's no more now than getting a phone call or a postcard."

"Y'all ought to put in for a plane ticket for that fool for one of those African spots. Get him down on that equator and it'll take the starch out of him."

Mrs. Jamison giggled. "You getting hungry?"

"Yes, ma'am. Hey, let me do the supper. You go watch television. I haven't cooked a meal in ages."

Mrs. Jamison dabbed her mouth with her napkin. "That was nice. I got some ice cream out there. Look in behind those snap ·beans."

Ruby served the ice cream with chocolate sauce and Nabisco

(283)

sugar wafers. Mrs Jamison snapped a wafer in half. "I guess you'll be seeing Mr. Spider Hornsby tomorrow when he comes sashaying home."

She ate her ice cream too fast and the cold stung the back of her nose. "Yes I am, and I don't want to talk about it."

"Well, I'm going to say one thing and get it off my chest." She drew herself up. "I think it's an absolute shame and disgrace to the city of Columbia and the state of South Carolina that that man can get a year and a day in a tax-supported penitentiary and the next thing you know he's home on Saturdays and up in church on Sunday mornings strutting around like a banty rooster. And that's all I'm going to say about Mr. Spider Harold Hornsby."

"Oh, Mama, you don't know thing one about it, so just hush up."

"Don't talk to me like that."

"All right. I'm sorry. It's just . . . oh, never mind." She began clearing the table.

Ruby eased her mother's wedding china in the warm water of the double sink. The twenty-seven-year-old Chinese pattern was chipped and cracked and the birds' wings, once blue and yellow, were faded and faint, the little eyes and brown beaks long gone. She handled them one at a time, washing, rinsing, and then carefully stacking them in the drain rack. . . . There was something nice about the kitchen. She'd missed it. Housekeeping they could keep, but cooking and serving for the right man was something else. She turned the hot-water spray on rinse, and as the fine needles bounced on the blue-edged plates and swirled in the cups she knew that even cooking for Spider would be better than living out of Big Boys and Bite Quiks and Krispy Kreme Donut Shops. Her skin was beginning to pimple and she knew she wasn't getting enough fresh greens.

"Ruby, ain't you about through?"

"Just finishing up."

She came out with two cups of coffee. "Mama, I just decided that most of the men I've met are creeps."

The Dean Martin show was on but she had the sound off. "You

(284)

shouldn't low-rate people like that. Everyone was put on this earth for a purpose."

"Just so long as it isn't mine. I swear everyone I meet reminds me of something a bat threw up. It's really a miracle you found Dad."

"Times were simple back then. Everyone's rushing around so now. They don't seem to be coming from anywhere, just going. Twenty years ago a person going to New York City or Chicago would be considered going somewhere. Land, there'd be a piece in the paper about it. Now they go up there and have dinner, see a Broadway show, and get back in the evening."

White doilies were on the arm and head rests of the three over-stuffed chairs and the deep sofa facing the cold fireplace and the color TV. The big chair where Mr. Jamison had sat was in the center, and on it an unnamed orange cat lay in the deep scooped-out seat left by his 280 pounds. Mrs. Jamison had taken his ash-tray stand to the garage and replaced it with a potted fern plant. "Lot of this new crowd go tearing from one place to another for no more reason than that cat there. . . . Your father didn't feature gadding about like that. He liked to sit and figure things out."

"But you really got along, didn't you?"

"Everybody's got problems, baby. Me and Otis, we had our share."

"You miss him?"

She turned the volume switch up on her remote control but Dean Martin was still talking. "Yes, I miss Otis."

The song started and she spun the dial. He was singing "When You're Smiling." "Darling, would you call up Mary? Tell her Dean's on."

As Ruby talked to Mrs. McCoy and told her Agnes was fine and sent her love, she watched her mother holding the remote panel in her lap like a box of assorted chocolates and watching the show. A twinge of sadness dipped and rolled inside as she realized how empty the empty chair was. She was glad she had the Westinghouse color set.

Mrs. McCoy was torn between talking to her and watching Dean Martin. She told Ruby to tell Agnes to write.

(285)

"Yes, ma'am, I won't forget. Bye now."

She joined her mother and picked up her cold coffee. Dean Martin was singing "Precious Love." She watched how he leaned on the piano, what he did with his hands, and the way he saved his smiles and used them when they mattered.

"Want some more coffee?"

"Yes, please." She patted Ruby's hand. "I just love Dean."

In the morning Ruby headed up the two blocks of Cooper to Cherry. She had gotten Spider's key from Virgil. The rain had swollen the door in its jamb and she bumped it open with her hip. Inside she laughed as she counted twenty-six beer cans scattered around the room; another eighteen were pyramided up on the coffee table as if they'd been used for target practice. The monkeys on the mantelpiece were snapped off at hear-no-evil, and a black burn hole the size of a five-pound lard can was in the middle of the sofa. Every dish, cup, saucer, bowl, and glass in the house was in the greasy water of the two sinks, and nine bags of garbage were lined up like feed sacks against the wall.

She switched her transister on to a c. and w. station and opening a beer turned the refrigerator off to defrost and began cleaning. Blonde hairs with dark roots were clogging the bathtub and washbasin drains. She clawed the wads out and flushed them down the john. Spider's pants were hanging heavily on coat hooks and wire hangers. Billy Lou had taken all but two of the wooden ones and every one of the yellow padded perfumed ones she'd bought from Belk's.

She cleaned until eleven-thirty and then went out on the front porch to wait for Spider. At noon he came home in a Yellow cab. He rushed across the yard, charged up the steps, and grabbed her. "God Almighty! Looka here! When you get in?"

"Last night. Surprised?"

"I guess so!" He kissed her and she kissed him back. He pushed her out to look at her micro skirt and jack boots. "Some outfit. Man! Is that the way they've been wearing them up there?"

"You like?"

"Love it. Really shows off your legs."

(286)

They were on the couch. He had his arm around her.

"O.K., I want to hear about everything. Everything. You know you ain't been gone no weekend."

"I'll get us a beer first." She called from the kitchen, "I wrote you most of it."

"Yeah, I know. But I want to hear it. Damn, I'm really glad you're back."

She sat on his lap. "Well, let's see now. We've done four or five club dates. Nothing special except those nights with John Harmon. I wrote you about them. Then we bombed at the recording session." She sucked in. "That was the absolute low point. Oh, the hell with me. I want to know about you. How you doing down that hill. Wait till I catch that Hooty. I'm going to snatch every hair out of that bastard's head."

Spider told her about the trial. How Roebuck had shouted that the raid had been inspired by the Lord and that Maynard should be the new sheriff.

"That must have been something."

"You bet your ass. Judge Wheeler leaned into that one. Said if the Lord wanted to hand down some legal decisions and some political suggestions he was going to have to go through the proper channels. Old Roebuck hit the ceiling and got slapped with a two-hundred-dollar-fine for contempt. Then Wheeler racked his ass about how low-life it was, the way they'd used Hooty, and if he had anything to do with Maynard Moody's political future he was putting him up for sewage inspector. . . . God, I wish you could've been there, honey."

"Me too. But you coming out of there with a year. I hate that, Spider, it's rotten."

"It ain't too bad. How many convicts you see coming home on Saturday?"

Spider was in the bathtub shaving. Ruby sat on the john seat, her feet on the tub rim. "It's a crazy town, Spide, crazy. Everything's going on. Music, records, song writing—I mean everything. We even ran into a couple of movie makers. . . . We still haven't had the right break we need but I just know it's coming."

He sloshed water on his face and rinsed off the lather. "I can't get over how good you look in that outfit."

"It's wilder up there. No lie—beads, bells, bushed hair. It's a lot like Hollywood."

"Hand me that towel." Spider rose. He was brown from his neck to his waist but the flesh around his stomach was the slick texture of waterlogged soap.

"Hey! You have lost some weight."

"I've been cutting down on bread and sweets."

She grabbed a handful of meat around his hips. "Used to be a big old handle right here. . . . I ought to know."

"Wasn't there some bird wanting you to run a spot for him?"

"Gus Gillespie. That was more our idea than his. Now you talk about a character."

"Might be a good investment. What if I bought him out and you and Agnes ran it?"

"No. I can't be tied down like that. I want to keep loose. I got to keep looking around."

He flipped the towel over the door. "Well, what in the hell you been doing?"

"Looking, and I'm going to keep on. That is, if it's all right with you."

"Well, hell, honey. I thought all this time might have changed things. You know how I feel about you."

"Yeah, Spider, I know. But you got to see my side of it. I'm just about ready to hit. I can't be saddled up running no honkytonk. Lord, I might be in Hollywood tomorrow."

"O.K. Forget it. . . . Want to go out tonight?"

"Love to. How about O. J.'s or Pete's?"

"Afraid not. Sheriff says I got to keep kinda low. Word gets out I'm raising hell and honkytonking, I could get some good people in trouble. We'll eat out and hit the drive-in."

"O.K. Fine with me. Hey, Mama says you're back in Washed in the Blood?"

"Damn right. And this time I'm staying. Me and this new fellow Peterson are good buddies. He comes by four or five times a week."

(288)

"Does he drink?"

Spider smiled and sprayed his armpits. "Does a goat stink?"

After a rib dinner at Osco's and a horror show at the drive-in they went home. Ruby wanted to make love but held back, waiting for Spider to make the first move.

"How about getting us a couple of beers?" When she came back his naked body lay shining on the sheets. She slipped out of her dress and heard him sigh as he reached for her. "That's nice. Mmmmm, you feel good."

She stretched out alongside him. The deep draw almost rolled her out. "Hey, I'm going to spill."

"I got you." He took the beers. "That's what I'm doing next Saturday. Buying a new mattress and a bigger bed. What do you think of a king size?"

"Be close. You couldn't make it up. A queen should fit. I'll measure it tomorrow."

He pulled her to him, and she snuggled in close with her eyes closed. He dried his beer-can-cold hand on the sheet and began stroking her thigh. She closed her eyes and gently rocked her head, trying to feel tender, trying to feel better about being with him. She felt nothing but a longing for him to try harder, to say something nice, special. He finally spoke. "Be sure and remind me about that bed in the morning. It's a damn wonder your spine ain't twisted trying to keep out of this hole." She touched him behind his ear, hoping he would say more, then stroked it and burrowed in under his chin. His whiskers felt good and she worked her toes in between his. He made a soft whistling sound through his teeth. "Nice. Nice." She felt his hands slide away.

He made love as if it didn't matter. It was slow, tired, strange. She tried to fit his mood but didn't know what he was doing. He could have been rowing a boat; he could have been with anyone. She started to say something, but then it was too late. He quivered slightly as if he was having a chill and came. "Jesus!" He was breathing hard from supporting his weight. He slid off. "Something's wrong. I'm about to pass out."

She thought he was having a stroke. "You all right?"

"I think so. Feel weak as hell."

"Your heart's going a mile a minute. You ain't on those diet pills, are you?"

"No. Maybe I'm getting old." He sounded as if he wanted to be talked out of it.

"Oh, silly, you're just out of practice."

He was flat on his back, his left hand patting her right. "Yeah, but forty-four, that's getting up there."

"Lord, you're the same age as Charlton Heston."

"Charlton Heston, yeah. Wait a second, I know what's wrong. I been going to bed at dark. That's it. It must be two o' damn clock."

"And me being on Nashville time doesn't help either. You just go to sleep now."

She was used to the darkness, and what features she couldn't see she could imagine. His feet were together, the ten toes straight up and squared. With his hands folded on his chest and his nose pointed straight at the ceiling boards he looked dead. He farted softly. She touched his shoulder and traced her finger down to the top of the sheet. Four months of being with him had made her comfortable with him. That's what he was; he was comfortable. A girl could do a lot worse than be comfortable. He would be a safe marriage. Almost a guarantee. A tune title flashed in her mind: "There's No Warranty in a Marriage Vow." It was too long, and warranty would be hard to rhyme. Some people wouldn't even know what it meant. . . . In the half-light she imagined Jimmy Lee's white and gleaming face and thin tense body stretched out in Spider's depression. He would be turning, twitching in his sleep like he was on a barbecue spit, talking show business and la-de-deeing old tunes and snatches of new bad ones. He slept like a dog with summer worms: always moving, spinning, mumbling. Barber-poling his pajamas around him until he couldn't breathe, then jumping up to straighten them out before they strangled him or rip them off and hurl them to the floor. Violent, sudden movements, then a spinning, scratching whirl, until he'd wake up with the bottom sheet snaked around his throat and the blanket halfway across the room. . . .

(290)

If Jimmy Lee slept like a sick dog shifting to find a cool spot, John Harmon was like a hog-tied bull. He'd lay panting as if not getting enough air and then, heaving a thundering sigh, as if wounded, would thrash violently, sometimes jerking the box springs from the runners or smashing over the clock, the lamp, and the telephone. He slept sprawled like a runner or a human swastika and always with his mouth an inch from the mattress seam and his closed eyes staring at the floor. He had to get away from whoever he was sleeping with, and the farthest point was the edge. He claimed he needed the air, and during the night he'd shift, flail out, and work his way toward whatever breeze or air-conditioner stream was blowing.

Spider was different. He was secure. He would lay perfectly still, his feet and hands squared, his back flat on the mattress. In the morning the sheet and blanket would be exactly where it was when he folded it down over his chest. The bed didn't even have to be remade. . . . Ruby had watched and listened to them all while they slept. Watched them closely, bending over to study and search for some clue to herself. Trying to figure out why three men as different as morning, noon, and night would want her. Something was there in common with all three if she could only find it. And once finding it she'd know what she was like. The "Know Yourself" quizzes in the papers and magazines revealed nothing except she had a strong character, liked things her own way, and was occasionally moody and ambitious. And asking Agnes was hopeless. "You're nice, Ruby. Really nice. . . . Why, you're the best friend I've ever had. I don't know what I'd do without you."

She'd overheard men talking about her. "Ruby's fun. Ruby's wild as hell, but fun." And, from Spider to Virgil, "Ruby's O.K. A real sport. You can count on her." If she could only find out exactly what she was like. If some gypsy or someone off the street would suddenly rush up and give her a card with three or four lines that she could memorize or hold in her hand. She could check it when she was in a jam or had to make a big decision. She could figure out where she belonged. If she had any talent. Who she should live with. Love. Marry. Or if she should stick it out in Nashville or follow her mother's never-ending advice and go back to Southern Bell.

Spider moved and spoke. "Don't forget about that bed in the morning."

"I won't. Sweet dreams now."

She lit a cigarette and went out to the porch. Maybe Southern Bell was right. And then she spoke out loud. She wanted to hear it. "Maybe Southern Bell's O.K. for Mary Lou Tyler and Thelma Jean Hooker and the Hopkins twins and Agnes McCoy, but I'm going to tell you something, pussycat: it's not good enough for Ruby Jean Jamison. Because tomorrow morning, doll baby, you're getting back on that big old Delta bird and it's look out, Nashville."

23

When the one o'clock sun sliced away the awning shade at Checkerboard Feed, Ridge Porterfield, the subpoena server from Carolina Bail Bond Company, moved around the corner to The Advance Loan-on-Anything lobby. It was 99 degrees, and the Palmetto State flag on top of the capitol hung straight down. Since 8:15 Ridge, a short red-faced man in a light peach-colored suit that wrinkled easily, had been on the even side of the 1400 block of Assembly watching the Hollywood Charm School at 1419½ and waiting for Raymond La Mer. In his spiral memo pad, Ridge had noted how Lorlene Tisdale, the secretary, had arrived for work in her hair curlers and kerchief at 8:30. At 10, with her blonde hair combed out, she had gone to the Dixie Dew Diner for coffee and grapefruit. She returned at 10:15. At 12 she came down for lunch, bought a newspaper, and returned sharply at 12:30. No one else had entered or left the office. The Venetian blinds in Raymond La Mer's office were closed, and with no moisture condensing on the casement Ridge noted that the air conditioner was broken or off.

At 1:15 Ridge had lunch at the Eat Right Cafe, a stand-up grill down the block where he could watch while he ate. He squeezed mustard and catsup down his onion-piled foot-long chili dog and sliding a large Pepsi to the end of the counter kept his eyes on 1419½. In his diary he itemized the lunch at 47 cents. He added another dime and picked up a Peter Paul Almond Joy. Shaking out one half and folding the other up tight in the glassine wrapper for later, he figured he had forty-five minutes before he had to catch the bus. At 3 he was due to serve a summons on a fourth-mortgage restaurant owner in Wales Garden. Wiping his mouth with the half napkin provided by the Eat Right, he started across the street for the Hollywood Charm School.

Upstairs, Ridge told Lorlene he was from the Better Business Bureau and was making a survey of the number of employees and current salaries in Columbia. Lorlene, who had just finished brushing her hair 750 times to keep her mind off of her screaming hunger after her grapefruit and yogurt lunch, was dying to talk to anyone. She told him she received $35 a week take-home pay but over $120 a week in extras and went on about how Raymond La Mer singlehandedly had brought her down from a size 20 to a 16 in three short months. "I wouldn't tell this to just anyone, but last week I bought my first pair of panty hose."

Nothing could stop her, and she rolled on about how she couldn't understand why business had dropped off so sharp and why the phone seldom rang. Ridge, studying the big glossy on the wall of Raymond La Mer smiling in a three-quarters shot through a soft focus, told her that money was tight all over. "Household Finance and Beneficial are eight per cent as of next month. . . . Good-looking rascal, ain't he. This an old shot?"

"Land, no. That was last year. Sat for it out in Hollywood. Nice, ain't he?"

Ridge nodded. The thin hawk face, black eyes, and slick hair would be easy to spot in Columbia. He reminded himself to mark down *Mediterranean floorwalker.*

"His eyes always that dark?"

"Yes. He's French. Latin, you know. La Mer, it means the sea." She checked his simple card announcing Ridge J. Porterfield over

(294)

a telephone answering service number. "I figure it was the luckiest day in my life when I walked in here. Absolutely my luckiest. You should have seen me then." She shook her head with her eyes closed as if she painfully could. "A sight. A real sight. Oh, I just wish you could meet him. Maybe that Better Business crowd could send him some customers."

"But he advertises. I hear them on the radio and see them in the papers, even bus cards. I figured he'd be swamped with clients."

A subpoena for nonpayment of rent against Raymond La Mer and five New York kited check summonses nestled in Ridge's coat pocket. "Not many talent offices like this around the South."

His financial investigation had revealed the only people Raymond La Mer—alias Manuel Ortega, alias Raoul Del Mar, alias Vincent Polotsi—had paid in the past five months were the Southern Bell Telephone Company and now Lorlene.

She ripped an emery board across her fingernails. "If you was to ask me, I'd say he was too good for this dumb town. He's years ahead of these lintheads. If they only knew what an inspiration that man was, they'd be coming in here on their bended knees."

Ridge felt his energy dropping as he thought Lorlene was sounding as if Raymond had left or was leaving town. He felt his fifty-dollar service fee sliding away. "How long's he been gone?"

"Week and a half."

He told her Raymond had to sign a Better Business form and he'd drop by the next time he was in the neighborhood.

"You better phone first. I wouldn't want you to go out of your way."

"Well, where is he now?"

"Last call came in from Spartanburg. Said he was leaving there and heading out for Atlanta or Memphis or someplace west. Mister, Raymond La Mer is one man that really covers ground. Now let me see. I believe he said . . ." Ridge waited. Lorlene rummaged in her foot-wide purse for her lipstick. It was the new pale shade, and pursing her lips in tight she wiped it on carefully. "Oh, I can't think straight now. But if you ask me why he's so scarce it's that doggone preacher's fault."

"Would that be Roebuck Alexander?"

"Yes, it would be. We were getting along wonderful until he showed up. Seems like he just took over everything. And then he turned like that."

"Like what?"

"Like a snake, that's what. And after Mr. La Mer had practically rebuilt that man's whole personality. If you ask me, he's crazy as a loon."

"Don't believe I follow you."

She snapped her purse as her eyes narrowed. "We had us fourteen customers signed up when that Holy Rolling jingo blew in here. Now we got only two. He's one and I'm the other."

"That's too bad." He checked his watch. The fifty dollars was as good as gone; he would make only his regular two dollars an hour plus bus fare. "It's been nice talking to you. What if I dropped by, say in the morning? I might be up this way."

"Well, I'd like to see you. You know you're pretty interesting yourself. But you'd better call first. If he's up in Memphis—that's it! That's it, Memphis! I knew I'd get it."

For Ridge she might as well have said the Sea of Tranquility.

"Well, I'll just stick my head in one of these days. It really isn't that important."

"O.K."

"Good-by now, Lorlene."

"Bye, Ridge."

In Memphis at the Ticonderoga Motel Raymond La Mer was at his wits' end. He slid a quarter in the Magic Fingers bed vibrator and spread-eagled out to relax. For two weeks he and Roebuck had barnstormed across South Carolina, North Carolina, and Tennessee over three thousand miles of superhighways, intermediates, and gravel, doing one-night stands in high schools, tent gospels, and 5 to 7 A.M. radio spots. His weight had dropped from 151 to 136. None of his clothes fit.

Roebuck had gained weight. In his J. C. Penney brown plaid jacket with solid brown sleeves and his tan slacks, he stood before the mirror jutting his jaw and thrusting out his stiff hands,

miming the finish to his big sermon on atomic revelation. In the
three weeks on the road he had been watching Dean Martin, Tom
Jones, and Billy Graham on television. He had picked up Martin's
smoothness, the sudden energy of Jones, and Billy Graham's hawk-
like thrusts and flashing eyes. For message he had been true to
himself, sticking close to hard literal Old Testament. Sin was
spelled out capital S, capital I, capital N. The Ten Command-
ments were as absolute as the freezing point of water, and Eve
was made from the dust of earth and the rib of man.

Roebuck ripped off the white glassine from a glass and, rinsing
it in hot water, then cold, filled it. He sipped the water slowly,
swishing it around in his mouth like vintage wine before swallow-
ing. "I don't suppose you're familiar with Revelations?"

Raymond's eyes were closed in pain. The Magic Fingers, the
Salesman's Friend, rattled on. "You're right."

Roebuck sat on the bed opposite him. "That shaking ain't going to do you a lick of good. Your problem ain't nerves."

"Leave me alone, baby."

"I don't want you calling me baby any more. I done told you
about that."

"O.K., O.K. Let me get some rest."

Roebuck rose, studying the empty glass as if he was reading
some message in the moisture. "I'm going for a walk. I want to
do some thinking."

"Good. . . . Wake me up about seven. I don't feel too great."

Raymond sighed as the door closed. Every minute alone from
Roebuck was heaven. Every minute with him hell. He was un-
predictable, irritable, and—in the last three nights he had finally
accepted the cold fact he'd been dodging for two weeks—he was
absolutely crazy.

In Chapel Hill at the roller dome, Roebuck had seated over
4,000 and grossed $8,900. Of the $8,900 he had given back $8,700
to the twenty needy families the Chamber of Commerce had provided him to sit on the platform. He had given away everything
but $200 and had ended his sermon by holding up ten twenty-
dollar bills and accounting for every dollar. Winston-Salem,
Raleigh, Clinton, and Charlotte, the home of Billy Graham, had

never seen anything like it. Of their twenty-one appearances they had grossed over $96,000. The net Raymond had in his pocket came to $906.45.

The Magic Fingers slowed down and stopped and he shoved in another quarter and spread out again, this time on his stomach with his head lolling over the side. He worried at the embossed flower design in the rug following one line and then the other as the vibrator jiggled, easing the tension in his throat and at the back of his neck. He would call Lorlene in the morning and tell her to call Budget Rental to pick up the furniture and typewriter, mail the autographed pictures on the wall to him c/o General Delivery in Newark, New Jersey, and close the office. She had worked for six months and was eligible for the $65 a week unemployment money.

The trip had been a nightmare. He still couldn't believe he had misjudged a character so badly. He concentrated on the flower pattern but in his mind, like a photograph appearing through the developer, the 4,200 cheering faces in the Peabody School in Charlotte were suddenly upon him. They were screaming, shouting, and waving five- and ten-dollar bills as Roebuck flailed them into a higher and higher pitch during the collection. He had been sitting in the wings wishing he had a washtub or a polyethylene garbage can liner to rush out with and begin gathering in the bills like leaves; there was no silver. And then Roebuck, waving away the collectors, who were poised at the back, and rolling on about salvation, redemption, and the healing powers of charity, came down from the podium and slowly and systematically collected the money himself. The audience helped him count it out and sort it. When he collected $250 he remounted the stage and gave it to one of the twenty needy families praying, crying, and screaming behind him in full view of the 4,200.

Again and again he made the trip from the contributing audience to the thankful needy. Each time Raymond's heart sank: 17, 18, 19, 20 . . . $5,000. When the twenty were finished, Roebuck, soaking wet and shining, joyfully pulled Raymond out to the center of the stage and introduced him to the crowd as the brains and power behind him. Raymond, smiling on top of the surging anger, felt like he wasn't getting enough oxygen. Roe-buck's arm was around him. "Folks, Mr. La Mer here's been like a brother to me. A brother." For three weeks Roebuck had called him Mr. La Mer in his strange sarcastic way. "I want you to give Mr. La Mer a great big hand of thanks. . . . Now, folks, I'm sure that when Mr. La Mer and I get back to our motel room he's going to be telling me I gave all the money away again and we didn't even earn our expenses." The crowd loved to hear Roebuck talk like this. "He's the only business brains I got. . . ." He smiled craftily. "I guess I got other things on my mind." He quieted the crowd's laughter and then spoke as if the message was for them and not Raymond. "I keep telling him that Jesus Christ wasn't no Certified Public Accountant like a lot of your preachers flashing around this part of the country in new Cadillacs and Chris-Craft motorboats, dragging water skis and having teatime with the Presi-dent. But him being a businessman, I just don't know how much gets through to him. So tonight I want Mr. La Mer to speak up right here and now. I want him to tell you exactly how much our little visit here in this fine city of Charlotte is costing us."

Raymond had known the crowd would gladly have given an-other dollar apiece. Another flat $4,200. He also knew there was no way on earth of justifying it. He had stammered out, "Three–four hundred dollars ought to cover it."

Roebuck shouted, "Hey, now! Hey, that's pretty high on the old razorback for two cotton choppers like us for just two nights. Guess a lot of you nine-to-fivers could feed a kitchen full of kids on something like that for a month and have something left over to see a picture show. I'm going to tell Mr. La Mer to step back and sharpen his pencil."

Raymond whispered, "Air fare, Roebuck; we rented a car. We're down to three hundred."

"Folks, Mr. La Mer tells me we flew in and we got to fly out and we need a car on both ends. O.K. Let's see, now. . . . If every one of you will dig down deep and come up with a dime, that'll just about do it. Only a dime now, no more, no less. . . . All right, I'm asking my manager and dear friend Mr. La Mer to

(299)

pass down the center aisle with his hat. . . . And I want to hear it jingling."

The Magic Fingers trembled as Raymond remembered the long walk down the center, thanking the faces and feeling his forty-dollar Tyrolean lose its shape under the flood of dimes. Roebuck led the crowd in "Bringing in the Sheaves" as he shuffled through the most embarrassing walk he had ever taken. He remembered the 4,200 dimes and the 420 tiny stacks on the Howard Johnson dresser in the room that night and the bewildered look on the cashier's face when he led her into the room to change them for bills. But he remembered even clearer, stronger, stranger, the betrayed look on Roebuck's face when he told him there would have to be some changes made.

"Roebuck, you're a big hit and you're going to get bigger. But you're going to have to pass that plate better than that. We're barely breaking even."

Roebuck had grabbed him by the shoulders, almost ripping the seams from the padding. "You don't understand. None of you mouthers understand. You just claim to. It's right there in the Bible. When the Lord passed the plate around in the deserts of Sinai it wasn't empty. It wasn't a collection plate! He had something on it. You don't even know what the multitudes were fed on!"

Raymond's voice went flat; the honeymoon was over. "In the hard lard idiom of your twin Carolinas, catfish and hoecake. . . . And baby, you better get those credits straight. Moses made that gig. Jesus wasn't even alive that season."

The Magic Fingers stopped and Raymond put in a station call to Jimmy Lee in Nashville. "I'm cutting out, Jimmy Lee. This cat's gotten to me. Only thing that fits me is my socks. I've lost fifteen pounds."

He filled him in on Roebuck's charity.

Jimmy Lee said, "Jesus, a real winner. I thought you had a gold mine."

"We were both wrong."

"What's your next move?"

(300)

"North, friend, north. As far north as I can get. You can take these great subtropics and shove them up Robert E. Lee's ass."

"I take it Roebuck isn't invited."

"In the circus jargon of a few years back, I'm leaving this bastard on the lot. Tomorrow when I have breakfast it's going to be no grits, no biscuits, no ham gravy, no goddamn twenty-minute grace, and no Roebuck. Here he comes. So long, Jimmy Lee."

"Keep in touch, Bennie."

24

As Cecil pulled the car out of the Bite Quik at Thompson's Junction, someone shouted, "Stop! Stop! It's me!"

He braked and they saw a tall blonde climbing out of a white Mustang.

Agnes said, "It's that Irene Cash."

Irene stuck her head in the window. Her heavy chorus girl make-up and eye liner looked purple-green in the hot noon light. "Hey, y'all."

"Hi!"

"Ruby, you got a second? I been trying to reach you. It's sort of personal."

They sat at the red, white, and blue steel umbrella table. The clerk hollered out if they wanted anything. Ruby told him two B.Q. Colas. "What you been doing?"

Irene crossed her legs slowly. She looked like a tall cheerleader in her dark blue stockings and yellow miniskirt. "Drawing unemployment."

"I thought you had a deal out at some honkytonk."

(303)

Irene shucked the paper sleeve from her straw. "John Harmon really screwed me up. And I mean royally." She told her how they had lived together for almost two weeks. How she did his laundry, cooking, cleaned out her savings account to pay his bills, and answered every incoming phone call to keep the alimony people off his back.

Ruby chewed her ice.

"He promised to marry me and put me in the act. I was going to dance while he sang. We even rehearsed it."

"You aren't going to tell me about Marvin Clarke, now, are you?"

"Christ Almighty! You? You too? Why, that crummy rotten two-timing son of a bitch. . . . You didn't go?"

"Hell, no. Did you?"

Irene was pale and nervous. She crumbled her Coke straw into the built-in ash tray. "Two weeks with a raving lunatic. He almost killed me."

"Lord, you poor thing. I knew that Clarke was rotten. I could smell it. And no songs, right?"

"He wrote nine. All dead copies of some old junk. . . . John beat the shit out of him. Broke every bone in his jaw."

"Wow! Then what?"

"No songs, no marriage. He's bad news, Ruby, bad, bad news. The lawyer wanted me to sue for breach of promise, but I said no. I might wind up having to have to marry that prick."

"Two weeks with Marvin Clarke. That must have been some kind of hell."

"That's why I'm wearing these stockings."

The bright sun glare made her eye make-up look like a raccoon's mask. "He worked me over like a piece of Italian veal." She sniffed and Ruby tore two napkins from the holder. Irene sobbed. "No phone, no car, no nothing. I had to stay. The only kicks I got out of that little love nest was when John creamed him." She blew her nose and checked her eyes in her pocket mirror. "Oh, Christ, look at me. Ruby, I swear he hit him on account of the music. It didn't have a thing to do with me."

"That figures. How about your job?"

"I'm stiff as a board. I can hardly move."

(304)

"Lord, what did he use on you?"

"Bit me. Every time we made love he'd start biting. I mean all over."

"Didn't you do anything back? I mean—damn."

"Kept hitting him with a piece of stovewood. The bastard loved it."

"That's terrible. Jesus, I never heard of that kind of freak. Is there anything I can do for you?"

"I don't think so. . . . Misery loves company. Thought I'd warn you about him. I think he still likes you."

"Lucky me. Maybe he wants us to start up a fan club. Where you living?"

"With a little drummer over on Tisdale out by Garden Center."

"Near that Howard Johnson when you first hit town?"

"Yeah, about a mile. You near there?"

"We're at the Capri Plaza on Murfreesboro."

"Hell, I've been there!"

"Well, listen, come over for a swim. It's half piss and chlorine but it's still a pool."

She wiped her eyes. "O.K., you're on. Is Harry Coffin still there? Plays drums."

"Don't think so. Listen, we gotta make tracks. Come on over. We get off around four."

"I'll do that. Say hello to Agnes. Ain't that her name?"

"That's it. We'll see you, now, hear?"

"O.K., Ruby."

The sun was straight up and straight down as they drove along Montgomery Road near Bullitt. Cecil tapped the p.a. mike. "You all ready?"

Agnes said, "Let's do 'Lovesick Blues.' "

"O.K." Ruby sang but her mind was back at the Bite Quik with Irene and the Airstream trailer with Big John Harmon.

Agnes nudged her during a bridge. "Come on, you're laying back."

"O.K., O.K." She pushed through to the end. "Do the next one by yourself. My throat's scratchy."

(305)

During lunch at the truck diner she told Agnes everything. She couldn't believe it.

"You know something? That's really sick. What you reckon gets into a man like that? He looked like such a quiet old thing."

"You find out, you tell me. . . . Agnes, now you listen and you listen close. I don't know what your plans are, but mine are for sticking it out here."

"I'm with you, Ruby. You know that."

"Bull. Next time Virgil says pee, you're squatting. You willing to nurse a week-old kid in between Bite Quik stops? I'm talking long range."

"I know. . . . Well, I hadn't thought that far ahead."

"Well, I have. I'm thinking of it right now. Couple more weeks and Moses is dropping us off like dirty laundry."

"But what do you want me to do? I can't help it. I swear I can't."

"Oh, hon, it ain't your fault. Don't let me get you all upset. It's me. I'm the one that's scared. I don't want to be left alone in this rat trap. . . . I'll probably wind up with some snake like John Harmon wrapped around me."

"But you got Spider."

"The hell with Spider."

"You don't mean that and you know it."

"Maybe I do and maybe I don't." She balled up her napkin and pushed her chair back. "I'm so mixed up I don't know what I mean."

Cecil had had lunch at a bar across the road and had his feet up on the dashboard, listening to the radio. He smelled of beer and whiskey mixed. Ruby asked him if he was able to drive.

Leveling his eyebrows, he looked her straight in the eye. "Are you inferring that I've been drinking?"

It was a new word, a drunk word. "Well, I'd hate like hell being in your shoes if they slap you with an alcohol test. Cecil, this road's crawling with Law."

He looked down the shining asphalt and scratched his ear. "I understand that alcohol test is pretty fierce. They can pick up the least little drop."

(306)

Agnes sat forward. "Let Ruby drive. You can put your head out the window. That'll straighten you out."

After the last Bite Quik they left him off at home. He touched his cap bill with one finger. "Moses Shugin said you were the best girls he's had. You know something? I'd have to go along on that."

Ruby asked, "You there when he said it?"

"No. I got me a buddy named Clarence, he works in the men's room." He winced and frowned. "My head's acting up. I want to thank you ladies for that driving."

He limped off, keeping his head smooth and balanced.

Ruby swung a U turn and headed home. She slowed to let a dog cross the road. It was clear and hot and the black asphalt flashed like patent leather. "That pool's going to be nice. Hey, I told Irene to come over. She only lives about a mile away."

"O.K. with me. . . . I sure don't remember her being that tall. Wish I was taller. Then I wouldn't be putting weight on so fast."

"Hon, you're supposed to. Lord, you make it sound like a sin or something. You're perfect. There ain't a gal in this town that wouldn't trade figures with you, including yours truly."

In Moses Shugin's outer lobby, Ruby leafed through *The Restaurateur, Grain and Seed Produce*, and the bible of the bread trade, *The Cracker Barrel*.

The receptionist finally sent her in. Moses shook her hands. "I'm sorry, Ruby. I was talking to California. Crazy state. You know, if I had it to do over again that's where I'd begin. If you can sell those monkeys, the rest of the country's easy." Vanderbilt lay below them, green and moist and disappearing into the thick magnolias and live oaks. "You ever been out there?"

"No, sir, but I'd like to. Me and Agnes would go in a minute."

He sat down sighing, smiling and folding his hands together. "That's what I like, loyalty. How's the route going?"

"Pretty good."

"You don't sound too enthusiastic."

"Well, I wouldn't want it as a permanent career."

His smile faded from his lips but stayed in his eyes. "I'll lay it on the table, Ruby. You kids are so good you got me over a barrel.

(307)

How does a three-month contract with two hundred dollars more a month sound?"

She took a deep breath. "Mr. Shugin, we sound like a couple of dying ducks in a thunderstorm in all that tile and glass. It's immortally hell on music. And—well, we're worrying about our careers." She crossed her legs, smoothed her skirt, and examining her cigarette avoided his eyes. He was drumming on the desk with a paper knife, trying to speed her up. "I mean"—her eyes shot up and caught his—"you know yourself that anyone big in the music field has got a lot more things to do with his time than go lining up for hamburgers and twelve-cent French fries." He was on his feet, his face in a half smile, half frown. Ruby was scared he was going to snatch out the contract and rip it to pieces. "Well . . . Mr. Shugin, will you sit down? You look like you're going to jump down my throat." She went on in a voice that wasn't hers. It was higher, metallic. "Agnes and me want you to sponsor us on a morning radio show." She sighed. She had said it and he'd heard it. The rest came tumbling out. "We don't care how early it is, just as long as it ain't all records. We figure we could play a couple and talk to the folks and then sing directly to them."

Moses's blank face was giving nothing away. "Combination talk show and music. That it?"

"Well, not much talk, sir. We know our limitations. We aren't educated enough to go answering a lot of current event questions and all. We're thinking about someone calling in with an old song and we'd play it along with them."

"Never heard of anything like that before. Who'd be calling in that time of morning?"

"Women cooking breakfast and getting ready to wake up their husbands. Maybe old folks and insomniacs who don't sleep much anyway. Mr. Shugin, most stations just read off a bunch of names and say happy birthday or happy anniversary and then play a record. We'd be sort of family like."

The telephone flashed red but he ignored it. "Sounds good for a couple crossroads but Ruby, this is Nashville, Tennessee. We got four hundred thousand people out there we're trying to reach. . . . Hold it." He was up and moving across the room. He touched

(308)

her chair, one of the bronze Restaurateur of the Month plaques, the door knob, and then worked his way back toward her, running his fingers around the bird dog scene on the lamp shade. "You might just have something. The personal touch. Personal. No one's done it big. We'd be letting them know that underneath the Bite Quik seven hundred million hamburgers and four hundred million cheeseburgers we're human beings that care about them. We care about the individual. That's how I see it."

"Yessir, and if you sell an old biddy in the morning, when it gets around suppertime and they're out in the car they're heading for Bite Quik."

Moses was shifting pencils and scratching at his leather calendar. "Wonder how much it would cost to get fifty thousand watts for thirty minutes? I wouldn't want some fertilizer king or funeral plan Shylock coming in there on top of us. Ruby, you got a merchandising head on your shoulders. The husbands don't care where they go as long as it's close. Well, by God, Bite Quik is close." He laughed, looking over the tiny gold, red, and black flags of the Bite Quik Tennessee and mid-South profile. Tennessee was solid with high-performance gold and red markers clustered at the interchanges and swarming over the downtown areas and the shopping plazas. Out on the five-hundred-mile wheel rim more golds and reds with only an occasional black were flying in Kentucky, Arkansas, Mississippi, Georgia, and South Carolina. "We're closer than close. We're everywhere."

He grinned, nodding his head with his eyes closed.

"It's the woman in the back seat with the heat and the kids and the dogs climbing over her that steers that car. Ruby, right there is the key to it all."

"It could be like Queen for a Day, Mr. Shugin. We could give them free hamburgers and B.Q. Cola if their song was on that morning."

"Better than that. Free everything, for the whole family. For a week, a month. Hell, how much can they spend eating our stuff?"

He made a rapid series of notes and circled them. "Where's Agnes? She O.K.?"

"She's fine, sir. Just had the cramps this morning."

(309)

"You got to watch that. Lot of flu running around. I'll send my doctor out. He'll be there in the hour. Won't cost you a dime."

"No sir, she's O.K. It's her first day."

"Oh. Oh, that." He was on his feet and escorting her out. "I think we're onto something. You'll hear from me. Soon."

Three days rolled by with no word from Moses. Irene appeared on the fourth and after a ten-minute debate on whether she should show her bruises to the Capri Plaza crowd and the truck drivers who slowed their rigs at the curve to look over the stock, she listened to Ruby. "For God's sake, what's a bruise around this dump?"

"Yeah, but they're so cruddy. I wouldn't mind a black eye, but this is the damn end. Any fool can tell they're bites."

"Bull. This crowd's going to be looking at your tail, anyway. Tell 'em you were in a plane crash."

Irene put on her white bikini, wooden clogs, sunglasses, and a red sombrero and with a copy of *True California Romance* under her arm set off for the pool.

Agnes was right; she was tall. Five foot nine plus her three-inch clogs plus her four-inch sombrero brought her down the gravel path at six feet four. Almost everyone at the Capri Plaza came to the door to take a look, and one long wolf whistle broke into two perfect notes. Ruby swung a chaise around facing the sun. "Real class place."

She opened her magazine. "I've been this route before." She nodded up at the horseshoe of rooms. "I'd hate to be the rent collector. Not a dime in the place."

The black roots in Irene's hair matched her dark eyebrows and lashes. From a hundred yards she looked like show business.

"Who does your hair?"

"I got a crazy little fag downtown. Does it free. Tells me I remind him of Carroll Baker or Carole Lombard or someone."

"You do look like Hollywood. I swear you do."

"Wish I felt like it. . . . This fellow's named Freddy. I'll send you down. He loves working on redheads."

(310)

"I been thinking maybe I'd have someone take a shot at it. You know, something different."

"Freddy's your man. You see these roots? He says I'm the only broad in town that can carry them off. Says anyone else would look cheap. I look a helluva lot better under the lights. This sun ruins my color."

"Your color? How about me? If I'm out here forty minutes, it's freckle city."

"Tell you what, I'll take you down next week. He might want you to cut some off and reshape it. You'll love him. . . . Listen at this title: 'I Married the Man Who Raped My Daughter.'"

"Great. Sounds like a wild TV series. Why do you read that crap?"

"It relaxes me. Guess I see how miserable other people are and I appreciate what little I've got."

"You ought to write a story for them." She raised her hands like claws and imitated a hollow laugh. "'How I Spent Two Weeks with Mad Marvin Clarke.'"

"Wish I could write. I'd make this thing look like Brenda Starr, Girl Reporter."

Ruby handed her the suntan oil. "How long you been here?"

Irene was resting her chin in her fists. "Five years. I know every bastard breathing and some that ain't. Who's straight, who's fag, closet, you name it: I got the book on them. As we say in the trade, intimately."

"You didn't hook, did you?"

"I wasn't that smart. I didn't get paid."

Ruby dipped her hand in the overflow and began making patterns on the cement. "Irene. . . ."

"Wait a sec, I want to read this. God! Want to hear it?"

"No, thanks."

She sat up. "You got to hear this part."

"I don't want to."

"Just shut up and listen. Here's the old lady telling about the night her daughter came home after being raped. Get this: 'I looked at her'—that's the old lady talking—'Jennifer, my God, what happened? She was crying. I knew something was wrong be-

(311)

cause she could not look me in the eye. Again I asked her. She began sobbing. "I've been raped, Mama. Raped. It was Dempsey. It was awful. Oh, Mama." I held her in my arms and made her sit down and tell me everything. Tears were dripping on her blouse and the black hip-hugging bell bottoms I'd picked up for her at the Jubilee City White Sale. She looked so sweet in that outfit. Kind of Mexican but nicer. She has dark eyes and hair like mine. A lot of the time we are mistaken for sisters. I always loved to shop for her. It was easy because we wore the exact same size on everything but the bra. I had a thirty-eight C. She had a D cup. Jennifer is a lot like me in other ways; she never liked wearing socks and that night was no exception. She had on the open-toe gold sandals I'd bought at Wardway the week before. Dempsey had taken her dancing and then to a Carvel for a milk shake. It was hard for her to tell the rest, so I held her in my arms and waited. I remember dabbing at the tear stains and feeling her hair. It was greasy and I decided I'd wash it in the morning. She always loved it so when I washed it. Then I'd lay out my white sailor suit for her, that was her favorite dress. . . .'" Irene stopped and shifted out of the glare. "Will you get a hold of this broad. This gal could be hemorrhaging and here she is telling about a goddamn white sale."

"Read some more."

She finished the story, swam one length, then floated one and stretched back out on the chaise.

"Irene, John said you picked a little. You ever do any singing?"

"Sure. I turned the Opry down last week. They been after me for years."

"Come on, have you or haven't you?"

"Yeah, a little. Know what Jerry said I sounded like? A rabbit drowning in a shithouse."

Agnes woke from her nap and came outside. She shook hands with Irene. "Nice seeing you again."

Irene told her she liked her voice and said she wished she'd show her how to build some strength up in her left hand.

"I'd be glad to. I wish I had your long hands and fingers. I bet you can reach anything." She yawned. "Just got up and I'm sleepy already."

Irene shielded her eyes with the magazine. "How far you along?"

Agnes was startled. "What do you mean?"

"Preg. . . . How many months?"

She looked at Ruby and then back to Irene. "How can you tell?"

"You walk funny. Putting on weight, too, ain't you?"

"That's no lie, thirteen pounds."

"Well, you better be careful. You're going to blow up like a horse and it's going to be hell slimming back down." She fanned away a yellow jacket. "Why all the secret?"

"Well, me and Ruby don't want to go back home until we've really tried to make it here."

Her eyes swept over to Ruby, then back to Agnes. "Makes sense."

Ruby turned and said, in a low, very distinct voice, "Don't go dragging me in. If you go back, Agnes McCoy, you're going alone."

"Oh, Ruby, don't be so hateful. . . . I'm going to keep it quiet as long as I can."

Irene squeezed her hands on the small of her back, arched, and stretched up on her toes. "I don't want to get in the middle of this, but honey, anyone with two eyes can see that kid from twenty yards."

Two days later Irene came over to the pool cursing that she'd been disqualified at the Unemployment Center. "That creep at the Red Glove told them I'd quit. I not only don't get another dime, I owe them three weeks back money. Ain't that a bitch?"

Ruby didn't look up. "That's too bad."

"Now there's a sympathetic voice. What's eating you?"

"Everything. No phone calls. No mail, no nothing. And now Agnes is in there bawling."

"Guess this is probably the wrong time to hit you for fifty bucks, isn't it?"

"You said it."

The slanting sun was balancing on the Cinderella Bread sign

(313)

down the road, and long shadows from the short pines reached across the oil-streaked gravel.

"Much chlorine today? God, it really smells."

"'Bout the same. Sorry I blew off like that. This place is getting to me."

"I'm used to it. That asshole Jerry is about as sympathetic as a brickbat."

"Listen, go talk to Agnes. She isn't feeling too good. Maybe you can take her place tomorrow . . . but keep me out of it, hear?"

Agnes's skirt was too short and too tight on Irene, but she managed to squeeze into the vinyl vest and the red, white and blue blouse. They found a blue leatherette skirt at Sears and spent the rest of the evening going over the songs. Agnes showed her how to bridge her hand high so she could hold the strings flatter. Irene wrung and whipped it. "Damn, that hurts. It's all numb."

"You'll get onto it." Agnes cocked her left hand behind the neck. "See all that extra power you get. It's a wonder you didn't ruin your wrist. Come on, hit it again."

They practiced for two hours and then copied out the words to five songs on a card and Scotch-taped it to the guitar box.

Agnes was propped up on the pillow eating fried shrimp and curry sauce and watching a Batman rerun. Ruby sat on the john with the mirrored door cocked, telling her about the day with Irene. "We only sang one song at the place in Culver. You remember it, the one that was flooded so?"

"Yeah. You park on the side next to a welding shop. Little redheaded clerk?"

"That's it. She had that fool eating out of her hand. Told him she had a sore throat and played him two Beatle numbers on the juke. Ag, she can talk anyone into anything."

She came out, drying her face and hands, tossed the towel over the easy chair, and flopped across the bed. "Oh, Ag." The horizontal line-up was wrong and the picture was flopping. "Doesn't that bother you?"

"Yeah, I guess it does."

(314)

She fixed it. "How you feel, hon?"

"O.K., I guess."

"You in any pain?"

The shrimps and sauce, the side of fries and the cole slaw were gone and the paper plates were stacked neatly with the big one on the bottom and the small one on the top. "Just low, Ruby. I don't like this lying here like this and you and Irene out having a good time."

"Oh, Agnes, you're so silly . . . you're getting stir crazy. Come on, we'll hit the pool."

"Ruby, how you like working with Irene compared to me?"

"Come on, get your suit on. Hon, that gal can't sing lick one."

"But you like her. You said you do."

"Sure I like her. She's O.K. She's saving our ass; why shouldn't I like her?"

"I'm afraid you're going to wind up liking her more than you do me."

"Listen, fool, you're my best friend. You always were and you will always be. Now just hush up about it."

"But if I was to leave and go home, you'd be working with her."

"Oh, Jesus! What if I did work with her? You'll be home with your almighty Virgil and I'll be flat on my ass here with no one but that dumb blonde hooker. . . . She's the only girl I know besides you."

"I'm sorry, Ruby. Was she a hooker?"

"Oh, I don't know. I guess not. She just looks like one. Ain't you about ready?"

Agnes worked Monday and Tuesday but on Wednesday morning she told Ruby she wouldn't be able to make it. Ruby called Irene. She had just gotten in and sounded half drunk.

In ten minutes she was there, sipping black coffee and brushing her hair.

"Damn, how you going to make it?"

"I'll be all right. That Jerry is driving me crazy. I sure as hell can't sleep back there. How much time we got?"

"Two hours. Go on, lie down."

"I can't sleep now. I'll take a swim. That'll fix me up."

The first three hours on the road, Irene's energy was up and she played around with the clerks and joked with Cecil. "Come on, Cecil, tell me the truth. Once a week or twice?"

Cecil grinned. "Every morning, Irene. I wouldn't lie. Every morning. I wake up around six and there it is, like a telephone pole."

"Hell, I'm not believing that. My twenty-seven-year-old bass player can't even do that. You got some secret potion, haven't you? Some roots or something?"

"No roots, no dust. I got no secret. Just get up before the sun hits it. That's what drives it down. Some old fellow told me that a long time ago, and I've been doing it ever since."

"I can see that sorry-ass Jerry getting up at six."

He pulled into a Bite Quik. "Then I guess you got troubles."

After lunch she began to fade. Ruby said, "Cecil, how about a slow smooth road to the next one?"

"I'll cruise out to Lakewood. That's good for fifty minutes."

Ruby said, "You're a prince."

Irene slept all the way.

At the Gallatin Bite Quik the order clerk sat up on the counter. "Well, the Honkytonk Angels. Second time around; must be doing good. Hey, you're new, ain't you, Slim?"

"You approve?"

"Approve! You bet I approve! Man, if I'd known you were coming I could have stacked this place up. . . . Say, didn't you used to dance at the Red Glove?"

Irene slid up on the steel counter and leaned on the register. "Yeah. Funny I never saw you around."

"Couldn't afford the cover. I hung around the bar. You know how it is."

"Sure. Lover, you wouldn't have a stroke if we just sat here and talked a little. I don't feel like singing today."

"O.K. with me. Say, I got a bottle out in the car. Like a little nip?"

"Good idea. Draw me one of those B.Q. jobs first. I'm having visions."

The Ford air conditioner hadn't worked after lunch and when Ruby came home she was soaked and exhausted. She skinned out of her blouse. "Ugh, I can't stand these dacron jobs. Might as well be wearing Saran . . . Moses call?"

Agnes was propped up on the pillows eating Schrafft's chocolate turtles, drinking a Coke and watching a western. "No calls and no mail."

Ruby glanced around the room. "Damn, Ag, you ain't even trying."

She smiled and tried to make a joke out of it. "Guess I'm eating for more than one."

"More like nine. And look at it—candy, candy, candy, Cokes, and more candy. You know that doc didn't say cottage cheese and yogurt and fruit just to hear himself talk."

"Ruby, you know I can't stand yogurt. It gives me the shivers. I declare it does."

"Bull. You just don't give a rat's ass." She picked up a one-pound ingot of chocolate-covered cashews; another one, half gone, was on the night stand, and pecan praline wrappers were everywhere. "There's got to be three thousand calories in this thing and you know it. How many did you buy; three, four, five?"

"I don't have to account to you, not today or any day. Besides, they keep my strength up."

"Next time you buy them you better pick up a Greyhound ticket."

"Now you said it!" Agnes was up, stamping her foot. "Ruby Jean Jamison, you want to get shed of me! I know it! I know it!" she shouted. "You want me out so you can bring in that black-rooted blonde whore."

Ruby grabbed her shoulders. "Will you shut up? You're going to miscarry right here in the goddamn room. Jesus! Go for a walk. You look like death warmed over."

"I'm not going anywhere."

"Suit yourself." She picked up the candy, two bags of salted nuts, and a small fruitcake and dumped them on the bed. "Here!

Eat yourself into a goddamn sugar spasm." She snatched the door open, left, and slammed it shut.

Jimmy Lee was naked, standing with his foot up on a chair arm, polishing his shoes with a hand towel.

"Can't you knock?"

Ruby flopped in his easy chair as he wound a towel around his waist. "It's me and Agnes again."

"I just heard." He tossed the brush in the corner where two pairs of shoes, his dirty laundry, three bottles, and two record jackets lay. "That's too bad."

Ruby looked around. "Still winning the Good Housekeeping Seal of Approval?"

"Yeah, but it's getting harder every month."

She shook a cigarette out of his pack. "What's going to happen to us, Jimmy Lee? If I lose her I got no act. I got nothing."

He poured a shot of vodka and sat on the unmade bed. "What if I told you you never had an act?"

"I'd call you a rat-faced liar. We had a great act going and you know it."

His voice was calm, flat. "Agnes's got a good voice and you look good shaking your ass. But act, no. No act."

"Bullshit, Jimmy Lee."

He kept on as if he hadn't heard her. "You two had a little talent and a little charm and a lot of naïveté. If I had to do the jacket I'd say average, earnest, country, and uninspiring."

"You—you been rehearsing this, I can tell. Screw you, Jimmy Lee." She shot up. "Tell it to the walls because I sure as hell don't have to listen."

"Keep your pants on a minute; I'm going to give you some advice."

"Advice! All I've heard in this goddamn town is advice. Every two-bit no-talent's got nothing going but advice."

He pulled her back to the chair. "I've been with you for three months now. I know what I'm talking about. Now sit down."

"Oh, Jesus! Lights, camera, action. . . ." She framed her face in her hands and blinked her eyes in a phony stage smile. "My hero!"

(318)

"With Irene you've got a chance of making it. How does that grab you?"

"Like a dose of clap. Irene can't sing and I can't carry her. Hell, I can't even sing."

"O.K. But you and Irene are playing in close to yourselves. You aren't screwing around with songs you can't cut. Dammit, you two sound like you had a couple of drinks in your life and slept in a few double beds."

Ruby laughed and went for the vodka. "You're O.K., Jimmy Lee. I believe your heart's in the right place. But you know something, cowboy? You're about as full of shit as a Christmas turkey."

25

Saturday morning at eight, Virgil came tooling the big red Cadillac up the Capri Plaza gravel. Sitting next to him was Spider. "Agnes! Ag! It's me. . . . Come on, roll out!"

Agnes came to the door in her shortie pajamas and three-inch torpedo hair rollers. "Virgil! I didn't expect you till noon."

He kissed her and put his arms around her. "We drove all night." He worked his hands under her panty elastic and cupped them over the curve. "Jesus, Ag. What you been eating? It's all back here."

"I haven't been feeling too good. Lord, it's so squinty. Come on in. Hey, Ruby, it's Virgil."

"Jesus, what time is it, anyway?"

"Eight. . . . Come on, gal, I got somebody who wants to see you."

"Well, don't bring him in here. I'm a mess."

Virgil opened the door. "He doesn't care about that."

Spider stepped in, carrying three dozen long-stemmed roses and two quarts of Seagram's V.O.

(321)

"Spider! Spider!" She sat up, rubbing her eyes. "You fool, what are you doing here?"

"Came to see you. . . . Give us a kiss. . . . We drove straight through."

"But what about the pen? Damn, hon, how'd you swing that?"

He kissed her. "Connections, baby. Connections."

"You been paroled?"

"Just till Monday."

Ruby took her clothes to the bathroom as Spider opened a bottle.

"Got any ice around here?"

Ruby called, "Right outside. Take a right. Costs a dime." She pounded on the wall and hollered for Jimmy Lee. He came over, yawning.

"Hello, Virgil."

"Hi, Jimmy Lee. This is my buddy, Spider Hornsby."

"Glad to meet you. Heard a lot of good things about you."

Spider looked him over.

They drove to Fred's Gourmet Foods on the Pike and sat in the horseshoe booth at the end of the long orange room. Spider and Virgil squinted in the flat morning light and slid around so their backs were to the sun. They began lacing their orange juice with whiskey. Agnes shook her head. "It turns my stomach in the morning." She began spooning sugar into her coffee.

Virgil counted. "Four? I don't remember you having a sweet tooth like that."

"I always did like sugar. Always. You ask Mama when you see her."

Spider patted his stomach. "Take a look, Rube. Fourteen pounds in forty-two days. Not bad, huh? No bread, butter, or grease, and no sweets. I'm a new man."

"Looks good. Damn, it really does. No bread?"

"None."

"How do you eat eggs?"

"Hard boiled. Got so I love them. And apples and grapefruit. I'm knocking down a dozen a day."

"Maybe you can talk Agnes, here, out of a few candy bars."

(322)

Agnes wadded up her napkin. "Will you quit picking on me? It's my figure."

Virgil put his arm around her, grinning, and kissed her neck. "She looks fine to me. Fine as wine." He whispered something in her ear, and she blushed and giggled.

Ruby chased her straight whiskey with water. "True love, right, Jimmy Lee? Maybe you can whip up a song out of that."

The waitress told Virgil he'd have to keep the whiskey on the seat or under the table. "O.K., sis. You're the boss. If you want a jolt, just wink."

They drank through breakfast and then drove out so Spider could see the Old Hickory Dam. From there they cruised around the Nashville copy of the Parthenon and then downtown. As they circled the high hill in the center, Agnes pointed out the capitol. "When the sun sets it's supposed to look like ancient Athens."

Jimmy Lee said, "You ever been to Greece, Spider?"

"Nope, never made that trip."

At the eight-thirty Opry show, Spider sat on the front row with Ruby and Jimmy Lee on one side and Agnes and Virgil on the other. The church pew seats had no armrests, and they passed the bottle and sliced lemons back and forth during the warm-up introductions and commercials. Spider leaned forward, not wanting to miss a move or a note. He touched Ruby. "They sound better here than on their records."

She punched his arm. "Of course, silly." She kissed his ear. "It's alive. It's all the difference in the world."

"I can see why it's pulling at you so hard." She squeezed his arm.

Jimmy Lee stashed the bottle between himself and Ruby. "See that bass man? It's Jerry."

"Irene's?"

"Dig."

"Little son of a bitch, isn't he. . . . Wish someone would kick his ass."

"Somebody will."

"Doesn't Art sound good tonight?"

"Beautiful. Beautiful."

(323)

Spider licked a lemon. "You know a lot of them, don't you?"

"Guess we do. Jimmy Lee will introduce you around."

"You tell him I want to shake Roy Acuff's hand?"

"All set. We'll get him between shows."

"Maybe Marty Robbins. Hell, I don't know what I'll say to them."

"Say you're glad to meet them and you like their work. They eat that up."

"O.K., I'll get it ready."

"You got to meet Junior DeLoache. He's a dreamboat. He wrote 'Lighthouse Lovers' and 'Sixteen Gears Forward.'"

"O.K., if you say so."

Virgil at the end of the row, had his hand down the back of Agnes's skirt. "Oh, baby, did I miss you."

"Daytime or nighttime?"

"Both. Hell, I miss you right now."

"Hush up. I want to hear this. Now, stop it. You're just ruining my things."

The act changed and the announcer cleared the mike. "All right, folks, here's Lester Flatt and Earl Scruggs and the Foggy Mountain Boys!"

"Flatt and Scruggs!" Spider couldn't believe it. He squeezed Ruby's knee and slapped her back. "Great God! I didn't know they were on. Damn, Jimmy Lee, they're my absolute favorites. Absolute!"

Flatt and Scruggs and the Foggy Mountain Boys came on like race horses, steel sharp and as right as railroad spikes. Spider smiled and jiggled his fingers and toes, tasting it as the music came right at him, tinny, whanging, wild. The high-pitched banjo crawled up on top, the low fiddle growl held at the side, while the steady driving dobro underneath pushed it all together and straight out at him. It curled and skipped, danced and broke and raced forward, ricocheting off sheet metal onto some wilder level where heat lightning flashed and forked and waited. The Foggy Mountain Boys held the frenzied bridge for twenty-four straight bars, and Earl Scruggs tipped his white hat and stepped in tight. The rest backed. He came on somber-faced, expressionless, placid, and picking like a madman. High, shrill, and quick as a lizard. His jaw was set and his eyes were riveted to the twin spider hands as his ten fingers with twenty different things to do walked back and forth on the ebony-black and mother-of-pearl five-string frets. He went to the top of where he was going, held it, and then slid down in a machine-gun shower of sharp C, G, and A notes that moved like a ribbon and streaked out over the crowd to be heard a country mile away. He bowed quickly and stepped back as Lester Flatt, his guitar up high with the box to his ear, moved in. He sang with his eyes closed, his head cocked for range, and threw out his nasal, perfect tones in a short sowbelly arc that rose and fell, gathering in all the mountain folds, wood smoke, and purple twilights of the Cumberland Mountains. He was unconscious of the crowd, the back-up men, of himself. He heard only the music which raised him on his toes and twisted him around until his jaw was pointing to the back of the long curved hall. No one in the crowd spoke, coughed, or shifted. They strained forward, not wanting to miss a beat, a sound, a flash. The cameramen slid back, waiting for the song to end. It was an old song, "I Still Think the Good Things Outweigh the Bad." It wasn't gospel but it was close, and as the words hung in the heat and the hundred-year-old oak of Old Ryman it was gospel for Flatt. The back-up men moved in to pick him up. They were dark-eyed and haunted under their big shadow-throwing hats. Too many years and nights on the road had ground them down, but it had sharpened them and their music into the close-grained group they were. They heard each other and listened. They blocked for one another and dovetailed in right, building, breaking, and backing up with tight, close counterpoints. The fiddle player swooped in with wild slides and dips, stops, double stops and high, close, screech work at the top of the neck. They peaked and held, and then, easing off, they stepped aside as Mr. Earl Scruggs moved back in. He cranked the D tuner down, then up, on the peg head and slicing into a fresh key brought the house down with his blinding, showering finish.

The crowd rose shouting, whistling, rebel-yelling, and the flash bulbs exploded from everywhere.

Spider, grinning, slapped Jimmy Lee's back. "No one can touch them, can they?"

"No one so far." They applauded until their hands stung. "I'll introduce you backstage."

"Jesus, fine."

He wiped the sweat down. "Man, now that really was something!"

When the first show ended, they crossed the street and went down the alley to Rosie's Bar and Grill. Rose shouted over the hot dog warmer, "Hey, Jimmy Lee, you scamp. Where you been keeping yourself?"

"Hello, Rosie. You getting much?"

"All I can handle." She screamed across the room at a fiddle group drinking stingers. "O.K., Mule Skinners, let's get that booth cleared." She shook Jimmy Lee's hand. "Stupid jerks get drunk in here and then can't play and I get blamed. . . . O.K., move in there before someone beats you to it. Where's your friends from?"

"Columbia, South Carolina."

"Hell, I got kin down there. Drinkwaters. You all know them?"

Spider shook his head. Virgil said, " 'Fraid not."

She drew beer. "Sorry-ass people. Been on relief far back as I can remember. . . ."

Two song writers called Jimmy Lee over to a corner. Spider nudged Ruby. "What's going on? Looks like trouble."

"They're looking for songs. . . . It's a tough market."

"He got any?"

"He's in a dry spell. But you never know about that fool. He's full of surprises."

"Guess he is. . . . This is a great place. Know something? I like your friends. They got a lot going on."

"Don't they, though. Wish old John Harmon was here. He'd take us right into Marty Robbins's trailer."

"Where is he?"

"On the road. Hon, you wouldn't believe how many miles this crowd puts in every year."

Jimmy Lee bought double Seagram's V.O.s for everyone and waved over three side men from the Blackhawk Mountain Boys.

(326)

"Boys, this is Spider, Virgil, Ruby, and Agnes. . . . One of the greatest quartets going."

Virgil was red-faced and getting louder. "You tell 'em, Jimmy Lee. We got to have a name. We can't go running around loose with no damn name."

Spider raised his glass. "The Four Flushers."

Ruby laughed. "No. How about the Four Commodes. . . . Sounds better. Y'all sit down. Scrooch around there, Ag."

Spider tried to stand up but could manage only a crouch from the crowded booth. "O.K., let's have one for the great state of South Carolina and the glorious memory of Cotton Ed Smith."

One of the older Blackhawks frowned. "Man, that goes back some." He drank fast.

Spider smacked his lips and frogged him on the arm. "Don't you go losing any sleep about us beating your time around here. We ain't singers. But now these two little babies here; that is an entirely different story. They are red hot!" He finished his drink and lopped his arm around Jimmy Lee's shoulder. "You're O.K., Whitey. You're O.K. You're the kind of a guy a man can get along with."

"You're O.K. too, Spider. I mean it."

"I mean it too. Guess I should have kicked your ass about Ruby. But I say live and let live. If it hadn't been you it would have been some other saxophone player."

"I don't play saxophone."

"Well, comb or jews'-harp, whatever it is. Only thing matters is you're taking good care of her. Now I want the straight word, little buddy. You think she's got a chance in this crazy-ass town?"

"I wouldn't be handling her if I didn't."

"That's double talk. Give me a couple more cards."

"They need songs, Spider."

"Well shit, pardner, you're the song writer; get 'em. If there's any question about money, phone me up. Old Spider will take care of that end."

"It ain't that easy." He ripped open a pack of potato chips with his teeth. "What happens when you get out?"

(327)

Spider finished his drink, wiped his mouth, and waved for another round. "Going to make her an honest woman."

"But say she wants to stay in Nashville. Say she hits it big up here?"

"She'll come home. Ruby's no fool. Ruby's smart. She knows a good deal when she sees one and, friend, you are looking at the best damn deal in the Palmetto State. Because when I promenade out of that pen next year I'm a rich man. Rich, you hear that? Then all she's got to do is sit back and figure out some fancy ways of spending it."

"Makes sense."

The Blackhawk Boys signaled for a fast drink, drank, and rose as one. "So long now, nice meeting you."

"Take care, fellows."

Ruby leaned over with a cold cigarette in her mouth. "What are you two sawing at?"

Spider's Zippo lighter flashed. "The national debt and the price of fence posts."

Someone shouted from the doorway, "Jimmy Lee Rideout, you little son of a bitch!" It was Smiling Jim Gibson in his rhinestone-studded hat, guitar, belt, and boots. Two young girls with heavy make-up and beehive-teased hair were with him. He moved in and shook hands. "Why didn't you phone me? I'm in the doggone phone book."

Jimmy Lee introduced him around. Smiling Jim sent his girls to the bar and slid into the booth. Rose shouted over the noise. "Jim! Jim Gibson!"

"Yeah, Rose."

"I ain't serving these gals. They ain't even fifteen!"

"Well, let them sit there!"

"Hell, no! They got to get out! What in the hell's wrong with you anyhow?"

Jim told the girls to wait for him at Ernie Tubbs's Record Shop. He shook his head, grinning. "That Rose'll do anything to attract attention. Louise is an Avon girl. Hell, she's twenty-eight."

When Jim Gibson grinned most of his face disappeared into deep troughs and heavy pock marks. The lines were etched so

(328)

deep it could have been joy or intense pain; there was no seeing the narrow eyes.

"I'm not lying. She's been working North Nashville for nine years. She just takes good care of herself."

Ruby rattled her ice. "She ought to give lessons." Agnes giggled and drank.

Smiling Jim honed in on Jimmy Lee. "You hear how I handled that Buchanan from the Atlanta *Globe*?"

"No."

"He wanted a quote for the Sunday supplement. I told him all I wanted in this here life was a place to hang my hat and a warm place to take a shit. Wild, right?" He grinned and searched Jimmy Lee's eyes as he twisted and popped his knuckles.

Jimmy Lee said, "How 'bout a drink, Jimbo?"

Jim shook his head. "No, better not. I got a little something going. I better not mix it. You like what I told Buchanan?"

"Yeah. . . . He print it?"

"Oh, crap, Jimmy Lee. Don't you get it? Sure you do. You're putting me on. Damn if you ain't something." He smiled at Ruby. "This old stampeder will really get you going. You got to watch him. Hey buddyroll, you wouldn't happen to have a couple songs sticking out of your back pocket, would you?" He smiled as he pleaded. "I'm beginning to sweat, Jimmy Lee. If I don't hit with a single soon, church is going to be out." He grinned like a dog scooting his tail over a shag rug. "Got the man from I.R.S. following me like a shadow."

"Sorry, Jimbo. Haven't done a thing in two months now. I'm trying to dig up something for the girls here. Looks bad all over."

"Bad, you better believe it. What you gals call yourselves?"

"The Honkytonk Angels." Ruby touched a treble clef set in green stones on his sleeve. "Jim, I got four of your records home. I just love your 'Green Dreams.'"

"Thanks, honey. Wish I had another one like it right now. Didn't I see you two out at the Tulip Club?"

"Yeah, that was us."

"You looked good. Now I got it. You used to go with Big John?"

"It never made *Billboard*."

"How's he doing?"

Jimmy Lee took one of Spider's cigarettes and broke off the filter. "He's holding his own."

"Anything in the oven?"

"Nothing worth talking about."

"Who's plugging for him?"

"Marvin."

"Marvin! Jesus, the original loser. The Black Curse. He played me a kid's song couple weeks back. Bad, really bad. He's cracking up, Jimmy Lee. You know, I think this whole town's cracking up. You hear about the Glipper Brothers and Snuffy?"

"No."

"Cut a single with a Hallmark Mother's Day Card."

His girl friends were rapping on the window and waving at him. He held up a one-minute finger. "Jimmy Lee, do me a favor. You know, for old times' sake." A blue temple vein writhed and pulsed as sweat beaded his pale face. "Anything, Jimmy Lee. I'll cut anything. Hell, I'll do a Vietnam recitation." His voice dipped. "You know me, old buddy. I don't have any politics. I'll take either side."

"I'll see what I can do, Jimbo. And you see something for the girls, call me at the Plaza."

"It's a deal. I better roll."

Jimmy Lee grabbed his arm. "Jimbo, you're going to wake up dead if you don't knock off on those pills."

"Thanks, Jimmy Lee." His face lit up. "I am getting a lot of feedback. You're a buddy for giving it to me straight. Tomorrow morning, Jim Gibson is clean. And baby, I'm staying there this time. So long, South Carolina. Don't forget me, Jimmy Lee."

Spider lit a cigar. "So there's the famous Smiling Jim. Looked like someone took a hatchet to him."

Ruby said, "Feedback! What's that fool on, Jimmy Lee?"

"Uppers, downers, sidewinders, anything he can get."

Spider still couldn't take it in. "I've been listening to him for twenty years. Now there's something you got to see to believe."

Jimmy Lee spoke through his potato chips. "Stick around. You can get an education around here."

Spider was slurring his words. "Well, I ain't having Ruby doing

(330)

that and that's the word on that. Honey, the day I get out is the day we're getting married."

Jimmy Lee proposed a toast. "He's going to be a rich man."

"Right. Richer than hell and no one to spend it on but Ruby Red."

Ruby had her arm around Spider. "Hey, that's what I call a helluva proposal. You serious?"

"Damn right. What do you say?"

"Sure, I'll marry you. We'll make it the first cell-block wedding in South Carolina history."

Spider handed the waitress two ten-dollar bills.

"Keep 'em coming, sugarfoot. No, I ain't getting married in no cell block. I want the full-dress treatment at the old Washed in the Blood of the Lamb."

Jimmy Lee let out a yip. "Washed in the what?"

"In the Blood of the Lamb."

"That a church?"

"You damn right."

He folded his hands in prayer. "I don't suppose that's a high Episcopal job, is it?"

Ruby flared up. "Don't get smart-ass, Jimmy Lee. . . . Spider, this peckerhead gets smart-ass every once in a while. Pour something on him."

The no food and straight bourbon had gotten to Spider. "How about it, Ruby, we getting married or not?"

Ruby jabbed her cigarette out. "Sure, any time. Jesus, talk about your Hollywood endings." She finished her drink. "Come on, Spider, let's get out of here. I wanna go to bed."

"SPIDER!!!"

"Yeah. Right here. You O.K.?"

"You awake?"

"What the hell you think I am."

"I can't marry you."

"You're too drunk to talk. Go to sleep."

"I'm not drunk. . . . I'm clear as a bell. I like you, hon. But I can't go marrying you."

"We'll talk about it in the morning. Run your finger down your throat."

"I ain't sick. We'll talk about it now. Spider, I ain't studying spending your money. That's so close to nothing it ain't even funny. I want something different."

"You're drunk and you're tired. Save it till morning. It'll keep."

"No, it won't. Spider, I'm staying put in Nashville and I ain't meeting you at the pen gate with no orange blossoms."

"Sweet Jesus. I'm going to sleep."

She cut the light on. "No, you're not. We're nailing this thing down right here and now. I don't know when I'm coming home. Maybe never. . . ."

"What if you don't make it?"

"I'll cross that bridge when I get there. Hon, I don't want you waiting on me, I swear I don't."

He turned the light off and lit two cigarettes. He handed her one. "What if I came back up here?"

"You wouldn't last. You don't fit in."

"Didn't I fit in tonight?"

"Oh, hell, I don't know. Quit asking me so many questions. I don't know anything."

He reached over and took her hand. "Tell you what. We'll just go on like we been with no promises. When you come back to Columbia is your business."

"And no money from you, Spider. I don't want to have to be thinking that you own me all the time."

"Any way you want it. But if you get in any trouble you'll holler, won't you?"

"I'll holler. . . . Want to make love to me?"

"No way, baby."

Ruby watched Spider shaving. He had his shirt and undershirt off and had a hand towel aproned under his belt. "Hon, you have lost some weight. No lie."

"Thanks." He patted on after-shave lotion and cupped his mentholated hands around her face.

"Mmm, cool . . . that's nice. . . . I'll take this thing off, O.K.?"

(332)

"O.K."

She lay in Spider's arms, watching the cigarette smoke bluing against the sun streaks. It was after one o'clock. "Like old times, isn't it?"

He squeezed her. "I'm going to miss you."

"I'll miss you, too."

"If you get scared or in trouble you'll call me, won't you?"

She nodded into his neck.

"And if you change your mind?"

She hesitated and snuggled down close. "Just hold me, Spider."

"O.K., Ruby."

At two o'clock Spider got up and dressed quickly.

Ruby said, "You'll take care of yourself now?"

"You too, puddin'." He kissed her. "And write me."

"I'll write." She wiped her eyes. "Bye, Spider."

"Good-by, Ruby."

When Ruby went back to her room she found Agnes's guitar on top of the dresser. She knew what the note under the strings would say.

Dear Ruby.

I'm glad you are sleeping. I couldn't have faced you. Virgil knows that I am pregnant and he is putting his foot down. He wants me home now and he will not stand for me staying up here another single day. I honestly tried to talk him out of going back but I think he has the right idea. You and Irene can borrow my guitar. Look in the top drawer, there are some more picks and sheet music there. You can have my outfits if they fit (ha ha). Good luck in anything you try. I feel awful leaving you like this. I hope you understand it wasn't my fault.

Your best friend,
Agnes.

P.S. Virgil says if Irene keeps working for a while you are to send me the pay check and I'll sign it over to her—say good-by for me.

Suddenly Ruby was crying. She sat on the luggage rack, her arms wrapped around her legs, silently shivering. Tears slid down

(333)

her face to her knees. Agnes's dresser drawers were open and empty and her side of the closet was bare. She had made up both beds, centered Ruby's comb and brush set in the middle of the vanity mirror, and even thrown out the tiny paper cups her chocolate-covered cherries came in. Ruby stared at the strange, quiet order and knew that now she was finally alone.

She bought a Coke and a package of Lance's peanut butter and cheese crackers from the vending machine and knocked on Jimmy Lee's door. There was no answer. There was nothing to do but wait, and shaking away the thought that now there was nothing to wait for she began brushing her hair five hundred slow, smooth strokes.

At three o'clock the phone rang. She let it ring five times, hoping it was Agnes calling from the road, saying she was sorry and heading back. It was Moses Shugin. He wanted to see her right away.

Ruby watched Moses while he spread out contracts, research reports, and complicated accordion-folded graphs on the desk. He was distant, strange, worked up and frantic. "Where's Agnes?"

"Shopping."

"That's right, you said that. You look tired. You aren't on some kind of pill?"

"No sir, just blue. Me and my boy friend just broke up."

"I know how you feel. But a gal like you will bounce back. Give it a week and you'll be good as new."

"I hope so."

"O.K. I didn't bring you down here to discuss your love life. Down to business. My staff has come up with something, and if I'm going to keep any peace around here I'm going to have to give it a try." He explained how they were all for the half-hour radio show on fifty-thousand watt WOIX but weren't sure the Honkytonk Angels were the right couple to do it.

"But it was our idea."

"That doesn't mean anything around here."

An icy pair of fingers inched along inside her stomach.

(334)

"We're having agents send in tryouts. Ruby, the staff feels B.Q.'s got to have the best talent that's available."

"But we haven't a prayer against the big-time singers, and you know it. This town's loaded."

"Then I pay you off and we shake hands. Remember our agreement?" He slapped his palms on the glass-top desk. "That's it, Ruby. Short and sweet. But I want to wish you all the luck in the world."

26

"Jimmy Lee, we ain't got a Chinaman's chance." They were at the Big Boy, drinking coffee and looking down the highway at the evening church traffic.

"Not if he advertises . . . but that bastard owes you that job. You dreamed the whole thing up."

There was lipstick on the coffee cup, and she spun it around to drink left-handed. "Wonder how many we'll be up against?"

"Singers are dying for a call like this. He'll get a hundred. It'll be like worms out of a hot log."

"A hundred!"

"Easy." He pulled out a pint of Scotch. "Knock that water down."

"I can't do it. Give me the bottle."

"No, the damn gal's watching." He drank her water off and did the bartendering on the seat. "Here, that'll hold you. You called Irene yet?"

"She doesn't answer. Oh, God, she's going to panic."

"Irene? No way. That's the least of your troubles."

(337)

By ten o'clock Ruby had painted her fingernails and toenails with a Cutex red-orange she and Irene had picked up at K-Mart and was watching a movie. It was Tyrone Power and Rita Hayworth in *Blood and Sand*. She'd seen it three times. Tyrone Power was working out with the small hornless bulls while Rita Hayworth watched him from the deserted stands. She liked the trumpet music but wanted things to happen faster.

Irene called. Ruby flopped across the bed. "I been trying to reach you all day. I got to see you."

"I'm beat. Ruby, I need some sleep. Agnes is still out for tomorrow, isn't she?"

"That's what I've got to see you about. Irene, dammit, you think I'd be asking you over at midnight if it wasn't important?"

"O.K., O.K." She heard her ask Jerry to drive her over. "O.K., you sawed-off little bastard," Irene shouted. "You just wait till you want something from me. . . . Ruby, I'll catch a cab. This prick says he's got a backache."

Irene rolled a joint and lit it. "Damn, you weren't kidding. Tell you what, I'll spend the night. Got something I can wear? We'll have a pajama party."

"You think you can take Ag's place?"

"Sure, why not? We ain't getting it anyway. You wouldn't happen to know who's judging this clambake?"

"Not a clue. Irene, this will probably sound crazy as hell, but Jimmy Lee swears you and me got more going than Agnes and me."

"Sure, sure." She picked up Agnes's guitar. "That before or after he slept with you?" She bridged her hand high on the neck and, fingering the strings for a G, strummed it twice. "Feels good. Let's get some sleep."

Ruby scratched a layer of sugar from her doughnut. They were having breakfast under a Bite Quik steel umbrella. "Cecil, maybe you could find out the judges from Miss Whatever-her-name-is."

"Miss Taggart? Shoot, she wouldn't give me a slice of bread. No, I'm putting Clarence on it. You'd be surprised how much a man will turn loose when he's at the urinal. You take some nervous cat and cut the water on him real quick like, and he's saying the first thing that pops in his mind."

"How come?"

"Tight. Tight crowd. They don't want to turn loose that quarter for a towel. Lord, I've seen them pretend they don't even use any hands."

Irene said, "Well, tell him to hurry."

Ruby wiped her fingers on a napkin and picked up her guitar. "Show time. . . . Let's do 'Jambalaya'. Cecil, stick close and listen. We might use it for the audition."

He lit his cigar. "Good strong song. Could be the right one."

The Bite Quik had two cab drivers and a Shell gas man at the counter. Ruby hit a long chord, smiling. "Hello, folks, we're the Honkytonk Angels." They came on with their hard-driving version of "Jambalaya." Irene backed Ruby up on the rising, looping song and kept the harmony close and her chords in tight. Ruby felt the strong foundation and began moving with the music like she was dancing, shotgunning her guitar and whacking the box on the big upbeats. The cab drivers put their coffees down and applauded at the finish. The Shell man stepped forward. "Wonderful. That's one of my all-time favorites. You know who wrote it?"

Before Irene could answer, Ruby said "Who?"

"Hank Williams. Right here in this city. You won't believe me but I'm the one who used to sell that scutter gas for his 'fifty-three Caddy."

Ruby said, "I'll be dogged. You remember him?"

"Like he was standing here right this second. Slim old boy. Slim as a reed. Used to drink Orange Crush and Nugrapes. Never saw him eat much. Always carried a big roll of money. Paid cash for everything."

Ruby said, "Was he nice?"

"The Lord never made a nicer fellow. I remember that Caddy, too. One of the best cars ever built. I watched that oil and greased it like it was sacred. That was the exact same car that man died

(339)

in." He pointed down the road. "Here, look, you can see our sign. That's where I serviced her."

"I see it." She winked at Irene. "Never can tell when we might be pushing Cadillacs around."

"If old Hank was here right now he'd be a huggin' you with both arms. You gals solid put your hearts in that song."

"Thank you."

He picked up his order in a cardboard carry-out. "I want to wish you all the luck in the world. I got me a hunch the good Lord is going to be watching out for you two."

Heading out for Brentwood, Ruby leaned over the front seat and checked her hair, lips, and eyes in the sun-visor mirror. "Reckon that old bird knew what he was talking about?"

"Not with that Jesus light shining. Probably thought it was a hymn."

"How in the hell you know what he thought? Sometimes you make me sick." They were crossing the Shelby Avenue bridge.

Irene watched the coal boats pushing up the Cumberland. "You asked me what I thought. I told you. We sound like holy hell, and you better damn sight start facing it."

"I been facing it. Cecil, you heard us. What do you think?"

"Sounded O.K. to me. I understood every word."

Irene laughed. "Well, at least we're clear."

Cecil angled his rearview mirror. "Y'all want to sing or ride?"

"Let's just ride." Ruby sat back hard. "Boy, this really pisses me. No one gives a flaming red-hot damn about anything around here."

They didn't speak for twenty miles of Interstate until Cecil slowed and sucked on his side teeth. "Now will you look at that. More new houses. Where in the world these folks coming from? And where you reckon they are going to work?"

Irene bridged her hand high on a G-fifth. She plucked the E, then the A, took a beat, and strummed the rest. "Probably ten thousand more guitar players."

By Friday Cecil had a name from Clarence. It was Larry McGraw, the Atlanta-based public relations man for Shugin Enterprises.

(340)

Irene phoned him. He was leaving to catch a plane but said he would meet them in thirty minutes in the poolroom at the Nashville airport. Cecil drove fast, missed the traffic by keeping on the Interstate, and came out on the airport turnoff in fifteen minutes flat.

Larry McGraw was playing snooker by himself on the back table at the Jet 'n' Cue. He was thirty-five and had a lean dark molelike face and a bad head cold. They shook his hand and agreed that summer colds were the worst and sat down to watch him run five balls. He explained as he shot how the red balls had to be knocked in first and how the pockets were smaller than regulation pool and the cushions faster. He hung the number four ball on the corner rail, sipped his beer, and chalked his stick. For a short man he had long arms and legs. His fingers were white with dusting powder and blue-tipped with chalk. He drilled in a red ball. "O.K., give me a rundown on the facts."

Ruby explained how the radio show was their idea. She picked her words carefully, phrasing everything as a question, asking for advice rather than giving any.

Larry used the stick bridge on a reach shot and tapped in the five. The red balls were gone and he stalked around the table like a hunter, lining up his shots and figuring position for the next ones. He ran three and stopped. "Keep talking."

"Guess that's about it."

Irene creased her leg in tight on the table. "Not quite, Mr. McGraw. We really want that job."

He drilled the last ball in and hung up his stick. He wiped his hands on the moist towel, then the dry one, and examined his fingernails. His eyes met hers. "And you'll do anything to get it?"

"Short of murder."

He slipped on his red silk-lined Tahitian print jacket. "How about sleeping with a couple clients?"

Her eyes stayed with him. "We might work something out."

"Just a few special people I have to take care of."

Irene rolled a chalk cube over slowly. "I can handle it."

"And Red here?"

Ruby looked at the long green table and then him. She nodded. In the dark bar he explained that in p.r. he had to do a few favors and provide an occasional romance. The men would all be high-type executives. "Nothing small, see. Nothing under a sixty-thousand-dollar-a-year man."

He held a Spanish onion from his martini on a toothpick as if it were a small microphone.

"I think we can work this out very comfortably." His long hand touched Irene's. "Of course, I don't want to set this up and then be left out in the cold. Follow me?"

She folded her cocktail napkin in half, then in half again. "We're way ahead of you. As long as I don't have to hear that my-wife-doesn't-understand-me ballad."

He laughed. "That's my trouble. She understands everything."

Ruby waited until he dried his eyes and blew his nose. "And no green stamps?"

Larry laughed again as he rose, paid the bill, and started across the lobby with them. He pressed Irene's elbow. "I'll be back up Sunday. I'll phone you around seven. That way we can talk things over and get to know one another."

The p.a. system crackled and blared. "Last and final call on Delta Fifty-seven to Atlanta and New Orleans. Passengers please report to Gate E-Nine."

Irene slid her hand around his thin waist. "Why don't I just meet you at your bar at seven?"

"You're on."

"Call if you can't make it."

He was backing through the gate. "I'll make it. Promise." The gate closed. She waved.

"He'll make it if he has to walk."

"Damn, Irene, I don't want you doing everything."

"Don't worry, you'll get your chance."

Ruby shuddered. "I can't stand him. He really turns my stomach. Ugh, I can't stand the idea of him pawing me."

"Wait till you see his sixty-thou-a-year buddies. You'll think the baboons have been turned loose."

Ruby slid a nickel in a mixed nut machine and cranked the handle. The machine delivered one broken cashew and half an almond; the rest were peanuts.

(342)

The last notes of "Jambalaya" were still ringing in the room as Ruby ducked her head through her guitar strap and sprung her hip out. "O.K., Jimmy Lee, let's have it."

Jimmy Lee had rolled a Hollywood Variety into a thin tube. He tightened it. "You're getting better."

"Fellow the other day told us we sounded great."

"You aren't great, so get it out of your heads. You're getting better."

Irene flipped through the TV Guide. "Think we can win?"

"You want the truth?"

Ruby yodeled a sigh and flapped her arms up. "No, no more truth. I'd like a big, fat, crazy-ass lie. Tell us we're wonderful."

"O.K., you're wonderful."

"That's better."

He tapped her head with the Variety. "O.K., fruitcake, let's try it again. This time look at the walls or close your eyes. Quit watching that damn mirror. O.K., imagine you see those shrimp boats and try and smell that gumbo . . . it might help."

Ruby chorded down, cranking the E peg. "But you doubt it?"

"I doubt it. All right, from the top: a one and a two and a three. . . ."

They played "Jambalaya" as hard as they could.

Ruby waited. "Any better?"

"I think so."

"It's not the wrong song, is it?"

"No, it's right. You can move around on it. Just pray there's no musicians on the panel."

He made changes on their phrasing and showed Irene where to weave in and out of the harmony to build up Ruby's lead. They did it again. Ruby rehearsed an exposed-tooth ghostly smile in the mirror. "That felt better to me."

Jimmy Lee went for the Scotch. "Let's break. We're killing it."

Irene, down on her spine with her knees jammed in the dash, smoked a joint as Ruby weaved through downtown traffic heading for Larry McGraw's motel. "Slow down, Ruby. Slow down. I can't get up with you playing cowboy. I keep seeing those beady little eyes. Greasy son of a bitch, isn't he?"

"I thought he looked like Steve McQueen."

"Yeah." She kept the joint below the window level and pulled on it hard. They passed the Ramada Inn. "It's no use. I've had it. I'll need a couple martinis."

At the bar they had two drinks and ordered a third. At 7:02 the bartender slid the phone over. "Irene Cash?"

"Present."

She listened, nodding, and kept drinking. "Be right back, sugar. O.K. if I bring Ruby? She wants to say hello."

In Room 161, Larry McGraw lay under three blankets, blue with chill and shaking. A thermometer was in a glass on the night stand, and lined up next to it were three bottles of medicine, some red and green capsules, and a two-quart pitcher of orange juice.

They sat on the bed opposite him. Irene said, "Damn, honey, what happened?"

"Asian flu." He could barely talk. "Hit me on the plane coming back. Almost passed out."

She patted him on the head. "You do look kinda green. Want me to get you something?"

He shook his head slowly, carefully. Ruby read the thermometer. It was 103. "You better call a doc."

"He just left. I need bed rest and liquids."

Irene sat closer. "How 'bout if I crawl in there with you? Maybe we could bring it down together."

A smile etched across his pale face like gray crockery slowly cracking. "No, thanks. God, I've really been looking forward to seeing you. . . ."

"You going to be O.K. for Tuesday? That's the big day."

He nodded.

Ruby read the thermometer again. "Jesus, I hope so."

"I'll be there. This little arrangement means too much to me."

"Us, too."

"I'll get the doc to boost me up with something."

Irene was running her fingers up and down his arm. "Poor Larry, baby. What a crummy deal." His eyes were closing and his nose was running. They didn't reach for the Kleenex.

(344)

"Come back in the morning. Gotta sleep now. Need bed rest. Quiet. Lots of liquids."

Irene kissed his forehead.

Five feet down the hall she broke out laughing. "You see that horny little mother. He's probably got triple pneumonia. He had that bug when he left here." She leaned on the wall. "Poor little sap. One hundred and three degrees, hot and cold flashes and hopping on that Delta." She swayed down the orange carpeting, rolling her hips and snapping her fingers. "Too much. Too much."

In the morning Larry was sitting up but still weak and sweating. Irene arranged some flowers she'd picked from the Traveler's Rest yard in his glass. "Cute, ain't they?"

"Thanks."

Ruby felt his head. "You're hot as a match. I thought sweating brought the fever down."

"I did too. The doc is coming back out. I'm getting more shots."

Irene stroked his throat and chest. "Poor sweetie." Slowly she moved her hand toward his legs.

His hand stopped hers. "No, honey, please don't. I'm too weak to even think about it."

"Just wanted to give you a little sample."

She arranged the flowers so their heads were all pointing at him. "How's that?"

"Cute. You're sweet, you know that?"

"Larry, baby, you're still in the contest, aren't you?"

"Damn right. You kids are a shoo-in. They love the idea in Atlanta."

Ruby said, "But are you sure you can make it?"

He smiled up. "If they have to carry me in there."

Ruby salted her tomato wedges on the side of her tunafish salad. They were having the buffet lunch at Quality Courts Motel. "I told Moses I'd bring you by. He wants to see what you look like."

"Lead on. Maybe he'll tell us something."

"I wouldn't count on it."

(345)

Moses shook their hands. "So you're replacing Agnes. That the way they're wearing their hair these days?" He was in a nubby West Coast white silk suit with black and white Italian shoes.

Irene whipped her legs crossed. "That's the way I wear mine."

"I see Ruby here's told you to speak your mind."

"She said you like the facts."

His head bobbed slowly as he smiled, pleased with himself. He tapped a long finger to a blue vein bulging in his skull. "Eighty-four years old, Irene, and it's like an IBM computer."

"I hear you speak five languages."

"Any shoestring-selling Arab can speak five languages." He faced the Vanderbilt campus and with his hands behind his neck raised up on his toes in a strange isometric exercise. "I often thought I'd have made a good teacher. But then, I guess I would have been too demanding. I would have required nothing short of excellence." He paused and softly hummed three toneless notes. "Ruby, Irene—by God, I like you girls. I like you. The average girl trying to snag that radio show would be bobbing her head, yessiring me like one of those little plastic birds you hook onto a glass of water. I hope you win it. By God I do."

Irene's legs flashed like a trout breaking as she crossed them. "Are you on the judging panel?"

"No . . . my hands are off the decision."

Ruby couldn't resist. "How about Larry McGraw? We hear he's in on it."

Moses grinned. "I'll bet you kids have turned this place inside out. Am I correct?"

"Yessir. But it hasn't done us a lick of good."

He shot his cuffs. "McGraw has nothing to do with this. If he told you differently he's lying." He sat back down. The sun glistened on his bald head as if it had been waxed. The long gray hairs curled out of his ears. "Girls, I admire that kind of spunk. That's the way I used to operate. Nothing stopped me. Nothing. But now I'm on the other side of the table. I got to keep this thing fair or it's trouble." He looked down a long sheet. "You're on at two-fifteen." He rose and stuck out his hand. "Good luck, Ruby . . . good luck, Irene."

Ruby squeezed his hand. "Moses, if you tell us the judges I'd be willing to consider everything equal. I mean, about us having the idea and giving it to you and all. Lord, we only got one more day."

"Afraid not, Ruby. You two are too attractive. It wouldn't be fair."

Outside, the sun was blinding and the shoppers were keeping in the shade. Cecil cut the ball game off. "Find out anything?"

Ruby cocked the air conditioner nozzle up. "Larry McGraw is out, O. U. T. And that, old buddy, is *all* we know."

The ride out to Cecil's house was in the five-o'clock traffic, and they crept along in second. Cecil finally broke the silence. "If I hear anything, I'll phone."

Ruby stretched her neck and rotated her head, trying to ease the tension. "Thanks, Cecil. I think we've had it."

Irene had her face pressed against the back side window, watching a jet plane moving into the final approach leg.

Later Cecil phoned and gloomily reported he'd seen Clarence again. No one knew anything except Moses, and Moses had his own bathroom. Ruby watched herself in the mirror, practicing a frozen in-pain smile. "Be sure and wear a black arm band."

Cecil said, "No, I ain't doing that. Good luck now. Say good luck to Irene for me."

"O.K. Bye, Cecil."

27

Jimmy Lee groaned. "Ruby! Now listen! Irene. Dammit, all you're hearing is yourselves. I can't even tell if you're trying." The song was sounding worse. "Here, let's try this." He positioned her on Ruby's left. "Now don't move. Stay with her and keep in tight. You're running off by yourself. There's too much separation."

Ruby cranked the B tuner up. "Ready?"

"No, wait a minute." He told Ruby to fill a cold spot on the first bridge with a G seventh and a quick beat on the box. "Now don't go thinking about it and getting all tensed up. Do it loose." He lit a cigarette. "Slide in there when you feel it going soft. O.K., from the top."

They did it again.

Ruby smiled. "Hey, O.K. I liked that. What'd you do, Irene?"

"Don't know. It felt better, though. I swear to God it did."

Jimmy Lee stabbed his cigarette out. "I should have known it. You're left-eared, you dope."

"Come off it."

(349)

"No lie. It's simple; you hear better on your left side. I'm the same damn way. Let's don't argue. All right, one more time. This time I'll tape it. Don't move. One and a two and a three!"

On the playback he stopped it four times to show them the space between the melody and the harmony was perfect. "Damn, you're really getting it licked. You're beginning to sound like something."

"Come on, Jimmy Lee. Let's not go too far overboard."

"Ruby, as God is my witness." He raised his right hand. "It's the truth . . . hell, you can hear it. You can't argue with tape."

"Maybe not."

"O.K. Let's get some supper and relax. Then we'll come back and hit it again."

Ruby stuffed her blouse in and spun her skirt straight. "Jimmy Lee, I want you to know we appreciate this."

By eleven o'clock they had done the number six more times. Five of the takes were taped. Jimmy Lee turned the tape reel over. "Great. O.K., one more time and that's it. This time cut loose." Ruby hipped and wiggled and Irene did two complete turns and moved in low with her shoulders and breasts jiggling out the strong two-beat rhythm. Their voices blended like eggs and milk and Ruby, feeling the solid foundation under her, pushed out into higher, longer, wilder sounds. . . . Jimmy Lee applauded. "Fantastic. Fan-goddamn-tastic!"

Ruby checked herself in the mirror. She was shining with sweat. Her eyes were bright, her lips moist. She slung her guitar off and rubbed where the strap had cut. "I'm bushed."

He patted her on her tail. "You're beginning to work. Feel the difference? You're putting out."

"Well, something's happening."

"You used to walk through a number like you were thinking about your next meal. Now you're cooking." He poured three drinks. "You gals are going to make it." He took a long drink, closed his eyes, wiped his mouth, and sighed. "Tell you what. You miss out tomorrow, I guarantee I'll come up with something for you. Hell, with that sound there's just no way to miss."

Ruby pushed her ice cubes down with her nose. "And you're

(350)

not lying? Don't forget, cowboy, I saw that swill you poured out for Ruth Ellen."

"I wouldn't lie. This is too important."

At eleven-thirty Jerry phoned and told Irene he was lonely. "O.K., O.K., got any grass? Listen, I ain't staying all night. We got a big day coming up."

Ruby was trimming her toenails and watching Johnny Carson interview Jane Fonda.

Irene snapped on her wrap-around skirt and scratched the car keys out of the hairpins and combs on the dresser. "I won't be long. Maybe he can settle me down. I'm about to jump out of my skin." She watched Jane Fonda. "I think she's so pretty. Will you look how relaxed she is? She wears some of the greatest clothes. Who else is on?"

"I don't know. . . . Hey, take the key. I'm going to sleep."

The Carson show ended, and when the Nashville Sermonette came on Ruby switched over to Channel 2. It was all news and weather reports. She got up and, rewinding the tape, played the sixth take again. She wet her lips and closed her eyes, listening as hard as she could. Jimmy Lee wasn't lying. They did sound good. Maybe better than good. Maybe great. She leaned in close to the mirror, and as the music climbed she whispered through half-closed eyes and eyelash tips, "You're great, you bastard. Great! Ruby Jean Jamison, you hear that?"

She stood up and spinning around stiffened and fell back spread-eagled on the bed. Sudden tears were in her eyes, and the back of her neck and the tips of her fingers tingled as the last notes rose and hung in the room. A sweet, clear coolness pulsed up from her stomach into her throat. Jimmy Lee wasn't lying. They didn't need Moses or Larry or anyone. They had it all, right there. He had said it: "You can't argue with tape."

She clicked the machine off. They were good enough to walk off with the job, and from morning radio it would go to daytime radio, and from there it would only be a matter of a few personal appearances before they were looking over contracts for network television.

(351)

She heard Jimmy Lee come in. She waited until she was sure he was alone and went in.

"Gal, you should be sleeping."

"Don't I know it."

He threw his shirt in the corner. "I got to get me a laundry done." His white skin looked pink in the red neon leaking through the blinds. "Still scared?"

"Little bit. Listen, Jimmy Lee, you swear you aren't pulling another Ruth Ellen on us?"

"No, honey, I'm not. You're good, really good. Now forget it before you worry it to death . . . where's Irene?"

"With Jerry."

"Hope she lays off the booze. I want you two looking good. Listen, it's one-fifteen. You better check out."

"I can't sleep. I've tried."

"I'll walk you down for a swim."

"No, I just washed my hair."

"Looks nice. Damn, it really does."

"Irene trimmed the ends. Jimmy Lee, I just can't be alone tonight. You got room for me?"

"Sure, baby, sure. Let me fix you a nice tall drink. I had some limes around here someplace."

They made love and lay back under the air conditioner breeze, smoking and watching the shadows on the ceiling.

"Ruby, that was better, wasn't it?"

"It was." She laughed. "I'm going to make a lover out of you yet."

He held her hand. "You think you're through with Spider?"

"I don't know, Jimmy Lee. I wish you'd quit asking me about it. It just spoils everything."

"Groove."

The diesels downshifting and backfiring rumbled over the cement slabs on the highway, and in the distance a freight train sounded its lonesome coon-hound sound.

"Jimmy Lee, one last time. I just can't help it. You weren't lying, were you?"

"I swear to God, Ruby. Honey, I'm so tickled about it I don't know what to do. But you got to promise if you lose you're hanging in there and working with me."

"I promise."

"Now go to sleep."

At three-thirty the phone rang in Ruby's room. When she got to the door it stopped. "Hung up before I got there. Probably Irene."

"Come on." He patted her leg. "Go to sleep."

Jimmy Lee's phone rang. Irene was crying. "I figured you'd be there."

"What's wrong?"

"Jerry and me had a fight. I drove the car in a ditch."

"Damn! Are you O.K.?"

"Yeah. The garage is coming to pull me out. The car's O.K. I didn't hit anything. Ruby, come out and get me. That little bastard beat me up. I think he broke my nose."

"Oh, Lord! Listen, where are you? O.K., I'll be right out." She slammed the phone down. "He broke her nose. Now how's that for an intro in the morning?"

Jimmy Lee jerked on his pants. "Shit!"

The flashing red lights of the tow truck lit up the Bite Quik Ford head down in the drain ditch. It had caught on the soft shoulder and spun in sideways. Irene was leaning on the rear bumper, crying. Ruby hugged her. "Poor thing. There, there now. . . . Damn, what a break." She pushed Irene's hair back. "You could have been killed. Oh, honey, what a shame."

Irene dried her eyes. "My nose. I just know it's broken. Oh, Ruby, I'm going to look like an old wrestler."

Ruby led her around to the headlights. "Doesn't feel broke. Your eyes are kinda funny. It's your eyes! Oh, Lord! Hey! It's mascara. Irene, that's all it is! Jesus! I thought they were black." She whistled two quick notes and slapped her on the back. "Are you lucky."

After the mechanic pulled the car up and cranked it, Jimmy Lee paid him and the cabbie and started home with Ruby in the back seat holding Irene.

It was almost five and dawn was streaking in the east. An Eastern Air Freight jet was crossing the road ahead of them. "You're O.K., hon, everything's going to be fine."

Jimmy Lee turned around and squeezed her knee. "Check your teeth, Slim. See if they're loose. You're lucky you weren't wiped out." He cut the radio on as a d.j. stepped on the last line of a Motown record with a bail bond commercial.

"O.K., out there, now let's hear from Big Ben."

Jimmy Lee said, "Catch this."

A siren wail grew louder, tires squealed, and a heavy fist pounded on a door. Behind it a voice trembled. "It's da Law."

Another smoothed in. "It ain't a sin to be locked up but it's a downright crime to have to spend the night in jail. The next time you're down there you make that one phone call to Big Ben, the Bail Bond King. . . . Here's Ben now."

A 300-pound voice rumbled in. "This is Ben. You call me now, you hear? I guarantee I'm getting you out of there. Because if I can't"—his voice dropped lower—"I'm getting in that cell with you."

Jimmy Lee said, "Cool?"

Irene laughed and wiped the tears away.

Their luck fell through in front of the mirror. It wasn't mascara. The black welts had spread. A perfect blue-black circle had formed around her left eye, a sharp deep black was under the right. Ruby's shoulders collapsed and her arms flapped down helplessly. "We're through . . . Look! Look at you!"

"What in the hell you think I'm doing?"

Ruby was crying. She screamed, "You dumb cunt! I told you to leave that bastard alone. Now look what you've gone and done!"

Irene spoke in a small jerking tear-streaked voice. "I could wear sunglasses."

Jimmy Lee dropped down in the chair. "Sure, and carry pencils and a German Shepherd."

"Bull." Ruby took three steps and whirled back. "Shit! Bullshit!"

Irene was pressing ice cubes wrapped in a washcloth to her eyes. She spoke through her tears. "Jimmy Lee said we were good enough to win it on our music."

(354)

Ruby snapped, "Oh, shut up. . . . You're going to look like something they let out of the insane asylum."

Irene lowered the ice. "You're a big comfort. What if I said screw it and sent you down there alone?"

"Oh, shut up. . . . That ice isn't doing any good. We need raw meat. Reckon anybody's open?"

Jimmy Lee took a drink. "Christ, what a night. Keep it on till I get back."

He returned in thirty minutes with two pounds of hamburger and two large frozen pork chops. Ruby covered each of Irene's eyes with a pound of the 98-cent ground round and put the pork chops in the sink to defrost. "Now don't move. I'll turn it for you."

Irene said, "Don't you need some sleep?"

Ruby's voice shot up into a rasping, mimicking screech. " 'Don't you need some sleep?' Of course I need some sleep, moron."

"Listen, Ruby. If you're going to act like this, maybe we better end this little act right here and now." She sat up, holding the meat like two big red sponges. "Because, sister, I don't have to take this shit from no one."

"Everything was going so perfect. Perfect."

"I know. Why can't I wear shades and say I was in a car wreck?" She sat up holding the meat over each eye. "I could put Band-Aids on my jaw and maybe limp in."

Ruby eased her down. "Stay still. I think you got to keep the blood in your head."

Jimmy Lee was at the door. "Y'all get some sleep."

"Jimmy Lee, I'm sorry—"

"It's O.K., Slim."

"Night, Ruby."

"Yeah."

"Ruby, come on now. Please lie down. I feel bad enough already. I can't stand the idea of keeping you up all night."

"I can't sleep now."

"We'll split a joint . . . hand me my purse."

They lay still, smoking silently and concentrating on relaxing.

Irene spoke. "Nice feeling, isn't it?"

"Yeah. . . . I guess I do feel better."

"Can you sleep now?"

"I think so. . . . You finish it, I can't hold it down that close."

"Ruby, I'm sorry I'm such a drag."

"It's O.K., hon, go to sleep now."

Irene took the last toke and Ruby put it out.

Jimmy Lee woke them at eleven. Irene sat up. "How does it look?"

"Like two black eyes."

Ruby was stretching and scratching her scalp. She shuddered. "Oh, Lord, it's worse."

Irene hurried into the bathroom. "Oh, Ruby, it's terrible. Terrible! I can't go see anybody."

Jimmy Lee whispered to Ruby, "What in hell you going to do with her?"

Ruby called out, "Hon, you're wearing my big shades like we said last night." She fished a cigarette out of his shirt pocket. "We're saying she was in a car wreck."

After breakfast at Shoney's Big Boy they ran through "Jambalaya" twice. Jimmy Lee gripped his head. "No! You're all tensed up. Slim, forget that damn mirror." He hung a towel over it. "O.K., now, from the top and this time loose."

Jimmy Lee was snapping his left fingers and patting his right on the vanity top. "Better, much better. You're closing in on it. Now hit it again. A one and a two and a three. . . ."

It was twelve-thirty, and he popped his hands together. "Now you're cooking. Keep it right there. Ruby"—he held her shoulders; his light eyes met hers—"you and Slim got it locked. It's going to be a piece of cake." He patted her tail and put his arm around Irene. "Just keep her away from the mirrors."

"I will."

"And get in there and wail."

On the bottom floor of the Davis-Dalton Building a sign read *Bite Quik Contestants Please Follow the Arrows.* The trail led to the reception area on the twentieth floor and Miss Taggart,

(356)

sitting under another sign: *Information*. Twenty-eight contestants with their guitars and violins were lined up on folding chairs facing a fifty-four-cup coffee service and a stack of fruit- and cheese-topped Danishes. Ruby introduced themselves and before Miss Taggart could ask anything told her that Irene had been in a terrible automobile accident and would appreciate it if the judges knew ahead of time. Miss Taggart looked at her suspiciously and told them to help themselves to the coffee and pastry. They would be called at 2:10 sharp. It was 1:30.

"I guess you don't remember me. Irene and me are on the Bite Quik route."

"I remember you."

Her tone said the conversation was over, but Ruby knew it was her last chance. "Did Mr. Shugin come back?"

"He did."

"Miss Taggart." She lined her fingers up on the green desk blotter. "We been here two months and we been putting out like crazy. Couldn't you let us know who the judges are? . . . Lord, we're going to find out in forty minutes."

"You'll have to wait like all the others, Miss Jamison. Please sit down now."

They sat next to two girls dressed in matching pink vinyl cow-girl outfits. *Sally and Gloria* was stitched to their vests and set off with tiny black semiprecious stones. Gloria was reading the New York *Variety*. Sally was pushing her cuticles back with an orange stick. Both had on mirrored sunglasses.

Ruby said, "Where y'all from?"

Sally spoke around a wad of gum. "New York. How about you?"

"South Carolina."

"I got a boy friend there. Fort Jackson, near Columbia. He says it ain't much of a town."

"It's O.K. You don't happen to know who the judges are, do you?"

She shook her head. "I don't know from nothing in this cow town. Our agent told us to buy these outfits and go hokey, and here we are."

Irene leaned over Ruby. "You ever do any radio stuff?"

(357)

"Radio? We did three Ed Sullivans. What happened to your eyes?"

"Car wreck. Last night out on the Memphis Bristol. Damn near got killed."

"Whew! You're lucky. The way you rebels drive around here, it's a wonder you all ain't dead."

Ruby said, "Ed Sullivan. Tell me what you did, maybe I remember the show. Could you take off those mirrors? They give me the creeps."

"Sure thing." Her eyes were dark, deep-set and Latin. "Song and dance stuff. Did a couple twist numbers way back. Last time on it was a Bossa Nova and a song from *La Mancha*. Dig?"

"Sure. Anything else?"

"Sure. We even worked Hollywood."

"No kidding. How'd you make out?"

"Tried it three years." She glanced around the room at the other contestants. "Out there you have competition . . . not this freak show." She thumbed her pink vinyl and raised her voice. "If our friends saw us in this we'd be laughed right off the Strip."

A girl down the line snipped, "You're getting laughed at right now, sister. You ought to feel at home."

Gloria snapped her *Variety* down. "You rat-faced little bitch. What whore house gave you two hours off?"

Miss Taggart rapped a pencil on her desk. "Girls, girls, we'll have none of that."

Ruby said, "How close you come to getting in the movies?"

Sally said, "That little bitch!"

Gloria cut through. "We had two boy friends who were there eleven years. One got a job making waves in the tank with a two by ten for *Mutiny on the Bounty*. The other broke his ass doing showcases and got a spot shoving apples under Alan Ladd."

"Apples?"

Sally was touching up her eye liner. "Six-inch lifts. They call 'em apples."

Irene said, "I only saw him on TV. I didn't know he was that short."

"Next time watch how they shoot up on him. Hell, you never see his feet."

(358)

Ruby said, "Either of y'all see the judges?"

Sally nodded. "They stuck their heads out just before you got here."

"You saw them! What'd they look like?"

"Couple cowboys. Lot of glass and big boots. Real creeps."

"Young or old or what?"

Sally looked at Gloria. "Forty, fifty. Hard to say. Hell, I'm no Perry Mason."

Ruby kept after her. "Two, though, right? Could be the James Brothers. They have on white suits with red and gold flowers?"

"No, more like blue or green. It wasn't white, I know that much."

"Damn, now who could that be? Think, Irene, think; who's in town?"

"Jeffrey Brothers? No, there's three of them. Hiltons? I forget their colors. Damn, I don't know."

Miss Taggart announced, "Laverne and Linda Hathaway, you're next. Good luck now."

Irene asked Sally where the contestants went when they left. "Out the back. It's like Fort Knox around here."

By 1:45 three more duos had gone in. Sally and Gloria were next. Ruby asked, "You nervous?"

"Not any more; these things are all alike. Creeps singing and creeps listening."

Irene touched Ruby's arm. "Think Miss Taggart's got a needle and thread? I forgot to sew a button down."

"Oh, Lord, what next? . . . I'll see." She picked up a pineapple Danish. "Miss Taggart, my girl friend's got a loose button. You wouldn't happen to have a needle and thread, would you?"

"No, I'm afraid not." The buzzer sounded and the board room door opened. "Sally and Gloria Duval, you're next. Good luck."

Ruby peered in but all she saw were big windows and bronze plaques.

Miss Taggart exhaled. "All right, Miss Jamison. We can do without that."

"Sorry."

Irene said, "I could make it pop off. It might get a ripple."

(359)

"No, I mean, yes. If you hold it on you'll just freeze. Why in the hell didn't you check it earlier?"

"Get off my back, will you?"

"I wish I had a drink."

"I wish I had a joint. I've forgotten everything Jimmy Lee told us."

"Me too. Irene, we're going to bomb. I just know it. I won't even be able to open my mouth."

"I'm the one that's going to get the fish eye. Oh, my mouth's solid cotton."

"We'll pretend we're back at the Plaza and no one's listening. Listen, for Christ's sake, keep pushing me. If you let your voice drop I'm dead. How's my breath?"

"I can't tell. How's mine?"

"O.K."

Irene touched her loose button. "It's only three minutes."

"Miss Taggart." Ruby stood up. "Did you tell them Irene's been in a wreck?"

"I did."

"Ruby, how do I look?"

"Awful."

"Ruby!"

She sat down and laughed two strained barks. "I'm just kidding."

"Thanks, thanks a lot."

Ruby beat a finger tattoo on her guitar case. "How about me?"

"Pale as death. Pinch your cheeks. One more minute. I'm about to have a stroke. Ruby, I'm afraid to pop that button. They'll think I'm hooking."

"You got no choice. We got to dance their asses off or we're dead. Promise me you'll do it."

"I promise. Oh, Ruby. It's time."

The buzzer sounded. Ruby took a deep breath. "Jesus wept."

"Ruby Red and Irene Cash. O.K., girls, be sure and take all of your things."

Ruby slid by. "You sound just like Delta Airlines, Miss Taggart. Be sweet now."

(360)

28

The two judges had just escorted Sally and Gloria out the back and were at the small bar in the corner mixing a drink. They were Nashville singers. One had a purple cowboy suit on with a bar of music across the back. Under it was spelled out "Green Dreams." It was Smiling Jim Gibson. Ruby nudged Irene.

The other turned and she saw the diesel truck and the red and yellow forked lightning. It was Big John Harmon. Her voice broke and came out in a strangled whisper. "John."

Irene's guitar was dragging the ground.

John rushed forward. He started to shout but checked himself and touched his fingers to his lips. "Quietly, quietly. . . ." He came across, giant-stepping, tiptoeing, and grinning like an ape. "We got to disqualify anyone we know." He took their hands and hugged them together. "It's like old times, old times."

Jim Gibson remembered Ruby. He poured them stiff drinks and shook Irene's hand. "You look like you been in a wreck."

"Have, last night. Out on the Memphis Bristol. Head-on collision."

John peered in over her glasses. "Pretty clean job for a head-on. Sure it wasn't that dobro man?"

"You go to hell. I still haven't forgot that Marvin Clarke deal. You pervert bastard."

"You seen him lately? His jaw's so wired he can pick up Mexico City. I'm sorry he roughed you up like that."

"I bet."

Ruby asked, "How come you didn't spot us on the list?"

"I should have. There aren't many Ruby Reds running around loose. Guess Irene threw me. Where's Agnes?"

"Went back home. Pregnant."

"Well, you can fill me in later. We got to hear something. What's it going to be?"

Ruby hit a G chord and slid into E minor. " 'Jambalaya.' "

"A brand new one, right? I'm just kidding. O.K., now, do twenty-four bars or so and warm up. Then stop and start over. We'll tape you when you get into it. Hold it, Irene, you're sharp. There, that's it."

"Thanks."

"Don't mention it. Ready?"

"Ready."

"Good luck . . . AND HIT IT."

On the tenth bar Irene's blouse button popped straight out and bounced on the table. John caught it, shaking his head and blowing. Ruby slowed as Irene went weak-kneed and voiceless. They stopped dead.

John laughed. "What a goddam act." He looked down Irene's front. "See you're getting plenty sun. You kids should have gone with Gladstone Films."

Jim grinned.

John said, "O.K., now let's quit fooling around. This time let's see you move those glasses. All right, hit it. I'll tape when you're right."

In the middle of the fourth line Ruby felt Irene blocking in tight underneath and pushing her up. She was where she wanted to be and, loosening up, she began weaving and bobbing her guitar neck at John and Jim and bucking her hips in a stepped-down boogaloo. Irene stayed in tight and they climbed together. For Ruby it was like being back in the Twilight Zone. The dancing came out of the singing; where one stopped the other began. They lapped and folded over as Ruby, half cobra, half alley cat, felt herself crawl into the core of the song, knowing it was their best version yet. She was sorry Jimmy Lee wasn't there to see them. They finished hard, and with the last chord ringing in the air, cocked their hips and shotgunned their guitars at John and Jim as they'd practiced at the Capri Plaza. Ruby knew they'd been good. Better than good. She saw Irene grinning and she knew she felt the same. She slapped the guitar box and winked. "O.K., Big John, what's the verdict?"

He nodded. "Pretty good. Pretty good."

"Pretty good! Come on, John. You can do better than that. How about you, Jim? What did you think?" He was mixing himself another drink.

"O.K. by me."

"O.K.!" She looked from Jim to Irene and back to John. "That was our best take yet. We've never done it better. What's going on here?"

John hugged them both. "Ease up, Ruby. Ease up. We liked it. I swear we did. Honey, we've heard twenty-seven numbers since ten o'clock. We've had it. I'll play that tape back again when I get my breath. Maybe I missed something."

"But John, you don't understand." He was moving them to the door.

"No buts, honey. Now you scatter before that secretary starts sniffing around."

"But you're promising to play it back?"

"I promise. . . . Take care now. Be good, Irene."

Ruby pushed the car to 95 on the Dickerson, rushing back to the Capri Plaza.

They dashed into Jimmy Lee's room without knocking. He was sitting on the john and closed the door to a small crack. "Be out in a second."

"Well, hurry! Jimmy Lee, it's terrible!"

(363)

He flushed and came out, buckling his belt.

Irene was rolling a joint. Ruby lit a cigarette and was pouring a drink into a dirty glass. "Guess who's judging?"

"Mantovani and his thousand strings. Come on, no games."

"John Harmon and Jim Gibson."

"You're kidding. Jesus! Wild! We can walk in."

Irene tipped her tongue down the blue gum line. "Yeah, walk in. He said we sounded O.K."

Jimmy Lee unzipped his fly and straightened his shorts.

Ruby grabbed his arm. "Jimmy Lee, were you lying or not?"

"I wasn't lying. Quit bugging me. I got to call John."

Miss Taggart answered, saying she couldn't put the call through until after five but she would give him the message.

Ruby said, "I want to be in on this. I'm getting Clayton to put us on the same line."

Jimmy Lee was snapping his fingers and pounding his fist in his palm. "Suit yourself. But keep quiet."

The call came through at five-fifteen. They were lying across the bed with the receiver between them. Ruby's right hand was plastered to the mouthpiece. John said he was calling from the drugstore downstairs in front of Shugin's offices. Jim was at the counter getting a prescription filled. Jimmy Lee sounded tentative, as if he didn't know what he wanted to know. "You all about through down there?"

John said, "Finish tomorrow at noon. Seeing about fifteen more. A real ball buster."

"Anybody any good?"

Ruby grabbed Irene's hand and squeezed.

John said, "Yeah, a couple up from Shreveport and another from Mobile. The Mobile one knocked me out."

Jimmy Lee said, "When Ruby and Irene coming in?"

Ruby stared at Irene. She stared back. "Came in today. Come off it, Jimmy Lee."

"I didn't know when they were on. O.K., let's have it."

"You'll keep it quiet?"

"Got my word, John."

"They ain't got a prayer."

(364)

Ruby's eyes froze on Irene's.

"You tell them that?"

"I didn't have the heart. I even played it back. It's grim, old buddy, grim."

"What did Jim say?"

"Same thing."

"Who's got last say up there?"

"We cut the field down to five and play the tapes for a Shugin character."

"But you can recommend someone, can't you?"

"Forget it, Jimmy Lee. They can't hold a candle to ninety per cent of this crowd. Bunch of pros made the call."

"You been wrong before, John."

"I can still smell shit when I step in it. Jimmy Lee, what do you want anyhow?"

"John, I got five new songs."

"You're putting me on. You'd have called earlier."

"I just finished them last night. They've got your name written all over them."

"Good?"

"Beautiful. I wouldn't kid around. I've been dry too long."

"Who's seen them?"

"No one, John. You've got first shot."

"I'll be right out. What do you want?"

"I want the girls to win that dumb-ass show."

"No way, Jimmy Lee. No way. This Shugin's an operator. He's a multimillionaire. He can ruin me around town."

"Play him the four lousiest tapes and then the girls. Tell him they're the best. You're a star, John; he'll listen to you."

"I gotta hear those songs first. Can I come out?"

"Sure, come on. They're waiting for you."

"Jimmy Lee, I don't want to be running into the girls again."

"I gotcha."

Ruby was stretched across the bed with her face in the pillow. Jimmy Lee rubbed her back. "Sorry you heard the old nitty grit. But you can't believe everything you hear from John Harmon."

(365)

Her voice was muffled. "You really strung us along, didn't you?"

"I said you're good and I'm standing behind it. The hell with John Harmon. You got potential."

She sobbed. "Potential what?"

"Talent for a great act. I'm telling you, you really wailed in here. You sounded damn good."

Irene was sitting in the dark corner with the meat on the armrests, smoking a joint. "You said great this morning. Now it's dropped to good."

"O.K., I gave it a little hype. I wanted you in there confident. Don't cry, honey."

"I ain't crying because you lied, Jimmy Lee. I'm crying because we ain't no good. We're no good now and we never will be."

"O.K., so you can't cut the Supremes. For my money you got plenty going for you. Plenty!"

Irene said, "It's called ass."

"No. You got class and personality and you can carry a tune. You're better than half the people you hear around, and I mean it."

Ruby propped herself up on one elbow and pushed her wet hair back. "Name one."

"The Claussen family."

"Oh, Jesus, thanks a lot."

"O.K., Fred Roach—you've heard him—Lyle and Sandy Greene, the Glipper Brothers and Snuffy." He snapped his fingers. "Arthur Godfrey."

Irene groaned. "Godfrey? He can't sing."

"I'm talking about an act. Singing, talking, doing spots, and plugging commercials. He knows how to do it and that's the league you're in."

Irene was on a bummer. She threw the joint in the john, sat back down, and pressed the ground round to her eyes. "If we read a few commercials and do the weather and hold our singing down to one number, we got a show, right?"

"Listen, I can't be wasting time. John's coming out."

Ruby rolled over and stared at the Indian brave looking down

(366)

the dark canyon. "Park the car out back and tell him we ain't here."

"O.K., but no noise."

She snuffled. "Where you getting all those songs from, Jimmy Lee?"

He was snapping his fingers and ticking out his little two-beat rhythm through his teeth.

Smiling Jim Gibson headed straight for the whiskey as Big John flopped down in the easy chair and kicked off his boots. "Man, we been putting out. Ten to five, Jimmy Lee, thirty-four straight acts."

"Got any phone numbers?"

Jim served John a tall bourbon. "Remember that couple I told you from Mobile? They're twins and just hit town. What do you say me and you show them around? One of them's out to here."

"Maybe we'll do that."

John raised up and unhooked his belt.

"Where's the girls?"

"They didn't come home. Probably catching a movie."

On the other side Ruby and Irene had their ears plastered to the wall. John's big voice came through strong. Everything else was muffled.

Jimmy Lee handed him the lyrics to "Alimony Jail" and "Please Tell the Kids I Won't Be Out Today."

"Nice titles."

"Yeah. O.K., here, I'll show you how they run."

They went through both songs.

"I got seven just as good, and if that isn't an album I'm eating them."

John read them slowly. "Good lines, nice. O.K., let's hear them."

"John, you got to take my word on the tune. I'm not too hot on piano and the good stuff doesn't come through."

"You ain't making sense. Come on, unwind it."

"Listen, I can build up the theme. What I got in mind is—"

"O.K., O.K., no more sales pitch. Play it."

(367)

He punched the play button; the song came on. John's face creased in concentration, trying to flesh it out. "Damn, Jimmy Lee, it doesn't get up. It just lays there. You don't even have a bridge."

"It was that damn piano. I couldn't get the feel of it. Right here." He pointed to the first line. "That's all different. It starts off with two E's and then a hard G. . . . Like this: da, da, de, de, dada. . . . Then we move into 'You'll find them all,' then WHAP! 'at old Alimony Jail,' now we go dadada. . . . Get me your guitar."

Between the time he had faked the first bar and when Jim came squinting back in, adjusting his tuning gears, Jimmy Lee knew he had the tune he wanted. It had come streaking in through the beer, cigarette, and soft drink commercials and all the old songs that had been burying him. It came with a fresh strong melody etched in the first ten notes, rose up fast in a hairpin bridge, and leveled for thirty-six bars before sliding into a curling, rising refrain, another bridge, and out. It was rich enough for two songs. Three. He couldn't wait to get his fingers on the strings, for in behind "Alimony Jail" another tune was rising for "Please Tell the Kids I Won't Be Out Today." He was sweating, he was cool. He adjusted the strap and closed his eyes, cradling the big Martin. His fingers came in tight on the frets, sliding smoothly into the opening refrain as if he'd been playing it all his life.

John, his hands in his tight back pockets, squeezed himself. "Terrific. I'll take it." He was smiling in confusion. He didn't know whether to hug Jimmy Lee, play back over the song, or go on to the next one. He hunched forward, blotting up his every breath.

On "Please Tell the Kids," Jimmy Lee moved through the song as if walking in a familiar room in the dark. He knew exactly where everything was: the walls, the tables, the chairs. The melody rose, curved up, and tucked into the bridge and then came back onto itself, blocking out perfectly on the first pass and ending on the last word. John Harmon took the guitar and, humming "Please Tell the Kids" again to let it set up, dropped back into "Alimony Jail." He sounded even better. While John played and Jim Gibson

(368)

studied the lyrics, Jimmy Lee winked at himself in the mirror. He knew that whatever desert he had been through was now behind him. Another tune came up behind his eyes, and behind that still another. He had opened up a whole new layer that seemed to stretch out as far as he could see and as deep as he wanted to go. He listened to the melodies for a minute and then pushed them down, knowing they would keep. They would be there when he wanted them. Two were enough for John. "I'm on the Long End of Leaving and You're on the Short" was so good it made him tremble.

John smiled. "They're beautiful, chief. Beautiful. I love 'em. I swear I do."

"How do you like the image?"

"You saved my life, Jimmy Lee. I'd give my front teeth to dump that diesel route. This is ME!"

Jim was nodding and patting Jimmy Lee on the back. "You came back, horse. You came back. We knew you would. Dammit, we knew it."

John said, "I'll dump that 'monkey suit' and come on in a blue serge suit or maybe a stripe. Look like I'm going to court or getting dressed to see the kids. And brother, let me tell you there is one helluva audience out there for *that*."

Smiling Jim slapped John on the back. "Just like the old days, hey, buddyroll?"

John said, "Better, Jimbo. Much better. O.K., Jimmy Lee, I want these two and anything else you got. How many pints of blood you want?"

"Straight royalty split, no cash."

"And the catch is the girls?"

"You got it."

"You're on. I'm putting them in the winner's circle."

"Screw the winner's circle. I want you guaranteeing they win."

"I can't, Jimmy Lee. This Shugin's got the last word."

"Stick with him. Tell him they're the hottest thing in the South."

"Then he gets in another opinion and my ass is on the platter."

"John, dammit, how many of these self-rising gigs are carrying decent singing? It's all personality. You think that bullfrog God-frey can sing? Hell, no, but he can solid-talk and sell those soap products. Get him thinking like that."

"They're talkers, all right."

"And lookers. They'll look great in the ads and on appearances. That hoecake and biscuit crowd will eat 'em up. They'll kill 'em at the bake-offs."

"I'll tell him about Godfrey." He closed his eyes and tubed his lips. "Jimmy Lee, I got to have those songs."

"Get them contracted and they're yours. And first crack at the others."

"Jimmy Lee, I love you, baby. You have saved my ass. Those are great songs. And you can knock off a couple of tear jerkers for Jimbo, can't you?"

"No sweat."

John's arm was around Smiling Jim's shoulders. "Come on, good buddy. Me and you got to sell old Shugin a load of seed."

Moses Shugin silently clapped his hands. "Well, well, well." He motioned for them to sit and turning the desk corner sideways, examining Irene's eyes, then Ruby's, sighed as he sank in his deep red leather. "Well."

Irene's eyes had gone from deep purple to dark blue, but at the edges it was light blue and clearing. She still had on her glasses.

Ruby had counted four "well"s and wondered how many more would come. Remembering her Helpful Hints from Hollywood Charm on the flattering placement of legs and hands, she care-fully crossed to the left, giving Moses a leg view and no hip, touched her skirt hem smooth, and folded her hands. She sat straight and met his searching eyes. "Miss Taggart says you wanted to see us." Her heart was thudding and she could see her pulse flicking in her wrist. She turned it over. Irene's stockings slicked together as she recrossed her legs.

Moses pronounced. "That was some pretty strong medicine you girls poured down Mr. John Harmon and Mr. Jim Gibson." Ruby's stomach turned over cold and slow as Irene ducked into her purse for a cigarette. Moses pushed the cheeseburger-shaped

(370)

ash tray to her and honed in. "Not only have they recommended you without reservation, their enthusiasm I'm sure could be compared to that the young Caruso received."

Ruby was determined not to get on the defensive. "Mr. Shugin, I hope you're not going to start beating around the bush."

She knew it was the wrong thing to say, but she felt better knowing her voice wasn't going to tremble and split.

"I'd like to finish. . . . Your friends Mr. Harmon and Mr. Gibson not only insist you are the best singers to ever cross the state line but have agreed to come along as guest stars for the first year of the contract."

Irene shook out a match. "Wild!"

Ruby said "Jesus!"

A faint smile touched his lips and danced in his eyes. "Yes, I believe the man from Galilee would be the proper person to acknowledge."

Ruby said, "Does that mean we get the job?"

"Ruby, Irene." He was on his feet with his back to them. The window was open and a breeze up from the Cumberland was spinning the maple leaves and rattling the magnolias. "I understand you used to keep company with Mr. John Harmon, so I can understand part of this rather inordinate enthusiasm. But as a businessman I am at a loss to decipher the rest."

Ruby sat up on the arm rest, smiling. "Come on, Moses. Do we get the show or not?"

Moses's head was bobbing like the drinking bird he once described. "There's no doubt about it, a five A.M. show with those guests would be the last word in morning entertainment. I'd be a fool to say no."

"Then you're saying yes."

"I am."

Ruby bounced around. "Great, Moses! Great! Wow!" She kissed him.

Irene hugged him tight. "Oh, Moses, you old dreamboat. It's too good to be true."

Ruby flopped back down in her chair. "Our own show! Jesus!" She stretched her arms up over her head and her feet out until

(371)

her arches twinged with cramp. "Irene, old baby, we're rolling. We are rolling."

Moses was beaming. He buzzed Miss Taggart to serve brandy. He toasted them, they toasted him, and they toasted the gold, red, and black flags of Bite Quik. He toasted them again. "John Harmon didn't have to promise me anything. I thought you two were wonderful."

Ruby couldn't resist. "You must have heard a jillion tapes."

"No, I don't have that kind of patience. I heard nine or ten. Enough to know what I was getting. Girls, I'm announcing that guest list, center spread, in our kickoff advertising over the whole South."

Ruby said, "Hey, how far does that station reach? I think I heard it down home."

"Usually around three hundred miles. But when the weather's right we'll get clear over to Florida."

"Lord, wouldn't that be something!"

"Now, I've got a couple new girls coming in for the route tomorrow morning. I want you to keep fresh and in top shape for the broadcasts."

Ruby began laughing. "This is going to be one wild show. Can't you see John Harmon and Jim Gibson rolling in at four-thirty?"

Irene was wiping her eyes carefully. "Too much."

Moses tapped on his calendar. "O.K. Everything's set. Next Wednesday morning, WOIX contracts are being prepared, and I'm giving you each a car." His smiling eyes narrowed. "There is something I'd like to know. It's off the record."

Ruby said, "Shoot."

"Hasn't John Harmon been married a number of times?"

Ruby giggled. "He doesn't want us, Moses." She told him about Jimmy Lee's songs.

"I see. I see. So that's it." He held his handkerchief to his mouth to prevent a laughing seizure. He was finally able to speak. "The original house of cards. You're brilliant. Brilliant. You've got looks, stamina, talent, and the rarest commodity on the market today, brains." He toasted them with the last of his brandy. "Take it from an old duffer who's seen the tinsel flash and heard the deep voices of our time, you two—if you'll pardon the rather pedestrian expression—are where it's at." He punched his call buzzer. "Miss Taggart, put down lunch for Ruby and Irene for Friday. And Miss Taggart, I want you to see that they have fresh flowers in their office. Every day."

It was 4:58:25 A.M. on the IBM clock at WOIX, out on the Gallatin Road. Ruby and Irene had been there since 3:30, drinking coffee, tuning their guitars, and practicing their introduction. Two mikes were side by side on their work table, two more were on the floor, knee high for their guitars. In front were cue cards for station breaks, Bite Quik commercials printed up on stiff white board, and four volumes of country and western lyrics. At 4:59:45 Fred "Buddy" McIntire cleared his throat. "Testing, testing. Ready, girls?"

"Ready."

"O.K. Just relax." His voice turned golden and dipped down a half octave. "McIntire here, Buddy McIntire. Good morning. Good morning. Good morning. . . . And here we are again at the top of your dial with fifty thousand clear-channel watts of your favorite listening pleasure beaming out to you from station WOIX. This morning, ladies and gentlemen, your friends, the famous Bite Quik people, located in over four hundred and fifty convenient spots from the bluegrass of Kentucky to the South Carolina coast line, are proud to present a bright new package called 'Sunrise Songs' starring two new stars direct to you from the singing and swinging stages of Music City, the sensational Honkytonk Angels—Irene and Ruby Red."

Irene hit two chords and held the third. "I'm Irene. Morning, folks."

Ruby came on strumming. "And I'm Ruby Red. We'd like to dedicate our very first number to two close personal friends who helped make this dream of ours come true. One friend is here right now with us but the other is in a place where he might not be able to hear it. Anyhow, for Jimmy Lee Rideout of Nashville, Tennessee, and Spider Harold Hornsby of Columbia, South Carolina, here's one of our favorites, 'The Midnight Special.' "

(373)

They played it twice and finished soft with Irene holding onto the last chord and Ruby humming. The phone rang and Ruby snatched it up.

"Hello, Ruby, Irene. My name's Pearl Weaver from Duck River, Tennessee. I'm seventy-four years of age and I want to be the first one to welcome you. You played that thing beautifully."

"Thank you, Mrs. Weaver. Now where in the world's Duck River?"

"Most folks call me Pearl. Well, girls, you head out the Interstate and you cut off at Tidwell, then you just keep on going till you hit it. You know where the dog food plant is?"

"I think so."

"Well, we're about a mile from there. Matter of fact I can go out on my front porch the minute it gets light and I can see it. You girls got to come out some morning and we'll sit and have a nice visit."

"Well, Pearl, that's certainly a nice offer."

"I make my own blackberry preserves and I always keep something in the oven for visitors."

Ruby said, "Pearl, sit back a second. I got something I want to read. Folks, every Monday, Wednesday, and Friday we are going to have two of your favorite singing and picking stars from the Grand Ole Opry. Ladies and gentlemen, none other than Smiling Jim Gibson and Big John Harmon and his Sugar Mountain Boys!"

Pearl's voice came through loud and clear on the microphone. "Land, how does a show this early afford talent like that?"

Irene smiled into her mike. "Well, Pearl, we've done a few favors for them, and you know how we like to stick together in show business."

"Well, it's certainly nice of them. John Harmon at five o'clock. That's going to be something. Maybe you can talk that scamp into doing some gospel."

"We can do even better than that. I think we can get him to do *all gospel*. Now how'd you like that?"

Pearl said, "Remember now, you said live. No records or those tape things."

(374)

Ruby cut in, "Darling, you can call in and talk to him. Now that's about as live as you can get."

"Oh, that would be wonderful. Wonderful."

Ruby strummed an open C. "Now, Pearl, we want you to sit back, and Irene and me are going to play something for you. You name it and we'll see if we can do it. Now don't make it too hard now."

"You girls know 'I'm Thinking Tonight of My Blue Eyes'? Me and my husband Omar courted to that tune up on the Kentucky border."

"Let's see now. . . ." Ruby flipped through the index. "Yes, ma'am, we got the words right here. Tell you what, Pearl, if you'll hum a little bit of it, Irene and me will pick up the tune and we can sure try it."

"I used to have an uncle who could do that. You could whistle a tune or hum it through a cigarette cellophane, and that scutter could play it right back at you. It's a gift, Ruby, a gift. Oh, I like you all's names, Ruby Red and Irene, that's nice. Oh, if I had me a gift like that I'd sit out on the porch and pick out old songs all day. I always say the old songs are still the best."

"We think so too, Pearl. Now come on, hon, let me hear you hum it."